AIRBORNE

Robert Radcliffe was born and educated in London. A journalist and advertising copywriter, he also spent ten years flying as a commercial pilot.

His first novel, *A Ship Called Hope*, was published in 1994. In 1997 he sold his house and business and moved to a cottage in France to write. The result was *The Lazarus Child*, a book that sold more than a million copies worldwide.

In 2002 he published *Under An English Heaven* which was a *Sunday Times* top ten bestseller. This was followed by *Upon Dark Waters* (2004), *Across the Blood-Red Skies* (2009), *Dambuster* (2011) and *Beneath Another Sun* (2012). Other works include theatre drama and a BBC radio play. *Airborne* (2017) is his eighth novel.

Robert and his wife Kate, a teacher, live in Suffolk.

Also by Robert Radcliffe

A Ship Called Hope
The Lazarus Child
Under An English Heaven
Upon Dark Waters
Across the Blood Red Skies
Dambuster
Beneath Another Sun

ROBERT RADCLIFFE

AIRBORNE

HEAD
of ZEUS

First published in the UK in 2017 by Head of Zeus Ltd.

9 7 5 3 1 2 4 6 8

A catalogue record for this book is available
from the British Library.

ISBN (HB) 9781784973827
ISBN (XTPB) 9781784973834
ISBN (E) 9781784973810

Typeset by Ben Cracknell Studios

Printed and bound by CPI Group (UK) Ltd,
Croydon, CR0 4YY

Head of Zeus Ltd
Clerkenwell House
45-47 Clerkenwell Green
London EC1R 0HT

WWW.HEADOFZEUS.COM

For my Father

CHAPTER 1

The first time I ever have a proper conversation with Theo Trickey, as opposed to listening to his fevered ramblings, it is ironically about Erwin Rommel.

By early 1945 we're prisoners in Ulm, which is an attractive small city on the Danube, surrounded by hills and forests, down in southernmost Germany. Ulm's two claims to fame are Albert Einstein, who was born there, and its cathedral, which boasts the tallest church tower in the world. Climb its seven hundred steps, and on a clear day you can see the Alps glinting to the south. We're based at a POW hospital near the city centre, me as senior Allied MO, Theo as one of my patients, and by now we've been together, shunted round Germany like itinerant tramps, for four months, since our capture at the Battle of Arnhem in September 1944. Of the many places we've visited on our wanderings, Ulm is one of the more pleasant. Or was before the bombings started.

Apart from my duties at the hospital, I service three or four satellite camps where I tend to sick or injured prisoners, and run twice-weekly outpatient clinics. By now many of my patients are German civilians, who are courteous, mildly wary of my British uniform but not hostile. Indeed they are grateful for whatever medical succour I can provide, which, with supplies limited, is often pitifully little. In the months since my capture I have made strides with their language, such that I can converse with them reasonably. They speak mostly of lost menfolk, their fears for their children and the daily struggle for food.

One day some time in mid-January, I'm halfway into my morning ward round at the hospital when I hear boots, and turn to see two German officers approaching. Both are majors, dressed in the field grey of the army, immaculate in shiny boots, gloves, peaked caps, medals, the lot. Somewhat startled, I rise to meet them.

'We are seeking Captain Garland,' one says in clear English.

'Er, well, yes, that'd be me.'

They look me up and down. Wearing a grubby collarless shirt, with rolled-up sleeves and surgeon's apron, apparently I'm not quite what they're expecting. 'You are Garland, the senior Allied medical officer for this municipality?'

'Yes, I suppose so.'

'Then we request that you accompany us.'

'Accompany you?' Startled turns into concerned. Am I being arrested? Is this about the British bombings? Have I angered Commandant Vorst once too often? Has he found the secret memoir I'm writing? Or my stockpile of pipe tobacco, or private letters?

'Yes, Herr Doctor. To visit a patient. Nearby. An important dignitary.'

'An important. . . But why doesn't he just call his own doctor?'

'For reasons of discretion firstly,' the major goes on. 'Secondly because you are the senior Allied medical officer. And thirdly because you are recommended.'

'I am?'

'Yes. Also, it is not *he*. The patient is a lady.'

A VIP, and a lady, presumably civilian: it could be worse, and at least I'm not being arrested. I smarten myself up, don my French army greatcoat and red beret, gather a medical bag and descend to the street with the two majors. Outside a car waits at the kerb, engine idling. The air is thick and cold; fresh snow has fallen, draping the rubble and grime like a clean new blanket. We board the car and set off, passing a burned-out tram, queues of townsfolk hunched outside food shops and parties of Russian prisoners in rags clearing debris from bombing raids. Above the snow-laden rooftops the cathedral pokes defiantly skyward; so far it has escaped destruction but the surrounding damage is considerable, with whole districts demolished. Casualties, I have learned, are heavy, and I see more than one body at the roadside.

Soon we are leaving the city, heading west, and then almost immediately entering a wealthy suburb with leafy avenues lined with imposing-looking residences. 'Herrlingen', the sign says. We pass two or three houses; then we crunch into a driveway and pull up before a large house with gabled roof and half-timbered façade. The front door opens and a butler steps out, greeting me with a wordless nod. Leaving the two majors in the hall, I follow him up a carpeted staircase to the first floor and along a corridor to a door. He taps and gestures for me to enter.

'Good morning, Herr Doctor, we are very grateful that you have come.'

My host is a schoolboy of about fifteen. Although clearly a youth, he is wearing the uniform of a Luftwaffe cadet. He is of medium height and build for his age, handsome-faced with a flinty grey gaze. There is something familiar about him, in the gaze and in the angle of his jawline, and the slight cleft of his chin. I glance around; we are alone in a lady's salon, like a sitting room. On a table by the window stand family photographs in silver frames. One, of an officer dressed in the uniform of a field marshal, is instantly recognizable.

'My name is Manfred Rommel,' the youth continues. 'I am son of Generalfeldmarschall Erwin Rommel. It is his wife, I mean his widow, my mother, who we have asking you to visit.'

'I see. May I ask her name?'

'Frau Lucie Rommel. She is in the next room. Shall we proceed?'

'Just a minute.'

'Yes?'

'You – I mean, the general, his family, live here in Ulm?'

'That is correct. This is our home for a few years. My father is buried in the churchyard.'

I think back: a newspaper glimpsed in a waiting room, two or three months ago, Bergen it was, at Inge Brandt's hospital. Front-page photographs of a lavish state funeral. *The Hero Has Fallen*, the headline read.

'And who are the two officers downstairs?'

'Loyal associates of my father's. And trusted friends of the family.'

'Trusted?'

His gaze wavers. 'These are most troubled times, Herr Doctor. For us, and for the Fatherland. Can we visit my mother now?'

'Of course.'

He turns to a door. 'I am sorry but she speaks no English. I will interpret.'

'I understand. Can you tell me what is the problem?'

'Her heart is broken.'

The bedroom is dark and airless, heavy with the scent of rose water. The curtains are firmly shut and only one small table-light burns. A large bed with a canopy stands against a wall bearing a wooden crucifix; a slight figure lies motionless beneath the covers.

'Mama? Mama, it is me. I have brought the British doctor.'

I speak enough German to follow this. And also her response.

'No doctor.'

'But, Mama, we agreed you would see this man, who is a renowned expert in matters of the mind. And the heart.'

This I half understand, and then don't understand at all. In any case, having attended dozens of German patients with or without interpreters, I feel it necessary for Herr Doctor to take the initiative.

'Please reassure your mother of my best intentions, and tell her I will try to help.'

He translates; there is no response.

'Now inform her that as a matter of procedure, I must

make an examination of her physical condition first. For this I require the curtains to be opened, for the light.'

He translates, his voice imploring, but still nothing, so I rise, draw back the curtains and throw open a window.

'*Das ist besser, nicht?*'

The woman is in her forties, with angular features and shoulder-length prematurely grey hair. She submits to my examination passively; with Manfred's help I assist her to a sitting position, listen to her heart and lungs, take her temperature, pulse and blood pressure, check her ears, pupils, reflexes and oral mucosa. I find no significant abnormality except that she is underweight and listless, moving for me as though a mannequin, and staring sightlessly at the wall throughout. As I progress through the examination I find, despite her lack of symptoms, that I am becoming uneasy. Eventually I allow her back on to the pillow, where she lies gazing at the ceiling.

'How long has she been like this?'

'A few weeks.'

'Since your father died.'

'Yes. She refuses food; nor will she accept medication.'

'They were devoted?'

'Completely. They are married thirty years, you know. He writes letters every day he is away, hundreds she has keeping, and he never forget our birthdays or anniversaries and always telephoning and sending presents and flowers.'

Manfred's voice is becoming strained, the child struggling hard to be the man. And as I study his mother's face, once pretty, now pinched and limp, she looks up at me, and a single tear runs down her cheek to the pillow. Then she crushes her eyes shut and turns away.

'Manfred. I need a few minutes alone with your mother.'

'But—'

'It's quite all right, she is safe. You should take a little time for yourself.'

'Yes, but the interpreting. . .'

'I believe we understand one another.'

He leaves and we are alone. Peace descends, broken only by the patient's soft breathing and the ticking of a clock on the mantel. I wait at her side, watching the snow fall silently beyond the window and searching, in any language, for something helpful to say. Words are such primitive tools, I reflect, so blunt and unfeeling. So inadequate.

'Frau Rommel?'

Her back remains turned.

Tentatively I reach out to her shoulder. 'Lucie?'

Still nothing. I lean closer. '*Ihre Mann. Was sagt er?*'

The grammar's wrong – *What does your man say?* – but it's enough and I feel her tremble beneath my hand like a frightened animal. Seconds more and she's convulsed with sobbing.

'Good. *Das ist gut, Lucie.* Be strong, *meine Frau*, that's what he says. Be strong for our son. *Für Manfred.*'

Gently I turn her, and lift her, until she's crying more easily, less violently. The door opens and Manfred's worried face appears; I beckon to him. He comes to the bed, his own eyes tearful, and takes his sobbing mother in his arms.

A few minutes later I return downstairs. 'She should not be left alone for any period, nor allowed to decline in bed,' I tell the majors. 'She must take nourishment and exercise and interest in her surroundings, and especially her son. He is the key.'

'He is attached to an anti-aircraft battery in Munich.'

'Then he should seek compassionate leave.'

'Will she recover?'

'She can be helped if she chooses.'

'Will you visit again?'

I hesitate. 'If she requests it.'

They escort me to the car. 'Our driver will return you to Ulm, Herr Doctor.'

'Thank you.'

They exchange glances. 'His loyalty to his country is beyond question.'

'I beg your pardon?'

'The field marshal. When the war is over, the world should know, *history* should know, that his loyalty to his country was beyond question.'

And that's what I recount to Theo Trickey.

I return to the hospital, partake of the usual cabbage soup lunch, supplement it with hoarded Red Cross prunes, fill my pipe and write up my notes – including the extraordinary events of the morning. Then I head upstairs to complete the morning's abandoned ward round, finishing as usual at the bed of Theo Trickey.

'Hello, Private, and how are we this afternoon?' I enquire, studying his chart. No response comes, nor do I expect one, because Theo has been largely comatose since he was found with severe head wounds amid the wreckage of Arnhem. In fact I only know his first name from a letter in his pocket. I chat to him out of habit, and because we've been together so long.

'Well, the temperature's down a little, I see, which is good. Perhaps that swelling on the brain's reducing at last.' I check his pulse, still thready though possibly firmer, enter it on the chart, and then begin carefully unwinding the bandage on his head.

'You will *not* believe what happened today.' And I proceed to tell him: the two majors, the drive in the car, the house, the butler, young Manfred and finally my encounter with his mother.

'Rommel's wife, Theo, can you believe that? The Desert Fox himself!'

'Lucie.'

I freeze. It's barely a whisper, more an exhalation, like a sigh. 'Theo?'

'Lucie.'

'Good God, you're awake! Don't move. Orderly!'

'Water.'

I grab the cup at his bedside, and carefully lift his head. He swallows, nodding, then sinks back on to the mattress.

'Dead?' he whispers again.

'Private, don't talk. Here, drink again, slowly now.'

'Is he dead?'

He's talking about Rommel. 'Yes, well, yes, he is.'

9

He nods. 'They killed him. Said they would.'

'He said that? Private, are you telling me you knew Erwin Rommel?'

His eyes flutter shut.

'He was my *mentore*.'

CHAPTER 2

Some might consider it ironic that an army medical officer's first taste of blood in the field of battle should be his own. I'll leave that to the pundits and philosophers. What to me is unquestionably ironic, however, is that after years of prevaricating, months of training, weeks of waiting and hours of frantic preparation, my operational service with the army lasts precisely eight days.

Which is quite enough.

My first direct encounter with war comes at 1.30 p.m. on Monday 18 September 1944. I am seated in the thunderously noisy interior of a Douglas Dakota aircraft, flying over the board-flat fields of Holland, which glisten in the afternoon sun because the Germans have flooded them to deter landings. I can observe this because I am positioned near the gaping doorway of the Dakota, the door itself having been removed, so am afforded a wide if draughty view of the countryside below, as well as some of the hundreds of other Dakotas flying across Holland with us.

Inside mine sit twenty men, facing each other in two rows down each flank of the fuselage, their expressions ranging from bored, to amused, to focused, to pensive. Some chat and crack jokes, some doze, a couple read newspapers, many smoke. Two are playing chess with a pocket set. Heavily equipped and dressed for action, all are experienced, battle-hardened veterans of this unique form of warfare, and know exactly what to do, and how to do it, effectively and efficiently.

Except one.

'All right, Doc?'

The man on my right nudges me. He is closest to the door, in the number-one jumping position, and rightly so for he is our leader, Lieutenant Colonel George Lea. He commands 11th Parachute Battalion, which is comprised of some eight hundred men, for whom I am the newly assigned medical officer. We are currently on our way, in the company of four other battalions, to meet up with six more battalions who flew here yesterday. In other words, a total of something like ten thousand men, an entire division, with more still to come, descending upon a picturesque little city in Holland.

'Fine, thank you, sir.' I force an anaemic smile. 'Just be glad when, you know. . .'

'Yes, shouldn't be long now.' He turns back to the doorway, closely studying the geography unfurling two thousand feet below, then points, and away in the distance I glimpse the curling glint of a river, which means we must be getting close. Above Lea's head are mounted two lights, one red, one green. These will dictate our egress from the Dakota and are thus magnetically compelling, but right now both remain stubbornly off, so I turn away and try to ignore them, together with the growing knots of tension in my stomach and bladder. Across the fuselage my orderly sergeant, Bowyer, amused no doubt by my discomfiture, catches my eye and winks. I disregard this insubordination and glance once more towards the front of the Dakota, where an American airman wearing baseball cap and headphones stands chewing gum. Despite his modest rank and nonchalant demeanour this man has been closely monitored ever since he appeared from the cockpit five minutes ago, for he is our dispatcher, the flight crewman who will preside over our departure. And after weeks of tense waiting, no fewer than sixteen cancelled missions, and an unwelcome extra delay this morning due to fog, we'd all very much like him to get on with it. Especially me. But presently he's blowing a bubble with his gum and studying his fingernails, so with departure clearly some time away I turn back to the gaping doorway and the view beyond.

And as I do so, war happens.

A little puff of soot-black smoke appears behind one of the following Dakotas, then another, and another, and a moment later I hear a faint popping sound. A second after that there's a monstrous crash and our aircraft bucks, hard, like a bus hitting a pothole. It is sudden, violent and terrifying, I feel the Dakota tilt, sense the pilots struggling with it, smell burning and taste cordite. A mist of smoke fills the fuselage. I'm certain we're on fire and crashing, and without realizing it begin to rise from my seat, a single thought in my head. Get out. Now. But before I can move a hand pulls me firmly back down. It belongs to the man on my left, Crawford, the battalion intelligence officer. 'Steady, Dan.' He grins. 'Just a little flak.'

13

The next ten minutes are the worst in my life. A cacophony of explosions outside, accompanied by a crashing of shrapnel on the hull, as though we're being attacked with hammers, and all the while the poor Dakota jerks and heaves about the sky, engines roaring, like a doomed bull. The noise and the motion are appalling, the urge to escape uncontrollable; staring round in wide-eyed panic all I can do is cling to the frame of my seat and pray. Even my steel-nerved colleagues are affected, I note, which makes it worse, hunched into their seats with heads down, teeth gritted or, as in Bowyer's case, eyes tightly shut. Through a window above his head I can see the starboard wing; it has a gaping hole in it and a furiously fluttering mess of wire and metal where an aileron used to be, and something black and liquid is leaking from the engine. Beyond it the sky is thickly pocked with dark balls of exploding flak. A flash catches my eye and I watch in horror as a Dakota bursts into flames, drops away and spirals towards the ground, while another is slipping back from the pack, trailing smoke. Then with a crash another shell bursts close by ours, and stars of daylight appear through holes in the roof. Then a blessed shout: 'Stand by!'

It's the dispatcher, at last. Quickly we stand, only to be immediately thrown down again as the Dakota bucks in another burst. 'Fuck this!' someone shouts. We regain our feet, secure our helmets, fumble our parachute static lines on to the overhead wire, check them with a tug, check the harness of the man in front, check the huge kitbags strapped to our thighs, the haversacks on our chests and, in the case of the combatants, the weapons and ammunition festooned about

14

their bodies. Another crash of shrapnel: the Dakota lurches and we all lean towards the rear, pressing instinctively for the doorway. There's no question now, no bravado; every one of us wants out, and badly. Colonel Lea's in the doorway, hands gripping either side, legs braced like a sprinter, his eyes on the lights, ready to fling himself out. 'Hold firm back there!' he commands angrily as we press behind. Second in the queue is his batman, then I'm number three, followed by Bowyer and Crawford, and then the rest. I'm so desperate to get out, so close to panic, that I almost push past them. Almost.

But suddenly it's green light on, and away we go, charging through the door like lemmings off a cliff. Lea goes, his batman goes, I follow so close my boots are inches above his head. Then it's the buffeting slipstream, the momentary dread plummet, then the wondrous tug on my shoulders, the crackle of unfurling cotton and the jerk of the harness as the chute bursts open.

The relief is instant and euphoric, like waking from a nightmare, like deliverance from evil. I was in hell; now I'm out, I'm alive, and drifting gently to earth. Above and behind the rumble of aircraft engines recedes, as too the crump of anti-aircraft fire, while all around dozens, scores, hundreds of parachutes fill the sky. It's an awe-inspiring spectacle and in my gratitude and relief I want to shout aloud for joy, but there's no time for joy, there's war to be fought and the battleground is fast approaching. Fumbling at my waist I unfasten the strap holding my kitbag to my leg and lower it until it dangles twenty feet below. Beyond it, the ground appears heath-like and partially obscured by smoke. Then I hear a new sound, the crackle of small arms, and looking down see brown earth spurt up and

15

outward like a flowering tulip. 'Shelling!' someone shouts, away to my left. 'Watch out, boys, they're shelling the DZ!'

There's nothing I can do: the drop zone is rushing up, and I'm oscillating wildly back and forth like a child on a swing. I reach up and heave on shrouds to try and check the motion, preparing, legs together, knees bent, as best I can for impact. My last thought, as the ground hurtles up at me, is to try and catch the swing as it comes forward, then all might be well. But I hit the ground in full back swing, land badly, crack my head a stunning blow, and have the knockout completed by the haversack on my chest smashing me in the face.

Time passes: it seems long but is probably minutes at most. The first thing I am aware of is blinking up at a milky sky, now devoid of aircraft or flak, while being dragged slowly across the ground on my back. Feebly I bash at the parachute release on my chest with a fist, but it's no use, so I struggle to my feet, still pulled by the chute which billows in the breeze like a sail, until finally, exhausted and dazed, the release opens and I'm freed.

I sink breathlessly to my knees to take stock. The back of my head throbs damnably, and my mouth and nose are pouring blood from the haversack blow. I summon a handkerchief, probing a chipped molar with my tongue, and start mopping and dabbing, all the while looking around for the others. But incredibly I see no others. Not a one. I'm alone, in the wide open, behind enemy lines. Nor can I see the landmarks we were briefed on: the factory to the north, the forest to the east, the roads and tracks. Panic rises again; hundreds of us are here in the vicinity – thousands – surely I should see someone? For a moment I wonder if I've dragged clear out of the DZ, but then I glimpse another parachute nearby, its occupant gone, and with my head gradually clearing, common sense prevails. I'm not alone, and I haven't dragged more than a few yards, so it must be the terrain. Get oriented, our instructors drilled endlessly, as soon as you're down get oriented and head for the rendezvous. Fast. I clamber to my feet. The ground around me is uneven and thickly tussocked, thus concealing anyone lying or crouching on it; it's also masked by drifting smoke from signal flares and fires in the scrub. I hear the distant crackle of small-arms fire and the whump of a mortar and remember, belatedly, that I'm in a war zone and people here want to kill me. My need to urinate is insistent and I even begin hastily divesting myself of kit, but then there's a zipping noise in the grass beside me and I realize it's a high-velocity bullet, missing me by feet. The bladder must wait. I fumble at a pocket and produce the compass we all carry. Southeast, the briefing said, rendezvous at a wooded area in the southeast corner of the DZ. I raise myself higher and set off at the run. A moment later I'm crashing heavily to the ground once more, felled by the kitbag still attached to my leg. Winded, cursing and bloody, I can only laugh.

A mere fifteen minutes later, military order, as is the wondrous way with the Paras, has been fully restored. We may arrive in some disarray, someone famously said, but once arrived we don't fuck about. How true. Breathless and sweating I reach the rendezvous, kitbag on shoulder, to find Colonel Lea and his staff calmly manning a temporary HQ beneath the trees. Maps on trestle tables, radio operators twiddling knobs, runners bearing messages; there are even mugs of tea appearing. And men, everywhere, converging on the area from all directions, joshing and cracking jokes as if on a Sunday jaunt. Without fuss they begin forming up into 11th Battalion's four companies, then their individual platoons and sections. NCOs bark orders and people move at the double; everywhere I see bustle and organization. Jeeps are arriving, dropped aboard gliders together with motorcycles, bicycles and trailers of weapons, ammunition and supplies. Even the sporadic shooting heard earlier has died away, and off to one side I spot a forlorn gaggle of German soldiers, hands on heads, being guarded by a Sten-gun-toting corporal. It's the first time I've ever seen the enemy close up, and I'm not impressed.

'Captain Garland?'

A tap on the shoulder and I turn to find Sergeant Bowyer, and my batman Sykes, and others from my medical team. 'There you are, sir. Hello, been in the wars have you?' Bowyer cackles, to all-round mirth. Yet I detect relief, for although he may not have huge respect for his officer, he'd prefer not to lose him. High time, I decide, fingering my blood-caked face, to pull my socks up.

'Got separated on the DZ, Sergeant. Is everyone here?'

'Just about. Three or four still to come. Jeep's arrived and much of the supplies. Just waiting on the rest of it and we're all set.'

'Good. Any casualties?'

'Just one sir, so far. The colonel's number two, Major Lonsdale, caught a bit of shrapnel on his hand. I've already dressed it. Do you want me to look at your nose?'

'That won't be necessary. Double-check the inventory, if you please, get everyone into their sections, and be ready to move in five minutes.'

I wander a few yards into the trees to finally relieve my bursting bladder, gulp greedily from my water bottle, and then dribble some on to my handkerchief to clean up my face. By the time I return I feel calm and in control. Around the clearing Colonel Lea and his team are packing up.

He smiles. 'All set, Doc?'

'All set, sir.'

And with that, 11th Battalion moves off.

We set off along a sandy track towards Arnhem, which is some five miles away. Our job, as part of 1st Airborne Division, is to take and secure the bridge over the Rhine at Arnhem, so that the heavily armoured 30 Corps, which is motoring up from the south, can cross it, storm into Germany and effectively end the war. This ambitious plan, put together by Monty himself, is called Operation Market Garden and the first wave of Paras, including John Frost's 2nd Battalion, landed here yesterday and managed to reach the bridge. But now he's having a hard time holding it, so we in 11th Battalion are to reinforce him. Speed, Colonel Lea tells us, is of the absolute essence, and we must reach the bridge before nightfall.

After a while the sandy track becomes more paved, and a railway line comes in from our right. We keep to the north side of this; then we cross over and immediately enter a small village where, pleasingly, the population has turned out in support. Cheers and applause greet us, and we self-consciously fall into marching step, straightening our backs and swinging our arms as flowers are thrown, children wave flags, dogs yap at our heels and pretty girls bestow kisses on our cheeks. Many older inhabitants are movingly affected, openly weeping, scarcely daring to believe the five-year nightmare is over. One old man steps forward and clasps my hand, squeezing it fervently and nodding in wordless gratitude. Not knowing his language, I can only pat his hand and nod back.

No sooner do we enter the village than we leave it again and peace descends, leaving only the sounds of birdsong, boots on tarmac and the grinding of gears from the medics' Jeep following behind. The afternoon is pleasant and warm, with shafts of dappled sunlight piercing the autumn canopy and the scent of dog rose and river meadow rising from the Lower Rhine, occasionally visible off to our right. Locals still appear, smiling and waving flags, and every now and then a battalion motorcyclist speeds by, chivvying stragglers and checking the column, which is now spread out over a mile or more. Then after another hour, just as we're approaching some neat-looking suburbs, and with my watch showing 5 p.m., the column comes to a halt. As it does so, I think I hear the rumble of very distant artillery.

Primus and hexamine stoves appear, mess tins come to the boil, tea brews, cigarettes light, and banter banters, for the great British Tommy needs no instruction in taking a break. I gather with my section around our Jeep, which as well as carrying up to four stretchers also transports our supplies and baggage. Sykes hands me tea, Bowyer a cigarette, and bending over the bonnet I break out a map and take stock.

By my estimate, we've arrived at an Arnhem suburb called Oosterbeek, which is still a good two miles west of our objective at the bridge area. At the speed we're going it'll be nightfall before we get there, which could be problematic. Right now we're still moving in battalion formation, that's four companies of roughly two hundred men each. The likelihood is, as we draw nearer the objective, Colonel Lea will split the battalion and send the four companies in by different routes. Right now, up at the head of the column, small advance parties are already probing carefully forward, identifying possible routes, and checking houses, garages and street corners for signs of trouble. The battalion follows in company order, with the main medical section bringing up the rear. Each company has its own orderlies and stretcher-bearers equipped with field dressings and basic first-aid equipment. Should anyone get injured, they will do what they can on the spot, before sending the casualty rearward to us. Being at the back means we don't have to retrace our steps to help anyone. Also, as and when battle is joined, we're ideally placed to set up an aid post, from where we can properly stabilize casualties before sending them rearward once more to a dressing station. These are like temporary hospitals, under canvas or in requisitioned buildings, and manned by field ambulance staff complete with nurses, surgical teams and operating facilities. This rearward-moving system for casualties – front line to aid post to dressing station – is well established and works successfully. Usually.

All too soon whistles blow and the column moves off. But noticeably more slowly, and carefully. Within minutes we're treading lightly into Oosterbeek: neat rows of incredibly tidy houses with spotless paintwork and pretty gardens. Smiling residents still appear, but more guardedly, standing in a porch, or at a curtained window, perhaps at their garden gate but no further, knowing that danger lies ahead. And although we've seen or heard no sign of the enemy since the DZ, an instinctive wariness also comes over the men around me, who spread themselves into two files, one on either side of the road, and move cautiously, constantly scanning left and right, high and low, their weapons at the ready. They know this is ideal ambush territory, and with the rumble of distant gunfire growing unmistakably louder, they can sense the enemy nearing. We gradually advance in this fashion: forward for a few minutes, then all stop, at which point the men dart into gardens to squat behind walls, or go prone in a ditch, ready and watchful, until we move on again. Through the trees to our right the river grows more visible; rounding a bend we see the iron girders of a rail bridge, one of yesterday's secondary objectives. But the bridge has been blown, with the central span lying drunkenly in the current. Which just leaves the road bridge, presently in the hands of an embattled 2nd Battalion.

A while after this, just as dusk is falling, word comes down that we're halting for the night.

My second day of war begins early. Having passed a cold, uncomfortable and mostly sleepless night in a hip-scrape in some Dutch person's garden, I am roused from restless slumber by my batman Sykes bearing tea.

'Bless you, Private,' I croak, 'you're a Godsend. Did you have a good night?'

'Mustn't grumble.' Sykes grins toothily. 'Found a mattress and blankets in a shed round the back.'

Mattress, blankets, shed. Shelter and comfort, in other words, while I'm lying in a flower bed picking petunias out of my hair. That's the difference between the seasoned regular and temporary volunteer.

'Good for you,' I say graciously. I haul myself upright. 'Any gen?'

Gen. News, information, gossip, rumour: together with tea the army runs on it.

'More of the same,' Sykes replies. 'Column moves off in half an hour.'

Out in the road I see sleepy soldiers in various stages of preparedness. 'Any enemy activity in the night?'

'Plenty up at the bridge by the sound of it. Not much round here.' He grins again. 'Too early for the dozy buggers!'

'Early?'

'We'll see. Here, Captain, pass me your oatmeal and I'll fix breakfast.'

I rise, breakfast, ablute, shave (officers must maintain standards), check on the team, the vehicle and the equipment, then wander up and down the column for a while, until the whistles blow and we set off forwards once more. The weather is more overcast than yesterday, and noticeably chillier; I wear my camouflage jumping smock over my battledress, which in turn is over vest, shirt and tie, and yet the night's chill lingers in my limbs. This mainly because our pace is so slow. Barely a crawl in fact, a few yards and stop, another few yards and stop again. By mid-morning we've covered perhaps half a mile. This cautious progress is frustrating, but understandable, for there are distinct signs of battle from the head of the column, with sporadic small-arms fire clearly audible, along with the rattle of machine guns and the occasional crump of a mortar. Self-evidently, the plan to relieve 2nd Battalion at the bridge is slipping badly behind schedule.

And then around mid-morning we receive our first casualties. Two men borne in on stretchers, one with a straight-through thigh wound, the other shot in the abdomen, which looks more complicated. Both are conscious but in pain. The section swings into action, orderlies break out supplies, Sykes fills out cards, while Bowyer checks on treatment so far received. I kneel next to each man and make a more thorough examination. Both will require surgery, so both will need transport to the dressing station which, we have learned, has been established back down the road in Oosterbeek. Satisfied their bleeding is under control and conditions stable, I re-dress the wounds and give each a shot of morphia.

'Not too serious, is it?' one mumbles as I finish.

'Not at all, old chum. Up and about in no time.'

'Thanks, Doc.'

'So, it's getting a bit lively, is it,' I venture, 'up at the sharp end?'

'Snipers mainly, and a couple of machine-gun nests. It's all these houses and alleys and so on: Jerry's got too much cover.'

'Hmm.' I check my watch to record the morphia shot on his card, noticing idly it is exactly 11 a.m.

At which point the world goes completely mad.

It starts with a single piercing shriek overhead, followed by a deafening crash across the road. I stare in awe as a pillar of earth and rubble explodes into the air while the ground shudders under my feet; then I hear Bowyer shout, 'Down!' and fling myself rather belatedly to the pavement. A second later the bombardment begins in earnest. It's mortar fire, I learn later, a concentrated barrage designed to break up the column. It works. You hear the whistle overhead and then feel the whump of the explosion in the belly and bones as well as the ears. The shells come over in clusters, three four five in quick succession, then a pause, then another cluster, slightly nearer as they fine-tune the range, until it feels like giant stamping feet are approaching up the road. Choking smoke clogs the air, which fills with flying debris, shrapnel, clods of earth and shattered masonry. I lie there on the pavement, rigid with terror, my hands covering my head, and wait for it to end. The men on the stretchers are but a yard away, vulnerable and unprotected, yet there's nothing I or anyone can do while the bombardment lasts. Except pray.

Suddenly there's a lull, and I feel someone tugging at my boot.

'Round here!' Bowyer again, gesturing from behind a garden wall. I scrabble round on hands and knees and flop breathlessly down.

'Christ, that was close!' I gasp needlessly. 'Where's it coming from?'

'Up there' – he points – 'somewhere behind the houses.'

'Is it finished?'

'Doubt it.'

'We should get the stretcher cases under cover.'

But another shrieking whistle drowns his reply, and the world erupts into the ear-splitting, smoke-choking, debris-flying madness again. I topple sideways behind the wall, bent double, arms on head, eyes tight shut, like a child in a thunderstorm. I feel the ground quiver with each concussion, taste smoke and cordite, hear the patter of falling debris all around, and my own gasped breaths.

Then it stops. Five seconds, ten; I straighten a little, raise my head. A burst of machine-gun fire comes from behind the houses, and distant shouting. Bowyer scrambles to his feet.

'Quick!'

'What now?'

'Our boys are after them. But they'll be back. They're repositioning, so we must too.'

'Where?'

'There!' He points down the road, the way we've just come. 'Out of the line of fire. Where we can be of use.'

'But we can't just turn round and go back!'

'Yes we bloody can! We're no use to anyone dead and that's what we'll be if we stay here!'

Fair point, and as if to emphasize it I see men running rearward, hell for leather, heavily laden with weapons and ammunition, which seems sensible but not quite right. Then a Jeep comes reversing down the road towards us at high speed, a young lieutenant at the wheel. He spots me and squeals to a halt.

'Captain! Thank God. Listen, they've split the column. We've got to get a section or two round behind them. So pull back a hundred yards to those trees there, set up defensive positions – one forward, one rearward – while we try and nail those bloody mortars.'

'Defensive. . . What?' I can hardly believe my ears. 'Yes, but I mean, what about orders? Colonel Lea, and Major Lonsdale – what about them?'

'They've got their hands full up front, believe me! We've got to protect the flank and rear before they break us in pieces. There's a crossroads a quarter-mile ahead; I'm going there to set up, you get the rear covered, then as soon as we clear the area we'll link back up, got it?'

'Well, I. . .'

'Jolly good! Oh, and watch out for tanks!'

With that he throws me a salute, crashes the Jeep into gear and speeds off.

No plan, the soldiers' saying goes, survives contact with the enemy. How true. Ten minutes ago we were advancing in good order upon our objective. Slowly, yes, but tidily, methodically and in accordance with the Plan. Now we seem to be like headless chickens, running about setting up all over the place with no plan at all. I stand there in the road like a rock blocking a stream as men flow round me, and try to order my thoughts. Disregarding for a moment that a lieutenant has just *ordered* a captain to set up a firing position, the simple fact is that the captain hasn't a clue how to go about this, because he's a doctor not a combatant. So what the hell should I do? And tanks? Nobody said anything about tanks. Until he did.

A soldier trots by, hefting a Bren gun on his shoulder.

'You! Private!'

'Me, sir?'

'Yes. Where's your commanding officer?'

'Christ knows. We got split up.'

'Then who are you reporting to?'

'CSM Barrett, sir. He's down there with the others.'

Company sergeant major, thank heavens, somebody who'll know what to do. I head for Bowyer, who's busy loading our supplies on to the Jeep. The two stretcher cases are already aboard, securely lashed. 'Is that everything?'

'That's the lot. Better get going before shelling starts again.'

'Right, and there's a CSM I need to find.'

I send the Jeep on ahead and fall into hurried step beside him. Around us the exodus continues. A man jogs past bearing a PIAT anti-tank gun, while two more push a trolley full of ammunition.

'Technically speaking, Bowyer,' I puff, 'isn't this retreating?'

'Paras *never* retreat!' he scolds angrily. 'They withdraw.'

'Ah.'

'And regroup.'

'I see.'

And he's right, for five minutes later we arrive to find CSM Barrett and two other NCOs busily restoring order, with men setting up positions on both sides of the road, behind walls and trees, in ditches and culverts, under hedges and even on garage roofs. I also spot more injured, mostly walking wounded but two more stretchers and three sitting against a wall. I approach Barrett, who salutes me warily.

'Sergeant Major,' I reassure him, 'clearly you have matters in hand, so I'll not interfere, but I do need to set up an aid post, somewhere out of the way, and would welcome your advice.'

Barrett looks relieved. 'Yes, well, ah, I'd suggest back a little, sir, in one of the houses maybe. Be safer once the shooting starts.'

'And how long have we got before then, would you say?'

He checks his watch and grins. 'Noon's my guess, Captain.'

'Very well. Thank you. And good luck.' We salute again – it seems appropriate – turn and part. Fifteen minutes, he estimates. I head down the road a little, select a house with double garage and knock loudly on the door. There's no reply, the occupants having wisely departed. I scrawl a note of apology and push it through the letterbox, then nod to Bowyer who forces the garage doors to reveal a cavernous and mostly empty interior. The orderlies remove the rest – furniture, tins of paint, a canoe – into the garden, Sykes drapes our Red Cross flag over the gate, we move the supplies and injured in, and 11th Battalion Medical Aid Post No. 1 is open for business.

A few minutes later, precisely at noon as Barrett predicted, the shooting begins.

It's from this moment really, this midday on Tuesday 19 September, that everything changes. From familiar to alien, recognizable to indescribable, normal to deviant. The outside world, the one beyond the once-peaceful suburb of Oosterbeek, recedes into non-existence. Time expands and contracts seemingly at random, hours racing by in an instant, minutes slowing to a crawl or stopping altogether. There is no 'before', nor any 'after' worth bothering with, only the immediate 'now' has consequence. Life's routines and rhythms – eating, sleeping, washing, thinking – all cease except as sort of splintered fragments of their recognized forms. Existence evolves into a book hacked to shreds by a madman with an axe. The words are all there, somewhere, but any order, any sense, any narrative structure, any *meaning*, is gone.

Battle is joined, furiously and pitilessly. Nor will it be stopping, not for days. Not until the dead number in the thousands, with thousands more lying in wounded agony, and the rest, the spent husks of the survivors, both victor and vanquished, finally fight themselves to an exhausted standstill. In time it will be known as the Battle of Arnhem, and largely remembered for the ferocity of fighting and 2nd Battalion's heroic stand at the bridge. But for the majority of us participants, and the beleaguered Dutch people living there, it will always be the Battle of Arnhem–Oosterbeek. For although John Frost and his boys do astonishing work at the bridge, the fact is most of us will never see any bridge, nor even Arnhem itself, but will play out our part in the drama within a steadily shrinking circle of death centred on a crossroads in Oosterbeek, which the Germans will come to call *der Kessel*. The Cauldron.

CHAPTER 3

11th Battalion Medical Aid Post No. 1 lasts seven hours. Renewed enemy mortar fire heralds the recommencement of hostilities that Tuesday noon, but only briefly, mercifully, as our forces are already infiltrating the streets above and behind us, converging on the enemy who swiftly pack up and move on. After that it's a cat-and-mouse business, them probing our defences with sniper fire, machine guns and the occasional mortar, while patrols of Paras hunt them down and our boys in the street return fire with everything they've got. Then the enemy move off and try again from a different direction. For the men patrolling it's urban warfare at its most raw – and tense stuff: you literally never know what's round the next corner. To add to the pressure, increasing signs of fierce fighting are heard in several directions, with the thump of artillery now added to the mix of mortars, rifles and machine guns. More rumours of tanks too, although thankfully we don't see any in our little stretch, which comes under repeated fire but holds good. CSM Barrett has deployed his force wisely; the boys are well dug-in, with good lines of sight and plenty of ammo. Cheerful too: as each exchange of shooting dies down, ribald shouts and banter soon follow.

'Shove that up your arse, Adolf!'

'Nice work, lads. Say, Nobby?'

'What!'

'You still alive over there?'

'Course I am!'

'Pity. I rather fancy your missus.'

'Up yours. Pop over and lend us a fag, would you?'

'Ha bloody ha.'

Banter aside, as the afternoon wears on and fighting intensifies, casualties inevitably occur. Not many from our position, but several from actions happening elsewhere in the area. Apart from our 11th Battalion, we hear that 1st and 3rd Battalions are fighting their way towards 2nd Battalion still stuck at the bridge, 156th Battalion is assaulting high ground to the north, with 10th Battalion to their left, while the South Staffordshires and Scottish Borderers cover their rear. All are taking casualties, some of which find their way to us.

We manage as best we can, but the garage soon fills, and we're forced to park stretchers on the driveway, with walking wounded arranged around the garden like wilting plants. This is far from ideal as it provides little cover and we're frequently forced to duck as missiles whistle overhead or we're showered with debris. We've five medics there: me, Bowyer, Sykes and two orderlies, with various stretcher-bearers coming and going. As we work, I constantly find myself wondering about the rest of the battalion: Colonel Lea, Major Lonsdale and the others. Being so cut off is disconcerting, like getting separated on a school outing; we have no radios, no messengers, no information, the last direct contact was with the lieutenant in the Jeep this morning, and he hasn't been seen since. And with sounds of heavy fighting coming from their last known vicinity, I can't help worrying how they're doing, and whether we're ever going to link up with them again.

But with the trickle of casualties rising to a flow there's little time for worry. Nor does it get you anywhere, as I learned in training; instead you must empty your mind and just get on with it. So we do. We're operating a triage system, with each new casualty given a swift preliminary assessment and then treated in order of priority. Which sounds logical, but in reality means that midway through dressing an arm, a victim will arrive with a head wound needing urgent attention, so you turn to deal with that, but then another turns up with severe bleeding, so you drop everything for him. It's like fighting bushfires in a drought, and my least favourite way of practising medicine: hectic, wearisome and seemingly ineffectual; just when you think things are under control, somebody else staggers in and off you go again. All you can do is cope as best you can.

After hours with no respite and no end in sight, I'm beginning to buckle. At one point Jack Bowyer suggests we force entry into the house to give us more space and better cover, but some ingrained sense of decorum stops me. In any case it would be temporary at best, for as the afternoon wanes it becomes obvious the situation out in the road is untenable, despite the best efforts of Barrett and his men. Small-arms fire grows noticeably louder, the smack of bullets hitting masonry more frequent, and as the enemy closes on our position I fear we'll be overrun. Most of my injured require hospital, many require surgery, none wish to fall into enemy hands, so my priority becomes getting them out. Towards dusk I totter wearily from the garage and go in search of Barrett.

Who concurs. 'We can't hold on much longer anyway.' He shrugs, accepting my proffered cigarette.

'Any chance of rejoining Battalion?'

'Not the way we came, that's for sure. Jerry's got it well covered.' He gestures up the road, now heavily cratered and littered with rubble. His face is grey and fatigued, he has a bullet hole through one sleeve and a graze on his temple, probably from a shell fragment. Like so many Paras he chooses to fight in his red beret rather than a steel helmet. He'd say it's because the helmet's too heavy and confining, but really it's because the beret scares the enemy and he's proud to wear it. As a doctor I cannot condone such recklessness, but as a Para I can't help admiring it either.

'What about 30 Corps? I thought they were due by tonight. Tomorrow latest.'

He glances south to the river. 'Who knows? They might turn up; they might not. But we can't hang about on the off-chance.'

'What do you suggest?'

'Well, Jerry generally don't like fighting in the dark – we learned that back in Tunisia – so chances are he'll knock off at nightfall, then me and the lads might make it back to Battalion, if we're quick at it, you know, slipping through houses, over garden fences and so on. . .'

But not with us, by implication, clearly, with our garage-load of stretcher cases. I draw smoke, watching as a mortar shell bursts not seventy yards away. A day ago this would have shocked me profoundly, now it's a minor inconvenience.

Barrett's waiting, and watching, for he knows he needs my permission to attempt a break-out.

I put him at ease. 'You should definitely give it a try. But not with us, we'd only hinder you.'

'Thank you, sir. And the wounded?'

'They need the dressing station, which is back the other way somewhere. Any suggestions would be most welcome.'

'Wait till nightfall, that's my advice. Then make a dash for it using the Jeep to ferry as many stretchers as you can, with the rest carried on foot. I'll detach some lads to lend a hand, then once you're safely clear we'll make our break for it.'

He had it all thought out. So in the absence of a better plan that's what we do. I return to the garage, force one of Sykes's bully-beef sandwiches down my throat and resume work. Before we know it darkness descends and soon, like magic, the shooting duly subsides, until only sporadic small-arms fire is heard, together with a far-distant rumble of artillery and the incongruous warble of a nightingale. Then, moving by torchlight and speaking in low voices, we prepare for evacuation, loading five stretchers on to the Jeep and sharing the others between us and Barrett's boys, who also help with the walking wounded. I instruct the Jeep driver to go with his lights off as fast as he dare into Oosterbeek, find the dressing station, drop the stretchers and come back for more.

'Only if it's safe, mind you, and for God's sake don't take chances.'

Behind us flickering flashes illuminate the night sky as fighting continues in the bridge area; ahead all seems quiet. The driver nods and thumbs the starter, shattering the silence.

We watch him pull out, weave round rubble and shell holes, and disappear into the night, ears alert for sudden shooting. Nothing is heard save the grumble of his receding engine, so, gathering ourselves into a ragtag parade, we step out into the darkness.

Oosterbeek lies three miles west of Arnhem. This we already know, having passed through it on the way in, a pleasant little suburb peopled by smiling residents delighted to see us, and featuring tree-lined streets of chalet-style houses interspersed with shops, hotels and bars. Now as we return, somewhat chastened, Oosterbeek doesn't look so good, with its tidy streets littered with smashed paving, broken glass, fallen branches and burned-out vehicles. Eerily quiet too, with not a light to be seen, and no residents bothering to come out to greet us this time. This is partly due to the blackout, but also because the war they thought finally over has just crashed back on to their doorstep. And that's nothing to cheer and wave flags about.

The dressing station is at the centre of town, on the crossroads of the main Arnhem to Utrecht road, in a hotel called the Schoonoord. A Red Cross flag draped from an upstairs window proclaims its presence as our motley procession arrives an hour later. Several orderly staff hurry through its doors to help us, together with stretcher-bearers, aproned medics, and to my surprise a number of female nurses who turn out to be Dutch. The station is manned by 181st Airlanding Field Ambulance, which is a sizeable and well-equipped outfit with surgeons, anaesthetists, operating facilities and even a dentist. All the better, I conclude privately, watching as our wounded are conveyed inside, for while walking an idea has formed in my head. And as soon as the handover of wounded is completed, I ask to see the commanding officer of the 181st in order to discuss it.

'Daniel Garland, sir!' I muster my best salute. '11th Battalion MO.'

'Do stand at ease, Captain.' Lieutenant Colonel Arthur Marrable eyes me through curls of smoke rising from his pipe. Mid-forties, with swept-back hair and a kindly face, he is standing at the hotel reception counter, which now serves as his HQ. Behind him an orderly bangs on a typewriter beside a radio operator, headphones clamped on ears, who is busy twiddling knobs.

'11th, you say?' Marrable continues. 'I hear they've had quite a time of it.'

'Yes, sir. Do you have any news? We lost touch this morning.'

'Very little I'm afraid, of the 11th, or indeed anyone.' He nods at the radio operator. 'Communications problems.'

'What about Brigade? Might they know something?'

'They might. HQ's across the square at the Hartenstein Hotel, but I warn you, Brigadier Hackett's in no mood to be bothered with lost doctors. Especially as his boss has gone missing.'

'General Urquhart? Missing?'

'Apparently. Nor can he contact Division up at the bridge.' He puffs smoke and lowers his voice. 'Frankly, Garland, it's a bit of a mess.'

'30 Corps?'

'No news. No radio contact.'

'Only the thing is, sir, I really need to get back to the 11th.'

'I could badly use you here.'

'Yes, but they're without their MO.'

'I'm afraid it may be too late. Rumour is they've been over-run. I'm sorry.'

At this point the conversation stalls rather, together with my great plan to grab Bowyer and Sykes, sprint back to Barrett's mob and head off in search of the 11th.

Marrable takes pity. 'Look, old chap, here's what I suggest. There's stew and spuds in the kitchens, coffee too. Go and eat, then head upstairs and find a room, freshen up and get some rest. Meanwhile I'll try and speak to Hackett. Maybe we'll have firmer news in a few hours. If I hear anything of the 11th I'll wake you, I promise.'

It's too good an offer. Weary to my bones suddenly, I find and brief Bowyer and Sykes, eat my fill in the kitchens and clump upstairs. Choosing the first empty room, and barely pausing to loosen my tie and kick off my boots, I'm asleep before I hit the mattress.

To be woken, having slept like the dead, at precisely six the next morning, by an express train hurtling past the window. A massive explosion follows, the whole building shakes, my window shatters, a picture falls from the wall. I jerk upright, wondering what on earth has happened, and hear it again, a sound like the sky tearing apart followed by the explosion of a hundred cars crashing. Then another, and another. This is shelling, I realize, scrambling beneath the bed, and no piddly 3-inch mortar stuff, this is big, heavy artillery, 75-millimetre or even the dreaded 88s, fired from miles back. They're shelling the hospital, I curse in disbelief as the next rounds crash in, the fucking Germans are deliberately shelling a clearly marked hospital, with red crosses on roof and walls, and filled with unarmed wounded, non-combatant doctors and female nurses.

But then maybe not. For as the bombardment goes on, the walls tremble and plaster settles from above like snow, I gradually sense that the barrage, although thunderous and terrifying, is not aimed directly at me, but perhaps a little way off. Crawling to the window, I risk a peep. Outside the scene is hellish: smoke, dust and desecration, rubble and craters, a truck in flames, trees blasted asunder, their torn limbs stark white. But as the next salvo crashes in, it does appear to land a few hundred yards away, in the direction of the Hartenstein Hotel and Brigade HQ. Five minutes pass. I keep watching, the barrage goes on, some of it in our vicinity, some of it not, the Schoonoord shakes, the din is appalling, and then through the smoke I glimpse khaki-clad figures in a doorway, weapons at the ready, and watch as they sprint off at the crouch. Our boys, and they're still fighting. A lull comes; I grab my boots and dash downstairs.

Colonel Marrable is at his reception desk, calmly puffing his pipe and studying a clipboard. Around him stands a cluster of medical officers.

'Ah, Garland, there you are. Sleep well?'

'Um, I – Well, yes, thank you, sir, but—'

Another explosion rocks the building. Everyone ducks; Marrable carries on regardless. 'Good, good. Now, this is

Dixon, Cartwright, Spencer and Poutney. Chaps, this is Daniel Garland, come to lend a hand from the 11th.'

This is news to me and I'm about to query it, when another shell bursts and a ceiling light crashes to the floor. So we all shake hands instead, as though it's a pub social. 'How d'you do, delighted, jolly good, what-ho.'

Marrable consults his clipboard. 'Now, Garland, we've a busy day ahead, quite a list for surgery. So I've rostered you in with Clifford Poutney here. We've got a little operating theatre going in a storeroom round the back – a bit rudimentary but I'm sure you'll manage. . .' He breaks off, regarding me quizzically.

'Sir?'

'Ah, your tie, Garland old chap, is askew rather. And you might want to shave before you start seeing patients. Boots could do with a brush-up too.'

I can scarcely believe my ears. Here we are being bombed to buggery, and he's complaining my tie's not straight. It's like being back at medical school; even the others, all smartly turned-out, I note, are smirking like schoolboys. I open my mouth, desperate to ask about the 11th, but now suddenly doesn't seem the moment, and Poutney is catching my eye and shaking his head. So with no other option, and with everyone watching in amusement, I plod off upstairs to clean up.

Ten minutes later, tidy and fragrant, I descend once more. Poutney is waiting.

'Sorry to keep you, Captain,' I mutter.

'Think nothing, old boy,' he replies from behind an impressive handlebar moustache. He extends a hand. 'I'm

Cliff, and don't worry about the old man, he's a stickler and likes a tight ship, but he's a solid CO and terrific doctor. Come on, I'll show you around.'

We do the tour and, I admit, despite the mayhem outside, all looks immaculately ordered. The Schoonoord's dining room has been converted into a large ward, with rows of stretchers occupied by tidily arranged casualties sporting clean bandages and tucked-in blankets. Orderlies move smoothly from bed to bed checking pulses and temperatures, adjusting drips and jotting notes. The nurses I'd seen last night are evident too, straightening blankets, mopping brows, bathing faces and sweeping up debris. Everything appears calm, well organized and spotlessly tidy.

'This ward's full now,' Cliff says. 'We've a second in the lounge but it's filling fast. After that we'll have to start using the bedrooms upstairs.'

Another salvo crashes in. As one, everyone breaks off, cringes, then dusts themselves off and carries on as before. Like some surreal parlour game.

'When did this lot start?' I ask.

'Yesterday. Brigade says they're softening us up for a counter-attack. But our boys are giving as good as they get. Apparently.'

'Terrific.' Overhead a light bulb swings. 'Power's still on, I see.'

'Yes. Water and drains too. God knows how long for though.'

'Medical supplies?'

'Enough basics – blood, morphia and penicillin – for about forty-eight hours. After that we're in trouble. Air drops are promised but we've seen none yet.'

41

We continue our rounds, occasionally stooping to offer encouragement or light cigarettes for casualties, who in the main seem remarkably chipper. The resilience of the British Tommy. Eventually we find ourselves at the rear of the hotel, and Cliff pushes open a door to reveal a small storeroom. Inside stands a trestle table covered by a rubber sheet. Masks and gowns, anaesthetics, dishes of instruments, disinfectants and other surgical paraphernalia lie ready. To one side is a basin for scrubbing up.

'Right.' Cliff hands me a gown. 'I suppose we'd better get started.'

The long day passes. As the war rages outside, Cliff and I work in that cramped little storeroom on its victims. Borne in on stretchers, some are unconscious, others have to be anaesthetized. Some cry out in their pain; most endure it with grace and forbearance. Even occasional humour: 'Don't take the foot off, Doc, it's one of a pair.' In short, the job of the battlefield surgeon is to save life and stabilize the patient for rearward evacuation to better facilities. Casualties fall into three categories: firstly those needing urgent resuscitation or surgery for severe bleeding, respiratory obstruction, open chest or head wounds and penetrating abdominal wounds. Second come those needing early surgery, such as those with multiple wounds, compound fractures or large muscle-tissue injury. Thirdly come all the others. Most (but not all) combat injuries are caused by blast and/or missile penetration, they just vary in location, severity and complexity. A bullet might pass right through soft tissue and cause little damage, but the same bullet hitting chest or abdomen can wreak havoc to vital tissues and organs. If it hits the head the results can be catastrophic. Bullets are famously indiscriminate. Many battlefield injuries involve orthopaedic trauma, with around 70 per cent musculo-skeletal. Fractures account for a quarter of all injuries, while abdominal wounds have the worst recovery rate. These are mere statistics. Shock and blood loss are the principal killers, as are contamination and infection, particularly if injuries are allowed to fester. Debridement, which is the cutting away of infected tissue, plus the use of anti-bacterials such as sulphanilamide and the antibiotic penicillin are effective. Time above all is crucial. Get them on the table as quick as possible and work fast: that's their best chance. We do our best to. And soon, as is the way with surgery, the outside world retreats, and horizons shrink, until nothing remains but the man lying there, his injuries and needs, and brief muted exchanges.

'Retract there a little, please, Dan.'

'Debride more anteriorly?'

'Yes, and irrigate above and below. That's it.'

The patients come and go. The mental effort is intense and wearying, so much so that soon I'm barely noticing the incessant thunder of barrage. Time swiftly passes. At one point Marrable pops in to check on progress; Sykes and Bowyer also make an appearance. Then we suffer our first fatality. A stretcher is carried in, unusually accompanied by one of the Dutch nurses, who is holding the injured man's hand.

'Shell burst,' says the orderly. 'Hit in the chest.'

'What's she doing here?' Cliff's fatigue is showing.

The orderly shrugs. 'He begged her to stay with him.'

'Well, it's damned cramped in here, you know. . .'

'I will not be in your way,' she says quietly in English.

Cliff and I exchange glances. She looks pale, and young. But determined.

'Oh very well, but please keep out of the way.'

I examine the patient, who is unconscious, unresponsive, has a thin irregular pulse, a sickly grey pallor and is breathing fast and shallowly. A large and bloody bandage surrounds his chest. He has freckles and tousled black hair and looks barely twenty.

'What blood has he had?' I ask the orderly. A bag lies on the boy's stomach with a drip into his arm.

'Three units so far.'

'Bring more please, quick as you can.'

We set to work, but as I cut away the bandages it's clear the damage is extensive and severe. A deep and gaping chest wound is revealed, packed with blood-sodden field dressings, the tissue shredded, rib bones smashed. Carefully removing the dressings with forceps, fresh blood quickly wells beneath, filling the cavity until it overflows and drips to the floor. I probe with my fingers. Somewhere inside a major artery has been severed; to have any hope we must find it, clamp it, then set about repairing it and the other damaged vessels. Meanwhile the boy is hypotensive, his blood pressure plummeting; he's also suffering shock, hypovolemia – catastrophic blood loss – and associated organ failure. We do our best, working fast, shoulder to shoulder, three-, sometimes even four-handed within the wound. More blood arrives, we connect it to his drip and set it flowing, his heart keeps pumping it, for a while, but mostly into his chest. Then it fails altogether. I can sense this because my fingers are touching it.

'Tachycardia!'

'We need more time, bugger it.'

But we don't have more time, and there's little more we can do. Battlefield medicine does not allow for complex and protracted attempts at resuscitation: there isn't the equipment, manpower, skills – or the time. As a last resort I stretch my fingers further into the heat of his chest, feel for the muscle of his heart, and begin squeezing. A minute or two passes in silence, but the organ remains unresponsive.

'Leave it, Dan.'

'Adrenalin?'

'No. Pointless. We did what we could.'

And that's that. We jot a note on his card and begin clearing up. There's a lot of mess, including pools of blood on the floor. I'm about to start mopping when a voice breaks the silence.

'Please don't do that, Doctor, I will get bucket.'

She has not moved or said a word throughout. Nor did her hand leave the patient's. Her face is still wan, her mouth small, expression downcast yet composed.

'Yes, well – yes, all right, that would be a help. Thanks.'

She nods and exits, leaving me, Cliff and the dead boy alone. The mood in the storeroom is sombre suddenly, sombre and angry. 'For God's sake!' Cliff explodes, and throws down his gown. Then the door opens and Marrable appears, as if by sixth sense.

'Right, you two, time for a break. Stew and spuds in the kitchen. Off you go.'

The rest of the day passes similarly. The Schoonoord is increasingly busy, while around it our circumstances worsen. After a hasty meal of rather less bully beef stew and tinned potatoes than yesterday, Cliff and I split up, he to 'Lounge Ward', me to 'Dining Ward' where I find to my shock that the earlier orderliness is fast disappearing. In fact it resembles a disaster scene more than a hospital. The first matter of note is the smell, which is badly foetid from blood, pus, bedpans and insufficient air. The windows, by now all blown out by the shelling, have been covered by wood and mattresses to prevent further injury from flying glass. As well as making the room stuffy, this casts it into deep shadow, relieved only by wall-lights which flicker feebly in the failing power. Meanwhile the number of injured has soared, with recumbent men filling every inch of floor space, on stretchers, bedroom mattresses, even the bare floorboards. Crossing the room is a tiptoeing affair, a hesitant two-step, yet even so it's hard to avoid standing on the occasional finger or foot. And even as I begin examining the newest arrivals, yet more stretchers appear at the entrance. 'Not in here!' shouts one of the doctors, his tone fraught. 'Put them in the corridor. We'll get to them when we can.'

And others I speak to during the afternoon sound similarly overwhelmed, including the wounded.

'How's the shoulder, Corporal?'

'Not so bad thanks, Doc.'

'Good. We'll soon have you out of here.'

'Fat chance. We don't stand an earthly, you know.'

'No?'

'They keep coming and coming, heavy machine guns, mortars, grenades, the lot. What bloody use is a rifle against that!'

'Not much I should imagine.'

'Too right. Three of my mates bought it.'

'Try not to worry.'

Later I spot Jack Bowyer picking his way through the stretchers.

'Hello, Captain.' He grins. 'Where the hell you been hiding?'

His good-natured insolence is almost heart-warming, but I ignore it, pumping him for news instead. 'What about Battalion? Any gen?'

He grimaces. 'Cut to ribbons is what I heard. Everything's to pot, practically the whole division. All the talk's of falling back here and making a stand.'

'Jesus. What about Colonel Lea?'

'In the bag.'

'What!'

'Injured apparently, then Jerry nabbed him.'

'Christ.' I picture the scene. No first-aid post, no dressing station, no hope of evacuation, no damn medical officer. All a casualty can do is throw himself on the mercy of the enemy. And I can't help feeling responsible, at least in part.

'Major Lonsdale's our CO now,' Bowyer says. 'Did you speak to Marrable?'

'I tried, but he says we're more use here. I'll try again later. Is Sykes all right?'

'He says we should make a break for it, with or without permission. I agree.'

'But you can't do that! It's desertion.'

'No, it's finding Major Lonsdale and rejoining our unit. That's proper.'

I'm stunned, but can see he's serious. 'No, Sergeant, I can't allow it. In fact I *order* you not to. Please, just hang on, at least until I get a chance to see Colonel Marrable.'

But it's late in the evening before that chance arises, and the outcome is no better. At dusk, the German barrage finally lifts and a glorious peace descends on the Schoonoord. The relief all round is palpable, and with the patients fed, medicated and settled for the night, the medical staff retreat to the kitchens for sustenance and respite. Cliff Poutney is there, together with others I met earlier. We haven't spoken since the blood-soaked ordeal in the storeroom, but he catches my eye and winks, clearly in better spirits. Talking of which, after supper (bully beef and biscuit) someone produces brandy, pinched no doubt from the Schoonoord's bar. Bottles circulate, cigarettes light up; soon the mood is lifting. And by the time Marrable arrives, pipe in mouth and clutching a sheaf of papers, it's almost optimistic.

He soon puts paid to that.

'Hello, chaps.' He gazes round, eyes narrowed. 'Everyone all right?'

Murmurs in the affirmative. Across the kitchen the Dutch nurses stand in a group, the young one from the storeroom among them. Our eyes meet briefly; she manages an ashen smile.

'Good.' Marrable shuffles papers. 'You'll be wanting the latest from Brigade.'

He gives us the facts, which are much as Bowyer summarized earlier. The good news is that General Urquhart, who's in charge of the whole division, has turned up safe, having been stuck in a house surrounded by Germans for two days. Also that 30 Corps is making slow but steady progress towards Arnhem from the south.

'When might they get here, sir?' someone asks.

'Tomorrow, hopefully, or the next day. Which means we must do everything to conserve supplies.'

'Penicillin's running low. Morphia too.'

'Yes, I know. However, an air drop is also promised for tomorrow, including medical supplies, which should ease matters considerably.'

Thus encouraged, we move on to the matter of Operation Market Garden.

'What's happening in Arnhem, sir? And at the bridge?'

Marrable glances at the Dutch nurses. He knows his every word will quickly circulate to their friends, relatives and neighbours – the much-put-upon inheritors of this mess. Evidently he decides they have the right to know.

'2nd Battalion is still holding the north end of the bridge, but sorely pressed, and all efforts to reach them have failed. They're not expected to survive much longer. The rest of the 1st Parachute Brigade has also been badly mauled, as have the 4th Parachute and Airlanding Brigades. High casualties and loss of life have been sustained across the whole division. German reinforcements including tanks and heavy armour are pouring into Arnhem by the hour, such that the situation there is untenable. So the plan now is to stage a phased withdrawal here to Oosterbeek, form a defensive perimeter, and hold out until 30 Corps arrives.'

'Withdraw the whole division?' someone asks incredulously. 'All ten thousand?'

'Yes, although it is feared as many as half have already been lost or captured.'

He pauses to let this sink in. Glances are exchanged and murmurs circle the room. One of the older Dutch nurses is openly weeping.

'But the main objective, sir. Market Garden, the bridge. We're giving up?'

'It looks that way. The main objective now is to save what's left of the division. Hold out here in other words, and pray to God that 30 Corps gets here before it's too late. And that inevitably means hundreds more injured coming our way, so resources will be stretched, and your services in high demand. I ask you all therefore to continue to do your utmost. . .'

More follows, including arrangements for the burial of the dead, news of a second dressing station at another hotel, a night rota system for keeping watch, and a typical Marrable plea about maintaining personal tidiness. A while later he leaves us and the meeting dissipates. In need suddenly of fresh air and solitude, I wander out to the rear garden for a cigarette. Beneath a starlit sky, the autumn night is cool and calm, with a faint breeze stirring the leaves overhead. The garden, once trim and tidy, neatly grassed and edged with beds, is now scarred by a sprinkling of shell holes, spoiling its charm like boils on a face.

In a corner I find the temporary graveyard Marrable mentioned. Twelve new graves have been dug, and filled, including one for the boy from the storeroom. Curious about his name, I bend to read the sticks that burial details use to mark casualties.

'That one,' a voice says from behind. 'Fourth one. His name is Web-stair.'

'Ah. Yes, I see now, Webster, thank you.'

'Nineteen years, from a place called Basil-don. Do you know it?'

'Not terribly well. It's in Essex, I believe, to the east of London.'

'Oh. That is all he told me. Before. . .'

'Yes.'

She's very slight of stature, perhaps five foot, and wearing a too-large man's jacket over her uniform. She's tying her head in a scarf.

'You're leaving?'

'Yes, I must. My father will be expecting me. It's only two kilometres.'

'Two kilometres? But you can't! There are Germans everywhere. With guns!'

'Oh yes?' A bright white smile suddenly appears in the moonlight. 'Don't worry, they won't shoot me.'

'How can you know?'

'Because I'm a nurse. And they don't shoot nurses.'

'But they might mistake you! No, it's too dangerous, at least let me come—'

'No.' She rests a hand on my arm. 'It will be all right, but not if you come. That *would* be dangerous.'

'Well. . . Are you sure?'

'Yes. Please do not worry.'

'Are you coming back tomorrow? I mean, if it's safe that is.'

'Would you like me to?'

'Well, I – of course, we're enormously grateful for all your—'

'Then I will.' She turns to leave, but then pauses. 'You did all you could. With Web-stair today. It cannot have been easy.'

Then she's gone, and I realize I don't even know her name.

CHAPTER 4

Days and nights fuse into a single seamless hell of screaming shells, shattering explosions, blood, death and desecration, punctuated by surreal intervals of nail-biting silence. The passage of time ceases; no world exists save the battered ark of the Schoonoord and its bloody cargo of dead and dying soldiers. Each day Cliff Poutney and I descend to confront the nightmare, threading our way through the mass of groaning bodies to our storeroom abattoir, where we slice and chop and saw like back-street butchers. Each night we repair to the wreckage of our bedroom, there to stare through the missing window at the stars, waiting in shocked silence, bleary with sleeplessness, for the coming of the hated dawn. Unsurprisingly we draw close. I find the shelling unendurable; Cliff calms me with stories of his Dorset home. Meanwhile he talks fearfully of captivity so I sing show tunes and crack bad jokes, until exhaustion overtakes us and we fall into unconsciousness for a few hours. Then six o'clock comes and the whole nightmare cycle begins again.

I lose track – a week passes, a month, an eternity? One night I'm nudged awake before dawn to stand watch and, leaving Cliff snoring, descend blearily to reception, boots in hand, there to find the radio operator slumped asleep at his post. Failures in radio communications have become a feature of the Market Garden débâcle and suddenly I'm incandescent with rage. But just as I'm about to kick the man awake, I see the fatigue on his face, and the bloody bandage on his knee, and the little crucifix in his hand, and I hesitate. He's doing his best, I realize, like everyone, in his own way, calling and calling into the ether for help, and never getting a reply.

I leave him, and tiptoe away along the corridor to check on the wounded. This hour is the quietest of the cycle and I almost relish it. Almost. By now the entire floor of the Schoonoord has injured men lying on it. Most are sleeping, having received morphia to provide a night's rest and respite from pain. When it wears off, we can expect our services to be in demand, but for now only one or two are awake and in discomfort. I settle them with reassurance and analgesics, then return to reception to wait for the day to begin.

Which it does, exactly at dawn, with the hated artillery barrage. I have been bracing myself, as I do every day, praying that this day may dawn differently, but with Teutonic precision, at six on the dot comes that shrieking, tearing sound, like tortured souls from hell, followed by an appalling explosion that shakes the poor Schoonoord like a dog with a toy. I grit my teeth, cursing volubly, while the barrage grows, gathering strength like a hurricane, until it is in full flow.

With further rest impossible, weary staff begin appearing from all directions. Breakfast is tea without sugar or condensed milk as both have run out, as has the water, which now comes from the radiators. Then it's down to work amid the familiar patterns of the day: the Schoonoord falling to bits round our ears, the nerve-stretching onslaught of the barrage, the stench of cordite, blood, suppuration and sewage, and the never-ending procession of incoming stretchers. If anything more arrive than yesterday, and certainly more dead; by mid-morning we're stacking new wounded two high using chairs on tables, and a melancholy queue of fatalities waits in the garden for burial. Walking wounded must find space where they can. Injuries are not just from artillery fire either; many arrive showing evidence of closer combat, as our troops struggle to repel the encroaching enemy. Rifle bullets, hand grenades, one victim arrives having been stabbed by a bayonet. Still the barrage accounts for most, some shells exploding so close that they compound injuries with flying glass and shrapnel, and bombard us with debris and dust. I seem to spend my time in a permanent crouch, crawling on hands and knees between new arrivals, assessing and processing, trying to find places to accommodate them. Jack Bowyer crosses my path occasionally, but we have neither time nor inclination for chit-chat. The little Dutch nurse is also in evidence, and once, after a particularly loud blast which blows the lights, we look up and exchange a vacant stare, like startled rabbits. Later still my batman Sykes appears, bearing boxes of supplies.

'Power's out,' he puffs. 'Water too: the main's blown.'

'Any chance of repairs?'

'No, they're buggered for good. Drains too.'

'That's a pity.' I glance up at him. 'What have we there?'

'Last of the morphia. Be right up shit creek when this runs out.'

'Air drops later today, Private. We can hold out till then.'

'Right. Er, did you speak to the old man? You know, about rejoining Battalion?'

I gesture around. 'In this! Are you mad? And where would you look for them? 11th Battalion's gone, don't you get it?'

'So you're not going to try?'

'No, Sykes, and neither are you! It's insane. And we're needed here.'

He's offended, I can see, and maybe I have gone too far. But his attitude irks, and the notion of wandering through bombed-out streets crawling with Germans, searching for a battalion of men that doesn't exist, is beyond ludicrous. Anyway, I'm too tired and jittery for niceties. He stalks off in a huff. I immediately feel guilty and am about to call after him when there's a thunderous whoosh overhead. Everyone looks up, a second whoosh, Marrable appears, somebody cheers, Bowyer catches my eye. Aircraft, we realize. Supply drops! And not a moment too soon.

We charge into the street like over-excited children. No Dakotas are seen, nor parachutes; however, the engine noise persists so we wait, hoping they're circling back for the drop. I look around. It's days since I was last out here and it's a shock. As though Oosterbeek has been struck by an earthquake. Barely a building stands undamaged, few have windows, many are roofless or show gaping holes in walls. One or two are on fire. The streets below are littered with wreckage and debris, burned-out vehicles, fallen telegraph poles, smashed trees, shell craters and mounds of rubble. It's a scene of utter desolation, yet incredibly men are here, and busy at work all around.

Our men. Through drifting smoke, anti-tank guns and other artillery pieces can be seen on junctions and corners; elsewhere machine-gun and mortar positions are dug in behind walls or in doorways. These are the targets of a relentless barrage, yet they're still manned, still alive, and still shooting back. Up at a window I glimpse figures in khaki. One of them is waving, so I wave back, and he shouts a response.

'GET THE FU—!'

Whoosh! Engines thunder overhead. I glimpse black crosses on mottled wings and the next instant everyone's diving for cover and a hail of machine-gun fire is ripping up the road around us.

'Back!' Marrable shouts. 'For God's sake, get back inside!'

After lunch (half a mug of tinned soup) it's back to the storeroom with Cliff for the afternoon operating list. Though others have been working here, the place is much as we left it, apart from an absence of running water to wash with and electricity to see with, and rather more bloodstains on the floor. We scrub with Lysol, pump up a primus lamp for lighting and set to work. A succession of casualties follow, exhibiting the usual range of impact and blast wounds to heads, chests, abdomens and extremities, some superficial, many not, some predictable, others a total surprise. We carefully remove one man's head bandage to find relatively minor blast wounds to his face, but one of his eyeballs lying on his cheek. Upon questioning he tells us he has dizziness and 'blurred vision'. Examining the organ we find it bloodshot but undamaged, and still attached by the optic nerve and retinal vessels, so having inspected and washed it, we replace it in the ocular cavity and bandage him up.

Another young patient arrives in a state of high agitation.

'Shot in the bollocks,' the orderly reports perfunctorily. We all wince.

'Save 'em, Doc!' the man pleads. 'For God's sake, save 'em, I'm getting married next month!'

We save one, lose the other, repair a badly lacerated scrotal sack, assure the youth his prospects for fatherhood remain favourable, and send him on his way.

Hours pass. As usual, the task absorbs us so completely that we barely notice the passage of time, or subtle changes to our environment and conditions. Midway through stitching a thigh wound with cat-gut, Cliff breaks off and cocks an ear.

'D'you hear that?'

'Hear what?'

'Voices. Outside. Thought I heard voices. Shouting and that.'

We duly listen, but nothing is heard, although we do notice less artillery and more small-arms fire.

Cliff shrugs. 'Must have imagined it. Who's next?'

The next patient is an amputation, a procedure I've never carried out and have been secretly dreading. The victim, a corporal of the Royal Engineers, is brought in semi-conscious, rolling his head from side to side and mumbling incoherently. Cliff and I examine his leg, which is grotesquely angled, hanging by sinew and completely shattered below the knee.

'Put him under, Dan, it'll have to come off.'

I prepare the anaesthetic, a syringe of sodium pentothal, and, rolling up his sleeve, straighten the arm and swab the fold of his elbow with disinfectant. But the poor man has lost so much blood his veins won't stand up, and despite repeated insertions of the needle my attempts fail and I'm forced to withdraw.

'Try and make a fist, old chap,' I murmur in his ear. Slowly his hand closes. Meanwhile Cliff twists a tourniquet around his upper arm until at last a faint line of blue appears beneath the skin. I slide the needle in again, probing further and further, at the same time plucking back lightly on the plunger. Seconds pass. I stop breathing, feel the sweat break on my brow and a pulse banging in my throat. Deeper I probe; then suddenly a cloud of crimson floods the syringe, discolouring the clear anaesthetic. I nod to Cliff who loosens the tourniquet, and slowly advance the plunger, watching until the man's face slackens and the first deep breaths of unconsciousness overtake him.

'He's out.'

'Good work. Right, let's get that leg off.'

But there's no saw. We rummage through boxes, poke among trays, search high and low, but find no sign. The all-metal sterile bone saw with detachable blade specially designed for amputation is missing.

'Surely it was here yesterday?'

'I don't know, I don't recall seeing it.'

'My God, perhaps it never arrived.'

'Well, we'd better find something, and quick. This leg needs to come off now.'

'I'll get the orderlies to—'

'Hold on!' I retrieve my battledress jacket from a hook and begin feeling along its seams. 'Yes, here it is. Hand me that scalpel.' A moment later I'm slitting the seam of my battledress and removing a thin package wrapped in greaseproof paper.

'Escape kit! Good thinking, Dan!'

I unwrap the hacksaw blade, issued to all Paras in case of capture, and drop it in a dish of disinfectant. Along the corridor somewhere a commotion of voices seems to be starting up. Cliff examines the blade. 'How are we going to use it? With no handle or anything?'

We clip Spencer Wells forceps to both ends, and then, standing on opposite sides of the table, him holding one end and me the other, we begin gingerly sawing.

It works surprisingly well. But then the door crashes open and a fully armed German soldier stamps in.

'*Was machen Sie!*' he shouts. Then he sees what we're doing and goes pale. A second later he exits, slamming the door behind him.

Cliff and I look at each other. 'Christ, we've been over-run.'

There's nothing to do except finish the operation, which goes well, with the leg's blood vessels ligatured, a skin flap closed over muscular tissue to form a stump, and a cannula added for drainage. Having bandaged the wound, we administer morphia and antibiotic, cover him with a blanket and carry him out to the ward.

All medical officers are ordered to reception. We gather in an uneasy semi-circle, Marrable at our head. Before us stand four fully armed Germans. With their jackboots and coal-scuttle helmets they look huge and imposing, yet smell, peculiarly, of carbolic soap. Odours aside, their demeanour is hostile. Standing with them, I note with consternation, is the little Dutch nurse.

The lead German steps forward. *'Sie sind Gefangene des deutschen Heeres!'*

'You are now prisoners of the German army,' she translates quietly.

'Sie werden Ihre Arbeit im Krankenhaus fortsetzen.'

'You will continue your work at the hospital.'

'Dann werden Sie in Gefangenenlagen transportiert werden.'

'Then you will be transported to prison camps.'

And that's that. Checkmate. The end of the game. More follows, including strong warnings about hidden weapons or attempts at escape, both of which will result in severe punishment. We half listen, scarcely able to take it in, yet alone believe it. Half an hour ago we were free men, beleaguered yes, under pressure yes, but free men pursuing a just cause. Now we're the worthless flotsam of war, irrelevant, subjugated, doomed to incarceration. Cliff looks wretched, his worst fears realized, while a leaden gloom settles in my stomach. We're not marching to Berlin as victors, we're beaten men going to prison. For as long as the war lasts.

The German is still talking, loudly, and it's beginning to irritate. Then halfway through a harangue about ration shortages and the illegal use of water, Colonel Arthur Marrable steps forward and holds up his hand.

'Be so kind as to tell the sergeant,' Marrable says to the nurse, 'that he will stand to attention when he addresses a senior officer, and also speak respectfully. Furthermore he will do up the top button of his tunic.'

'What?' Her voice is a terrified whisper.

'Do it, if you please, nurse.'

She translates, we hold our breath, Marrable takes out his pipe. The German's eyes widen and blood suffuses his cheeks. He looks fit to explode. But then slowly he reaches up, fastens the top button of his tunic, and brings himself to attention.

'*Heil Hitler!*' he shouts, and stamps off.

'Obnoxious lout,' Marrable mutters. 'Anyone got a match?'

The rest of the day, somewhat surreally, continues much as before. German soldiers come and go, their cumbersome presence a repeated reminder that we're now beaten men. But in other respects the situation improves, particularly for the wounded. For a start the shelling stops, so we're able to tend to them properly, undisturbed by ear-splitting explosions or falling masonry. We even unblock a few windows to allow in light and fresh air – badly needed now the drains have failed. The orderly staff and Dutch nurses set to work emptying latrine buckets, mopping and cleaning, sweeping and wiping, before an evening meal of sorts is prepared and circulated. An army padre arrives, passing from bed to bed offering solace and encouragement, taking letters, sharing a joke. Later we follow him into the garden for a service for the dead, now duly interred by a burial detail. All the Dutch nurses attend, including the small one. Afterwards we linger for a word.

'What will you do?' I ask.

She shrugs. 'Continue as before. German rule is nothing new for us.'

'It is for me. I don't think I'll like it.'

'You learn to adjust. And be patient. And have faith it will end.'

'Yes.' I hesitate. 'I'm sorry.'

She looks up. 'Sorry?'

'We came here to kick them out, to liberate you. Yet we brought nothing but misery and death. Now we'll be taken away and you'll be left with this mess.' I survey the wrecked garden. 'We failed you.'

Her hand touches mine. 'You tried, Captain. That is all that matters.'

'It's Daniel.'

'And I am Anna.'

'Right. We should probably go inside. Curfew and that.'

'Yes.' She turns to go. 'Do you?'

'Do I what?'

'Have faith it will end?'

'Of course.'

Inside, the evening ritual is under way: patients settling for the night, last-minute urgencies seen, medication issued, night staff posted. I report to reception, now lit by candle, to learn that Cliff and I are on duty at four so ordered to rest. Quite where is another matter. With the top floor out due to a smashed roof, and our bedroom now crammed with wounded, options for a quiet billet are dwindling.

Cliff grimaces. 'It looks like you-know-where!'

We scrounge a spare stretcher and head to the storeroom, candles in hand.

'You take the table, I'll take the floor.'

After a cursory wash with no water, I arrange the stretcher beneath the operating table, remove my boots, gaiters and tie and flop down, sniffing distastefully at the stink of disinfectant, dried blood and my socks. Above me the table squeaks in protest as Cliff stretches out.

'You a regular, Cliff?' I ask after an interval.

'Suppose I am. Joined in thirty-seven. Could see the way the wind was blowing, knew the army needed doctors, signed up for the RAMC, got posted to the 181st under Marrable, been with them ever since. Tunisia, Sicily, Italy, now this. What about you?'

'No. Not a regular. I only joined up a few months ago. This is my first op.'

'Last one too, by the looks of it.'

'Rather appears that way.'

'What do you think will happen?'

'God knows. I suppose we'll find out tomorrow.'

We bid each other goodnight and settle as best we can, but from the creaking of the table I can tell he's restive.

'You OK, Cliff?'

'Hmm? Sorry, I didn't mean to disturb you.'

'What's up?'

A worried sigh comes from above. 'Nothing. It's just. . .'

'What?'

'The shelling. And the gunfire and all that. I can take it, just about. God knows I've seen enough of it over the years.'

'Yes.'

'But captivity. You know, the whole idea of being locked up, as a prisoner, for months, or maybe years.'

'What about it?'

'It scares me stiff.'

I'm roused, rudely, by the door flying open and a blast of torchlight in the face.

'Wake up! All officers to reception right away.'

I force open my eyes, only to find it's my orderly sergeant bossing me around. As usual. 'Bowyer, what the hell are you doing? What time is it?'

'Half three. Jerry's scarpered. We've been liberated.'

'What! By 30 Corps?'

'No, by our lads. Marrable'll explain. He wants you both pronto. Also' – he lowers his voice – 'Sykes is gone. Slipped away in the confusion. Can't say I blame him.'

We struggle into our mildew-stinking clothes and hurry to reception, where we find Marrable and the others gathering in expectant silence. Outside all is quiet save for the hiss of rain.

'Right, chaps,' Marrable begins, 'listen carefully, here's the gen, hot from HQ. Arnhem's had it. We've pulled out. All remaining troops have been ordered back here to Oosterbeek. There's a chain-link ferry across the river here; our boys are to form a one-mile perimeter around it, and hold that perimeter until 30 Corps get here.'

'They're really coming?'

'Pray they do. The Polish Para Brigade is also due, if this rain ever stops. HQ calculates we can hold out here for another day, maybe two with air supplies, but if nobody comes they're looking at evacuating the entire division across the river. Either way, this bridgehead represents our only means of relief, in or out, so it must be held at all costs.

'Now, the Schoonoord lies on the eastern edge of the perimeter, which is both good and bad news for us. The bad news is we'll feel the full brunt of enemy attacks coming along the Arnhem–Utrecht road, which are likely to include storm troops, heavy artillery and tanks. Our lads will be trying to stop them, right here around the crossroads. So it's going to get bloody.'

Murmurs circle the room; then someone inevitably asks: 'And the good news?'

Marrable smiles. '. . . is that our boys have been quietly widening the perimeter during the night, with the result that Jerry has pulled out. We're free again. For now.'

More follows about new arrangements for surgery, revised duty rosters, and a complete inventory of all remaining stores. Once the medical matters are in hand, however, the conversation soon returns to military ones.

'So Arnhem Bridge has gone, sir?'

'I'm afraid so. 2nd Battalion held out superbly, but no one could get near them. A radio message was picked up at HQ, "Out of ammo, God save the King," then nothing more. It is feared barely seventy men are left.'

'Out of seven hundred.'

A shocked silence follows, then: 'What of other units?'

'A handful from 10th Battalion got through here in the afternoon. And from 156th. They were defending the rear but got surrounded. Hung on as long as possible, then broke out by bayonet charge through the enemy lines. Eighty or so made it.'

I have to ask. 'Is there any word of the 11th sir?'

'Yes, Garland. A Major Lonsdale put together a scratch force from surviving elements of 11th, 1st and 3rd Battalions and is currently holding the southeast corner of the perimeter from a church down the road. Doing a fine job too by all accounts.'

Major Richard Lonsdale, Dickie to his friends, our first casualty on the drop here, a flak fragment to the hand. I don't know him well, but his reputation is formidable. Should I try, even at this late stage, to rejoin him? To assume the role I was appointed to, yet abandoned so long ago?

Marrable reads my thoughts. 'It's all right, Garland, Lonsdale has an aid post nearby plus full medical support co-opted from other units. Everyone's mixed up together now, so I want you to stay here until the whole show's over.'

Decision made. It's almost a relief. I can only nod glumly.

'Scarcely seems possible, sir,' someone else says. 'Ten thousand men, a whole division, decimated in just a week.'

'I know. HQ estimates over half have been killed, wounded or captured, with much fighting still to be done.' He straightens suddenly. 'Which means, gentlemen, we're going to be busier than ever, so I want you now to go find sustenance, then clean up, smarten up and be back here ready to start the day at oh six hundred hours. And don't forget to shave!'

We disperse, freshen up as best we can, and after another breakfast of brackish tea, report to our various duty stations, eyes anxiously on our watches. Shortly before six, Anna and the other Dutch nurses appear from the cellar where they've been sheltering during the night. Despite noble efforts, they look rumpled and weary. As do we all.

The six o'clock barrage is louder, more ferocious and more sustained than anything we've previously experienced – and noticeably nearer. Less the lobbing of heavy shells from far away, more a furious assault by every weapon imaginable from just down the road. Plus our weaponry is now added to the mix, as we reply with mortars, Brens, heavy machine guns and the rest. Shells can literally be heard thrumming up the road outside, in both directions, scything anything in their path. Mortars thump and crash at minimum range, machine guns rattle from many directions at once, and above it all comes the incessant clatter of small-arms fire as Paras shoot back from upstairs windows, round street corners, behind barricades and down dug-outs. It feels as though everyone is just letting fly with everything they've got.

In the Schoonoord the effect is utterly devastating, beyond hell, beyond anything we've experienced, and completely incapacitating. Coherent thought is impossible, yet alone useful action, when the barrage first starts; all we can do is throw ourselves to the floor alongside the wounded, clamp our arms over our ears and wait to die. Shattered glass flies, shells punch through walls, dust and smoke choke our lungs, walls quake, floors tremble. I lift my head to the maelstrom briefly and see a patient writhing in agony, blood spurting from a fresh wound to his abdomen. A medic stoops to help him, only to fall dead from a stray bullet. Elsewhere an orderly slumps, his face a mask of blood, while a section of ceiling crashes on to wounded victims nearby. On and on it goes, an insane cacophony, assaulting the senses, violating body and mind. Rigid with terror, I lie there on the floor, willing, praying, begging it to stop.

Then it does. Or rather it alters. Like an adjustment, as though the players in this nightmare drama are shifting position, or changing tactics, or simply drawing breath. Whatever, the tumult pauses, and as it does so we raise our heads to new sounds: the groaning of wounded, a sob of terror, our own hoarse gasps. And something else, like the grumble of distant motors. We begin to move, instinctively grabbing the pause and filling it with activity, slithering like reptiles from one casualty to the next, then rising to a crouch, finally scuttling about on all fours like monkeys, swabbing, wiping, staunching, bandaging as we go. The pause stretches, the grumbling engine grows louder, and suddenly a fully armed paratrooper runs in, grime-stained, darkly stubbled, heavily laden with grenades, Sten gun and a PIAT anti-tank gun.

'Get the fuck down! Tanks coming up the road!'

Then he disappears and a moment later the mayhem restarts, shooting all round, thick and furious, but with the added crash of 88-millimetre gunfire as the lead tank's turret fires, side to side, smashing walls, exploding trees, demolishing vehicles. Slowly the grinding noise creeps nearer, and then comes a bang as the PIAT fires from right outside, followed by a whump as its shell strikes home. A storm of shooting follows, running feet, shouting and the crack of grenades, then a hoarse cheer followed by the roar of enveloping flames. 'By God, we got it!'

Ten minutes later the next tank is heard grinding up the road.

And so it goes, all day, back and forth, winning, losing, fighting, dying. Our presence seems redundant, our efforts at doctoring next to useless. There's no food that I can recall; we run out of medical basics, so we tip water bottles for the thirsty, sedate the agonized, drag out the dead. Existence becomes about surviving the next tank attack, the next aerial bombardment, the next infantry assault, the next hour. And we do, but inexorably, and despite early success and incredible resistance, the Oosterbeek perimeter, the Cauldron, begins to shrink, as our forces are driven back by the overwhelming weight of enemy. Finally, late in the afternoon, the Germans overtake our position once more, and we fall back into their hands.

This time it's for good. As yesterday, an armed detachment enters the hotel, checks everyone for weapons, warns us to behave and leaves. We're so dazed we can only shrug and carry on. A little later a contingent of German medics arrive under the leadership of a major called Voss. He doesn't shout, he doesn't gloat, he isn't armed, he merely surveys the wrecked hotel in awestruck silence before closeting himself in a corner with Marrable. They talk for a long time while we move slowly around, tending wounds and sweeping up, like pensioners in a trance.

'We've arranged for a temporary ceasefire,' Marrable explains to us in a while, 'to evacuate the most critically wounded. From both sides.' We're gathered back in what's left of reception, pale, shaken, weary, caked in dust. The ceiling's down, one wall open to the afternoon sunlight. I spot Cliff gazing out at the clouds, his arm in a sling from a shell splinter. Jack Bowyer has a bandage round his head, Marrable himself a bloody cheek. He looks utterly drained, and old beyond his years, the fight, the wonderful insistence on good form, gone from him. 'Major Voss here is arranging for transport to arrive in one hour. We'll need all hands to help with loading. That is all.'

At dusk the shooting duly dies away, until only sporadic rifle fire is heard, as both adversaries withdraw to rest and eat and lick their wounds for an hour. We begin carrying the wounded outside, preparatory to evacuation, but then an odd thing happens. Six German infantrymen are found in the garden, having set up a firing position there. Marrable tells them they must leave, that armed combatants aren't allowed on designated medical premises – it's against the Geneva Convention. Major Voss agrees and backs him up.

But they refuse. 'If we walk out of here we'll be shot,' one protests.

'No you won't, there's a ceasefire.'

'Fuck ceasefire, if the Red Devils spot us they'll shoot us. Or we'll shoot them.'

Voss prevails, promises all will be well and orders them on their way. They slip out of the back gate and run for the road. Immediately a burst of gunfire is heard and they come charging back, red-faced and furious. Voss too is incensed, shouting angrily at Marrable about lies and betrayal.

Marrable can only nod in agreement. Then he beckons me over.

'Sir?'

'Garland. Some stupid arse of ours down the road is still shooting. Go and find them and tell them to bloody stop, or we won't be able to evacuate the wounded.'

'Me, sir?'

'Yes you, damn it, you're an officer, order them to stop if necessary, and be quick about it.'

This isn't real, I decide, it's a dream, and Bowyer will shake me awake any moment. But Bowyer doesn't come, and with fumbling fingers I find myself making ready. I don a medic's apron over my battledress, so it's obvious I'm not a combatant, then strap on two Red Cross armbands, one on each arm, for added emphasis. I stuff a Red Cross satchel with random kit and loop it over my shoulder, and I borrow a tin helmet with a large Red Cross painted on it for extra insurance. I still feel I'm walking out to face a firing squad.

'Wait!' a female voice calls. 'Take this!'

She's found a broom, and tied a Red Cross flag to it. 'Hold it up high, it will protect you.' Then she leans up and kisses me on the cheek.

Daylight is failing as I step through the gate and into the street. Broken glass crunches underfoot and a gust of wind blows drifting smoke; other than that all is deathly quiet. I set off, broomstick high, a nervous hum on my lips. *If you were the only girl in the world. . .* It's like a cowboy film, I feel, the lone survivor walking down the street after the shoot-out, while unseen eyes watch from windows. Except the dead bodies I pass are all real men, and the unseen eyes have real guns and lethal intent.

I move down the road, passing shattered terrace houses, a burned-out tank and a German half-track lying on its side, four bodies splayed around it like discarded dolls. I start calling, in an idiotic stage whisper, outside one house after the next. 'Ah, hello? Anyone there? Medic calling.'

'Don't move,' a voice growls. I stop beside a low garden wall. 'Don't move, don't turn, don't do anything, or you'll give away our position. Face down the road and stop waving that bloody flag.'

'Right.' I do as instructed.

'Who are you and what do you want?'

'I'm Garland. From the dressing station, at the hotel back there.'

'And?'

'And I've come to ask you to cease firing, for an hour, so we can evacuate the wounded.'

'Fuck that, there's Jerry everywhere. If I see him, I shoot him and he shoots me.'

Exactly what the Germans said in the garden, I note. 'Yes, well, you see it's an order, as it were. From Brigade. I'm here to pass it on, from Brigadier Hackett. I'm sorry.'

A pause. 'Do you know how long I've held this position?'

'No.'

'Three days and nights, no food, no water, and no relief. I've two dead in the cellar, two wounded covering the back, and three upstairs watching the road. I'm not giving it up. I'm not retreating, not surrendering, and if we cease firing, Jerry will only take advantage and reposition.'

'I understand. But—'

'We'll fight here until the ammo runs out, then we'll take 'em on with bayonets. We'll stand until we die.'

'Yes. I see.' Silence falls, for I have no answer to that. A shrill screech splits the air as swifts fly overhead in the evening calm. I rack my brains. 'All right, listen. I'm going to drop my satchel next to the wall here. It has bandages, dressings and a little morphia for your wounded. Water too.'

A grunt.

'And a packet of Players.'

'Cigs, Jesus!'

The magic of tobacco. I lower the bag, and an unseen hand reaches out and drags it from view.

'Thanks, Doc.'

'That's OK. We've run out of everything too, you know. Yet we've two hundred injured, including some from your unit probably, and nothing we can do for them. Jerry's bringing trucks. We can get them out of this, and take them to proper hospitals. They'll stand a chance. If not. . .'

I hear a cigarette lighting. 'One hour, you say?'

'One hour.'

'And Hackett ordered this?'

'The man himself.' I hold my breath. Then something comes to me. The ancient war cry of the Parachute Regiment, first heard in desperate fighting against Rommel's Afrika Korps in Tunisia. Now it's a password among wearers of the red beret. As a novice and non-combatant I have little right to use it.

'*Waho Mohammed?*'

'OK, Doc.' Another grunt. '*Waho Mohammed.*'

*

I meet Anna one final time in the garden of the Schoonoord.

'You're leaving?' she asks.

'Yes. Colonel Marrable's sending a medical team with the wounded. My name came up.' I force a wry smile. 'I think he's trying to get rid of me.'

'Where are you going?'

'I'm not sure. A place was mentioned. Apeldoorn?'

'Yes, it's about thirty kilometres north of here. There's a prisoner-of-war hospital.'

'Ah. And you?'

She looks around the ruined grounds. Pitted with shell holes, littered with fallen trees and rubble, it looks more like a building site than a garden. Except for the dead. Two rows of new fatalities lie waiting for burial, many uncovered and grotesquely mutilated. Some have been burned by flame-throwers; the smell of death and putrescence and burned flesh hangs heavy. Yet after so long we barely notice.

'I haven't seen my father in days. I have word he's unhurt, but our home is damaged and I must return to help him. Then I expect I will take up my job at the Queen Elizabeth hospital, and wait for the war to end. Once more.'

'Let's hope it's for good next time.' I hold my breath. 'Shall I write?'

Her eyes widen. 'To me?'

'No, to Father Christmas. Would you like me to? It seems I'll have plenty of time.'

'Well, I . . .' Her face clouds as implications sprout. Then a frown appears. 'What's that?'

'What's what?'

'That! My God, look, he's moving!'

I turn, mystified, towards the rows of dead bodies. Then a hand appears, hovering above one of them, as though suspended on a string.

'Jesus,' I gape. 'Jesus, that one's still alive!'

And that's how I meet Theo Trickey.

CHAPTER 5

Theo Trickey's father, Victor Trickey, met his mother, Carmelina Ladurner, in Innsbruck in the winter of 1921. Victor was twenty-six, fair, dashing, an officer of the British army, in Austria to train for the first-ever winter Olympics, due to be held in Chamonix. Carmelina (Carla) was eighteen, beautiful, headstrong, the daughter of a print-shop owner from Bolzano in the Italian Alps. Both were accomplished skiers, but hurtling down Nockspitze Mountain one day that November, their paths crossed; they collided and fell. Carla twisted an ankle, so Victor, strapping their skis to his back, swept her into his arms and carried her the mile down to the lodge. Where it was love at first sight.

Victor stayed in Innsbruck four months, with Carla making repeated trips from her home to visit him. Though her grasp of English was modest and his Italian non-existent, their rapport was at once intuitive and intimate, founded more on physical attraction and a shared love of the outdoors than meaningful conversation. Victor lived thriftily and lodged in a males-only hostel, while Carla stayed with an aunt who allowed him to the door but no further. So each day they skied the region's famous slopes, before retiring to a tavern for the evening, there to sit entwined before blazing fires, sipping hot Stroh rum, listening to Tyrolean folk musicians and fictionalizing a future together. His army salary precluded heavy spending but Carla had money enough to finance these outings, and also the occasional trip away. One week she persuaded him to return with her to Bolzano to meet her family.

'They want much know you,' she coaxed.

'But the cost, old sport.'

'I pay!'

'In that case. . . Why not!'

Bolzano lies sixty miles south of Innsbruck in the far northern Italian province of South Tyrol. Wild, mountainous, spectacularly beautiful, South Tyrol had for centuries enjoyed semi-independence and a rich if confused cultural heritage. At various times coming under Holy Roman, Austro-Hungarian, Venetian, Bavarian, Italian and even Napoleonic jurisdiction, following the First World War South Tyrol lost its prized autonomy and became formally annexed to Italy, an arrangement many inhabitants deplored. By the 1920s unrest was growing in the province, with some residents seeing themselves as Austrian or German, while others sympathized with the new Italian nationalism under Benito Mussolini. Many simply wanted to remain as independent South Tyroleans. Factions developed, communities split, neighbour fell out with neighbour, even families feuded. Bolzano, as the region's capital, became the focal point for this ethnic turmoil.

The event was a family celebration, the baptism of Carla's niece, held in a church hall near Bolzano's famous Castello

Mareccio. Victor wore his uniform, which impressed the gathering almost as much as his wit and charm. An English officer of the Great War, handsome, dashing, amusingly mannered, was a notable catch by the young Ladurner girl, whom most family elders considered flighty and irresponsible. For his part Victor was surprised and bewildered by Carla's clan, which was large and diverse and managed to embrace all sides of the ethnic argument. Strong views were held, he soon learned, and expressed, loudly and in a variety of tongues including German, Italian, a local dialect called Ladin, and even occasionally English. Despite the internal feuding, the British, he found to his relief, were well regarded, especially in matters military.

'What is you regiment?' Carla's father Josef demanded, pouring him schnapps.

'I'm a second lieutenant of the East Surreys,' Victor recited. 'The Young Buffs.'

Josef slapped his thigh. 'This is *fantastisch*!' and launched into a long and complicated story, which Victor already knew from Carla, about how Josef had encountered the East Surreys in the field of battle.

'This most famous battle Piave River, the sixteenth of June 1918. You remember, of course?'

'Well, now you mention it—'

'Yes, yes, very near to here. But first I fight at Caporetto under the young lion Rommel. You know him of course.'

'Um, Romm. . . Who? '

'Rommel! Move quick and make them panic, he always say. With just one platoon running fast we take two thousand prisoners in one day! Anyway, then he leave and we fall on the enemy at Piave River and poum! A crushing victory for Italy!'

'Ah. Congratulations.'

'NO! It is *katastrophal*! I fight for Austro-Hungary, of course!'

'But they lost?'

'Yes, I just say this! Were you not there?'

'Well, as it happens—'

'Your East Surrey boys reinforce useless Italians. This is why they won. They were *fantastisch*!'

'But they were the enemy.'

'NO! Well, yes, but, pah, I no surrender to useless Italians but to your East Surrey boys. Gentlemen, very fine gentlemen, most respectful!'

This exchange typified the region's ethnic confusion, which, Victor realized during that long afternoon, extended right through Carla's family. Having met her rather nervous mother Eleanora, he was introduced to her grandfather, also bewilderingly called Josef, a sinewy ancient who carried the Ladurner name, spoke only Ladin, and was descended from South Tyrol's most famous folk hero, Andreas Hofer. Meanwhile the old man's wife was from Slavic peasant stock and spoke no recognizable language at all. By contrast Eleanora's antecedents, Carla explained, were part southern Italian plutocrats, and part Austro-Hungarian Jewish aristocracy.

'So I am Habsburg also, see, Victor?'

'Does that mean you're rich and own a castle?'

'Ha!' She patted his rump. 'No rich no castle. Oh, but see my uncle Rodolfo there? He very rich!'

'Let's meet him.'

'No! He is southern *Fascista*. My father detest him!'

'His own brother?'

'No! He family Zambon from my *mother* side. Victor, you must learn these if we are to marry.'

It was two weeks before she could visit him again, as her travels depended upon permission from her mother and cash from her father, neither of which could be taken for granted. She and Victor both found the separation hard; in the meantime they corresponded, daily and with growing fervour, such that by the time she finally stepped from the Innsbruck train and into his arms their passion was uncontainable.

'I miss you so many!' she gasped, showering him with kisses. 'I want us be one.'

'Yes, well, yes! But shouldn't we, you know—'

'Kiss me more, Victor!'

Ten minutes later Theo Trickey was conceived in an archway beneath the rail bridge at Mühlau. It was January of the new year 1922.

For Carla, a committed if wayward Catholic, consummating their union meant marriage was a given. This may have been her intention. Victor was not her first affair, but the first to offer the possibility of release from Bolzano and her family. Nor was the attraction just physical, for, war hero and Olympic contender apart, Victor was clearly a man of means, with business interests outside the army in retail, property and commerce. He lived in London, which was capital of the world's mightiest empire, and the British had recently won the greatest war in history. England was therefore the place to be. Victor was her ticket there.

For his part, marriage was a rather vaguer notion, something to be savoured for the future, although naturally, and with minimal prompting, he honoured their physical congress with a formal proposal.

'Next winter perhaps,' he mused over dinner that evening. 'Or what about the one after, at the Games in Chamonix!'

Carla squeezed his hand. 'Next winter, Victor.'

'Yes, of course.'

Thus the plan was agreed. He would return to his regiment in the spring as intended, notify his superiors and family of the good news, obtain a promotion, make the necessary arrangements for Carla's immigration, then return to Bolzano in November to claim his bride.

'Perfect, Victor.' She beamed. 'Everything will be perfect.'

But nine weeks after their archway tryst, and with his time to leave Austria drawing near, he received an urgent telegram summoning him to Bolzano. He arrived to a cooler welcome than before, Carla pale-faced at the door, a thunderous-looking Josef, Eleanora standing behind sniffing into a handkerchief.

'What is it?' he whispered to Carla as they waited. 'Did someone die?'

'I have baby.'

A few minutes later a heavily revised plan was laid out before him in Josef's office behind the print shop. No schnapps was offered.

'You are already propose my daughter Carmelina.'

'Yes, sir. With great honour and—'

'There is British legation of trade in Bolzano. They will make licence.'

'Licence?'

'Tomorrow you marry Carmelina. Then you return England and make arrange import Carmelina and baby to London. You agree?'

'Well, yes, sir. Of course.'

'Good. All is settled.'

The following day and with the usual formalities miraculously waived, Victor Trickey married Carmelina Ladurner by special licence at the British legation on Via Dante followed by a Catholic blessing at the nearby Cappella di San Giovanni. There was no wedding party, and by the evening Victor was on the train back to Innsbruck. Two days later he returned to London.

Theo was born in Bolzano that September of 1922. By this time South Tyrol's ethnic troubles were becoming acute. In Rome Mussolini ordered a programme of compulsory 'Italianization' for the region, and installed a grim-faced senator called Tolomei in Bolzano to oversee this cleansing process. Nicknamed 'the Undertaker', Tolomei ruthlessly instigated a thirty-two-point programme aimed at ridding South Tyrol of any vestige of autonomy, and erasing all trace of its indigenous heritage. These steps included the appointment of Italian-only municipal officials, civil servants, teachers, judges and senior police, enforcing Italian as the only permissible language, cash incentives for southern Italians to settle in the province, banning the teaching of German or Ladin in schools, and, most repressive of all, the Italianization of all place names, many of them centuries old, from mountains, rivers, towns and villages right down to streets and houses. To add further insult, this draconian and deeply unpopular measure included the Italianization of new babies' names.

Theo was baptized Andreas Theodor Josef Victor Ladurner-Trickey, in the same chapel in which Carla and Victor were married and by the same sympathetic pastor. But registering these names proved less straightforward. Soon after the baptism Carla presented herself nervously at the register office, her unusually pale-skinned baby in her arms, while a scowling registrar scrutinized her choice of names. Unknown to him, 'Andreas' was blatant civil disobedience, being the name of Josef's famous ancestor Andreas Hofer who had fought for South Tyrol's independence. But since it was also an Italian name the registrar, ignorant of the symbolism, ticked it with his pen. 'Theodor' met with less approval, which was ironic as Carla had only included it as a sop to her pro-Italian mother who had relatives bearing the name. Unfortunately the relatives were Hungarian and spelled it differently from Italians. 'Theodor' was thus swiftly changed to 'Teodoro' by the pen-wielding registrar. 'Josef' meanwhile, in honour of Carla's father and grandfather, was immediately rejected by the tongue-clicking registrar for being too 'Germanic'. Striking his pen through it, he scrawled the Italian version: 'Giuseppe'. Then, with his patience already waning, he got to 'Victor'.

'Are you mad? What is this!'

'His father's name, sir. He is English.'

'I don't care if he's double Dutch! Victor is a name of Anglo-Saxon or Teutonic provenance and utterly banned.'

'But his father. . .'

'Italian names only! Those are the rules.'

Five minutes later, having exhausted the registrar by explaining Theo's surname, Carla fled clutching his new birth certificate.

Despite the inauspicious circumstances and a quarrelsome domestic situation, Andreas Theodor/Teodoro Josef/Giuseppe Victor/Vittorio Ladurner-Trickey was a contented baby. He and his mother lodged with Carla's parents in the house above the print shop in Laubengasse, where the four rubbed along in an atmosphere of strained forbearance, despite their political differences. These invariably centred on the ethnic question. Josef was an ardent South Tyrolean separatist, whereas Eleanora's sympathies lay with Mussolini and Rome. As a couple they had learned to tolerate each other's position, but Carla's presence upset the balance – she sided with Josef – so arguments regularly flared. And when other family members visited, their opinions served only to fan the flames of disagreement, such that the clamour of raised voices became the background to Theo's childhood. And not just at the print shop, for by then disputes were spilling on to the streets to engulf whole communities. Factions developed, graffiti appeared – much of it racist – leaflets and posters circulated urging action, gangs roamed, goading the black-shirted militia. Civil unrest became a feature of Bolzano life. One night Senator Tolomei removed a statue of the Austrian poet Vogelweide from the main square. Word quickly spread, and in no time protestors were gathering, clamouring for its reinstatement. Opposition parties clashed, abuse was hurled and then sticks and bricks, a mêlée broke out, and the *carabinieri* were called to disperse it. Josef and Carla were in the thick of it.

Meanwhile Eleanora sat at home with the toddler Theo, who despite the family's disagreements had become the darling of the clan. Fair, chubby, cheerful, right from birth his smiling face and placid demeanour had a calming effect. Eleanora was especially fond, often retreating with him to her room when disputes flared, or wheeling him to market to be admired by neighbours, his fair complexion and china-blue eyes a diversion from the incessant quarrels. Sometimes he'd be lying on the floor surrounded by arguing relatives, and then, just as matters were turning unpleasant, he'd look up and chuckle, and the tension would melt into laughter.

But even Theo couldn't melt the tension over his father.

A modest trickle of correspondence had arrived in the months following Victor's departure from an address care of his Greek landlady in somewhere called Kingston upon Thames. Carla dutifully responded, painstakingly transcribing her replies into English using a dictionary. This was laborious, as on average she wrote three letters to Victor's every one, and also because decoding his appalling handwriting and abbreviated style was not easy: 'Pub meet Rose and Crown with Arthur G next Tues interesting trade proposition auto spares' was a typical sentence. Mercifully his letters were short. Soon they were even shorter, such that by the time of Theo's birth they were half a page every three weeks or so. His final missive arrived a month later; it congratulated Carla on the birth, applauded her choice of names, and assured her all was proceeding to plan vis-à-vis his return to Bolzano to collect them. That was October. November came and went, then December and still no word. By then Carla was writing almost daily, short plaintive notes desperately appealing for news. Finally, and at considerable expense, she sent him a telegram: *why you not here victor stop we wait in worry stop respectfully carmelina and teodoro please please reply*. A week later she received her reply, also by telegram. Standing at the door of the print shop, Theo on her hip, she tore open the envelope, then sank to her knees: *regret you inform vic tricky dead accident skiing scotland stop popodopoulos eleni.*

Carla was heartbroken, not just for the man she loved, but for the life they'd dreamed of together. All through the long months of pregnancy she'd waited, and the weeks following Theo's birth, patiently ticking off the days, writing lists, planning her emigration, boasting to jealous girlfriends, working at her English, only to have her dreams shattered at the bottom of a Scottish mountain. Her instincts were to travel to England immediately and to find and reclaim her poor Victor somehow, yet in her heart she knew it was impossible: she wouldn't know where to start, and anyway there wasn't the money. Instead she sank into a well of despair, staying in her room, barely eating, not sleeping, relinquishing Theo to her mother. Weeks passed, then months, until one day she emerged from her room, picked up her son and gazed into his eyes.

'Are you there, Victor, my love?'

Theo chuckled up at her, blue eyes beaming, and the healing began.

So he grew up fatherless, but not without father figures. Erwin Rommel would become an important one, John Frost another, but in the early years his family served, principally his grandfather Josef. A staunch separatist with strong views and an anarchic streak, it was Josef who inducted him into the culture of his motherland. From an early age Theo spent long evenings at Josef's knee, poring over photos and picture books, wrestling with German and Ladin texts, and listening to Josef's endless stories of strife, struggle and ancestral heroism, while Tyrolean folk music played on the gramophone. Josef also, at Carla's insistence, taught him what little he knew of Theo's paternal homeland, spinning made-up tales of great kings and queens, far-flung empires, eternal rain, a *presidente* called Lloyd George, and a poet called Shake-a-spear. Theo listened in rapt attention, fascinated by his two homelands, both the real one of snow-capped mountains, rushing rivers, Tyrolean streets and Grandma Ellie's strudel, and the imagined one of his lost hero father, with its fearsome kings, pea-soup fog and week-long games of 'criquet'. Greedily he devoured all information put before him, which was as well for Grandpa Josef brooked no backsliding. Stoutly built with piercing eyes and stiff hair that stood up as though electrified, he had a gravelly voice and smelled of printer's ink, and could anger quickly, especially over matters political. But he was rarely short with Theo, and as time passed the pair grew close.

Meanwhile Josef's father, Josef the elder – Theo's great-grandfather – took charge of the boy's physical education. In his eighties, short and wiry with wispy hair and a drooping moustache, Josef senior enjoyed legendary personal fitness, having grown up a goatherd in the mountains. From an early age, in all seasons and weathers, Theo found himself frog-marched into the Alps, gasping to keep up, there to learn hiking, map-reading, making camp, making fire, reading the stars, shooting straight with a rifle, and how to avoid freezing to death in the storms that blew in without warning. One March evening when he was eight, such a blizzard forced the pair to take refuge all night in a snow scrape. Shuddering with cold and terrified by the shrieking wind, Theo whimpered in the darkness while the old man stumbled about. Then he heard tutting in his ear, felt dried meat and raisins being pushed into his mouth, then a drink that burned in him like fire. Before he knew it he was being trussed up within a canvas sheet and gripped tight by wiry limbs, there to lie cocooned like a moth in a web till morning. Striding down through the snow into Bolzano next day, Theo sensed a change within him, as though a test had been passed. 'Take action and be brave, Theodor,' Josef said quietly in Ladin, 'for it is fear and inaction that kills.'

Another male influence was his uncle Rodolfo, Eleanora's brother, a Fascist Party functionary who lived partly in Bolzano and partly in Rome. He was rich and elegantly dressed with oiled hair, a glamorous wife and a daughter Theo's age called Renata, and he would arrive outside the print shop in an open automobile to whisk the children off to cafés for hot chocolate and ice cream. There he would extol Mussolini's vision for a strong and united Italy, the importance of ethnic purity to achieve this, the need for discipline among the proletariat, and a sturdy governing class. Much of this passed over Theo's head – he was more interested in Renata's ribboned curls – but Rodolfo promised to show him Rome one day, and the ice cream was delicious.

Around the same time he began at a new school. He was already attending an 'official' one, where only Italian was spoken and only an approved curriculum taught. Oddly this included English as its second language, but of Ladin, or German, or South Tyrol as a cultural entity, there was no teaching. Then one afternoon Carla met him at the gate and led him by the hand through Bolzano's back streets to an unfamiliar part of town. As they went she kept looking behind, as though checking for followers.

'Where are we going, Mama?'

'Somewhere secret, somewhere you must tell no one about.'

They were called *Katakombenschulen* – catacomb schools – secret hideouts where the language, literature and culture of Austria and Germany were still taught. Many South Tyroleans aligned themselves with these northern influences, as opposed to the Italian nationalism of the south, but under Mussolini's directives their study was strictly forbidden. Hundreds of German-speaking teachers lost their jobs, but some braver ones clubbed together in attics and basements to continue their work in secret. South Tyrolean children attended in their hundreds.

Theo's *Katakombenschule* was located in the cellar of a disused chemist's shop smelling of mothballs. It housed thirty pupils between eight and twelve, and one teacher, a kindly girl in her twenties, called Nikola Angeletti. That first evening Nikola gave a brief introduction to the basics of German grammar, then took out a book by the writer Wilhelm Müller and read them poems about a broken-hearted man on a long winter's journey. She read slowly, pausing to ensure her students understood before resuming in a clear melodious voice. Theo was entranced, both by the story, and by Nikola, who unlike his 'official' teachers was quiet and gentle, and seemingly oblivious to her shabby classroom and the subversive nature of her work. Looking round the dusty basement, pin-drop silent, he saw all his classmates were likewise captivated. When she had finished reading Nikola moved to a box in the corner.

'Here are Herr Müller's poems again, children,' she said, cranking the handle of a gramophone player. 'Only this time they are sung to music by an Austrian man called Franz Schubert.'

The teaching Theo received at catacomb school, combined with that from his official school – despite its prejudices – ensured he grew up well educated. He was no maths scholar, angrily struggling with calculus, geometry and algebra, but was strong in history and geography, and especially languages, becoming fluent in German, Italian, English and Ladin by his early teens. His greatest strength, however, lay in all things outdoors. Thanks to a competitive streak, years of fitness training from Josef senior and a growth spurt that transformed him from portly to statuesque in twelve months, he was soon leading the field in sports, particularly athletics, cross-country and running. He was also an accomplished skier, proudly telling classmates he inherited his skill from his late father, the

British Olympic champion Captain Victor Trickey, tragically killed smashing the downhill record in Norway. The same Victor Trickey, he would add, who won medals in the Great War leading the charge at Piave River. His male friends may or may not have been impressed, but, by now tall, strong and fair, with generous lips and alluringly Slavonic eyes, he was certainly stirring the girls.

By the mid-1930s the South Tyrol Question, as it was by then known, was reaching a climax. It had also spread beyond the tiny province to be taken up by governments across Europe, some insisting its autonomy be recognized, others urging diplomatic compromise. One government in particular, under its energetic new leader Adolf Hitler, paid special attention, as Germany's influence widened towards the Saar in the west, the Sudetenland to the east and then down towards Austria itself. Eager to secure his southern flank, Hitler entered direct talks with Mussolini over South Tyrol's future. And from these talks a diabolical pact would in due course emerge.

In the meantime life for Theo continued much as before: strudel and sedition at home, Carla and Josef embroiled while Eleanora clucked disapproval, bustling streets with shopkeepers, market traders and placard-waving protestors all jostling for trade, and the final stages of a twin-track education, although catacomb schools were ruthlessly suppressed by Tolomei's thugs. Winters were long and hard; Theo and his friends passed them at the chocolate parlour, or the outdoor ice rink, or Bolzano's first department store, or at the cinema where he held hands with a girl called Mitzi Janosi and watched newsreels about persecuted Germans in Czechoslovakia.

But once the spring thaws came, the town's youth were released like caged birds, scattering to the Alpine sunshine to hike and fish, camp, canoe and shoot. These mountain adventures were sometimes organized into competitions by scouting groups such as Wandervogel or Pfadfinder in Austria, or the new Hitlerjugend movement in Germany, and in the summer of 1936 Theo and his friend Otto Wörtz were selected to represent Bolzano at a regional jamboree in the Bavarian town of Mittenwald. Over four days they competed in target-shooting, athletics and cross-country events. Otto won a bronze medal in the javelin; Theo to his astonishment finished second overall. On the final evening he, Otto and the other winners were formed into a line, down which a party of dignitaries processed presenting medals. At their head was a compact man in his forties, wearing the grey uniform of the German army. He was a major, Theo saw, with an impressive row of battle ribbons on his chest and a much-coveted Iron Cross at his throat.

'Congratulations, young man,' he said in German upon reaching Theo. 'A very commendable silver medal. What is your name?'

'Theodor Victor Ladurner-Trickey, sir.'

'Quite a name. And where are you from?'

'Bolzano, sir.'

'Ah. A most beautiful town, in a most troubled province. So are you Italian in your sympathies, or German?'

'Well, I, um – Neither, sir, really. I am sort of South Tyrolean, you see. Although I'm half-English – my father. . .'

The German's eyes narrowed. Beneath them a chiselled jaw ended in a cleft chin. 'You mean you don't know?'

Theo's head spun. 'Well, yes – I mean, no, sir, that is – Oh goodness, I don't—'

'Then you must decide, Theodor. Because it is perfectly all right to be South Tyrolean, or Italian, or German, or even half-English. As long as you *know* it. Because if you don't know it' – he pointed at Theo's medal – 'then this and everything it stands for is meaningless. Do you understand me?'

'I. . . Yes, sir.'

'Good man.' And with that he was gone, moving up the line like a passing squall.

Otto sniggered. 'Nice going, champ.'

'Who the hell was that?'

'Rommel, you idiot. Head of the whole Hitlerjugend!'

Erwin Rommel's question to Theo was pertinent, for within months notices were going up around Bolzano announcing yet another edict from Rome. But this one was different.

'My God, have you seen it!' Carla shouted, brandishing the newspaper.

Josef glanced up. 'Don't look surprised, we knew it was coming.'

'But not like this! Not so... so cut and dried. It's inhuman!'

'It's the new reality, Carla, the new order.'

'What will we do?'

'Resist. As we always have.'

The edict was called the South Tyrol Option Agreement. Hammered out in private between Hitler and Mussolini, it required everyone in South Tyrol to adopt either German or

Italian citizenship. No exemptions, no abstentions, no third choice: South Tyrol was to vanish from the map. Inhabitants choosing Italian nationality could remain in the province, those choosing German must leave; everyone had six months to decide and another six to relocate as necessary. In the meantime the entire population must register full details of their birth, marriage, residence, national identity, ethnicity and religion. There was one more clause. Young men of military age, having made their decision, would automatically be enrolled for service in the Italian or German armed forces.

'What will your family do, Otto?' Theo asked his friend at the cinema one night.

'Germany, of course! Father has relatives in Munich, and a job waiting at the university. We'll get an apartment, I'll join the army – it'll be terrific.'

'And you, Mitzi?' He turned to his girlfriend. The Janosi family were neighbours of the Ladurners and known pro-Italians.

Mitzi shrugged. 'Father says we'll sign and stay. And you?'

Theo stared at the screen. 'God knows.'

Once again his family was split. On his grandmother's side – Eleanora, Rodolfo, cousin Renata and the others – their choice was already made: register Italian and be done with it. But for the Ladurners the matter was less clear-cut. Josef and his kin had German ties, he had cousins in Austria too, he spoke German, he could probably find work and settle there. But Bolzano was his home and he was damned if he'd be exiled from it. Ellie agreed. You don't need to be exiled, dearest, she pleaded, just sign the paper, adopt Italian citizenship and we can stay together right here. But signing the paper and accepting Italian nationality was for Josef the ultimate betrayal. If he signed, everything he believed in, everything centuries of freedom fighters had striven for, right back to his ancestor Andreas Hofer, would have been for nothing.

'I can't do it, Ellie,' he told her at the table one evening. 'I am not German, nor am I Italian. I am South Tyrolean and always will be. So I am refusing to register, and will stay here and continue the struggle.'

'Me too,' Carla added. 'I'm staying.'

But she was mistaken, for within months events overcame them and everything changed. Firstly, at dawn one morning and without any warning, Josef was arrested. Pounding on their door, a gang of Blackshirts stormed in, ransacked the shop and then dragged Josef off. No explanation was given, no arrest warrant offered. After a week of frantic enquiry, Carla learned he'd been transferred along with scores of other dissidents south to Trento, where he was being held in prison. The charges against him, apart from disobeying the Option edict, included riotous assembly, incitement to civil disobedience and, most seriously, the production of treasonable propaganda, this last from leaflets and posters found hidden at the print shop.

Then in an unconnected development his wife Eleanora was summoned to Bolzano's town hall for interview at the newly opened Bureau of Ethnicity.

'Is this about my husband?' she asked anxiously.

'Your husband?' the official replied. 'No, *signora*, this is about you, and the registration card you filled in.'

'Oh. What about it?'

'It says you are one-half Jewish.'

'Well, indeed, that is correct, on my mother's side. She was Frederica Hartmann – from Hungary, you know, descended from the Habsburgs.'

'Really.'

'Yes. Is this important? My husband, you see—'

'Yes, it is important. A register of all Jewish or part-Jewish persons is being compiled for the authorities.'

'What for?'

'It is a condition of our treaty with Germany. Now, your husband is Jewish?'

'No. He is a Catholic. So am I, in fact.'

'Children?'

'One daughter. Widowed.'

'Grandchildren?'

'I have one grandson. His name is Victor Trickey, he is fifteen and registered British from birth.'

'British?'

'His father was an officer of the British army.'

'British, very well.'

'Will that be all?'

'For now, yes, thank you.'

Arriving home an hour later she found Carla slumped ashen-faced in a chair and Theo sobbing in his room.

'Carla, what has happened? My God, it's your father!'

'No, Mother, not Father. It is Grandfather. He is gone.'

Theo's beloved great-grandfather, Josef Ladurner senior, his indestructible physical coach and mentor, was dead of heart failure at ninety-two.

The three travelled to Trento to break the news to Josef. Though normally a short train ride across the border into Italy, their journey was frustratingly protracted, with everyone's papers repeatedly checked, at Bolzano Station, at the Italian border at Salorno, then a third time disembarking at Trento. And gaining entry to the *centro di detenzione* proved practically impossible, with warning notices, patrolling policemen and high walls topped with barbed wire barring their way. Circling round, Carla eventually found a wooden doorway with bell-pull.

'Go away!' an angry voice replied when she rang.

'We've come from Bolzano to visit my father. On a matter of domestic urgency.'

A peephole slid open. 'No visitors allowed, now clear off.'

'Please, *signore*,' Carla murmured, moving close to the hatch. 'It is my father, Josef Ladurner. We have news of a sad bereavement.'

An eye studied her through the hatch. She forced a smile. 'Please?'

'Wait there.'

They waited. Finally the hatch opened again. 'You only. Ten minutes, that is all.'

Eleanora nodded. 'You go, Carla. I'll stay here with Theo.'

She followed a guard through clanking doors and a maze of dank corridors smelling of sewage until she came to a windowless room with no furniture save a table and two chairs. Josef was waiting there, pale, thinner but defiant. The guard smirked, and took up station stood by the door.

'I'm so sorry, Papa,' she said when she'd told him. 'He was in good spirits and suffered no pain.'

'A great man gone.' Josef shook his head. 'How I will miss him. He is interred?'

'In the cemetery beside Grandma Maria. They are both at rest now.'

'Thank you.' He gestured around the room. 'It was this, you know.'

'This?'

'This struggle. It's what killed him. Fought for our liberty all his life, only to be betrayed by the fat crook Mussolini. This is what will kill us all.'

At the door the guard glanced up. 'One minute left!'

Carla shifted uneasily. 'Papa, how is it in here? Do they feed you properly?'

'Pig swill. But the food doesn't matter – our spirits are strong.' He nodded at the walls again, pointedly, holding her gaze, then down at the clenched fist of his hand. 'What of other news from the outside?'

Carla recounted Eleanora's story about the summons to the Bureau of Ethnicity.

'I heard about these things already. Danger lies everywhere. For us all. Poor Ellie. She is not strong enough for this.'

'Time!'

Josef stood suddenly and embraced his daughter. As he did so she felt crumpled paper being pressed into her hand.

'Go!' he hissed in Ladin. 'You, Theo, get out before it's too late.'

'What? But go where, Papa?'

'Stop talking!' And before they could utter another word, she was pulled away by the guard and escorted from the room.

Dearest Daughter,

I have one minute! Your name is listed. Treasonable offences same as me – I have seen this. They will come for you. You must leave now. Your marriage certificate and son's birthright will give you entry to England. Victor's relatives and friends and his regiment must help. Separatist sympathizers, too, in government. Go and continue the fight, Carla! Tell Ellie she must go south to her brother; she will be safer in Rome. GO, dearest daughter, and remember me always,

your loving father,

Josef

CHAPTER 6

The town of Apeldoorn lies fifteen miles north of Arnhem. I arrive there that Sunday 25 September aboard a motley convoy of trucks and ambulances crammed with wounded. Theo is among them somewhere. Though short, our journey is slow, hindered first by the wreckage-strewn streets of Arnhem, blocked every few yards by fallen trees, burned-out vehicles, shell holes and mounds of rubble. Bodies too, scores of them, both ours and theirs, lie piled at the roadside. Later, as we clear Arnhem, a different human wreckage impedes our progress, as long lines of civilians retreat from their ruined city. Grinding along tree-lined roads, we force a passage through this listless horde, which parts to either side, their worldly remains loaded in carts, wheelbarrows, prams, or in bundles tied on their backs. They are mostly women, children and the elderly; I stand in the truck watching this melancholy procession unreel behind us, and can only share their mood of gloom. Some of our boys call out cheerily, and make V for Victory signs, but the Dutch don't reciprocate; indeed, many shake their heads, a few spit and one old man brandishes his fist. His gesture says it all: we came to liberate them, and only made things worse.

Then, to add final insult to injury, we get attacked by our own air force. The refugees hear it first, scattering in panic into the ditches and fields beside the road. Then the truck lurches to a halt and our driver leaps out and sprints for cover. Next comes a thunderous roar followed by the crackle of machine-gun fire and two RAF Typhoons hurtle past, guns blazing. There's no time to do anything, certainly not unload stretchers; all we can do is gape in indignant disbelief. Our pilots are already unpopular, having failed to stop the Luftwaffe attacking us and then dropping our much-needed supplies into the hands of the enemy. Now to top it off they're shooting at us. As they circle round for another pass, we wearily disembark the trucks and start waving white handkerchiefs, Red Cross flags, rude gestures and anything else we can think of. Mercifully they see the signals and break off, rocking their wings sheepishly.

'Useless fuckers,' somebody mutters as they depart.

A while later we drive through the gates of a wire-fenced compound and pull up. Before us stand the blocks of a large modern-looking barracks. Other convoys have arrived before us, and the compound is busy with revving motors, barked orders and figures in khaki scurrying to and fro with stretchers and crates of supplies.

An RAMC captain strides up with a clipboard. 'Who are you lot then?'

'Oh, um, Daniel Garland, 11th Battalion.'

'11th?' He checks his clipboard. 'That's odd. I've seen no one from the 11th.'

'No, well, you see, I got separated, ended up attached to the 181st Airlanding Field Ambulance.'

'Marrable's mob! At the Schoonoord?'

'That's right.'

'Good show!' The officer pumps my hand. 'I'm Redman, 133rd Parachute Field Ambulance. Got captured at the bloody DZ, been in the bag ever since. Speak a bit of German too, so they've got me doing liaison. Come on, I'll show you round. Got plenty of your chaps here already.'

I follow him indoors to the main assembly area, which is low and cavernous. It resembles many barracks halls, except this one is carpeted to the farthest corner with stretchers. Hundreds and hundreds of wounded lie, sit, squat or stand, occupying every available space, waiting as ever to be processed and treated. A desultory murmur of massed male voices echoes like plainsong in a monastery and the familiar tang of putrescence assaults my nostrils, while a haze of damp air and cigarette smoke hangs above the multitude like mist. It's too much, almost Biblical, and my heart sinks at the sight, overcome suddenly with unbearable weariness and a sense of utter despair. Last night, following my insane flag-waving adventure outside the Schoonoord, I tried to rest, crammed into a corner of the storeroom with Cliff Poutney. But after a week living knee-deep in festering wounds, shattered limbs and spilled guts, the air toxic with the stench of pus and excrement, with only the crash of shells and cries of the injured to listen to, my nerves are in shreds and no sleep comes. At dawn I rise and wander aimlessly from room to room, trying to make sense of it all, and half hoping to find my Dutch nurse Anna. But Anna is long gone and there's famously little sense to be found in the madness of war, so I give up and sit on the hotel steps waiting for the end to come.

'You all right, old chap?' Redman asks.

'It's just. . . I mean, how many are there?'

'Oh, upwards of a thousand, so far. More still to come of course, from the various dressing stations. We're sharing them out between the barrack blocks.'

'It beggars belief.'

'Does rather. Listen, chin up, supper's in an hour. Grub's not bad either. I expect you could do with it.'

I expect I could, for food, I realize then, real food in the form of a proper square meal, has not passed my lips since breakfast on the day of the drop. 'Well, now you mention it.'

'Splendid. Feel like helping out while we wait? It'll help pass the time!'

So I dump my haversack, roll up my sleeves and set to work, just as before, passing among the wounded, checking pulses and temperatures, adjusting bandages, updating casualty cards. Time does pass, more stretchers arrive, and some familiar faces. I spot Jack Bowyer – we exchange a nod – and then Cliff Poutney, his arm bandaged, who manages a thumbs up; finally Colonel Marrable himself strides in, pipe in mouth, thus heralding completion of our exodus from the Schoonoord.

'Say, Garland?' Redman calls. 'Is this one of yours?'

He's kneeling by a body on a stretcher. The victim's entire head and torso are bound in bloody bandages, his casualty card is signed by me, and shows only the information from his identity discs: name Trickey TV, rank Private, followed by his service number and religion, which is RC. A letter in a bloodstained pocket begins 'Dearest Theo, how I long for you. . .' Common decency prevents me reading on, but at least

I know his name. 'Try and save him,' Anna had said in our final conversation. 'He is lucky we found him, and lucky to be alive. Perhaps he will be lucky for you.'

Redman grimaces. 'Multiple wounds to cranium, upper body and extremities, internal bleeding, organ damage, failing life signs. Doesn't look good, old chap.'

'I know. We found him among the dead.'

'Not surprised.' He lowers his voice. 'Extra morphia and a visit from the padre. It would be kindest. And quickest.'

'Somebody already tried that. It didn't work.'

'Then it's major surgery you're talking. Complicated cranial stuff and still no guarantees. And there's a hell of a queue.'

I think of Cliff Poutney, and me, working away in our blood-soaked storeroom. Cutting, chopping, sawing and stitching all week like butchers in an abattoir. *Try and save him*, Anna had said.

'I'll do it.'

Carla and Theo arrived at Victoria Station, London, one showery autumn day in September 1938. Theo had just turned sixteen. With their baggage strewn about them, they peered round the crowded concourse, and at the scrap of paper bearing their only contact. An hour later they were labouring up Kingston High Street in a downpour; finally they found the address and knocked.

A middle-aged woman in slippers appeared. 'Sorry, full up.'

'Oh, ah, *Signora Pakadap-alapish, per favore?*' Carla tried.

'What you say?'

'*Scusi*. . . Signora Papa-daka. . . Oh Theo, you do it!'

Theo cleared his throat. 'Excuse, madam. We have searching the domicile previous of Lieutenant Victor Trickey of famous East Surrey regiment. Please.'

'Vic? Blimey, he long gone, my dears.'

'Yes, this we know most sadly. We are searching his family.'

'His family? What for? And who you are, heaven sake?'

'His family.'

'Eh?'

'His family from Italy. This Lieutenant Trickey's wife, Carmelina, my mother. And his son. Theodor. Me. How do you do.'

'How do—' The woman gaped. Rain still fell. A cat scampered in, a red London bus splashing noisily by behind. Carla rummaged through her handbag.

'Here, *signora*, this you sent me since many years.'

It was the telegram, from Victor's landlady, informing Carla of his death. As she read, the woman's hand rose slowly to her cheek. 'My heaven, my lor', blimey, you mus' come in, my dears!'

Eleni Popodopoulos, a widowed Greek emigré, ran a boarding house off Burton Road in Kingston upon Thames, not far from the barracks where the East Surreys were headquartered. Victor Trickey, she explained over tiny cups of sweet tea, or 'Vic' as she called him, had lodged with her for a few years following the Great War.

'Although I never know if he in or he out or where he is half a time. Sometimes he disappear weeks on end.'

'With the army,' Theo said. 'Secret missions?'

'Army? I don' know about that but lots of secrets yes. And alway with the skis – he love that damn snow.'

'Olympics training. This is how Lieutenant Trickey met my mother.'

'Oh yes?' Eleni appraised Carla anew. 'Yes, he have eye for handsome lady.'

'Did you know his people?' Carla ventured. 'Any his relatives?'

'Relatives, no, my dear, he never talk of this. Friends, yes, a few, you know –business types. They come and go.'

'What happen then, with the *accidente*?'

'Oh, I don' know nothing about that. Vic go off yet again, some weeks, I know not where. Also' – she lowered her voice – 'also he pay no rent for quite some while. Anyway, I keep getting letters and so on, then come this telegram, you telegram from Italy.'

'You open it?'

'Yes, my dear, sorry, but I need find him, you know, for rent and that. Anyway, a few day after I hear knock on door and this man come who I never see before.'

'What man?'

'I don' know! I just say I never see him before!'

'*Scusi, signora*. Please finish.'

'Well, like I say, he come to door, he very polite, he say he friend of Vic Trickey and bring sad news of Vic killed in accident. He give me money, not much, and ask me send telegram to lady-friend in Italy to break sad news.'

'Lady-friend? But I am wife!'

'Like you say, my dear. Anyway, that end of story.'

Carla sensed it wasn't, but now wasn't the time to press matters. She sat back, biting a nail pensively, more rain spattered the window, Eleni's tea cup clinked, Theo stroked the cat. Three days of trams and trains, alien landscapes, unknown tongues and strange food, only to end up at a dead end in this land of featureless grey. Carla stared around. Old photographs of men in Greek costume adorned the mantelpiece; a flight of plaster ducks ascended one wall, a large Orthodox crucifix dominated another. A moment later she was sobbing into a handkerchief.

'No blimey, my dear! What is this tears?'

'We have nowhere to go, *signora*, nowhere to stay.'

'You mus' stay here!'

'But you full up.'

'Pah! I always say this first. You never know who coming at door.'

'We have little money.'

'Money tomorrow, no worry today. You'll see. Now then, young man Theodoros – this is wonderful Greek name, Theodoros, you know? Theodoros, you carry you bags for Mama quick.'

And so they moved into Eleni's boarding house, one room on the top floor with two single beds, a washstand, and a view of a scruffy back garden. Three other lodgers were in residence, all men, two travelling salesmen and a young teacher called Clive Greenhough from the nearby grammar school. Carla and Theo unpacked, spent the weekend reconnoitring their strange new neighbourhood, visited the park and river, scoured the shops for anything familiar to eat, and then on the Monday Carla descended to breakfast dressed for a mission.

'Where is fortress East Surrey *reggimento* please?'

One of the salesmen looked up. 'You mean the barracks? It's in King's Road, five minutes away.'

'Why, Mama?' Theo looked her up and down. Elegantly attired in her best cream dress, the one from Neumann's with the buttons down the front, her raven-black hair brushed into a clasp, she had rouge on her lips, powder on her cheeks, and she smelled of scent. Her demeanour was self-conscious but determined. Around the breakfast table, the two salesmen gawped in open-mouthed awe, while Greenhough rose noisily from his chair.

'Thank you, *professore*,' she purred as he seated her. 'May we speak later?'

'Of course, *signora*.' Greenhough blushed.

'Why, Mama?' Theo repeated.

'To discuss your education, of course.'

'No, why are you going to the barracks?'

'I am going to speak with *il colonello* of East Surrey *reggimento*. I am widow of their officer Victor Trickey; *il colonello* has responsibilities: to me, to you, even a pension maybe. I am going and will not leave without satisfaction.'

Three hours later she returned, muttering angry excuses and without satisfaction, but the next morning she went again, and the next, until on the Friday she returned with something more than excuses.

'Everything is arranged, Theodor.'

'What is?'

'I have a job, you have a school, we have a friend.'

'The colonel?'

109

'Not the colonel, he is arrogant. No, but his *aiutante* is very nice man. Very *simpatico*. Captain Henry Winter-Bottom. We are dining this evening. At a pub apparently, whatever that is.'

'What of Papa? They have information?'

'Henry is looking into it.'

'What is your job?'

'Henry is arranging it.'

'And the school?'

'Henry is arranging it with Mister Green-Huff. You will go to his school near here.'

That evening Henry Winterbottom escorted Carla to the Rose and Crown pub for beer and haddock; the following Monday she began work in the barracks laundry and Theo started school at Kingston Grammar.

After a passable supper of sausage, potato, veg and fruit – all tinned – and a blessed night's rest on a proper army cot in a room with walls and ceiling, glass in the windows and no dawn shelling, I arrive in reception next morning in rather better spirits than I departed it last night. While I slept, others have clearly been working, with the result that order is fast emerging from the ashes of chaos. Over breakfast of black bread and tea we learn that the assistant director of medical services for the entire division, Colonel Graeme Warrack, arrived here late in the evening plus a staff of assistants, orderlies, clerks, typists and all the rest. He and his team immediately set to work drawing up lists and rosters, allocating jobs, designating spaces and nailing up direction signs, with the result that the place has turned from a barracks into a hospital. It even has a name – the Airborne Military Hospital – giving it a homely official feel. Nearly all wounded have been moved into 'wards' in the various blocks, and treatment rooms, operating theatres, admin offices, stores, even a dental clinic have been set up, plus messing facilities for officers, NCOs and other ranks. It's extraordinary what good military organization can achieve, and refilling my mug with tea I can only reflect rather guiltily on my defeatism of yesterday.

I'm rostered to work in C Block, which is allocated to 181st Airlanding Field Ambulance, alongside my old friend Cliff Poutney, and under the ever-fastidious Arthur Marrable, so I make sure I'm clean-shaven, with tie straight and boots polished, before reporting for duty. Standing before the mirror, I can't help pondering the past nine days, and the changes they have wrought. I certainly feel different from the person who jumped from a Dakota so long ago, and ties to home and family seem very tenuous. On a whim I rummage through the haversack for my red beret and brush it down. Marrable's insistence on appearance is no mere affectation, I realize, heading for the stairs, it gives you identity and purpose, it makes you feel you belong, and it bucks you up. Everywhere I look, men are walking straighter this morning, they swing their arms and puff out their chests; there's even some saluting here and there. Far from being cowed, as you'd expect after such a thrashing, the Paras are proud of who they are. Even the Germans are impressed.

The day passes in a blur of the usual activity. C Block houses some sixty patients under the care of three medical officers and twenty orderlies. More wounded arrive during the day, recovering ones are transferred to 'convalescent' wards, while two serious cases die. We work in shifts with proper time allocated for rest breaks and admin tasks such as writing up case notes. It's a far cry from the madness of the Schoonoord but still very busy, with much the same work to be done. Only two noteworthy matters come up, three if you count the welcome arrival of Red Cross cigarettes. One is a briefing from Colonel Warrack; the other is news of Theo Trickey.

He's not housed on C Block, so as soon as practicable I send Jack Bowyer off in search, half expecting him to return saying Theo died in the night. But the news is he's hanging on, firstly, and secondly I won't have to perform neurosurgery on him as someone more qualified is doing it, thank God. The orderlies have given him odds of six-to-four against, Jack tells me cheerily, adding he's arranged for Theo to be transferred to C Block after his surgery.

Colonel Warrack's briefing takes place in the officers' mess at dusk. He begins with a summary of Market Garden statistics, which makes for sober listening. Of the 1st Airborne Division, he reports, that's something over 10,000 men, just 2,500 have managed to withdraw across the Rhine following their heroic last stand at Oosterbeek. The rest, some 8,000, are casualties of war, either killed, wounded or captured.

'Not the result Monty was hoping for,' he goes on gravely, 'although he says that with the bridges at Eindhoven and Nijmegen taken, the operation can still be considered a success.'

A few glances are exchanged at this, but no one comments.

'As for the wounded,' Warrack continues, 'around two thousand are now with us here at Apeldoorn, with this figure likely to peak tomorrow as the final casualties arrive. Now, I know we're stretched, but we must do all we can to receive and treat them properly. And' – he lowers his voice – 'hold on to them, gentlemen, because the Germans plan to start shipping them out.'

Mutters of concern circle the room.

'I know, and I've complained to the commandant about it most strongly. But he's adamant: this facility is needed for their own troops, so we're to vacate it, ready or not. Apparently special trains are due at the railway station, and as our injured become fit enough to travel, they'll be moved by rail to POW camps. In Germany. That process begins tomorrow with three hundred walking wounded—'

He breaks off, holding a finger up for silence, and for a moment I wonder if he suspects the Germans of listening at the door. But then I hear it – we all do – like a far-off train passing, or a gust of wind through hills. The rumble of very distant artillery.

'30 Corps.' He smiles. 'They may make it yet. And if they do we could be liberated in days. So we must try our best to keep everyone here for as long as possible.'

'Daft laddie then, is it, sir?' someone quips.

'Precisely. The commandant wants lists of those fit to travel by noon tomorrow. Make sure he doesn't get them: lose them, delay them, make minor injuries sound serious, demand second and third opinions, tell the lads to act sicker than they are. He'll send his own medics to chivvy things up: be polite to them, and appear to be helpful, but slow them down, insist they make detailed examinations of every patient, insist they write proper reports, then misplace them, and make them do it again. In short, use your best delaying tactics, gentlemen, for every hour we hold up Jerry is an hour nearer to being relieved.'

Fighting talk, and something of a Warrack trademark, we'd soon learn. Someone then brings up another matter of relevance.

'What about escape, sir? Apparently the perimeter fence has weak spots, and some of the lads are desperate for a crack at it.'

'Then they should give it a try, if they're fit enough. But they must get approval from their CO first, and only in ones and twos: no mass break-outs or the Germans will come down hard.'

'What about us?' Cliff asks. 'Can we have a go?'

Warrack shakes his head. 'Our duty is with the injured. Later, if the numbers fall, then perhaps we'll consider it, but for now every one of us is badly needed, so I'm afraid I must forbid any escape attempts by medical staff. I'm sorry, but that's an order.'

The days pass as he predicts. Apeldoorn swells with the last of the Arnhem casualties, but also with German medics who strut about bossily selecting wounded for transportation. We do our best to hinder them, and have some fun in the process. Jack Bowyer is a natural at confounding the enemy, and our wounded groan so dramatically whenever a German appears that we almost believe them ourselves. My speciality is the thermometer-in-hot-tea schoolboy ruse. Every time a German approaches one of my patients I wave a thermometer at him. *'Ernstes Fieber!'* I say, as Redman taught me, which means 'severe fever', and so they move on.

But not for long, and soon it's clear that time is running out, for by the second week half our injured are gone, and the sound of distant gunfire, which was always desultory, fizzles out altogether. A few of the fitter wounded manage to slip out under the wire, melting into the countryside in the hope of linking up with our forces or the Dutch Resistance, but hopes of being liberated by an advancing 30 Corps wither on the vine. Nineteen forty-four's Allied offensive, it appears, rather like the mild autumn weather, is over, leaving us with nothing but the chilling prospect of a winter in captivity.

Quite where becomes the next burning question. By now we're down to the last few hundred wounded, and these are the more serious cases. Rumours circulate of special hospital trains to convey them to camps in Germany, Poland, Czechoslovakia and all points east, and that doctors and orderlies will accompany them. Each day we scan the noticeboard to see who's for the chop and who's to be spared, and sure enough one morning a list goes up of the remaining wounded from C Block, and my name's on it, along with Poutney, Redman, Bowyer and others. My heart sinks at the sight; only now do I realize how much I'm dreading the notion of prolonged captivity. Ten hundred hours next morning we're to report. I spend my last day at Apeldoorn packing, gathering supplies, writing up case notes and preparing the wounded men for travel. Like me, many are understandably anxious.

'So what's this train like, Doc?'

'Well equipped, I hear. Fast too. Should only take a day or so to get there.'

'Where's that then?'

'Good question, Sergeant. Special hospital camp apparently. Top notch.'

'Pity 30 Corps never made it.'

'Indeed.'

Theo's on the list too, although he remains critical, unconscious and dangerously ill with a high fever – not caused by hot tea. I kneel at his side to check him over and then jot down his condition: pallor grey, heartbeat irregular, temperature soaring, respiration fast and shallow. Adjusting his bandages, I recall how he was found, a single arm rising from among the dead during a moonlit meeting with a nurse in a garden. Emboldened by the memory, I take up my notebook again.

Dear Anna,

Well, it's only been two weeks, yet feels much longer.
I hope you are well, your father too, and that life in
Oosterbeek is returning to some kind of normality.
Our 'lucky' patient and I are still together, and on the
move again, although I have learned nothing more of
him, nor of our destination, except it is deeper into
Germany which

'It's a wonder he's still with us.' A familiar figure appears from the shadows, wreathed in pipe smoke as usual.

'Oh, Colonel, hello. Er, yes, it is. Heaven knows what keeps him going. Willpower perhaps.'

'An example to us all.' He hesitates. 'Do you have a moment?'

'Of course.'

'I just wanted to thank you, Garland, before you leave, for everything you've done here, and at the Schoonoord. The 181st isn't your unit, and I know how much you wanted to rejoin the 11th, but I'm grateful you decided to stay.'

Ordered to stay as I recall, but now isn't the time for nit-picking. 'Sorry about Sykes, sir, running off like that. Will it go on his record?'

'Not from me. If he made it back to his unit, and survived till the end, then all credit to him.' He puffs on his pipe. 'I'm not coming with you tomorrow, Garland, I've been asked to stay on and help Warrack wind things up.'

'So I gather, sir.'

'Colonel Alford's in charge of your train. CO of the 133rd, a first-rate chap.'

'I see.'

He pauses. 'How well do you know him?'

'Colonel Alford? Not at all, sir.'

'No, I mean this young man here. You had him transferred from D Block, so I assumed he was a friend, or acquaintance. From the 11th perhaps.'

'Oh, no, sir, I – That is he was found among the dead at the Schoonoord, and I sort of took him under my wing. I don't know him at all.'

'Beware that Chinese proverb, then. The one that says if you save a man's life, you're responsible for it for ever.'

'I'll bear it in mind.'

'Good. Because as far as I'm concerned, your duty to this unit has been more than honourably discharged, and you're free to consider your options, when the moment is appropriate, if you follow me.'

'Yes, sir, I believe I do. Thank you.'

'No, thank you, Daniel, and the best of luck.' And with that he strolls away.

With just twelve months of peace remaining to the world, Carla and Theo settled in at the Burton Street boarding house in Kingston. Carla's job at the barracks occupied her three days a week; the rest of the time she shopped and cleaned, helped Eleni Popodopoulos with the boarding house, or met up with the few Italian expats living in the district. Not all were sympathetic to the South Tyrolean situation, but one or two were like-minded separatists, and together they gathered in Eleni's front room writing to community leaders, MPs, local councillors, churchmen, diplomats and anyone else they could think of, rallying support for the cause. At the same time she wrote weekly to her mother in Bolzano and jailed father in Trento, receiving long angst-ridden replies from one and only worrying silence from the other. Money was tight but seemingly not problematic, and meanwhile her social diary remained full, with the East Surreys adjutant Henry Winterbottom leading what Theo saw as an irritatingly large pack of suitors.

'Who are these men, Mama?' he would complain. 'Why do they come here?'

'Be nice to them, Theodor, they help us.'

'How?'

'They take care of our problems.'

'What problems?'

'You for a start! Your rooming, food, schooling, clothes, pocket money – these things don't happen by themselves, you know. Anyway, these men are polite, they treat me nice, make me feel, you know, *speciale*.'

'But what about Papa?'

'He is gone, Theo. Left us without so much as one lira, threw himself down a mountain and vanished. He never helped us and never will. Everything is down to me.'

At which point the discussion generally ended. And if over the months Theo noted a certain hardening of Carla's heart towards Victor, his own schedule was probably too busy to dwell on it.

He was an immediate hit at Kingston Grammar, walking in behind Clive Greenhough that first day to wide-eyed stares and gasps of wonder – tall, assured and exotic, like some foreign prince. Thanks to Nikola Angeletti and his Bolzano teachers, he was academically superior to his peers in most subjects, except maths, which still eluded him, and his grasp of English, which he learned to modulate from formal to colloquial. Outside the classroom he was equally strong, trouncing all comers at athletics, gamely learning football, and even sculling on the river. That winter of 1938 to 1939 he joined the chess club, the debating club and the drama club, for which he delivered a suitably typecast Mercutio in the Christmas production. He made friends: Romeo was played by a boy called Kenny Rollings who taught him snooker and called him Ted, and Juliet was a redhead called Susanna Price who dubbed him 'Theodorable' and kissed him on the cheek backstage.

In the spring he joined the school's Army Cadet Force and proudly donned the uniform of the British army – even if it was coarse and scratchy and smelled of camphor. Better yet his unit was affiliated to the East Surreys, which meant he wore their cap badge too. 'If war comes,' he told Kenny, lovingly caressing the badge, 'I will fight as my father, and die bravely if I must.'

Kenny shrugged. 'If war comes God help us.'

Carla also eschewed any talk of war. 'You will go to college, master the business of retail, and become a successful owner of shops,' she told him one evening in May.

'Yes, my dear,' Eleni added, 'like that Mark and Spencer. He was penniless Polish chap, you know, and that Fortnum too they make huge bloody fortune for their family.'

'Yes but if war does break out I must do my duty. Like Papa.'

'Vic? Blimey! And anyway, boy, who your duty? You half-German!'

'Shush, Leni, and he's not, he's half-South Tyrolean.'

'What's a difference, God's sake?'

'Mama, but listen—'

'No, Theo, you listen.' Suddenly she was speaking Ladin, a language they rarely used and no one understood, including Eleni. 'Your duty is to me, to your poor grandparents, and the oppressed peoples of your birth. You have no right to leave me for a war that is not ours. I will never permit such a thing, do you understand? And that is my final word.'

But six weeks later, to her horror, Theo was called up to the territorial reserves. Within minutes of the letter arriving she was dialling the barracks on Eleni's new telephone.

'Henry, for God sake, what 'appen?'

'Calm down, Carla,' Winterbottom soothed, 'everything's fine.'

'Calm down! Are you crazy? You promise nothing like this ever 'appen!'

'Well, that's not strictly true, is it, old girl? Our arrangement is that the regiment contribute towards the cost of his upkeep and education, in return for his services as a reservist. And that's precisely what's happened. It's called sponsorship.'

'But you promise no danger, never!'

'I promised to keep an eye out for him, and make sure he gets in no trouble, which is precisely what I'm doing.'

'What you mean? It says here he mus' report to this, this, two/six territory thing! He's sixteen, for God sake, Henry, he still a schoolboy!'

'It's the 2/6th Territorials, Carla. They're reservists, back-room boys. There's no danger, don't you see? I fixed it. He finishes school next month, and doesn't report until he turns seventeen in the autumn. Even then he's a Territorial, a part-time reservist, you know, weekends and evenings and so on. He can carry on as before, go to college, get a job, whatever you want!'

'What if war 'appen?'

'Hardly likely,' Winterbottom scoffed. 'You must've heard Chamberlain on the wireless. But in the unlikely event, he'll be posted to some depot in Wales somewhere, hump stores for a bit, then leave with a good service medal and carry on with his life. He'll probably be out within a year.'

The Apeldoorn hospital train turns out to be the real thing: long, modern, with tiered bunks for the injured, a galley for hot food, a well-equipped operating theatre and proper accommodation for medical staff. We embark that afternoon, about three hundred injured plus thirty medics and orderlies, all under the command of Colonel Alford. Before boarding we're lined up on the platform and given a stern lecture by our escorting officer, a German major, who explains in clear English that we're free to move through the train to treat our injured, as long as nobody attempts anything 'foolish', by which we assume he means escape. Infractions will be dealt with severely, he adds. We officers are then shown to our carriage, which is two from the rear, and introduced to our guard, a gormless-looking corporal we christen Boris.

Several hours pass. We settle the injured, a meal is served, but the train stays firmly in Apeldoorn Station. Redman quizzes Boris, who tells him nothing will happen until after dark, as it's too dangerous, thanks to: 'your *verdammt* Royal Air Force!' Sure enough it's long after dusk when we feel the jolt of an engine being coupled; a few minutes later doors slam, whistles blow and we jerk slowly into motion.

Very slowly. The train's carriages are connected by little observation platforms at either end; shortly after departing we wander out on to ours to see what's what.

'East,' Cliff pronounces, peering at the tiny collar-stud

compass that we all carry as part of our escape kits. These are sown into the linings of our uniforms and include silk maps, a few gold coins and a hacksaw blade. I suspect we've all been checking them privately; mine's intact less the blade which Cliff and I used for amputating in the Schoonoord.

Gradually, and with the train still moving at a snail's pace, houses and streets give way to open countryside. A thick mist has descended; the night is dark and overcast. Five of us are crowded on to the little platform.

'It's too good to be true,' Redman mutters.

'Too good to pass up, you mean.'

'Down these steps, stand at the bottom, wait for a bend, then jump, tuck and roll. Easier than exiting a Dakota.'

'What about the guard's van?'

'Time it right, go at an embankment or ditch and they'll never see.'

We watch a little longer to be sure; then, fired up with schoolboy fervour, and conscious that every passing mile takes us deeper into enemy territory, we return inside to confront Alford. He's busy writing up notes, Boris dozing behind him. The five of us gather eagerly around, while Redman, aware that Boris might be faking, uses his hands to signal our intent. After a bit Alford nods.

'Your er, proposal for the, um, patient sounds reasonable,' he says carefully, 'however we are responsible for many other patients, and I must remind you what Colonel Warrack said about, er, this sort of procedure.'

Colonel Warrack said no, and Alford's confirming it. We're dumbfounded. After a week trapped at Oosterbeek, two more at Apeldoorn, and now being stuck on a train heading into Germany, we've had enough, and feel we've earned a shot at freedom. Seizing this God-given opportunity, before it's too late, suddenly seems desperately important. Mutinous glances are exchanged and orders may get disobeyed, but fortunately Cliff Poutney, ever the diplomat, reopens negotiations on our behalf.

'We do understand, sir; however, we feel there are enough medics to meet the needs of the patients, and Colonel Warrack's, er, instructions about this sort of procedure, were, we feel, only applicable at Apeldoorn.'

Well put, and in any case, ironically, Graeme Warrack was at that very moment preparing to seal himself into the roof of his office at Apeldoorn, where he would remain until successfully escaping some weeks hence.

But Alford's not having everyone jump ship. And Boris is stirring suspiciously.

'The procedure you propose involves too many staff.'

'How many would be appropriate, sir?'

'Two maximum. And that's my final word on the matter.'

A rather moody hiatus follows while Boris potters about carving himself a black-bread sandwich, and we feign nonchalance by smoking and staring out at the passing night. Then Cliff proposes cards, a pack is produced, and we five gather round. 'We'll cut, shall we?' he suggests. 'Highest pair wins.' Redman scores highest with a queen, Cliff comes second with a ten, then I, cutting last, unbelievably score an ace.

Redman and I make ready, surreptitiously donning as many clothes as we possess, loading our pockets with food and water, checking our escape kits. Meanwhile the others distract Boris with the card game, which he gladly joins. Cliff, I note, looks visibly crestfallen.

'I suggest we stick together,' Redman mutters, 'head west by night, lie up during the day, try and link up with the Dutch underground.'

'Sounds good. What about the jump?'

'Go at the same moment, you go off the steps to the left, I'll go right. Roll into the ditch, meet up when the train's out of sight.'

'Got it. When do we go?'

He glances around and then grins. 'Sooner the better.'

With that he calls out to Boris in German, saying we're going up the train to check the patients, and will be gone at least an hour. Boris, deeply engrossed and oblivious to our heavy attire, waves in dismissal. I catch Cliff's eye and he manages a smile; Alford, too, makes a tiny nod of assent. This is it.

Then the carriage door opens and Jack Bowyer strides in. 'Begging your pardon, gents, but can Captain Garland come?'

'What?' I gape at him. 'Why?'

'That young private of yours. Trickey. I think he's dying.'

My head reels, Jack waits, everyone freezes like players on a stage, even the card players hesitate. Then Redman speaks.

'You'd better go, old chap.'

'But what about—'

'Cliff can see your other patients, can't you, Cliff?'

Things then happen fast. Alford takes Cliff's place at cards, slapping one down with a laugh, Boris and the others quickly joining in. Meanwhile Cliff grabs his haversack and follows us outside to the observation platform.

'Can't you wait?' I plead to Redman.

'They can't keep Boris quiet for long, and we've only so many hours of darkness. Sorry, but we have to go now.'

Bowyer looks confused. 'What's going on?'

Cliff shrugs on his haversack and clasps my hand. 'So sorry, old man, maybe you'll get another chance. Wish me luck?'

With that he descends the steps of the platform, while Redman takes the other side. They lean out, pause, judging the moment, as steel wheels clank over rails, a dark verge rolls steadily by, and beyond that misty blackness beckons.

Redman glances up. 'Red light on!'

'Fuck me,' Bowyer mutters.

'Green light on. . . Go!'

They go. I hear a muffled whump and lean out Cliff's side, peering into the darkness. Nothing; then a shadowy figure appears, raises itself to standing and waves.

And a shot rings out.

We're stopped for an hour. At first all doors are locked, with no one allowed in or out, while guards run back and forth outside shouting angrily. More guards check inside the train, counting and recounting us repeatedly. Finally our door opens and the German major steps in. He beckons Alford forward.

'Two?' he says, holding up two fingers. 'And do not lie, Herr Colonel.'

Alford can only nod. 'Yes, two.'

They descend from the carriage. Five minutes later Alford's back. 'Redman made it, Poutney didn't,' he reports grimly.

126

'A guard was looking out his side. We can collect him now.'

I go, taking Jack Bowyer with me. Cliff's lying fifty yards behind the train, dead from a bullet to the head. His eyes are open; he looks up at me with disdain. As well he might. For the man who got me through the nightmare of Oosterbeek, camped with me in our blood-soaked storeroom, shared his tea and cigarettes and knowledge and warm good humour with me, has just died in my place.

CHAPTER 7

Theo Trickey arrived in France in March 1940. He got there
through chance, military expediency and personal machinating.
His army career had begun, as Henry Winterbottom predicted,
as a part-time amateur – a weekend warrior with the Territorials.
This undemanding role would have remained the status quo,
but for the outbreak of war, which changed everything. Within
days plans were in hand to send a force across the Channel
to help stop Germany advancing into France and the Low
Countries. This force, known as the British Expeditionary
Force, would soon number more than 500,000 men, amply
equipped with the latest in warfare technology: tanks, artillery,
anti-aircraft guns, support vehicles, plus a thousand RAF
fighters and bombers providing air cover. Ferried into ports
in Normandy, then transported east by train and truck, they
amassed along the borders with Germany, dug in beside their
French and Belgian counterparts, and waited for the enemy
to attack. But once deployed and growing daily in size, the
War Office soon realized it was short of men to support the
BEF. Every bullet, every tin of bully beef, every gallon of fuel
for its vehicles had to be shipped over the Channel, stockpiled
in depots, and then transported across France to the Front.

Tens of thousands of extra soldiers were needed to keep these supply lines flowing, and the reservists were first to be called upon.

Shortly after his seventeenth birthday Theo became a full-time Territorial. Eight weeks' basic training followed at the barracks in Kingston and on Salisbury Plain where he marched and drilled, learned to tie knots and dig trenches, ate field rations and bivouacked in the rain, mostly without kit – including boots, greatcoat and rifle – because there wasn't enough to go round. Nevertheless he passed with flying colours and by December was home on leave 'awaiting further orders'. Rumours were soon circulating that the East Surreys might be deployed in support of the BEF; impatiently he and his co-recruits wandered Kingston's wintry streets waiting for news. Meanwhile Carla was on the telephone to Henry Winterbottom.

'Nothing to worry about, old girl.'

'What you mean? He keep talking about going to France!'

'Not a chance. I'm sending him to an OCTU.'

'Oct— what is this?'

'Officer Cadet Training Unit. Down in Hampshire. It's a sort of military college, to teach him to be an officer. There's an induction first, then the course proper, so he'll be gone for months. If the 2/6th does get sent to France, it'll go without him.'

'But what 'appen after he finish this OCTU thing?'

'Good heavens, the war will be over long before then.'

After an uneasy Christmas with Carla at the boarding house, Theo reported to 167 OCTU in Aldershot one freezing day in January 1940.

Whatever his preconceptions about officer training, nothing could have prepared him for the reality. Firstly his fellow cadets appeared an odd breed, quite unlike his Territorial friends back in Kingston; all nasal vowels, buck teeth and braying laughs, they reminded him of Alpine donkeys. Crammed eighteen to a hut, with no heating, communal washing and abysmal food, they enjoyed no favours or privileges, despite their elevated status. On the contrary their treatment was uniformly harsh, with their instructors driving them like pack animals, bullying and bellowing until they dropped from exhaustion. Special emphasis was placed on physical training, which meant a run before breakfast, PT and drill after, forced marches in the afternoon, and a final run before bed. Sometimes a session on the assault course was added for variety, which involved climbing walls, swinging on ropes, crawling through mud and swimming an icy lake. Designed to root out the weak, this baptism of fire proved too much for some cadets, who were returned to their units as unsuitable officer material. The survivors, Theo included, could only collapse on their cots and wait for the ordeal to end.

Which eventually it did. One morning, instead of being sent running, they were taken to the rifle butts and shown how to assemble and fire a Vickers machine gun. The next they received small-arms instruction. Map-reading followed, and compass work; signals and radio were introduced, as was vehicle driving, including lessons on a BSA motorcycle which Theo declared the finest machine ever. Different instructors appeared who shouted less and addressed them as 'mister'; there was also classroom instruction with lectures on army history, command structures, conventions of war and something called officer-like conduct. January passed, February; they began to be allowed into town on Saturday nights, albeit to specified pubs, where they spent their meagre pay drinking watered-down beer and bragging to army-wise Aldershot girls. They also took turns queuing to call home on the telephone. As well as dutifully ringing Carla, Theo used his time to phone his friend Kenny Rollings, stuck in barracks back in Kingston.

'How long you going to be there, Ted?' Kenny always asked.

'Heaven knows. Months probably.'

'Your voice sounds different. It's gone all plummy.'

'Has it?'

'It's those bloody toffs you live with. I'll have to start calling you sir.'

'You can practise now if you like.'

'Piss off.'

'Piss off, *sir*. How's Susanna Price?'

'Walking out with Albert Fitch, last I heard.'

'Oh.'

'Got bored waiting for *sir*.'

'Piss off.'

Always he pestered Kenny for regiment news, which meant word of deployment to France. Kenny's replies were unchanging – no news, only rumour. But then one evening in March he heard the words he'd been dreading.

'It's happening!' Kenny shouted. 'We're off!'

'What! When?'

'Drawing kit the next couple of days, transport arrives Thursday, Portsmouth Friday, be in France Saturday!'

'Christ, you lucky bastards.'

The next morning Theo asked to see the colonel commanding his OCTU. After a long wait in a corridor he was finally admitted to a panelled office.

'Well, and who are you?' the colonel demanded.

'Officer Cadet Trickey, sir.'

'*Acting* Officer Cadet, if you don't mind. Aren't you supposed to be in lessons?'

'Yes, sir, only something important has happened.'

'That's a curious accent you have there, Trickey, where are you from?'

'Oh, um, South Tyrol, sir, it's in—'

'Ireland, yes. Well, that explains it. Now, what's happened that's so important?'

'My unit, sir, the 2/6th Territorials, of the East Surreys.'

'What about it?'

'It's leaving for France, sir. Tomorrow.'

'So?'

'I should be going with it.'

'Do you have orders to rejoin it?'

'No, sir.'

'Then it's out of the question. You will stay here and finish your course. Dismiss.'

He returned to his hut, packed his kit, borrowed four pounds from classmates and slipped away to the station. He spent that night and the next day hunched in a bus shelter outside the main gates at Portsmouth docks, closely watching the comings and goings. Traffic was non-stop, and vehicles were carefully checked by guards, but he saw nothing to indicate troops. Then at noon the next afternoon a convoy of army trucks pulled up, the lead one with East Surrey colours fluttering on one wing. As they waited for entry he approached the rearmost lorry.

'Two/sixth?' he murmured at the tailgate. No answer. He tried the next truck, and the next, then at the fourth, the canvas flap lifted.

'Who the fuck are you?'

'Trickey, 2nd Platoon, B Company.'

'Then you'd better hop in quick, you nearly missed the boat.'

The city of Caen lies on the River Orne in Normandy between the ports of Cherbourg and Le Havre. Although inland from the coast, it is an important commercial port with large docks connected to the sea by a six-mile canal. In 1940 it was one of several ports used by the British to supply the BEF. Each night the essential paraphernalia of war – vehicles, ammunition, weapons, fuel, rations – were shipped across the Channel to Caen and other destinations, there to be unloaded and stored before onward transport to the BEF. The East Surreys 2/6th Territorial Battalion arrived there in late March, with B Company initially detailed to a fuel dump on the outskirts, before being detached to guard Caen's vital canal link to the sea. Theo's 2nd Platoon was stationed halfway along the canal at a lifting bridge in the little town of Bénouville and billeted in a former convent. On the afternoon they arrived their company sergeant showed them the bridge and issued them their orders. Which numbered just two.

'See this?' He pointed at the bridge. Dutifully they nodded. 'Guard it with your lives. Now see that?' He pointed at a little café beside the bridge. Again they nodded. 'Keep the fuck away.'

'Why, Sarge?'

'Because they don't want scruffy little bleeders like you messing up the place!'

Bridge-guarding turned out to be routine, undemanding and hazard-free. After six months of phoney war the enemy still showed no sign of activity, and was in any case three hundred miles away on the German border. It was also facing the mightiest force ever assembled, so the chances of 2nd Platoon ever having to defend their bridge, no matter how much they yearned to, seemed remote. Even their rifles were empty. The nearest they came to warfare were the training exercises in which rival platoons simulated attacks, which they would enthusiastically repel. Then their turn would come to play the aggressor, creeping along the canal with twigs in their helmets, before charging the bridge, bayonets fixed and yelling like madmen. Often their efforts were embellished for the benefit of local onlookers, many of them girls, who came to size up the young Tommies. One such spectator, a waitress called Jeanette, made a point of congratulating Theo on his *bravoure*.

He blushed. '*Merci beaucoup*.'

'I work there.' She pointed. 'At the café.'

'Ah.'

April came, bringing a cold snap. Theo was rostered for night duty, which meant pacing endlessly back and forth across the bridge, rifle on shoulder, blowing on his freezing fingers and counting the minutes until he was relieved. Little traffic passed at night save for the occasional pedestrian or farmer on a bicycle. Periodically the bridge operator arrived, climbing the ladder to his cab, there to manage the lifting mechanism allowing ships to pass beneath. Once or twice Theo was invited up to watch.

One evening it began to snow, lightly at first and then heavily as it grew dark. Crossing the bridge towards the end of his watch, frozen to the bone and with his greatcoat soggy with snow, he glimpsed a bundled figure waiting on the far bank. Forgetting to shout 'Who goes there?' he walked over.

'Can I help you?'

It was Jeanette, muffled up in coats and scarf. 'Madame invite you come café for hot chocolate,' she said in halting English.

'Ah.' Theo peered through the gloom. 'Only the thing is, we're not allowed. . .'

'Who will know, apart from Madame?'

Ten minutes later he was telling Madame his life story. In German.

'I was born in Alsace,' she explained, pouring his hot chocolate. 'So German is my second language. And you are the boy from South Tyrol, which means we are practically neighbours.'

'But how did you know, *madame*?'

'I have my spies!' She smiled, glancing at Jeanette who was busy washing glasses. 'Now, *Theodor*. . . Or should I call you Teddy like your friends?'

'I don't mind, *madame*.'

'Theodor then. So tell me: the separatist movement, that dreadful Option Agreement, the damned villain Tolomei, I want all the news.'

From that night Theo was a regular at the café, partly because of Jeanette who brought him soup and company on night duty, but mainly because of the café's proprietor, Thérèse Gondrée. Petite, attentive, with her humorous husband Georges and three little daughters, she quickly became like a favourite aunt. After the drabness of the convent and the lewd banter of his comrades, an evening at Café Gondrée provided a refreshing change from the norm. And a warm welcome – contrary to expectation.

'You know I am not allowed here,' he said one evening.

'Yes, and do you know why?'

'Because you don't want scruffy bleeders.'

'Nonsense!' Thérèse laughed. 'It's because I can speak German. It makes the British suspicious. They don't want their young soldiers being subverted.'

'But that's ridiculous.'

'People of the village mistrust me also.' She shrugged. 'It is human nature.'

Usually arriving late, he would sit by the fire, chatting to Georges or Jeanette and trying to read *Le Journal* newspaper. Thérèse would appear, work done for the day, hang up her apron and join them for talk. Conversation ranged from politics to the war, village gossip, the weather. Mostly she liked to talk about him, questioning him at length about his childhood in Bolzano, his flight to England, his lost father, imprisoned grandfather, anguished grandmother, and his aunts and uncles divided by ethnicity.

'It is sad when families divide like this,' she said late one night. 'Perhaps we can do something.'

'What can we do?'

'Your grandfather, for instance. We could write to the authorities in Rome, perhaps through an intermediary I know, and try to obtain news.'

On another night he talked hesitantly of his relationship with his mother, their difficulties and disputes, the men friends, money problems and the constant nagging.

'Your mother made great sacrifices,' Thérèse chided. 'Leaving her family, bringing her son to a strange country, making sure he has clothing, food, schooling. These are the actions of a courageous woman.'

Theo thought guiltily of Carla. Six weeks after absenting himself from Aldershot, and nervous of discovery, he still hadn't told her where he was.

'I could arrange something,' Thérèse suggested quietly. 'Through contacts in London. Trusted friends. She could be discreetly notified that her son is safe, without her knowing where you are.'

On one of the final occasions, Theo and Jeanette were playing on the floor with Thérèse's baby, while torrential rain thrashed the window like thrown gravel. Thérèse came in, wiping her hands on her apron.

'*Bald jetzt*,' she murmured, gazing through the window. 'Soon now.'

'Pardon, *madame*?'

'Spring. It will come very soon. And then they will come too.'

'Who?'

'The Boche. That's when they will leave their lairs and come at us. And they will come hard, Theodor, mark my words, so your famous BEF must be sure to be ready.'

The order finally came on 9 May and for Erwin Rommel, chafing with impatience in his forest hideout, it came not a moment too soon. Sidelined during the Poland campaign the previous autumn, he'd lobbied hard for an active role in the forthcoming assault on Western Europe. Now he'd won his chance, the Führer himself awarding him command of 7th Panzer, one of the formidable new mechanized divisions tasked with spearheading the invasion. Since then he had spent weeks getting to know his officers, practising manoeuvres, testing his men and equipment, and studying every detail of the invasion plan until he knew it by heart.

It was called *Fall Gelb* – Case Yellow, and involved more than three million men divided into two army groups. One group was positioned up north on the German border with Belgium and the Netherlands. This was where the main Allied forces were, including the British Expeditionary Force, because this was where they expected Germany to invade. But a second army group, comprising forty-five divisions including his 7th Panzer, had for months been quietly amassing in the hilly forests of the Western Rhineland, some 150 miles to the south. Once battle was joined in the north, this second force would make a surprise attack west, advance a hundred miles through the thickly wooded hills of the Ardennes Forest, cross through Belgium and break out into France, whereupon it would wheel north and make for the English Channel, thus encircling the Allies in one giant pincer movement. If successful, the enemy would be crushed and Germany would win a swift and glorious victory in Europe. But if it failed the effects would be catastrophic, resulting in ignominious defeat for Germany and an early end to the war. *Fall Gelb* was without doubt ambitious, its objectives formidable, and its risks many; several in High Command harboured misgivings, and even Hitler was fearful, so it was rumoured, pacing the Chancellery night after night consumed with anxiety.

Not so Erwin Rommel, whose confidence, skill and daring, so ably demonstrated in the First War, exactly suited this kind of high-risk operation. He believed utterly in the plan, certain that success was inevitable – provided every man played his part, kept his nerve and showed boldness and conviction. Having received the attack order on the 9th he briefed his officers; then he spent the remaining hours visiting his men, moving up and down the columns, checking vehicles and equipment, offering a joke here, assurances there, dispensing good cheer and cigarettes. At midnight the signal came that invasion in the north had begun, and he retired to his tent to study his maps and write letters to Lucie and his children. Then early on the 10th he emerged into the forest's misty dawn, mounted his command vehicle and gave the order to advance.

But he was soon dismounting again, hurrying forward on a motorcycle to see what the hold-up was. They had anticipated early progress along tortuous forest tracks would be difficult, especially with so many men and vehicles to move, but by mid-morning barely five miles had been covered and the 7th was falling behind schedule. Arriving at the head of the column he found engineers struggling to remove concrete obstructions in the road while being shot at by Belgian units hidden in the trees. Swiftly assessing the situation, he ordered his leading tanks up and told them to bypass the roadblocks, flatten new tracks through the undergrowth and then rejoin the road further on. 'And for God's sake, don't stop!' he urged. 'The Belgians will fall back once they see us coming.'

He was right, and the 7th was soon on the move again, covering some thirty miles by the end of that first day. By the end of the second he was more than sixty miles from his starting point, racing through the forests, pulling ahead of his rivals in 5th Panzer and approaching the heavily defended Meuse River at Dinant. Here the plan called for a pause to allow slow-moving infantry units to catch up, but Rommel pressed forward, hoping to surprise the enemy and capture one of Dinant's bridges intact. He almost succeeded, but as his leading units entered the town, French engineers blew the last bridge. Undeterred and despite the late hour, Rommel ordered scouting parties along the river to search for possible crossing places, and in a while they returned with news of a narrow island midstream, linked to both banks by ancient stone weirs. White water cascaded over the weirs, which were narrow and precipitous; Rommel did not know how strongly the far bank was defended. Watching through binoculars, he sent a few lightly armed scouts forward into the darkness; they picked their way over the slippery stones and reached the far bank undetected. Swiftly reinforcing them with a company of riflemen, the first German bridgehead over the Meuse was secured.

But it was soon sore pressed, coming under heavy mortar and shell fire from Belgian and French artillery positions along the western bank. The imperative now was to reinforce his men with armour, preferably tanks, and for that he needed a proper bridge. Searching upstream he found sappers waiting amid lorryloads of bridging equipment, pontoons and rubber dinghies. 'Who are you?' he demanded.

'5th Panzer Division,' came the reply.

'Right, follow me.' And with that he appropriated them and their equipment and set off in search of a crossing place. Finding one near the village of Yvoir, he set fire to houses along the bank to provide smoke cover, and summoned his tanks forward, directing them to shoot at the enemy across the river. He then sent infantry across in the rubber boats to secure the far bank while the bridging got under way. Repeatedly he crossed and recrossed the river in the dinghies, often under fire, and more than once he was spotted thigh deep in the icy river helping lash pontoons together. By dawn the bridge was nearing completion, but daylight brought increasingly heavy fire from the enemy. German casualties began to mount; Rommel called up more artillery and radioed the Luftwaffe for assistance. As the Stukas dived in, he waved the 7th on to the bridge, leaping aboard the leading tank as it crossed over.

All day the crossing and the fighting went on. Rommel's tactic was simple, if contentious. Rather than securing the bridgehead and assembling a force to assault the enemy, he immediately sent tanks forward to bypass their positions, and even circle round behind them, staying off the main roads, skirting towns and villages, pressing ever further ahead, shooting and moving, shooting and moving, spreading confusion and alarm like wolves among sheep. Often he went with them, returning from one such sortie pouring blood from a splinter wound to the scalp. 'He's everywhere,' an orderly marvelled as the wound was stitched, 'like a whirlwind.'

But at the same time others were voicing concern, particularly in Berlin where High Command was growing exasperated. Not only was 7th Panzer way ahead of the main force, but it was becoming strung out and fragmented. Rommel refused to halt so slower units could catch up, he was always up at the front when he should be coordinating matters from further back, and worst of all he kept 'losing' radio contact, so Berlin often had little idea where he and his division were. He's wrecking the whole invasion, anxious heads warned, yet not everyone agreed, including Hitler who followed proceedings in breathless amazement.

By the fourth day the Panzers were in France and the 7th reached its designated goal of Avesnes, where it was to pause and regroup. But finding weaknesses in the defences everywhere Rommel pushed on, advancing as much as forty miles a day, driving men and machines relentlessly, brushing resistance ruthlessly aside. Whole Allied battalions threw down their weapons in panic; one city surrendered without him even stopping. 'Come out, French soldiers!' he shouted as he thundered by. 'It's over, you can come out.' And they did. By 17 May he had taken ten thousand prisoners for the loss of forty men. He left them behind and charged on, never stopping,

leading from the front, racing his fellow commanders to be
first at the coast. In the north the Allies wheeled to counter
this new threat, only to find the northern army hard on their
heels. Suddenly the enemy was to their rear and sides, as well
as circling round in front. By 19 May the Panzers reached the
Somme at Abbeville; by the 21st leading units could see the
glittering waters of the Channel, and the encirclement was
complete. Rommel's 7th was among them, and its achievements
legend. Feared in battle and fêted at home, the newspapers
dubbed it Gespensterdivision – Ghost Division – because
nobody knew where it would appear next. The public was
ecstatic, Hitler jubilant, even the critics in High Command were
silenced. That evening he finally sent them a laconic signal.

'I'm at the coast.'

What Germany had failed to do in four years of the First
War had been achieved in just eleven days.

In the Allied camp disbelief gave way to despair. Churchill
flew to Paris to bolster French resolve, only to find the generals
burning archives and preparing to flee the capital. The next
day, accepting the inevitable and with the BEF surrounded,
he began trying to save it. Mass evacuation by sea was the
only option. Boulogne was considered, then Calais, but both
soon fell to the advancing enemy. The noose tightened; total
destruction now loomed, but just as hope was fading there
came an unexpected reprieve. For no fathomable reason and to
the fury of his commanders in the field, Hitler ordered a halt.
The net was perfect: one army group to the north, another to
the south; all that was needed was the final drawing of the
string. Yet Hitler hesitated, and the neck lay open, leaving

the BEF a corridor through to the beaches of Dunkirk. And salvation.

But not for everyone. Such was the speed of the German advance that whole divisions of the BEF had been bypassed almost without knowing it. One such, comprising the ten thousand Scotsmen of 51st Highland Division, was based in Lorraine, thirty miles south of Luxembourg, and so ended up outside the encirclement. Days of crucial wavering followed while orders and counter-orders came and went; then with the stranglehold tightening in the north, the 51st was belatedly rushed to the Abbeville area to try and break it. By the time they arrived events had already moved on, and their task became less about assaulting the enemy's rear and more about stopping it from turning west. So while 350,000 BEF men escaped across the sea from Dunkirk, the lone Scotsmen dug themselves in along the Somme and prepared for the onslaught. When it came the fighting was sustained and ferocious, featuring infantry assaults backed by tanks and artillery on the ground, and dive-bombers hurling high explosives at them from the air. Casualties were heavy and with no support and supplies running short, the 51st was forced into a fighting retreat westwards.

'Don't let them capture Normandy,' Churchill warned their general.

'Then for God's sake send reinforcements,' came his reply.

One day Theo was sitting in a café by a bridge, listening to it on the wireless, the next he was in a convoy of trucks heading east.

'Where we going, Corp?' his friend Kenny asked their platoon commander.

'How the hell should I know?' was the reply.

All day they ground eastwards on roads clogged with traffic coming the other way, some of it civilian, much of it French military. That first night they bivouacked in a ditch by the road; the following morning they continued, passing north of Rouen towards Amiens, their progress stop-start in ever-thickening traffic. At the noon halt they disembarked at the roadside to hear the rumble of artillery far to the north. A while later three Hurricane fighters zoomed overhead, wings rocking. 'Dieppe,' went the rumour as they boarded once more, but upon reaching the port half their convoy peeled off while the other half, including Theo's 2nd Platoon, continued north towards Abbeville. Late in the afternoon they began seeing evidence of British troops: a line of artillery in trees, machine-gun emplacements at road junctions, soldiers wearing armbands furiously directing traffic. Finally they entered a village and turned up a track to a large farmhouse. A hand-painted sign read '51HD HQ'.

'Everyone out!' a Scottish voice barked as they pulled up.

They spent the next hour unloading the trucks into a pen behind the farm. As they worked they noticed men hurrying in and out of the house, many of them officers, some in kilts.

'Who are these Scottish people?' Theo asked Kenny.

'Christ knows, but that gunfire sounds bloody close.'

Having unloaded, they next found themselves loading again, this time back-breakingly heavy boxes of ammunition into Bedford lorries. A quartermaster sergeant directed them, his shoulder bearing the insignia of the Seaforth Highlanders.

'Right, lads,' he said when they finished, 'in you get, four to a truck, tin hats on and keep your heads down, we'll be getting close to the shooting.'

'Hear that, Ted?' Kenny grinned nervously. 'This is it.'

Four lorries left the farm, following a series of lanes and tracks until they came to another village, smaller, barely a cluster of houses on a road with a church. 'Oisemont' a sign said. Slowing to a crawl, two drove on while two, including theirs, parked under trees and switched off. Nothing happened; the breeze rustled leaves, dogs barked, the village seemed deserted and eerily quiet. The sergeant appeared.

'You two, down here.'

They jumped down. 'Now listen,' he went on quietly. 'See that wall over there? There's a machine-gun section behind it. You take a box of .303 ammo over. You go quickly and quietly, you keep your heads down, and come straight back. You got that?'

Grasping the rope handles, they manhandled the heavy box to the ground, picked up either end and made to set off.

'Not yet, for fuck's sake!' The sergeant grabbed Theo's arm. 'Wait for my signal!'

'Sorry.'

'You will be!' Crouching, he leaned out behind the truck, holding one hand raised behind him. They waited, still hefting the heavy box, while he stared towards a copse of trees at the end of the village. Suddenly he beckoned them forward. 'Go!' he hissed, and they were running out into the open. Low sunshine threw them into harsh relief, their boots rang on the cobbles like hammers, and Theo felt the raw terror of exposure, as if a hundred hostile eyes were suddenly on him, as if every window hid a German with a gun sighted on his head. They made it halfway, grunting with effort, before Kenny stumbled and dropped his end. 'Christ!' The urge to leave him and sprint for cover was overwhelming. He heard a hoarse voice urging, 'Come on!'; he tasted the dryness of his mouth and felt hairs pricking his neck.

Kenny found his feet. 'Sorry!' He quickly grabbed the handle and they went stumbling on their way.

'Jesus, lads, look, they're sending us wee kindergarten bairns!'

Ducking round the wall, they staggered into a courtyard. Five men were lounging around a Vickers machine gun, which was pointing down a road behind the house.

'I hope they remembered the ciggies.'

'Aye, and my evening newspaper.'

'And some beer and sandwiches would be nice.'

'Christ, they get younger every day.'

Relieved of their load they made it back to the safety of the lorry. Only to repeat the process with more boxes to more positions all round the village. Everywhere the Highlanders met them with ribald good humour, and some surprise.

'Who are yous two then?'

'Oh, um, 2/6th Territorials, the East Surreys.'

'Jesus, we've got the Boy Scouts!'

'English ones too. We must be desperate.'

By now dusk was falling, and after two days with little food or rest, and still no sign of any enemy, hunger and fatigue were slowing their pace. Their final delivery was boxes of 9-inch shells to a mortar position behind the church. Having delivered them, they jogged wearily back.

'When do we eat?' Kenny complained. 'I'm famished.'

'Yes, I could—'

A burst of machine-gun fire erupted from the trees, flinging staccato lines of fiery yellow tracer at them which struck sparks from the cobbles all around. Immediately the Highlanders responded in kind, filling the air with furious shooting from all directions. Shocked immobile, they stared about in panic. 'Keep moving!' someone bellowed; the next moment Theo felt Kenny dragging his arm and they dashed for the lorries.

Then it was over, as suddenly as it had begun. A shocked silence descended.

'That was aimed at us!' Kenny exclaimed. 'They were trying to kill us!'

'No, lad,' the sergeant chuckled. 'That was just a warning from Jerry. He says run faster next time!'

The next morning they were roused at dawn to load lorries again.

'HQ's pulling back,' the sergeant, whose name was MacLean, told them. 'It's getting too risky here.'

'What about the men in the village?'

'They'll cover our withdrawal, then follow as best they can.'

Theo and Kenny exchanged glances. Their 2nd Platoon had declined to just six men, the rest, including their platoon commander, having been dispersed to other locations. 'What about our unit?'

'You're under the command of Divisional HQ now,' MacLean said. 'Just keep your heads down, don't do anything daft and you'll be fine.'

'Where are we going?'

'Backwards by the looks of it.'

Within an hour the stores from the pen were all loaded. Next they helped empty the house, carrying supplies, boxes of files, radio sets, even tables and chairs out to waiting trucks and cars. As they laboured, they saw officers striding about bearing maps and charts, some with red flashes on their lapels. Their expressions were uniformly grim. At one point they dropped a crate on the stairs to salute an older officer approaching from below.

'Don't be bloody stupid!' he growled, pushing impatiently past.

'That's General Fortune,' an aide muttered, 'CO of the whole 51st and in no mood for niceties.'

A moment later they heard the rising whine of approaching engines, accelerating as if from great height, then a blood-chilling siren as the aeroplanes dived. Someone shouted 'Stukas!' The noise rose in a deafening crescendo and then a piercing whistle as the bombs released; the next instant the whole world shook with explosions. The floor trembled, the building shuddered, dust and plasterwork fell from the ceiling, ornaments and paintings crashed to the floor. 'Get down!' the general commanded. Theo and Kenny dived under a table, their arms over their heads. The next salvo came: shrieking sirens, roaring engines, the whistle, the thunder of explosions, shaking ground and splintering glass. Acrid smoke choked their lungs; behind them the staircase collapsed and a gaping hole appeared in one wall.

Then it was over and the Stukas were gone. Peace returned, broken only by the crackle of flames and incongruous squawking of chickens. Deafened and dust-caked, they crawled from under their table and staggered outside. Two lorries were burning furiously; one they'd just finished loading was now barely four wheels and a chassis. Elsewhere the farmyard was transformed, pocked with craters, littered with fallen branches, debris, smashed outbuildings and vehicle wreckage. And a single body, lying alone in the dirt in a twisted heap. Brushing the dust from their clothes, they approached. The body lay face down, its pose grotesquely contorted such that its legs were facing downward while its torso faced up. One side of its head was gone.

'Christ, Ted, d'you think. . .'

'I should think so.'

'What are you two gawping at?' Sergeant MacLean strode up. 'Have you never seen a corpse before?'

'We... that is, not so. . .'

'Well, you have now. And you know what to do.'

'Um. . .'

MacLean saw their faces. 'Christ, all right, listen. Get shovels and bury him, deep as you can, under those trees over there. Remove any personal effects from his pockets and one of his identity discs, and give them to me. Find a piece of wood or roof slate or something and mark the grave with his name and service number, and that's it. And get your bloody skates on – we leave in ten minutes!'

By mid-morning they were on the move again, part of a

lengthy convoy winding their way westward – the direction they'd come from yesterday. Once again progress was impeded by military traffic and long lines of civilians retreating wearily from the onslaught. Twice en route they sprinted from the trucks as Stukas attacked; on each occasion the Highlanders shot furiously back before returning to the vehicles as if nothing had happened. The verges were littered with discarded military equipment and personal belongings; from time to time they passed the smoking shell of a burned-out vehicle, sometimes with bodies inside. After two hours they came to a town and crossed a railway line and a narrow river, and then a bridge over marshy meadows. 'Blangy-sur-Bresle', a sign read.

The convoy stopped; the boys stared out. Vehicles were arriving from all directions, disgorging hundreds of men and tons of equipment along the river as far as they could see. Heavy artillery, anti-aircraft guns, self-propelled field pieces and a row of low-loaders carrying Vickers tanks.

'Do you think there's going to be a battle, Kenny?'

'I bloody hope so.'

MacLean arrived. 'You two, with me.'

'What's going on, Sarge?'

'The new front line. We've got twenty miles to hold between here and the sea, and barely a division to hold it with, which isn't enough. But we're to dig in along the river and stop Jerry crossing at all costs. Or go down trying.'

'What about us?'

'Division's setting up a forward command post a mile back. They need runners – you know, messengers and so on. I take it you can run?'

'Course.' Kenny shrugged. 'Ted's a bloody champion.'

'Is that true?'

'He won medals and that. He's an officer too, ain't you, Ted?'

'Well, I. . . Only a cadet. Acting cadet, that is, not—'

'Stop blethering and follow me.'

The forward command post consisted of a ring of vehicles in a woodland clearing. One was an ambulance with a Red Cross painted on it, another was a khaki caravan draped in camouflage nets; also there were radio vans, tents, staff cars and motorcycles. As they arrived MacLean directed them to a tent marked 'Signals'. 'Wait there and don't get in the way.'

They waited. Other messengers came and went. They heard the hiss and crackle of radios; cars and motorcycles drove up and then roared away again. Everyone seemed busy and preoccupied. An hour passed.

'Why did you tell him I'm an officer?' Theo asked.

'Cos we'll get better jobs, you idiot!'

At one point they were ordered to another tent and given tea and sandwiches, but then more Stukas appeared and a furious anti-aircraft barrage started all about them. No bombs fell, the aeroplanes departed, they finished the tea and resumed their vigil outside the tent.

A lieutenant appeared. 'Who are you?'

'I'm Private Rollings and this is Officer Cadet Trickey.'

'Um, Acting. . .'

'Ride a bike, Rollings?'

'Ah, well, no, not exactly, but—'

'Trickey?'

'Yes, sir.'

'Report inside.'

The tent was dark and stuffy. Two radio operators sat at their sets with headphones on their ears, next to a clerk banging on a typewriter. To one side a major pored over a table spread with maps.

Theo cleared his throat. 'Um, Trickey, sir.'

The major looked up. 'Christ, how old are you?'

'Seventeen, sir.'

'For God's sake. Right, Trickey, I'm Wilson. I take it you can read a map?'

'Yes, sir.'

'Good. Now we're here' – he jabbed a finger – 'at Blangy, and here, about four miles south, is Saint-Léger, which is apparently held by a mixed force of Sutherland and Argylls, some Black Watch, a few Borderers – frankly we've no idea as we can't raise anyone on the radio. But we need to know – and know their situation, got that?'

'Yes, sir. Their, um, situation?'

'Strength, disposition, composition,' the major counted off, 'weaponry, supplies, casualties, communications, and some bloody names while you're at it – who's senior officer, who's he got in support, who's liaising with HQ, and tell him. . .'

'Yes, sir?'

The major sighed. 'Well, tell him he's pretty much holding the end of the line. South of him are the French, but no one's sure of their positions, or their intentions, frankly, so he must assume he's on his own out there.'

'Yes, sir, I'll tell him.'

'Right, off you go. And, Trickey?'

'Yes, sir?'

'Be careful. They'll be coming at us any time.'

Five minutes later he was pedalling furiously south aboard a khaki-painted bicycle with loose chain and no brakes, with his tin helmet bumping on his chest and his rifle slipping off his shoulder. Over the other shoulder he carried a canvas satchel he'd been given containing map, compass, binoculars, notepad and, to his surprise, a clip of live ammunition for his rifle – the first he'd seen since training. Soon he was out of Blangy and riding a rutted track beside the railway, sometimes in open farmland, sometimes through shaded woods. Overhead the sky was overcast; a blustery wind kept his head down and progress laboured. From time to time the River Bresle, little more than a winding stream, appeared on his left; beyond it the countryside lay flat, and then rose towards dark forests. At intervals he met clusters of soldiers who called out or whistled as he passed. Some were gathered in rifle sections, some with anti-tank weapons, Bren or heavier machine guns, one or two manned small artillery pieces on wheels, all pointing towards the high ground beyond the river. He pedalled on, passing civilians pushing handcarts, an old man riding a donkey, grubby-faced children, a mother with a baby on her back: all heading in the other direction. Dogs chased him; a horse frisked restlessly in a field. Suddenly he saw a sign for Saint-Léger, stamped his boot in the dirt and skidded to a halt by the railway.

'And who might you be?' a disembodied voice called from behind a hedge.

'Trickey,' he panted, 'from, um, Division, back that way. From Blangy.'

'Not from Scotland, that's for sure, Tricky-dick. What if you're a Jerry spy?'

'What? No, well, you see, Major Wilson sent me, to report on your, um, situation.'

'Our situation's fucked, laddie. What's the password?'

'Password? I don't know, he never gave me one.'

'Correct. Continue up the road a-ways, you'll soon come to them.'

He pedalled on past a signal box and a farm; then houses appeared, with soldiers stationed in gardens, outhouses and upstairs windows. He reached a little square featuring a *pissoir*, a war memorial, a deserted café and a village hall. Beyond them the road led up and out of the village towards the forest.

'Over here, please, quickly.'

He pushed his bike over to the hall. A low wall surrounded it, behind which a four-man mortar section tended their weapon; nearby two more hefted anti-tank rifles, meanwhile two officers leaned on the wall, training binoculars on the distant trees.

'What do you think, Simon?' one murmured.

'That's them all right. Look beside that darker clump of bushes – you can see the barrels poking out.'

'Ah yes, 50-millimetre. That means Mark 3s. Question is, how many?'

'And when. Still three hours of daylight.'

'Hmm.' The first officer looked up. 'Hello, and you are?'

'Trickey, sir. From HQ at Blangy. I'm to report your situation.'

Chuckles of amusement were exchanged.

'Well, Trickey, I think I can safely report that our situation is a little precarious just now. Because the enemy are lined up behind those trees, and might be about to attack. Does that help?'

'Yes, sir.' Theo fumbled for his satchel. 'Should I write this down? I mean their, um, disposition?'

'No, my friend.' The officer picked up his binoculars. 'I'd say you should put on your tin hat, load your weapon, and prepare to meet them.'

CHAPTER 8

The first thing was an eruption of mortar fire from within the trees. A series of distant thuds, a crescendo of whistling as the missiles soared, a shout of 'Down!' and then the crash of explosions all around. Tense silence one second, a cacophony of destruction the next. At the first detonations he ducked reflexively below the wall, rifle forgotten, hands clamped on ears, staring in wide-eyed awe at the chaos unfolding around him: the café roof collapsing, a smoking hole instead of the *pissoir*, a telegraph pole stumbling drunkenly sideways. The noise was deafening, the power of the explosions visceral, a crash like thunder and then a fist-like blow to the stomach. On and on it went, pounding detonations that split the air and shook the ground, terrifyingly close one moment, farther off the next. Speech was impossible, coherent thought unimaginable; all he could do was hug the wall and pray.

But even as he cowered, part of him also observed. Firstly, the barrage, though intense and violent, seemed widely scattered. The war memorial exploded to rubble right before his eyes, but many more shells were falling far and wide – as if there was no central target for the attack. Secondly, the men around him were not cowering, like him. Crouching yes, squatting on one knee steadying their helmets as if in a gusty breeze, but doing so doggedly, even patiently, with heads cocked and faces impassive. As if waiting. Because the Germans, he realized, even as the assault began to wane, didn't know exactly where they were.

Then it stopped, as if on a cue, and an expectant hush filled the square. He held his breath. Seconds ticked; the silence grew and solidified. And a new sound came above the ringing in his ears. The rumble of distant engines.

He felt himself being pulled up by the collar.

'You might want to see this' – the officer handed him binoculars – 'for your report.'

He took the glasses, squinted, but his hands shook so much he saw only a trembling blur. Breathing hard, he steadied himself on the wall and searched again, scouring the treeline, and suddenly there they were. Tanks. Six beasts of the deep, grey, menacing, nosing through the grass like sharks through a sea. Behind each beast swam a school of infantrymen, crouching low as they moved, using the tanks for cover. Something solid settled in his stomach. This was it. The enemy. Men with guns coming to fight and kill. 'The barrage was to soften us up,' the officer was saying, 'like the starter at a meal. This lot's the main course.' He turned to the men with the mortar. 'Commence firing.'

The sound of metal sliding down a tube, a percussive thud as it fired – then it was all eyes on the approaching enemy. The shell landed long, throwing a fountain of dirt high in the air behind the tanks. But it surprised the German foot soldiers, who turned in confusion; seconds more and mortar shells were exploding all round them.

'Off we go, everyone!' Drawing his pistol, the officer vaulted the wall and set off up the lane. Simultaneously men around the square gathered their weapons and ran after him. Theo hesitated, immobilized by fear and indecision. Up that lane lay killing and death, perhaps his own death. By his side lay his bike and his runner's satchel, his notebook and map. Major Wilson had ordered him to report the situation, and he legitimately could. *Enemy attacking Saint-Léger with tanks,* he would say, *our forces repelling but hard pressed, send reinforcements.* He could leave now and no one would blame him. Yet men were running forward to fight, and he couldn't deny he felt a kinship, a rush of excitement, and something else. Duty. *Load your weapon, and prepare to meet the enemy*, the officer had said. He heard boots running; then a soldier came skidding round the corner.

'Get the fuck up here, you brainless tosser!'

He followed him up the lane. The growl of engines was much louder now, as was the crump of exploding mortars mixed with the sporadic crack of smaller weapons. They reached a cluster of farm buildings, figures in khaki busily taking up positions among them. Beyond lay the field with the enemy, now barely two hundred yards distant and still approaching.

'Stay here and don't move!' the soldier said, pushing him behind a shed. An unlit cigarette waggled in his lips; his battledress displayed a lance corporal's stripe and a shoulder patch with the word 'Gordons'. 'Davey, you ready with that Boys?'

'Aye, for all the good it'll do.' A second soldier lay on the ground sighting a Boys anti-tank rifle round the shed.

'It'll do just fine if you get him close enough. How many do you see?'

'Just the one coming our way, half a dozen lads following it.'

'Our boys'll take care of them; we fix that bloody tank. Here, you, laddie.' The corporal lobbed a bag at Theo. 'Know how to arm a Gammon?'

Theo stared at the sack. His mind reeled: Aldershot, weapons training, Gammon grenade, a flexible bag of explosives with a ball-bearing detonator. You throw it at a tank and it explodes on impact.

'Um, yes, you unscrew the cap.'

'Good. Do it. Don't drop it.'

Suddenly a deafening bang from beyond their shed as a tank opened fire. Theo ducked instinctively but its shell soared high overhead to strike a building in the village. The corporal winked and held a finger to his lips; all round the farmyard soldiers were crouching behind walls and buildings, still unseen by the enemy. Off to the left Theo glimpsed more creeping among the houses. Then came a yell: 'Forward the 51st!' and to a man they rushed from cover, waving their weapons and roaring like savages.

'Now!' The corporal ducked round the shed and threw the Gammon. Theo heard it explode, and then a crack at his feet as the Boys fired. The nose of the tank appeared, barely ten yards away, dented, dust-caked, shuddering, its turret hunting left and right. The corporal snatched another Gammon, the Boys fired again and suddenly explosions and gunfire filled the air: grenades, rifles, machine guns, mortars, a furious tumult of battle mixed with revving engines and shouting Highlanders.

A German infantryman appeared, turned to them in surprise and then fell to an unseen bullet. A second slumped to his knees holding his head; Theo glimpsed a kilted figure leap from a roof, another thrusting at something with a bayonet, a third charging a tank like an enraged bull.

'Gammon!' the corporal roared. Their tank was trying to reverse, its turret ablaze, engine protesting. Crack went the Boys again. Frantically he unscrewed another bomb and held it for the corporal, who hurled it at the monster, before vanishing round the corner in pursuit.

Then it was over, the attack repulsed. Gradually the sound of gunfire and engines receded; soon it petered out altogether, leaving only the crackle of flames, the occasional parting shot, and the triumphant cries of the Scotsmen. He ventured from behind the shed. Thick smoke drifted over the field; two tanks stood stranded, furiously ablaze, while a third limped away trailing smoke. The remaining three had escaped to the trees. The infantry too had vanished, leaving their casualties scattered about the yard. He counted at least twenty, with indentations in the grass showing where more had fallen. To one side a gaggle of survivors stood under guard, their hands on their heads. He propped his unfired rifle against the wall and picked up his satchel. Report, he muttered to himself doggedly, I'm supposed to *report the situation*. But all he could think of was the Scotsmen. Like savages, he thought, brave and honourable, but with so much fury it had scared him, as it had scared the enemy who had withered before it. Like bloodlust. If that's what's needed, he reflected, opening his notebook, if that's what you need to fight a war, then I don't have it.

'All right, laddie?' The corporal reappeared. *A-reet,* it sounded like.

'Yes, thank you. Um, I suppose we won.'

'Aye, we did that.' He cupped a lighter to his cigarette.

'And so what happens now?'

'We fall back.'

'Back? But if we've beaten them. . .'

'We've done no such thing, laddie. We've driven them off. But they'll be back, and double the strength' – he eyed the sky – 'soon as they've called in the Stukas.'

'What do we do?'

'*We? We* pull back to the railway, dig in, get some scoff and await orders. *You* go see the lieutenant and be on your way.'

'Oh.' He stared at his notebook, shaking in his hand.

'It's called a fighting retreat, laddie. Stick that in your report.'

'Right. Yes, I will.'

'You did all right. With the Gammons and that.'

A-reet, he found himself writing, then remembered Wilson's instruction: *Get some bloody names.* 'Thank you, um, Corporal. . .'

'Guthrie. Niall Guthrie, the Gordon Highlanders.'

He pedalled back to Blangy to make his report. Dusk was descending; a fine rain fell. On the way he noticed that the positions he'd seen soldiers in earlier were now deserted. Some showed signs of fighting: empty shell cases, an abandoned mortar, a burned-out truck. By the time he reached Blangy it was dark and he was wet through. He had not eaten since his sandwich of the morning. Dimly he wondered about Kenny, and what he'd make of his day.

But Kenny was gone. He turned along the track to the command post, only to find it empty. Everything – tents, caravans, lorries, motorcycles – all packed and gone like the travelling gypsy fairs of his childhood. He stared around the darkened clearing. Somewhere above the hiss of rain came the rumble of motor traffic, then distant shouts and the revving of engines. He set off towards it, pedalling head down along a woodland track until he broke out on to a main road.

A column of men and machines filled the road in both directions as far as he could see. Lit by torchlight and slitted headlights, it moved slowly through the night like a giant shadowy insect. The sound was of trudging boots and grinding gears; the smell was dank woodland, engine exhaust and cigarettes. Here and there a hoarse laugh or ribald curse rose above the murmur, and far up the column he thought he heard singing. Mostly they moved in silence.

A dispatch rider sped up on a motorcycle. 'Who are you?'

'Trickey. I was supposed to report to Major Wilson.'

'Wilson? What unit?'

'I. . . I don't know. He was at the command post, back there.'

'CP's long gone, mate, Christ knows where. You'd better fall in with this lot.'

'Where's it going?'

'Back.'

'Have you seen Private Rollings? He's—' But the rider sped off.

He found himself amid a company of Sherwood Foresters. They were not Scottish, they explained emphatically, but merely attached to 51st Highland Division 'for the duration'. After teasing him about his name, accent and strange manner, they welcomed him into their midst, feeding him ration-pack stew and hoarded chocolate.

'So, Tricky-dicky, where you sprung from, lad?'

'Well, it's a place called Bolzano, in the South Tyrol.'

'That's Ireland, ain't it?'

'Um, no, it's. . .'

'Not *where*, I mean what unit, you tit!'

'Oh, sorry. I'm from 2/6th Territorials, the East Surreys.'

'Christ, they're sending up the useless mouths.'

'We must be in the shite.'

It was an expression he'd begun to hear, to describe non-fighting support staff, like him. Useless mouths. It was not meant appreciatively.

They walked all night. After a while the rain stopped and the clouds broke to a ragged overcast. Weariness overcame him and he fell into a trance-like rhythm beside his bike which rattled and clicked at his side like a mechanical pet. Towards dawn the column faltered to a halt. Immediately the Foresters began boiling water for tea. Theo slumped down on the verge and dozed off.

A strident voice woke him. 'D Company fall in!'

'That's us, lads, come on, jump to it.'

He struggled groggily awake. Gradually the memories came: the miles of cycling, the mortar bombardment, Corporal Guthrie, the Gammon grenades and the battle with the tanks, and finally walking all night in the rain with the Sherwood Foresters. He was still among them, he noted, gazing sleepily around, perhaps a hundred men strung out on a road beside a wood. But the rest of the column was nowhere to be seen.

He yawned. 'Where is everyone?'

'Oh look, it's Sleeping Beauty!'

'Come on, Dicky boy, shake a leg.'

He rose to his feet, brushing moss from his tunic. Around him the others were assembling their kit. 'What's happening?'

'Column left two hours ago. We're covering the rear, lucky us. Oops—'

A sergeant was striding up. 'Who the hell's this?'

'Dunno, Sarge, runner from HQ gone astray. Latched on to us last night.'

'HQ? Fuck's sake, what's his name?'

'Ted Dicky. He's Irish. Useless mouth from the East Surreys.'

'Right, Dicky, who's your commanding officer?'

'I, well, there was, um, Captain Wells, back in Caen, then sort of a Lieutenant Somebody at General Fortune's HQ, then, oh, Major Wilson yesterday, but then another lieutenant at Saint-Léger, I wrote down his name here—'

'STUKAS!'

They fell from above like gannets from a cliff, the screaming engines, the whining sirens, the whistling bombs, just as before. The Foresters moved fast, diving under vehicles and into ditches, but the Stukas were faster, dropping their loads with deadly precision before pulling round to attack with machine guns. Theo, face down in the ditch, felt the earth jump beneath him, and the deafening concussion as the two bombs hit, and then the spattering of earth and stones on his back and legs. The engines receded; he looked up to see the two black shapes banked hard over, circling round for the second pass. On the road lay the wreckage of man and machine: a three-ton lorry blown on its back, a radio truck ablaze, weapons and equipment scattered. And where seconds before men had stood, joked and chatted, now they lay strewn about a smoking hole in the ground. Some were dead; some to his horror were not. He saw a man crawling, both legs blown to bloody stumps; another staggered to his feet holding a gaping wound in his stomach; a third lay on his back screaming for help. But the Stukas were returning and there was no time to help. Even as he watched, the Foresters were running for the trees, but also for position, he realized, many of them hastily manning weapons – a Vickers machine gun on a trailer, a Bren recovered from a ditch, rifles and small arms everywhere – and as the Stukas thundered in for their second pass, the Foresters opened up with them all. But to no avail, and in seconds the bombers were gone, and silence descended on the road once more.

There was nothing to do but continue as before. The dead were buried, the wounded attended to, smashed equipment discarded, then the company finally formed up into its three platoons, and an officer appeared to address them. Meades, his name was, Theo recorded, a captain, also noting he looked youthful, and world-weary beyond his years.

'These air attacks will only get worse.' Meades glanced at the bloodstained road. 'We must be more vigilant and not get caught in the open. So now we're ordered to hold out here until tonight, then withdraw to a new line being formed ten miles west. The 51st will stand and repel the enemy advance from there.'

'That's what they said last time!' someone quipped.

'And the time before that!'

'I know.' Meades held up a hand. 'I know, but there it is. Now, I want everyone well dug-in. Number 1 Platoon, you cover the road from that copse over there. Number 2, you're the other side: set up a mortar section behind that mound. . .'

The briefing went on; then at the end Meades asked for questions.

'What about the BEF, sir?' someone said. 'I mean, what's happened to it?'

'Well, there're rumours – unconfirmed, mind you – coming over the radio that some sort of evacuation's taken place. By the navy, off the coast somewhere up north.'

'What, all of them?'

'Most of them, apparently.'

'Except us!'

'Quite.'

'And we're supposed to stop the whole German bleeding army.'

'Indeed, so dig in well. Now, I gather we've a runner from Divisional HQ with us. A Private Dick from the Irish Fusiliers, is that right? Dick, could you see me please.'

Theo, it transpired, would not be staying with the Sherwood Foresters. Instead he was to rejoin the main column, taking two orderlies and three seriously wounded with him. On a pushcart.

'I'd let you have a vehicle but we've none to spare,' Meades explained, handing him a bundle of papers. 'Now listen, these are for my battalion commander, Colonel Graveney, and there's duplicates for Div HQ just in case. Stick to the back roads, don't tangle with the enemy, and for God's sake watch out for Stukas.'

Departure was delayed. As the cart was being loaded, one of the wounded, the man with severed legs, died, so there was a pause while he was unloaded and buried. Then, with the remaining two casualties, their kitbags, weapons and Theo's bicycle piled aboard, they set off. A hundred yards up the road he heard a cry: 'Ta-ta, Dicky boy!' and turned to wave, touched suddenly by the poignancy of the scene. A single company of Foresters, fewer than a hundred men, with orders to hold off forty divisions.

They walked all morning. The sky was clear, the summer sun hot, so soon they were shedding clothes, tying handkerchiefs on their heads and arranging shade for the two wounded, who remained unconscious from morphia. The cart had rubber tyres and two handles which the orderlies took turns at, while Theo was told to push from the side. They were regulars, both privates, called Foley and Stitt. Foley was from Derby and given to grumbling; Stitt came from Newark where he'd worked as a cobbler before joining up. A good pair of boots, Theo learned, was all a man really needed in life, while army boots apparently were 'cack'. Neither showed any regard for Theo, who as a 'useless part-timer' was fair game for abuse. Insults flowed, and while Foley and Stitt alternated between pushing and walking, he was given no rest. 'Put yer back in it, boy!' was a frequent rejoinder. Fortunately the cart moved smoothly and the terrain was mostly flat, varying between open countryside and shady woodland, but when presented with an incline the efforts of all three were needed, and twice they had to unload one of the wounded to surmount a hill. As instructed they kept clear of major roads and stuck to lanes and tracks, using Theo's compass for guidance, yet signs of war – discarded baggage, plodding refugees, abandoned military equipment – were never far from view. Towards noon they crested a rise to find they were travelling parallel to a main road about five miles to the south. Long lines of traffic moved along it in a westerly direction, throwing up clouds of dust that stretched for miles.

'Civvies,' Foley said, mopping his brow. 'Refugees and that.'

'You sure? Looks like military to me. French army probably.'

'I tell you, Stitty, them's civvies! Making for the city – what's it called? – Rouen.'

Theo took out his binoculars and steadied them on the cart. 'They're German.'

'Don't be bloody daft! How can they be?'

His hands were rock steady this time, his breathing calm and even. There was no mistake: what he was seeing was a German armoured column, trucks, tanks and artillery, several miles long, moving at speed. They weren't bothered about confronting the Allies, he realized, they were racing to overtake them. And cut them off. Again. He reached for his notebook. 'They're definitely German. Looks like a whole division.'

The mood in the afternoon was subdued. Heat, fatigue, hunger and the realization that the enemy was not just behind them, but beside and also in front, curbed the urge for talk. Which remained mostly speculative.

'So what d'you think, Stitty?'

'Christ knows. The rate they're going they'll have us all surrounded.'

'Yes, but our lot'll send the BEF back to relieve us, surely.'

'Re-equip a whole army? Then ship it over? It'd take weeks.'

'They've got to do something. They can't just wash their hands of us.'

Theo only half listened. He was watching the casualty nearest him on the cart. He'd become restive as the morphia wore off; after a second injection he was now quieter, although his lips moved and his eyes sought Theo's. Theo murmured reassurances as best he could, his mind pondering Stitt's question. What if France goes? He thought back to Caen, to the carefree days of the 2/6th and 2nd Platoon and Kenny, to Thérèse and Georges and hot chocolate at the Café Gondrée. And Jeanette. How she came to him at night, walking beside him as he paced the bridge, and pressing herself to him when they kissed goodnight. What would happen to her if France fell?

By evening they were catching the main column. Or scattered elements of it. They passed a stranded lorry, its crew busy changing a wheel, then an emplacement of Bofors anti-aircraft guns pointing skyward, a cluster of tents, and then discarded vehicles shoved in a field. A dispatch rider roared by on a motorcycle. More men appeared, until finally they arrived at a road junction controlled by a Transport Corps corporal wearing armbands.

'Unit, lads?'

'Sherwood Foresters, 2nd Battalion.'

'Brigade?'

'Christ knows.'

'Blimey, more strays.' He glanced at the injured men. 'Right, there's a dressing station a mile up the road. Get them dropped off, then report to Captain Willetts at the Logistics CP nearby. He'll sort you from there.'

'Um, I'm not with them.'

'What?'

'I'm not a Forester.'

'What are you then?'

'Well, I'm a runner. Sort of. With Division HQ. I've got messages, and a report.'

'Right. Division's another five miles, straight on, follow signs for "Osmoy" village. They're set up in some old pile back there.'

He retrieved his rifle and bicycle, said goodbye to Foley and Stitt, and his casualty, who gripped his hand so tightly he had to ease it free. Then he pedalled off into the dusk. An hour later and after several false turns, he found the building, a decaying château set at the end of a drive. He parked his bike and entered a musty hallway with trestle tables set up for clerks, typists, telephonists and radio operators. About twenty people were busy working; he gave his name and Meades's papers to a receptionist who sent him to the kitchens for food, then to a tattered armchair by the stairs. 'Wait there,' he was told. Within minutes he was asleep.

He awoke to the sounds of exasperation.

'The French are doing what?... But that leaves us wholly unsupported!... Supplies! Everything: ammunition, food, fuel, transportation, the lot, especially ammunition!'

An officer was speaking angrily on the telephone. Portly of bearing, about forty, with red face and moustache, Theo recognized him as the general he and Kenny had seen two days earlier. General Fortune, officer commanding the 51st. Two aides stood at his side taking notes.

'Le Havre? But that's sixty miles, we'd never make it before. . . Hello? Hello!' He slammed down the receiver. 'We're on our own,' he fumed. 'French are detaching most of the 10th Army to save Paris. They're leaving us a division.'

'What about the 2nd BEF?'

'Too late, too far west. They're pulling out through the Atlantic ports. Meanwhile we're supposed to fall back to Le Havre for evacuation.'

'As long as Jerry doesn't get there first.'

'Precisely. Rumour is they may already be north of Rouen. Although I find that hard to believe.'

'Um, it's true. I saw them.'

Fortune looked up. 'Who on earth are you?'

'I'm Trickey.'

'Hey!' One of the aides stepped forward. 'Don't be bloody impertinent! Give your full name, rank and unit, and stand to attention before the general, damn you!'

'Sorry, sir. Trickey, um, Theodor, 2/6th East Surreys. Private, well, Officer Cadet, um, Acting, that is, as I never finished—'

'Stop mumbling! What the hell are you doing here?'

'I, well, I was doing supplies, then was a runner for Major Wilson. . .'

'Wilson? Who's he?'

The second aide spoke. 'Isn't he intelligence officer with 152 Brigade?'

'Just a minute,' Fortune interrupted. 'Now, young man, what precisely is it that you think you saw?'

'I, we – well, sir, we were pushing two wounded men, on a cart, you see, and we stopped on top of this hill, for a rest. And looking to the south – I had my binoculars, you see, sir – I saw a long column of Germans, not walking but in lorries and half-tracks and other vehicles, and tanks too and trucks towing artillery and so on, and they were moving along a main road west rather fast—'

'Show me.' Fortune strode to a map on the wall. Theo followed, heart pounding, forced himself to study it, found Blangy, found the woods where he'd slept with the Foresters, found the roads he'd followed with Foley and Stitt, and pointed.

'There.'

'What time?'

'About noon, sir.'

He was woken by an artillery barrage. It started some distance away, permeating the clogged corridors of his mind like insistent knocking on a door. Gradually it drew nearer, and more insistent, until it was no longer knocking but more an unbroken peal of thunder. Then the ground shuddered and he opened his eyes. He was still in the château, still curled on his armchair in the hall. He was cold and stiff. A shaft of dawn sunlight slanted through the open front door, illuminating fiery dust motes stirred by the barrage which sounded about two miles away. Around him the trestle tables and chairs stood folded, the typewriters and radios packed and boxed, the map on the wall gone. A vaguely familiar profile appeared in the doorway, silhouetted by the sun.

'Ah, there you are, lad. Been looking for you.'

It was the quartermaster from the Seaforth Highlanders, the one who had showed him and Kenny how to bury the dead. 'Sergeant MacLean?'

'Yes, and I hear you've been having a fine time of it.'

Theo was to rejoin his unit, MacLean explained, or at least try to. 'East Surreys were last heard of in this area' – he pointed to Theo's map – 'three or four miles north. They're supporting the Argyll and Sutherlanders, what's left of 'em.'

'I met some Gordon Highlanders. Defending a village on the River Bresle. I don't know what happened to them.'

MacLean sighed. 'It's the same everywhere. We fall back to a new line; they creep up in the night, hit us with a dawn barrage, then follow through with armour and infantry. All we can do is hold on a few hours, then fall back and dig in again.'

'A fighting retreat.'

'That's right.' His eyes were darkly ringed, Theo noted, his cheeks hollow and unshaven. A shadow of the earlier man. He told Theo to collect food and water and said he could keep his bicycle. If he failed to find the East Surreys, he was to make his way to the Normandy port of Le Havre, where together with the rest of the 51st they would be rescued by ship and returned to England.

By the time he set off the barrage had eased, replaced by the sound of sporadic gunfire. This grew louder and more intense as he pedalled north: he'd hear a pocket of fighting off to his right, then an interval of pause, followed by the next pocket. After half an hour he entered an area of denser woodland and now heard the added rumble of approaching engines. A moment later men were crashing through the undergrowth towards him.

'Get the fuck back! Tanks!'

He leaped off his bike and followed the men, who were bearing rifles and a Vickers machine gun. They ran on through the woods; the engine noise gradually receded until only their hoarse gasps and tramping boots were heard. The trees began to thin, a clearing appeared and then a mud-filled ditch.

'This'll do,' the leader said. 'Quick now, get the Vick up. Rest of you, spread out along the ditch. You! Get that bloody bike out of sight!'

Theo scrambled into the ditch, which was knee-deep in black mud. Beside him three men were already assembling the Vickers: erecting the tripod, attaching the barrel and breech, filling the cooling jacket with water from a jerry can.

'You, boy! Those ammo boxes, quick.' Theo retrieved the boxes. 'Not this side, you pillock, the other side! Good, right, now stay there, keep your head down, and don't go shooting till I say.'

Another man appeared, splashing along the ditch towards him. '*A-reet?*'

'Um, yes thank you.'

'*Gud.*' He produced four hand grenades, arranging them on the rim of the ditch like ornaments on a shelf. Through the trees the sound of engines grew louder. Guttural shouts could also be heard. 'Right, so you wait for their lads, *ye ken?*' He nodded towards the noise. 'They follow behind the tanks.'

'Yes, I know.'

'Then you'll know not to shoot till you can smell their breath.'

And with that they were ready. Two at the Vickers, busy loading ammunition and adjusting sights, three to their left with a Boys and rifles, and the one on his right with the grenades. Theo picked up his own rifle, slid the bolt and fingered the safety lever, holding the wooden butt to his cheek. *Load your weapon, and prepare to meet the enemy.* His helmet sat heavy on his head, his feet were wet, his mouth parched. The moment seemed dream-like yet viscerally real, and also detached, as though he was experiencing it through someone else.

Shouts and shooting erupted from the woods, and suddenly figures in khaki were sprinting into the open. Others pursued them, grey-clad, running from the bushes and then dropping to one knee to fire. He heard zipping noises, saw clods of earth spurting around him, then came a shout: 'Get 'em, boys!' and the Vickers opened up, shockingly loud beside him. Two Germans went down in an instant; others dived for cover. Everyone started shooting at once; then with a deafening roar a tank crashed into view, turret roving, its machine gun spitting fire. The man to his right convulsed and slumped, his grenades untouched. More Germans appeared.

Theo raised his rifle to one but the man jinked from view; a Boys cracked to his left; he saw hits from the Vickers sparking off the tank – its machine gun was tearing up the ditch now, clods of soil and stone flying, branches and twigs splintering from above – then came a shout and the Vickers stopped.

'Here!' The gunner beckoned frantically. His loader was writhing in the ditch. 'God's sake, come on!' Theo found his feet and stumbled through the mud. 'Load!'

Theo fumbled for the belt, held it to the breech, the gun roared, the belt raced through his fingers, he felt hot metal, tasted cordite, saw Germans falling as the gunner swung furiously from side to side, then the man's head jerked and he reeled back into the ditch. Further along the man with the Boys dropped sideways. The tank was coming; then a stick grenade splashed into the mud at his feet, he heard shouts in hoarse German, '*Töten Sie!*' – 'Kill them!' and he turned and scrambled from the ditch.

He ran. Away from the ditch, away from the clearing, running as he hadn't run since his youth in the mountains. Through fields and woods, farms and orchards, ditches and streams, fleeing as though pursued, arms pumping, lungs bursting, legs buckling. On and on, until with the sound of gunfire receding, he came to a village, saw a low wall, hauled himself over and flopped to the ground. There he lay, sweating, gasping, staring giddily up at clouds, until his heart gradually slowed and his breathing steadied.

He was in the village graveyard. Slowly he sat up and took stock. Bees fussed at flower beds, a lark sang overhead, posies wilted in vases, photographs of the deceased gazed at him from headstones. He didn't know where the village was – he had little idea of the direction he'd run. And he'd lost everything. Bicycle, satchel, food, helmet, water. Worst of all his rifle, the gravest loss of all. Your friend, your saviour, your reason for being, instructors recited endlessly, lose it and you are nothing. Now it lay in a muddy ditch beside the bodies of men he didn't know. He hadn't even fired it.

He hauled himself up and began walking, following a presumed course westwards. Craving only to be alone, he stuck to footpaths and tracks, circumventing houses and villages, hiding himself when he saw vehicles or people. Hours passed; apart from patrolling aircraft and distant dust plumes he saw little military activity, and suspected he was wandering off course. He didn't care, it didn't matter, part of him wanted to keep going, to keep walking ever further from death and killing, the duty and obligation, the mud-caked boots, coarse khaki and shouting Scotsmen. To walk away from being a soldier and never come back.

Late in the afternoon he caught up with a slow-moving procession on the road ahead, and saw people in dark clothes leading horse carts, pushing barrows and carrying bundles. Refugees: wordless, homeless, the eternal victims of war. Suddenly exhausted with solitude, he fell into slow step with them. More time passed, no talk was exchanged; then an old man sidled up.

'*Où allez-vous, jeune homme?*'

'*Le Havre,*' he replied. '*Et vous, monsieur?*'

'*Le sud.*'

He'd been walking the wrong way. All day. He plodded on, calculating – ten miles? Fifteen? Then the old man spoke again.

'*Vous êtes déserteur?*'

'*Pardon?*' He had to ask again, to be sure. '*Pardon, monsieur?*'

'Are you a deserter?'

He begged bread, water and apples, turned and hurriedly retraced his steps. Dusk fell; he rested briefly and then set off into the night, heading north and west. Navigation was easier; artillery flashes lit a wide arc of sky across the entire sector and he headed straight for them. Towards dawn he rested again, waking two hours later to the unmistakable sounds of barrage, ate his last apple and pushed on. He passed through a village, saw discarded vehicles and equipment; among them he found a water canteen and filled it at a *lavoir*. There were no people to be seen; all around were signs of hasty departure. In the distance traffic sounds rose above the rumble of artillery. He left the village, hurried round a bend and came face-to-face with a machine gun.

'Blimey, who are you?'

'Oh, um, Trickey. I got separated.'

'I'll say. Where's your kit?'

'Lost. I lost it yesterday, in a battle in some woods.' He looked around. A deserted village, a single gun emplacement, four men, one Vickers, one box of ammunition, alone at a crossroads. 'What's happening?'

'Division's falling back.'

'Le Havre?'

'Le Havre's fucked. Now it's some place called Valery some such.'

'I'm trying to rejoin them.'

'Can't miss 'em. Main road's a mile north.'

'What about you?'

'We're covering the withdrawal.'

'But what if nobody—'

'Listen, fuck off or I'll shoot you myself.'

He hurried on across fields and an orchard, the traffic sounds growing in his ears until he crested an embankment overlooking a wide road. Trucks, lorries, cars and vans filled it in both directions. He scrambled down and set off after a lorry full of soldiers. 'Wait!' He glimpsed tartan shoulder patches and berets with bobbles. 'Wait, are you Gordon Highlanders?'

'Gordon bloody bollocks, laddie!' a shout came back. 'We're Black Watch!'

Despite the gaffe they pulled him aboard, found space for him and plied him with boiled sweets and biscuits. Having duly recited his story, he learned that with the entire division surrounded, the 51st was ordered to the seaside town of Saint-Valery-en-Caux, some forty miles short of Le Havre. Here they were to make a stand until the Royal Navy could come and rescue them. The Black Watch, along with others, was to form a defensive perimeter around the town.

By noon they were taking up positions above the port, which was under sporadic bombardment from Stukas and unseen artillery. Theo found himself attached to a six-man rifle section defending a narrow lane. A lance corporal led the section.

'Here,' he said, handing Theo a rifle. 'And don't go losing it, we've none to spare.'

Theo hefted the rifle, which looked old and careworn. 'What about ammunition?'

'Just what's in it. Eight rounds. More promised but don't hold your breath.'

Eight bullets. To stop an army.

'So what are you, then?' the corporal was saying. 'Name, rank, telephone number, all that malarkey.'

'Oh, yes. Trickey, um, Ted, Officer Cadet, 2/6th East Surreys.'

'Officer! Hear that, lads, we've Captain Ted come to save us!'

Ribald laughter and insults circled the lane.

'No, well, you see, I'm only an acting officer, I never finished OCT—'

'Listen, you can be a bloody general as far as I'm concerned. Just keep hold of that rifle and go easy on the ammo.'

All afternoon they waited, three on one side of the lane, three on the other. Shower clouds hurried by, borne on a brisk sea breeze. The taste of salt was in the air, surf crashed, seagulls cried; the grey waves of the Channel beckoned, with home and safety just over the horizon. But countering the optimism was an unnerving sense of encirclement. Shells whistled overhead to explode with a crump down in the town; dive-bombers patrolled offshore; tanks and artillery crept nearer. The enemy could not be seen, but they could be sensed: organizing their approach, manoeuvring for position, taking their time readying for attack. For some the waiting was worse than fighting.

'Bugger this,' a young rifleman grumbled beside Theo. 'I just wish the buggers would get on wi' it.'

'Careful what you wish, Billy,' his friend replied, 'they'll be here soon enough.'

Supper arrived, an urn of soup and packet of biscuits between six. It was all there was, they were told. Later a sergeant came by to brief them.

'Navy's due in port from midnight. Half the division's already down there. Div HQ's in the town hall. They've been having a time of it but they're holding on. When we get the word we withdraw into town for embarkation. We do it orderly, we cover our backs, we go home in one piece, *ye ken?*'

'Aye, Sarge.'

Darkness fell. The sky flickered with star shells and flares; the barrage went on. They dozed at their posts, brewed tea and smoked; the enemy stayed back. But no ships arrived in harbour, nor any orders to withdraw. And at dawn the whole area came under monstrous attack.

As usual it began with a bombardment, but one more intense, more destructive, more terrifying than any previous, with dive-bombers, tanks, mortars and heavy artillery all working in concert to pound the 51st into submission. Nor was there any escape, for surrounded on three sides and with the sea on the fourth, the besieged men had no place to run and no place to hide. All they could do was find what shelter they could and pray for it to end.

Which it did at nine. Shelling of the town continued from surrounding cliffs, but in the perimeter the barrage lifted, leaving the stage set for the final push by the enemy. Now they advanced, from all sides, in great strength and with the presumption of success. Yet warily, for after weeks fighting Scotsmen, they knew to expect fierce resistance.

Theo and his rifle section lay in wait in their lane. An hour passed, nothing happened, elsewhere in the perimeter battle was heard commencing.

'Listen! Over on the right, them's 88s.'

'Camerons are on the right; 88s won't bother them.'

'They bother me.'

'Maybe they ain't coming.'

'Aye, cos they heard we got Captain Ted!'

'Where you from anyway, Ted?'

'Oh, um, it's called South Tyrol.'

'Lancashire, is it?'

'Quiet, you lot!' The corporal waved them to silence, binoculars raised.

The first they saw was four infantrymen creeping along the hedge towards them.

'Hold your fire, they ain't seen us yet.'

Then they did see them, and a short but furious exchange of shooting broke out, which ended with two Germans dead in the road and the other two sprinting for cover. One rifleman suffered a flesh wound to his arm. They bandaged him up, repositioned the section, and waited for the next attack. This came twenty minutes later, with a cluster of hand grenades thrown over the hedge on to their previous position, followed by half a platoon charging up the lane. This attack too was repelled, although for the expenditure of much ammunition. Plaudits followed.

'There they go!'

'Black Watch for ever!'

'Up yours, Fritz!'

'Say, Corp! Did you know that in the right hands, the Lee Enfield can shoot twenty rounds a minute?'

'No, Billy.' The corporal peered down the lane. 'Did *you* know we've not twenty rounds left between us?'

'Christ, I've only got two.'

'Me six.'

'What about you, Captain Ted?'

Theo checked his weapon. He'd fired it at last. It felt different from his old rifle, and the ring-sight wasn't as accurate. He doubted he'd hit anything. 'I've got three.'

Then everything happened very fast.

Billy was speaking: 'D'ye think they'll come again, Corp?'

'Aye.' The corporal raised himself, binoculars in hand. 'Something's moving—'

A shot rang out, a single shot fired from a distance.

The corporal jerked and fell.

'Sniper! That was a fucking sniper got the corp!'

'Christ, look, they're bringing up a machine gun.'

'What do we do?'

Theo froze. 'What do we do?'

'You're the fucking officer!'

'I. . . I don't know.'

The injured rifleman snatched up his weapon. 'Let's charge 'em. Come on, boys!' And four youths set off down the lane, arms waving, yelling wildly, as he had heard the Gordons yell. He didn't go with them. He stayed, and watched, as he knew he would. None made it more than halfway: a German machine gunner kneeling at his weapon poured bullets at them, cutting them to the ground as though with a scythe. Theo stared in despair, hearing their cries, watching as they stumbled and fell. Then the gun stopped and they were still. He felt their lives ebb, felt his own life shift and change, felt the rifle slip from his hands, turned and walked away.

He passed the day and night in a crevice in the cliffs overlooking the town. Battle raged all around: it registered only as noise; he excluded it from his consciousness. He watched sea birds soaring above the cliff, he listened to the hypnotic breaking of surf, sometimes he rested his head on his knees. It grew dark, it rained; he had no food or water, but felt no want. He wondered if ships would come, then knew he didn't care. Instead he thought of Bolzano, and his childhood in the mountains. How proud and self-assured he had been then. And how ignorant. He thought of his teacher Nikola risking her life for education. Of his mother and her long fight for liberty – *the actions of a courageous woman,* Thérèse had said. Of his grandfather Josef choosing prison over surrender, and of his beloved great-grandfather: *Take action and be brave, Theodor,* he'd said, coming down the mountain. *Take action and be brave.*

Awareness slowly returned, and with it a sense of acknowledgement. Like acceptance. He had been tried, and found wanting; now it was over. When he properly awoke, cold, stiff and empty, the sun was already high. And the town was silent. He left his crevice and walked along the cliff until rooftops appeared; then the whole town spread out below him, with its church spires, sandy beach-front and little harbour bobbing with fishing boats. Smoke drifted from bombed-out buildings, wrecked vehicles lay everywhere, and a white flag flew over the town hall. He approached closer, and a low murmur rose to him like plainsong, as men in uniform, thousands and thousands both grey and khaki together, packed the roads and streets surrounding the harbour. In their midst stood a single German tank.

He found steps in the cliff and descended to the town. Everywhere Highlanders stood, sat or lay, weaponless, smoking, talking in low voices or sleeping. Here and there Germans corralled them into lines. There was no shouting, no shooting, and little animosity, only the weary resignation of the vanquished and the bustling efficiency of their captors. Somewhere a regimental piper played a haunting lament. Slowly he made his way to the harbour, and to where the tank sat. A pennant fluttering from its antenna bore the Roman numeral VII. The men around it were not lower ranks, they were officers, aides, adjutants and senior NCOs of both armies. At their centre, standing apart and conferring quietly, stood two men he recognized: Major General Victor Fortune and Generalmajor Erwin Rommel. Fortune's face was fatigued and downcast. Rommel's demeanour was business-like. As Theo approached, both glanced up, but then continued as before.

'What happened?' he asked a nearby aide.

'What happened? Where the hell have you been? We surrendered an hour ago.'

'To him?' He nodded at Rommel.

'To him.'

He turned to go, then a German voice stopped him.

'Junge, halt!'

The narrowed eyes, the chiselled jaw, the cleft chin. Unchanged in the four years since they'd met at the Hitlerjugend games.

'Come here please.'

Theo approached. Others looked on curiously. The conquering general and the nobody private. Nearby, an aide snapped photographs of the harbour scene.

Rommel plucked gloves from his fingers. 'So we meet again,' he said in German.

'Ja, Herr General.'

'I see you made your decision.'

'Sir?'

'About who you are.' He looked around the crowded harbour. 'A Scottish man apparently. I'm not sure you chose wisely, for they are all going into captivity.'

'I'm not Scottish.'

'No. Then what? Italian, perhaps?'

'Italian? No, um, well, half—'

'Because Italy just entered the war. On Germany's side.'

'What?'

'Yesterday, evidently. Although I must doubt the wisdom of this liaison. Reasonable soldiers, terrible officers, in my experience, the Italians.' He took out a silver cigarette case; the aide with the camera leaped forward with a lighter. 'Anyway, this puts you in an even more difficult position, wouldn't you say?'

Theo could only shake his head.

'Because in war, it's vital each of us knows which side we're on. And I'm not sure you do.'

'No, sir.'

'No. But you don't belong here, that's for sure. Tell me, do you still run fast?'

'Run? I don't. . .'

'There's a little village, five kilometres up the coast, that way.' Rommel gestured. 'It's called Veules-les-Roses. Rather charming.'

'Herr General.'

'A British patrol boat is there, five hundred metres offshore, picking up anyone who manages to swim out to it. A few have, I gather.'

'I don't see. . .'

'I have just instructed two tanks to drive to the cliffs above the village and open fire upon this ship. I expect it will then leave, rather quickly, don't you?'

'Yes, Herr General.'

Rommel checked his watch. 'You have thirty minutes before they get there.'

CHAPTER 9

Cliff Poutney's tragic death on the Apeldoorn hospital train casts a pall over every man on board: sick and injured, doctors and orderlies, guards and escorts, friend and foe alike. After the appalling carnage of Arnhem, losing yet another man to a bullet, just for some madcap escape attempt, seems wretched and pointless, and I can only shake my head in agreement with the German major when he points to Cliff's blanket-covered body and asks, 'Was this worth it?'

Grateful to be needed elsewhere, I go forward with Bowyer to deal with Theo. He's in a carriage for the most seriously wounded near the front and it takes some time to reach it. When we do, I find he is indeed *in extremis*. Rocking gently to the motion of the train, he lies completely comatose on his stretcher, and upon examination exhibits a sky-high fever, low blood pressure, breathing fast and shallow, and pupils alarmingly fixed and dilated. Even as I examine him, his body convulses in a seizure and I have to break off until he goes limp again. Then I unwind the bandage on his head, there to find the ominous signs of swelling I've been dreading, and can only conclude, weighing up his symptoms, that he's suffering a lethal build-up of cranial pressure caused by bleeding. In simple terms, a brain haemorrhage.

'Don't look too good, do it, Doc,' Jack Bowyer mutters.

'Not terribly.'

'Double dose of morphia?'

Suddenly this is the last straw. 'NO, God damn it!' And in a fit of frustration I let fly at Jack. 'I am sick to bloody death of you and everyone telling me to end this boy's life, Bowyer. You may think it inconvenient he's still alive, but that's his choice. Our job is to help him until he decides otherwise. Is that understood!'

'Totally. So what you going to do?'

'I have no idea!' And with that I stalk outside to the carriage platform where of course, fumbling with cigarettes and overwrought emotions, I immediately regret the outburst. Before I know it tears are starting. Not just for Cliff, whose death upsets me greatly, nor for Theo or the thousands of other Market Garden victims we've had no time to grieve for, but mostly, I'm ashamed to say, for poor old Dan Garland and all that brought him to this pretty pass. I never wanted this, I tell myself, I'm ill prepared, ill suited and hopelessly out of my depth. An unwilling amateur thrown among hardened professionals, who despise me. An imposter in other words, and an affront to the beret on my head.

I smoke and sniff and wallow in self-pity for a while; then fortunately Jack arrives to put a stop to it.

'I'm going down back with the others,' he grunts moodily.

'No. Listen, wait.'

He pauses.

'Sergeant, look, I'm sorry. That was uncalled for.'

He shrugs. 'Only trying to save him unnecessary suffering.'

'Yes, and God knows, it may yet come to that.'

'We all feel it, you know. The dying and maiming and that, it's not just you.'

'No.'

'And Doc Poutney, he was a good man, a good doc: we all feel bad he's dead.'

'Yes. Yes, we do.' I fumble for cigarettes and offer him one; automatically he tucks it behind an ear. 'It's just, well, that boy in there, he's fought damn hard to keep going, and I'm not ready to give up on him yet.'

'Fine. So like I said, what are you going to do?'

Trepanning, unbelievably, is what I'm going to do. Cut a hole in his skull to relieve the pressure. Right there on the train. It's extreme, and fraught with risk, but the only thing left. I brief Jack, whose eyes widen incredulously, send him off with a shopping list; then I go in search of Colonel Alford and the German major. Ten minutes later Theo's being manhandled into the train's operating theatre which, though cramped, is clean, well lit and surprisingly well equipped. We strap him to the table and set up blood and plasma drips. Anaesthetic won't be needed as he's already unconscious, but considerable care is devoted to disinfecting him, me, and a growing array of instruments and equipment. Soon Jack appears bearing the final items: a workman's hand-drill, an assortment of drill bits, and a drinking straw.

'What's this?'

'Sorry, no rubber tubing anywhere. It's the best I can do.'

'Oh. Well, at least you found a drill.'

'It's a Heller – German, you know. Came from the guard's van.'

'Good quality then, hopefully. Put the drill bits in the Lysol and then scrub up.'

'Me?'

'Yes, you. There's only room for two of us.'

'But—'

'You'll only have to hold his head, you won't even have to watch.' Still he hesitates. 'Look, Sergeant. Jack. We may not always, you know, see eye to eye. But you're still my orderly, I hope, and as far as I'm concerned, the best there is. I really do want you here.'

Colonel Alford arrives with the German major. 'Are you quite sure about this, Garland?' he asks.

'No, sir, but if the pressure's not released he'll die within the hour.'

'Very well. What's the procedure?'

I take a breath. 'Open a flap of scalp two inches square. Retract the periosteum layer to expose the cranium. Drill a burr hole in the bone using the half-inch drill bit, but only down as far as the dura mater. If the haematoma's extradural we should see blood escaping straight away.'

'And if it's subdural?'

'Then I tent the dura up through the burr hole using this hook, and make a cross-shaped incision to allow the matter beneath to release. I then suture this, er, tube to the incised dura to act as a drain.'

'A drinking straw.'

'Yes, sir. It should serve until we get him to a proper hospital.'

194

I glance at the German major, standing purse-lipped at the entrance to the carriage. 'If that might be arranged, er, Herr Major?'

'Perhaps.' He nods. 'And this operation can be concluded within ten minutes?'

'Yes.'

'Because I cannot stop the train for one minute longer.'

'I understand.'

And that's what happens. He barks an order and a minute later the train grinds to a halt. Suddenly all is pin-drop silent and everyone's waiting, so I nod to Jack who cradles Theo's head to one side, and set to work with scalpel and drill bit. The drilling noise is disconcerting, as is the smell of hot bone. Alford and the German exchange glances, and Jack pales somewhat, but I press on until a half-inch-diameter crater is created, then fractionally further until I feel the drill penetrating. The haemorrhage does turn out to be subdural, and there's a flurry of panic when the drinking straw is inserted but gets blocked by a blood clot which I have to suck out by mouth. Then there's a gout of blood and cerebrospinal fluid, the pressure is released and all that remains is to secure the straw and close the flap of skin.

And pray like fury.

The following afternoon the hospital train finally reaches its destination. 'Fallingbostel' the station sign reads, in Lower Saxony, Colonel Alford says, some thirty miles north of Hanover. Deep in the heart of Germany, in other words, and a world away from any advancing allies or grand notions of liberation. And our mood reflects this sense of isolation as we medics assemble along the platform, the orderlies distribute themselves among the stretchers and the walking wounded shuffle painfully into line. Battledresses filthy and threadbare, accessories dangling on bits of string, possessions slung in tied bundles on sticks: frankly we look more like a procession of tinkers than a column of Paras. Nor, as we tramp listlessly along the town's cobbled streets, do the local inhabitants give us a second glance; apparently the whole area is a patchwork of prison and labour camps, so another gaggle of foreigners wandering by is of no interest to anyone. Soon we're ascending out of town and into a forest of brooding pines. Rain starts to fall; conversation, already desultory, fizzles to silence. Even our guards seem subdued. I return to the head of the column following a visit to Theo, who is being carried at the rear.

'How's he doing?' Alford asks.

'Still with us. Just.'

'Infection's your greatest threat now. You need to get him on penicillin, quickly.'

'There should be some at this new place. They say it's well equipped.'

Wrong. For as we are soon to discover, 'they', who were the Germans at Apeldoorn, either had no idea or were simply lying. Another twenty minutes and the trees suddenly clear to our right and a wire fence appears, twelve feet high topped with coiled barbed wire. Then a watchtower heaves into view complete with guards, machine guns and searchlight. We round a bend, the fence stretches on and then a cluster of wooden huts appears. It's ominous, reminding me of newspaper photos of a camp in Poland where fifty RAF officers were recently massacred following a break-out. This one looks identical: barbed wire, watchtowers, guns, huts, the lot. We reach imposing wooden gates manned by guards struggling with snarling dogs. On the gate is mounted a sign: 'Stammlager XIB'.

'This is no hospital,' Alford growls.

He's right. It's a prison camp and a grim one. After another hour being processed through the gate we're escorted to the 'lazaret', which is a separate compound serving as a makeshift infirmary. As we draw near a British army padre hurries out to greet us, his expression anxious.

'Hello, Colonel, hello, chaps, we've been expecting you.'

'And you are?' Alford asks.

'Pettifer, camp padre and interpreter. Got bagged in Italy. Been here a year.'

'What is this place? We were told to expect a hospital camp.'

'Ah, well, it's a POW camp, sir, obviously, of sorts. A *Korrekturlager* in fact.'

'A what?'

'Correction camp. It's one of Hitler's latest edicts, you see, sir. He regards you airborne chaps as, well, sort of terrorists. Gangsters, is the word he uses. He says once captured you should be treated as such.'

Some of us smile at the notion of being gangsters. But not Bill Alford. 'That's a bloody outrage! I demand to see the camp commandant immediately!'

'You will sir, I'm sure, and soon,' Pettifer soothes, 'but I must advise caution in your dealings with Major Möglich. He can be very, well, unpredictable.'

'Unpredictable be buggered! I insist on a meeting, Padre. Please see to it right away. Meanwhile, the rest of you, let's get everyone housed and settled.'

The lazaret huts are damp, cold and cramped. Four have been allocated to us, each divided into rooms barely ten feet by twelve, and crammed with double-tiered bunks such that twenty wounded men are expected to be housed in each room – that's over a hundred to a hut. There are no washing or toilet facilities in the rooms, just bedpans and one small latrine area per hut, few signs of medical equipment or supplies, nowhere to treat the wounded, make examinations or operate, and no fuel for heating. Alford's right, it is an outrage, completely contrary to accepted conventions of war. As we work, settling the patients as best we can, we learn that the camp houses mostly Russian and French POWs, some of whom have been in captivity for years. There're also Dutch, Belgian and a few non-airborne Brits. The Russians are in the majority but in a particularly parlous state; their compound is fenced off from the rest and their treatment much harsher. The French rule the roost therefore; most have been in captivity since the fall of France and as a result have the 'system' fine-tuned to their advantage. They run the bath house, cook house and stores, their people liaise and negotiate with the Germans, they've cornered the market in tradable goods such as Red Cross chocolate and cigarettes, they even control the coal stocks for the stoves. 'How's your French?' someone mutters at one point. 'Because we're going to need it.'

At around six the 'evening meal' is served: buckets of watery cabbage soup and unpeeled boiled potatoes. No meat, no protein, insufficient to nourish a mouse. To their infinite credit, our injured make few complaints but gratefully swallow whatever we pour in their mess tins, if they're fit enough to swallow; for those with facial or abdominal injuries who can't manage solids, we mash their food into a gruel. The gravely ill, like Theo, get nothing.

We officers eat after everyone else, retreating to one room we've set aside as an office-cum-surgery. Though we try to put a brave face on it, our mood is gloomy and our spirits low, the prospect of permanent incarceration here almost unbearable. As we drain our tins of cold cabbage water, a stamping of boots is heard outside, the door crashes open and a delegation marches in: four German soldiers and the aforementioned commandant, Möglich, plus Padre Pettifer following behind.

'Colonel Alford,' he begins, 'may I introduce the commandant, Major Möglich.'

'Yes you certainly may! Now listen to me, Möglich—'

But Möglich holds up a hand, as though stopping traffic. Short by comparison to his escort, bald and paunchy but smartly turned out, he surveys us with a disdainful downturn of the mouth and then addresses Pettifer in German.

'The, er, major expresses some surprise at your, ah, appearance, sir.'

'He what?'

'To be exact' – Pettifer winces – 'he says he's astonished to find that the so-called elite British red devil stormtroopers look so, er, *schlampig*.'

'Which means?'

'Slovenly.'

Alford visibly pales. He's going to hit him now, I think, he's going to grab this Nazi bastard by the throat and punch his lights out. Following which we'll all be taken out and shot, and good riddance. But he doesn't. Instead he straightens slowly up to his full six feet, brings himself to attention, fixes his eyes on the wall above Möglich's head and speaks, slowly and quietly to Pettifer.

'Translate this word for word, Padre. This facility is an utter disgrace. It directly contravenes Article One of the 1929 Geneva Convention, specifically relating to the treatment of wounded ex-combatants. I am currently preparing a report in which I list its failures, shortcomings and abuses, which are criminal in nature, and for which Major Möglich, as commandant, is personally responsible. And the moment Germany loses this war, which Major Möglich knows will be very soon, I will file this report with the relevant authorities, and personally ensure he is brought to trial for his criminal complicity.'

We hold our breaths as Pettifer translates. Now it's Möglich's turn to go pale, then puce with rage. But before he can respond, Alford hands him a sheet.

'This is a list of our requirements. If Major Möglich will attend to it, immediately and without prevarication, I will consider modifying my report in his favour.' And with that he turns and marches from the room.

The very next morning Lieutenant Colonel Bill Alford is removed from our midst and we never see him again. Only much later do I learn that he survives the war, leaves the army and returns to general practice at his home in Scotland. Whether he ever files his report I don't know, but his threat to Möglich works to an extent, because over the next days and weeks the situation improves marginally. Extra hut space is allocated, medical equipment and supplies begin appearing, more bedding, precious Red Cross parcels too, to boost rations and provide currency for barter. Control over bathing, cooking and heating is slowly wrested from the French; the sick and injured receive treatment. Stalag XIB will never be a proper hospital camp, and will remain harsh and depressing, but the Paras will survive it.

Mostly without me, as it turns out, because later that second day I'm summoned to Möglich's office. After a sleepless night on a straw palliasse this comes as a shock, and as I'm frog-marched across the compound between two guards I can only rack my brains in apprehension. Did he see me nodding during Alford's outburst? Is it because I smiled at the Hitler gangster reference? Is it to do with the escape attempt on the train? None of the above, as it turns out, unforgettably.

'Three of your seriously sick are to be transferred to hospital in Bergen,' Möglich says through an aide who translates. 'You will accompany them and return with medical supplies. Transportation leaves in one hour. Dismiss.'

I've no idea where this comes from, but assume it's to do with Alford's list of demands and silently thank him, especially as Theo's name is on the list. Why I'm chosen as escort is a mystery, but to get out of that camp, even for a few hours, is a blessed relief. I'm even issued with travel rations: a paper bag with black bread, sausage and an apple, and an hour later, hastily washed and shaved and with the stretchers safely loaded, and me up front between driver and guard, the grey army ambulance rumbles out through the gates. Bergen is only ten miles from Fallingbostel so we're soon trundling along the cobbled streets of a trim-looking town and pulling up beside the hospital, which appears modern. With my charges safely inside I'm shown to a lobby and told to wait. Minutes pass. I sink into a seat, a German newspaper catching my eye. Front-page photographs portray a lavish state funeral. The glorious hero Rommel has died, it turns out, following injuries received fighting in France.

'Herr Doctor Garland?' A female voice stirs me from reverie. 'I'm Doctor Inge Brandt. How do you do.' Clear English, forties, petite, prematurely grey, white-coated, not smiling but warily polite. Startled, I get to my feet.

'Oh, hello, how do you do?'

'Shall we visit your patients?'

I follow her upstairs and we spend the next hour going through the details: names and service numbers, nature and description of injuries, treatment received so far, treatment proposed, medication required and so on. Throughout it all she takes notes but also watches me closely, and questions me, such that I start to feel I'm the one being assessed, not the patients, which is unnerving. We get to Theo last. He remains pale and unresponsive but it's a relief to see him in a proper bed with clean sheets and fresh bandages. As we arrive a nurse is setting up a drip in his arm.

'Ah, the craniotomy my husband spoke of,' Inge says. 'We're starting him on penicillin as you can see, and we've replaced the drain you installed, for something more... conventional? I hope you approve.'

I am now deeply baffled. 'What? Oh yes, well, it was only a temporary. . . Excuse me, did you say your husband? And now I think of it, how do you know my name?'

'Yes.' Her eyes brighten fractionally. 'I apologize, Doctor. My husband is Gerhardt Brandt, Major Brandt that is, the officer in charge of your train?'

Who watched so closely while I operated on Theo. And expressed such heartfelt regret at Cliff Poutney's death. The penny drops. 'He arranged this?'

'He said he would try to help.'

'But how? I mean, by what authority?'

'That is not your concern.'

Not Alford then, or even Möglich, but an unknown German major showing humanity. Or someone even higher. Inge returns to Theo, we continue discussing his case, she continues to watch me closely, and continues to ask odd questions.

'Would I be correct in thinking you are a man of your word, Doctor Garland?'

'I'd like to think so. Why?'

'No reason. Do you agree this patient's best interests would not be served by sending him back to your camp?'

'Completely. It would kill him in days.'

'I agree. What is your view of the progress of the war?'

'You're going to lose it! In the next six months probably. Why, what's your view?'

'I don't have one. Not on its progress. Only its effects.'

'Which are?'

'Never mind.' She looks at the window, pausing. Outside, late-autumn clouds punctuate the piercing blue. 'We're on a journey, the German people. Like a train. We thought we knew the destination, but we don't. Now it is unknown. But malevolent. Like that story by Conrad.'

'*The Heart of Darkness.*'

'Yes.' She turns back to Theo. 'You're on it now, you two. Germany's train journey. As, how do you say, spectators?'

'Reluctant ones, I assure you!' I lower my voice. 'Why do not the German people simply remove the driver?'

But she just stiffens, and starts tugging Theo's sheets straight, and changes the subject again. 'I understand you are lacking medical supplies.'

'Yes, dreadfully. The camp commandant seems less than helpful.'

'I will give you what we can spare. And try to arrange more.'

'That's very generous.'

'Although it is not easy – we are very short ourselves.' She gestures to the window. 'Out there. This whole area around Bergen, you know, has many tens of thousands of labourers, from all different parts of the Reich. They work in farms and factories for the war effort. And live in large camps.'

'Like the *Stammlager* I've just come from?'

'That is a small military prison, for soldiers, who are not forced to work. I'm talking about civilians, men and women. In huge forced-labour camps.'

'I don't know of those.'

Her eyes lock on mine. 'Would you like to see one?'

Much later I realize she and her husband must have discussed this, and somehow concluded I could be trusted not to betray them. Which is a huge leap of faith by any standards. Having procured my word not to escape, Inge leads me back down to the lobby, explaining that as medical director she has responsibility for several outlying clinics she is required to visit, and therefore has use of a car. At reception she signs forms and tells them she is escorting the British doctor to one of these clinics, in order that he can witness Germany's excellent healthcare system for himself. Then we walk unchallenged out into the sunshine. Just like that. Dazzled, I inhale deeply, smelling autumn leaves and rain-washed streets, revelling in the fresh air and freedom. No stench of latrines or putrefaction, no wires, no guards or guns, no soldiers, just a quiet road in a quiet town, mothers pushing prams, children playing, pensioners sitting on a bench. No war anywhere. It's blissfully refreshing.

'Remember your promise,' Inge says, sensing my thoughts.

'Of course.' I nod and open the car door.

She puts her hand to the key, but then pauses. 'What you are about to see is not known of outside Germany, do you understand?'

'Yes I do.'

'But it needs to be.'

Barely five minutes out of town we come to the place, past a village called Belsen. As we drive, the usual thick pine woodland suddenly gives way to a vast wired plain stretching away for miles, and filled with tents and huts and ramshackle shelters as far as the eye can see. A kind of dusty smog hangs over the place. Smoke rises from dozens of fires; the ground is littered with people, possessions and rubbish. Shanty town, is my first reaction, like a slum in India or somewhere, huge, overcrowded, filthy, seen in a picture in a magazine. We drive on along the fence, Inge watchful now, repeatedly craning her neck and checking the rear-view mirror; suddenly she brakes and turns down a dirt track beside the fence.

'This is part of the women's section. I make rendezvous here when I can. But we can only stop for a minute.'

A hundred yards on gaggles of people can be seen gathering near the fence. Drawing nearer I see they are women; as we approach they surge like a tide towards the wire. The car stops. Inge immediately jumps out and goes to the fence where perhaps a hundred women are hurrying towards her. All are grossly emaciated, barely skin and bones encased in rags, tattered home clothes or pyjamas made from a coarse striped sackcloth. Many wear crudely fashioned scarves and coats, few have serviceable shoes, most are barefoot. As I approach they see me and recoil, as though frightened by my uniform. '*Englischer Doktor*,' Inge soothes, and starts handing small packages through the wire. 'Medicines,' she explains. 'It's not much – everything is carefully inventoried, but we manage some analgesics, anti-bacterials and so on. Malnutrition is the worst problem, that and contagious disease.'

I draw near, dumbfounded. A terrible smell hangs over the place, like death and decay. A hand reaches to me through the strands, more a claw, the skin scabbed, parchment thin, the nails black and broken. I take it, squeeze gently, but it is cold and unresponsive; immediately it withdraws only to be replaced by others. I look at the faces, the expressions, not afraid now, only desperate and appealing, the eyes and teeth too big for the sunken cheeks, the hair matted and lifeless. I remember my ration pack and, pulling it out, pass it through. It vanishes in a second. I search my pockets: cigarettes, matches, a cotton handkerchief, all go through; still the hands beseech for more.

'We must go. Guards patrol regularly.'

I glance up, searching over the heads, but the size, the scale of the place are beyond comprehension. A city of suffering. 'How many are there?'

'In the whole camp? Nobody knows. Thirty thousand? Forty? Some estimates are as high as seventy.'

'Who are they?'

'Poles, Slavs, Hungarian, Jews, Gypsies, Russians. The Nazis house them here, feed them on nothing, work them until they die and then replace them with more. The women work in satellite camps, in gunpowder and armaments factories until they are too sick to carry on. Deaths from starvation and disease run at hundreds every day. Last year there was a typhoid epidemic which killed ten thousand. No outside medical help is allowed. Come, we must leave now.'

We return to the car. She starts up, manoeuvres it round and speeds off. I glance back: the women are still at the fence.

'I don't know what to say.'

'Don't say anything. Not now. The repercussions for us both would be fatal. You are a witness, that is all. A witness, remember that.'

We drive back along the road into the forest until the camp is swallowed behind us. As if it never existed. Then she pulls up and switches off. 'We can't go back yet. It would look suspicious.' I check my watch: barely fifteen minutes since we left the hospital. A clean, orderly environment in a tidy little town populated by normal German people. She opens the glove box and produces a crumpled pack. There's only one cigarette left. I light it for her – her fingers are trembling. Mine aren't. They're too numb to take it in.

'Don't they know?'

She blows smoke. 'What?'

'The people, the townspeople of Bergen. Five minutes from their door is a vast camp of people suffering terrible cruelty, with a population the size of a small city. Don't they know?'

'They know but they don't say.'

Fallingbostel. I recall the inhabitants' indifference, glancing away as we marched past. 'Why not, for God's sake?'

'It's called oppression, Doctor!' Her eyes flash angrily. 'The German people are oppressed, don't you know that by now? We exist in a climate of fear and reprisal. Disobey a rule, complain about something, express dissent, and you simply disappear!'

'But—'

'And I didn't bring you here only to receive a lecture!'

'No. No, you're right. I'm sorry.'

She draws heavily on the cigarette and then offers it to me. The faintest hint of lipstick stains the paper; the tobacco tastes coarse and bitter. Suddenly we hear the rumble of approaching motors. She stiffens and then presses against me in a fake embrace. We freeze. I sense the slightness of her body and a hint of scent. A column of army vehicles goes by in the direction of the camp. At its rear is an open staff car with officers in the back. One glances at us as he passes; seconds later the column is gone. Inge slumps back into her seat. Only now do I realize the risk she is taking.

'You are putting yourself in terrible danger.'

'There's more.' She lowers her head to the wheel. 'There's worse.'

'Worse? What could be worse?'

'East. Far to the east, in Poland. Other camps. Gerhardt told me, he knows of them. They are secret, and guarded by the SS.'

'What kind of camps?'

'Camps for killing people. By the tens of thousand.'

CHAPTER 10

Ironically it was in Portsmouth, from where he had left England so eagerly twelve weeks earlier, that the Royal Navy now deposited Theo, together with thirty other 51st Highland Division survivors. With only a salt-stained battledress and borrowed boots to his name, he clumped down the gang-plank to the dockside, where his details were recorded, he was issued with two pounds in cash and a travel warrant for the railway, and instructed to report to his regiment within forty-eight hours. But he didn't report, he stayed in Portsmouth, spending that night in the same bus shelter as in March, then several days wandering the city's streets. He ate at soup kitchens and a seamen's mission, slept on park benches or bus shelters, stayed out of doors and spoke to no one, walking miles each day or simply sitting on the beach and staring out to sea. Eventually his two pounds were gone, his borrowed boots split and his vagabond existence ended when a policeman advised him to 'cut along home' before the MPs picked him up.

Walking up the road to the Kingston boarding house that evening felt like re-entering a forgotten dream. He stood at the threshold, beset with memories; then he knocked, the door opened, and Eleni Popodopolous fell on him like the prodigal son.

'My Lor', my heaven!' she screeched, sweeping him into a bosomy clinch. 'Thank God you still alive! Where you been, you bad boy, we been so worry!'

'Hello, Eleni. I've been in France.'

'France! Blimey and look the state of you! Oh, your poor mother, so terrible, so terrible, my God! Winterbottom, look! Look, Theodoros here, he here!'

'So he is.' A uniformed figure appeared. 'And not a moment too soon.'

'Soon? Why? What's happened?'

'My God, he know nothing!' Eleni dissolved into sobbing. 'He know nothing!'

'Know what? Eleni, where's Mother?'

'She gone!'

'What?'

'She carted off bloody prison! Two days ago!'

She pulled him through to the parlour where between cups of tea and avalanches of questions, he learned that plain-clothes policemen had arrived unannounced at the door two days earlier and arrested Carla.

'But why? What did she do?'

'She didn't do nothing, my dear! She Italian!'

'What?'

'They rounding you all up like horses!'

'Rounding up where?'

'At the races!'

'What?'

'It true, I swear. Kempton, the horse-races place, they got a prison there!'

He shook his head, the dream illusion rapidly turning to nightmare. He looked at Winterbottom, watching from an armchair. 'Please, what is this?'

Winterbottom sat forward. 'It's called the Emergency Powers Defence Act, Theo. Following Italy's entry into the war, all Italian nationals living in Britain have been categorized according to perceived threat, "A" being high risk, "B" being medium, "C" being low. And those unfortunately finding themselves in the first two categories are subject to immediate arrest and, er, internment. Your mother, it turns out, included.'

'But she hates Fascism! She's spent her whole life opposing it!'

Winterbottom shrugged. 'It seems she cropped up on some Home Office list as "politically active" and that was enough for the authorities to haul her in.'

'She's active trying to get independence *from* Italy!' Theo was shocked. And bewildered. A week ago he had been fighting for his life in Normandy. Then days more mindlessly tramping the streets of Portsmouth. Now this. It was too much, beyond assimilating. 'I, um, I must find her, go to her, I—'

'No, Teo!' Eleni grabbed his hand. 'Not now, my dear. Winterbottom already trying on telephone – there's nothing no one can do more tonight. Stay here. I feed you something, you scrawny to hell and frankly my dear pong high heaven. Get bath, food, sleep an' tomorrow we find your mother.'

Winterbottom nodded. 'And, ah, you should also report to barracks. And explain to the CO what you've been up to. Since absenting yourself from OCTU.'

He protested feebly but, exhausted suddenly, gave in to

Eleni's nagging and an hour later, bathed and fed, plodded up the stairs to his old attic bedroom, slumped on to his bed and fell into unconscious slumber. He was woken twelve hours later by a dream. Erwin Rommel was standing on a beach, hands on hips, while Theo swam desperately out to sea. 'Make your decision!' Rommel kept shouting after him in German. But he knew of no decision to make. He kept swimming, increasingly desperate, his arms and legs numb with cold and heavy like lead, but he could find no ship, nor any hope of salvation. *'Treffen Sie Ihre Entscheidung!'* Rommel kept shouting. 'Make your decision!'

Eleni had cleaned his uniform in the night; he dressed and descended to the dining room where he found one other lodger, a paper salesman who introduced himself as Brown.

'Someone's popular,' Brown said, nodding at Theo's plate which Eleni had piled high with bread and jam. After breakfast he packed a bag of Carla's clothing while Eleni collected food for her; then, once she had donned her hat and coat, they set out for the bus together. Kempton Park racecourse was not far from Kingston and they arrived there in an hour. Closed since the outbreak of war, they found it encircled with wooden fencing and patrolled by a policeman who directed them to an entrance.

'We come see prisoner,' Eleni announced. 'She arrested by mistake.'

'No prisoners here, only internees. Name?'

'Madam Eleni Popodopolous. And this prisoner's son Captain Theodoros Trickey of famous East Surrey *reggimento*.'

'I, um, I'm not a cap—'

214

The receptionist rolled his eyes. 'The internee's name, not yours!'

'Oh, she Signora Carmelina Ladurner-Trickey an' very important lady so you mind your manners, young man!'

Following more confusion and delay they were shown to a waiting room, once an office, with a window overlooking the racecourse. Through it they could see a wired enclosure on the grass near the grandstand. Within it stood a cluster of tents and huts.

'What this bloody madness?' Eleni muttered. A few minutes later the door opened and Carla hurried in.

Theo hadn't seen her in six months, not since he'd left Kingston for OCTU the previous December. Cries of relief and tearful embraces followed; then she stood him back for inspection.

'You're taller,' she scolded in Italian, 'and thinner. You look like your father.'

'You're thinner too, Mama. Don't they feed you?'

'Pasta! They think that's all Italians eat.'

'When are they letting you out?'

She didn't know – nobody did, so little was explained. Soon she was tearful again.

'Mama, don't upset yourself.'

'I'm not upset! I'm angry.'

'What do the officials say?'

Her eyes flickered. 'They say I could be "A" Class.'

The Kempton camp, they learned, was just one of many across the country, set up as temporary transit facilities. And the facilities – eating, washing, sleeping – were basic and communal, while the regime was tedious and humiliating. Currently the camp housed four hundred Italian men and women aged between seventeen and seventy. Most, Carla explained, had been British residents for years, many for all their lives. Very few, in her view, were Fascists, or in any way a threat to the State. The rumour was that those with 'C' classifications would be sent home, while those classified 'B' were to go to permanent camps around the UK. 'God knows where. Scotland, Wales, some place called Orkney, people say. Hundreds of miles away.'

'What about the others? The "A" Class people?'

Carla's face fell. 'Deported. To special internment prisons, in Canada.'

Before they knew it their time was up and they were told to leave. Theo assured Carla he would do everything possible; Eleni promised to bring her more food and belongings. Carla embraced them both. 'Maybe Brown knows something,' she murmured to Theo, before being led away.

From Kempton he went back to Kingston and the King's Road headquarters of the East Surrey Regiment, where his reception was less fulsome. 'Where the fuck have you sprung from?' the guard on the gate said. Inside, the barracks were quiet: 1st Battalion on leave following Dunkirk, 2nd Battalion en route to Malaya, and the Territorials, including Theo's 2/6th, not yet regrouped following the chaos of France. He asked for Henry Winterbottom but was told he was unavailable; instead, after close questioning by an intelligence officer, and an angry grilling from a quartermaster sergeant – 'Where's your bloody rifle!' – he was brought before the colonel of the whole regiment.

Standing to attention on the polished parquet, some minutes passed in silence while the colonel read from a dossier.

'Sit,' he finally said, studying Theo over his spectacles. 'So, young man, and what do *you* propose we do with you?'

'I, um, don't know, sir.'

'No, and neither do I. Because it seems that nothing about you is quite as it appears, and that's rather troubling.'

'Sir?'

'Yes, damn it! You go absent without leave, turn up in France, vanish for weeks, then wander in here without a by-your-leave. Don't you find that troubling?'

'Possibly, sir, but I can—'

'And that's just the start of it! Your nationality, for example. It says British on your signing-on form. But that's not true, is it?'

'I am half-British, sir.'

'And half-Italian.'

'South Tyrolean.'

'Whatever that means.'

'I'm English on my father's side.'

'Ah yes, your father. That's another thing.'

'He was English, sir. And an officer of this regiment, in the last war.'

'No, he wasn't. We've checked, and there is no record of a Lieutenant Victor Trickey ever having been an officer here.'

'But—'

'Which all puts me in a very difficult situation, *Acting* Officer Cadet Trickey. Because Italy, as you know, has declared war on Britain, and we can't have Italians serving in the British army. Even Tyrolean ones.'

'But, sir. . .'

'In fact some might say you should be in an internment camp. Like your mother.'

Henry Winterbottom, he knew then, was at the root of all this. His mother's trusted friend, confidant and *amante*, he'd probably written the dossier himself and passed it to the colonel. Why? Because the Trickeys and their problems had grown too burdensome, and too complicated, to manage any more, especially since Italy's entry into the war. Or perhaps it was pique; perhaps Carla had simply spurned Henry for another – Mr Brown the new lodger, for instance. Or perhaps she was of no interest to him now she was interned. It didn't really matter, Theo realized, his gaze wandering to the window, their minds were made up; nothing he said would change anything. What did matter was that no Lieutenant Victor Trickey ever served with the East Surreys. That mattered, and it hurt. And even if deep down he'd sometimes harboured secret doubts of his own, having it expressed so plainly like that was painful. And heartless of the colonel. Who was still talking. Something about the seriousness of going absent from his OCTU. No mention of his eagerness to serve his country, or his excellent record at the bridge in Caen, or his messenger work with the 51st. But then no one knew about those things, he realized; those who did were all dead or captured, even General Fortune. The colonel droned on and he half listened, his mind suddenly on four young Scotsmen outside Saint-Valery. *You're the fucking officer!* they'd shouted, before charging to their deaths. And then his encounter with Rommel. *Make your decision!* Or was that in a dream? It was so hard to tell any more. A pigeon landed on the colonel's ledge, fluffing itself up against the glass. Beside the window was a noticeboard displaying standing orders, lists of names and units, and a couple of leaflets. *Ready for Action?* read one leaflet, and showed a crouching soldier holding a machine gun. *Volunteers required immediately for hazardous duties. All ranks eligible.*

He was to be sacked from the army, he learned at last, to little surprise. Cast aside because he was an embarrassment and a puzzle. The colonel assured him it would happen without fuss, his record showing he was discharged for 'administrative' reasons only. He was to leave the premises now and return tomorrow to hand in his uniform, pay book, identity discs and any other kit he still possessed. By noon he would be a civilian again. He was sorry, the colonel said, but it was best for all parties.

By which he meant himself and Winterbottom. Theo rose to go, then stopped.

'Um, one thing, sir.'

'Yes?'

'My unit. B Company, the 2/6th. What happened to it?'

'Still missing, most of them.' The colonel shuffled papers. 'So you can count yourself lucky.'

Back at the boarding house he paced aimlessly from room to room, trying to process all that had happened. His mother, Kempton Park, the huts and tents, deportation to Canada, then the barracks, *Where's your bloody rifle*, and the colonel, disowning his father, then sacking him, and losing everything he'd ever dreamed of. It was too much, more than he could bear, he couldn't absorb it, couldn't think. He remembered he had letters, a small bundle Eleni had left for him on the mantelpiece, and with nothing else to do he sat down in the parlour to read. Apart from the usual circulars, coupons and catalogues, and a bill from Aldershot OCTU for unpaid accommodation, there were just two items of interest, a letter from an address in Rome, and a picture postcard from Normandy dated three weeks earlier:

> *'Dear Theo, excusing my Anglish, the Boche will come very soon, these are bad days very sad, Madame Gondrée tell me send best wishes and bonne chance, think on me, sincèrement, Jeanette Bolpert x.'*

The picture was of the bridge over the canal, with Café Gondrée in the background. He fingered the card, recalling the scene. Guard duty in the snow, soup and stolen kisses with Jeanette, warm conversation and hot chocolate at the Gondrées'. Only three months ago, yet already another lifetime. German soldiers now guarded his bridge, he reflected, and German officers drank at the café. If Thérèse let them.

The Italian letter was from his uncle Rodolfo Zambon, his grandmother Eleanora's brother, who lived in Rome. Eleanora was in failing health, he said, with 'nerves', so he and his wife wanted to persuade her to leave Bolzano and live with them. He had written to Carla about this but she seemed reluctant, so could Theo perhaps intervene? Next, their efforts to secure his grandfather Josef's release from prison were ongoing, including pressure from outside agencies, but the old man was stubborn and refused to agree the 'terms', which Theo knew meant renouncing his South Tyrolean identity and heritage – something Josef would never do. In the interim Rodolfo hoped to get Josef moved to a prison for political offenders nearer Rome. Theo's cousin Renata, meanwhile, she of the ice cream and beautiful curls, was now eighteen, Rodolfo reported, and a noted beauty, which was causing him no end of headaches. She often spoke of her dashing cousin Theodor, he said, concluding somewhat facetiously that any time Theo found himself in Italy, he must be sure to look them up.

He folded the letter, recalling the family disputes, the riots and demonstrations in the street, the arrests and persecutions that were so much a feature of his childhood. And also remembering Rodolfo, with his oiled hair and fancy car, driving him and Renata for sweet treats and political indoctrination at the ice-cream parlour. Strong government and a disciplined proletariat, he said, were what a progressive Europe needed. Tyranny and oppression, in other words, with dissent ruthlessly crushed. As in Poland, and Belgium, and France, and even England it seemed, randomly throwing its foreign settlers in prison. What had the colonel said? *Some might say you should be in an internment camp. Like your mother.*

'Good news?' a kindly voice enquired. Mr Brown, the new lodger, had appeared in the parlour.

'Oh, um, well – no, not terribly. My family, abroad, it's complicated.'

'I'm so sorry. Anything I can do?'

221

'Thank you.' He hesitated. 'As I say, it's complicated.'

'When is it not with families! I say, are those foreign stamps?' Brown stooped beside him. About thirty, with a disarming smile and swept-back hair, he had a military bearing, despite civilian attire. 'Italy and France – heavens, may I take a look? My nephew's mad about stamps!'

'Oh, well, yes, of course.' Theo handed them over, watching as Brown swiftly scanned them before passing them back.

'Ah, pity, he has these ones. Never mind, thanks anyway.'

'Tea, my dears?' Eleni entered bearing a tray.

'Ah, Mrs Popodopoulos, how very kind you are. A veritable Hellenic treasure.'

'Get away you flattering!'

'Not at all. Oh and I wonder, when you have a moment, could you prepare my bill? I have to leave in the morning.'

'Blimey, so soon? You only jus' arrive three day ago!'

'Yes I know, but the company wants me up north for a bit. Blasted nuisance, but what can one do?'

And later that night Brown knocked on Theo's door.

'Hello, old chap, sorry to disturb and that. Wondered if I could have a word?'

Theo rubbed his eyes. 'What about?'

'Well, you seemed a bit down in the dumps earlier.'

'Um, yes, family, and other things. . .'

'I heard about your mother. You have my sympathies.'

'Thank you.'

'Listen.' Brown produced a business card. *International Research Bureau*, it said, with an address in central London. 'I sense you could do with advice: you know, careers guidance and so on. Go and see these people, ask for Captain Grant, tell him I sent you. They'll help.'

'Careers? Well, I suppose—'

'Good man!' Brown smiled. 'Go tomorrow, while the iron's hot, what?' With that he slipped the card into Theo's pyjama pocket, bade him goodnight and closed the door.

In the morning he was gone. Theo came downstairs with a list of questions, but Eleni said Brown had departed before dawn. Munching breakfast Theo studied the business card, wondering about Carla's mention of Brown, and what line of work International Research Bureau might be in. Baker Street the address said, in the West End, and at least two hours from Kingston, and another two hours back. He checked the clock: he was supposed to return his uniform and kit to barracks. And sign off from the army for ever. Before noon. He'd never make it.

The building was unlike any business premises he'd ever seen. A featureless red-brick house like many others in Baker Street, its exterior gave no hint as to its purpose or trade. He pressed a buzzer, was admitted, gave his name to a uniformed doorman and within minutes was clanking upstairs in a rickety lift. Exiting on the fourth floor a female receptionist ushered him to a dingy, cluttered office, occupied by a chain-smoking officer wearing a captain's uniform. The uniform was rumpled and ash-stained, it displayed no regimental insignia, the tie was loose, its owner looked dishevelled and unshaven.

'I'm Grant,' he said, hefting files from a chair. 'Do please sit. Sorry about the mess – we're at sixes and sevens rather. I take it you've seen this?' He handed Theo a leaflet. The same

Ready for Action leaflet he'd seen on the colonel's noticeboard yesterday.

'Well, I haven't actually read it.'

'No matter.' Grant returned to his desk, which was festooned with files and papers. Outside a typewriter clattered; somewhere a telephone rang. 'There, that's better. Now then, Theodor, isn't it? Or do you prefer Teddy? Or is it Andreas, which is your first name, I believe?'

'I. . . Theo's fine, sir.'

'Theo it is. So, Theo, tell me a little about yourself. Your family, upbringing, all that flummery. And especially about your recent adventures in France, of course.'

So Theo told him, at length, and all the while Grant watched him, and massaged his fingers, and chain-smoked, and said little except to prompt him about some detail or event, until eventually Theo faltered to silence.

'And, um, that's all, sir, really.'

'Extraordinary. And Rommel actually spoke to you. At Saint-Valery?'

'Yes, sir. He said it was vital each of us knows which side we're on.'

'How interesting.' Grant ground his cigarette into an ashtray and then immediately lit another. 'And how true. Now, tell me, Theo, do you know what a *Kommando* is?'

'No, sir.'

'It's a Boer expression in origin. It's a small unit of men, formed with a specific job in mind, operating autonomously, and often disbanded when the job's done. Do you follow me?'

'Kind of, sir.' *Hazardous duties,* the leaflet said, beneath the picture of the soldier with machine gun. *Volunteers required immediately for hazardous duties. All ranks eligible.*

'Good. Because we, the army that is, have been tasked with forming some of these units, bloody quick, to send into action against Jerry. Harrying tactics, a bit of sabotage, demolition, that sort of thing.'

'Oh.' Theo wondered what this had to do with International Research Bureau.

'Yes, the PM's very fired up about it.' Grant pointed at the leaflet. 'So every CO of every unit in the country has been sent that, with orders to get chaps to sign up.'

'I see.'

'But it's all taking too long.'

'Ah.'

More followed, dizzyingly fast. The very first of these new units, Grant said, called 3 Commando for some reason, was forming right that minute, and was already earmarked for a possible mission. But it was under-strength, badly in need of fit young men with good references and active experience to make up the numbers.

'You're an athletic outdoors type, I gather. Cross-country, mountaineering, all that malarkey.'

'I have always enjoyed being outside, sir.'

'Crack shot too. I gather you won an award at some Alpine games somewhere.'

'Did I?' Then with a jolt he remembered. The Bavarian Hitlerjugend competition of 1936. Rommel had given the medal. But how. . .

'That is true, sir, although it was a few years—'

'And you have excellent languages, no?'

'I, well, yes, I speak Italian and German pretty fluently, also some French.'

'Not forgetting English.' Grant smiled. 'Some pretty heroic swimming too, of course.'

Theo could barely believe his ears – and barely keep up. Grant went on without pause, smoking and talking, nine to the dozen, something about 3 Commando forming in Dartmouth because of sea training he couldn't talk about. Theo would be needed to travel there right away to join them. 'Assuming you're willing, naturally.'

'Well, I, yes, of course but. . .'

Then he stopped. Madness. This was all utter madness. Grant seemed to know everything, yet was missing so much that was important. Had he not listened? Did he not realize he'd been sacked from the army? That he was a threat to the State? That he was due to sign off at noon, a deadline he'd now miss, which was a military offence? That his mother was in custody for her politics, and his grandfather, and he probably too, any time? Nor could he just up sticks and head for Dartmouth with no notice. Carla needed him, and Eleni, and his grandparents. And anyway he didn't know what his plans were, he needed time to recover, gather his wits, decide what to do.

Which was all just prevarication, because the real reason he couldn't do this was that he wasn't worthy. Wasn't brave enough. He'd sensed it in training, and had it proved to him in France, repeatedly. Hiding behind walls, cowering in ditches, watching in terror as four men charged to their deaths. He'd even run away at Saint-Valery, throwing aside his weapon and fleeing along the beach for the last boat to safety. When tested, he now knew for certain, he came up wanting, and that was the nub of it.

Grant had stopped talking and was studying him, massaging his fingers and blowing thick plumes of smoke at the ceiling.

'It's voluntary, you know,' he murmured intuitively. 'That's the whole point. You're volunteers, from all walks and backgrounds. Nobody expects you to know anything, or be anything, because it's all new. You'll be supported and helped and trained, but if in the end you decide it's not for you, then you can simply walk away. No questions asked, no blot on your record.'

'Sir. Please don't think I'm not grateful—'

'It's a lot to take in, I agree.'

'My mother, you see. . .'

'We know. And will do what we can to help.'

'You will?'

'Yes.'

'But. . .'

'And we also know how well you did in France. We have that from various sources. You have friends, you see, Theo, referees if you like, people of standing, and reliability, willing to vouch for you.'

'I do?'

'Yes, but as I said, I can't tell you more. But rest assured your efforts have not gone unappreciated. And you have certain valuable skills too.'

Theo's eyes returned to the leaflet. Who on earth could have spoken for him? And where? Caen? Guarding the bridge was hardly 'hazardous duty', and anyway his sergeant called him a useless shite. But had Thérèse Gondrée not hinted at *trusted friends* in London? And what about that sergeant at General Fortune's HQ? MacLean, his name was. Or Major Wilson at the forward command post, who'd given him the job as runner? Or the Gordon Highlander lieutenant at Saint-Léger, or even General Fortune himself: *What precisely is it that you think you saw?* he'd said.

'This war's going to change, you see, Theo,' Grant was saying, 'very quickly now. The Germans may invade us, they may not – there's not much we can do about it: our army's in tatters, most of our equipment lying in ditches in France. But what we can do, what we *must* do, is re-equip, and rearm, and retrain, as fast as possible – but it will take months, years probably, to get back to full strength. So in the meantime we must find other ways to strike at them, in some limited way, until we're ready. And for that we're going to need strong, motivated young people with special qualities and skills. Like you.'

Just twelve days later he found himself clinging in terror to a scrambling net slung over the side of a Royal Navy destroyer, trying to jump on to the wildly pitching deck of an RAF launch far below. The night was tar black, the English Channel rough, and every time the destroyer rolled, the net swung away from the hull, only to crash painfully back, bruising his knees and skinning his knuckles. Much more of this pounding and he knew he would fall to the sea and drown. He must jump, and quickly. He looked up, only to see anxious sailors peering back down at him, while to either side others of his unit inched their way down the net like insects on a web. He'd known them barely a week; now they were going to war together. Timing his moment as best he could, he waited for the launch to surge upwards, let go and jumped.

'Christ's sake, Trick, you landed on my bloody foot!'

'Sorry, I couldn't see you.'

'Well, I'm right here, you Irish oaf.'

Then the motors roared and the launch was pulling away in a flurry of white foam, hurrying to join two more launches circling nearby. A wave struck it with a thud and clouds of freezing sea cascaded over the twelve men huddled on its deck. Within minutes, as the three launches sped away, everyone was soaked to the bone.

An hour later they were still in the launch, which was now alone on an empty ocean, and apparently steaming in circles. 'Bugger this for a lark.' Theo's companion ducked as another wave struck. His face gleamed wet and was curiously striped, sickly white streaked black with boot polish. 'What are we still doing out here anyway? We should have landed ages ago.'

'Maybe we're lost.' Theo peered into the darkness. 'No, look, Percy! There's rocks over there, rocks – see!'

'I can't see nothing and for God's sake don't call me Percy! I told you, it's Burns or Burnsy or they'll think I'm a ponce!'

'Sorry, Burnsy, I forgot. But look, we're definitely heading for that beach!'

'Thank Christ, I'm about to puke.'

Minutes later the launch suddenly shuddered to a halt thirty yards short of a rocky cove. 'We're aground!' the coxswain shouted. 'You'll have to jump for it.'

The twelve jumped, only to find themselves chest deep in freezing sea.

'Jesus!'

'Christ, it's cold!

'Nobody said nothing about swimming!'

'Form a chain!' their officer ordered. 'Form a chain and get the equipment ashore. Quick as you can – we're way behind schedule.'

Struggling through the breaking surf they unloaded the launch, which then backed away into the darkness, leaving them gasping on the beach amid a soggy pile of weapons and equipment. As they began sorting through and kitting up, their officer, a young lieutenant named Copeland, consulted his map.

'Right,' he pronounced hesitantly, 'well, chaps, welcome to Guernsey. I think. Now, I can't be sure, because the coxswain on the launch wasn't either, but I believe we're here' – he gestured at the map – 'with the rest of B Force deployed along the coast, here and here. As you know, our job is to head inland, link up with them, then make for the airfield where the Jerry garrison's based. Once there we disrupt their infrastructure as briefed, causing a diversion so A and C Forces can raid the garrison, before withdrawing back here at oh three hundred hours for extraction aboard the launch.' He checked his watch. 'Unfortunately, because of the delay getting us here, we have less than two hours to complete the whole mission. So let's get cracking.'

They made ready, attaching webbing, filling ammunition pouches, strapping on grenades and bayonets, shouldering rifles. Theo rubbed more boot blacking on his face and adjusted his helmet, which was camouflaged with sackcloth, then he and Burnsy hoisted a large drum of wire on to a pole between them.

'Christ, Trick, it weighs a ton!' Burnsy gasped. 'And what's it for anyway?'

'Who knows. Disrupting the infrastructure, do you think?'

'Whatever the hell that means.'

The group set off, climbing slowly from the beach up a steep cliff path on to scrubby heathland. There they paused while Copeland, revolver drawn, checked for sentries. Finding none they pressed on. The sky was moonlit but overcast, so there were few stars to guide them, no recognizable features on the ground or villages or roads, and no radios to contact the other groups. Copeland navigated using map and compass but seemed unsure of his position and changed direction often. After nearly an hour trudging heavily through the darkness, and having seen no sign of the other groups, or the enemy, or an airfield, or any other humans at all, he called a halt.

'This can't be right,' he panted, 'we should be at the airfield by now.'

'Maybe Jerry scarpered. You know, when A Force attacked.'

'No, Sergeant, we'd have heard something, and seen flashes, gunfire and that.'

'Yes, I suppose.'

Theo raised his hand. 'Sir, there's a pole over there.'

'What? What are you saying?'

'A telegraph pole. Um, over there.'

Sniggers of amusement from the others, a sigh from Copeland. 'Yes, thank you, Private, I can see it's a telegraph pole. What of it?'

'Telegraph poles lead somewhere. They always do – to houses, a village, a road. We could follow it.'

It led to a cluster of farmhouses, one of which showed a light burning in a window. After reconnoitring for signs of the enemy, Copeland ordered everyone to wait while he investigated. Gratefully they slumped to the ground, shedding stores and equipment. Weapons were discarded, cigarettes lit; lowering their drum of wire Burnsy and Theo sat on the tussocked grass.

'Bit of a balls-up, wouldn't you say, Trick?'

'Looks rather like it.'

He was right. Ten minutes later Copeland returned.

'This isn't Guernsey.'

'What?'

'It's Sark. There are no Germans here, no airfield and certainly no A and C Forces. We're on the wrong blasted island.'

'Christ! So what do we do?'

'There's nothing we can do. Except abandon the mission and head back to the rendezvous.'

'We could cut the wire, sir.'

'What?'

'The telegraph wire, sir, we could cut it.'

'To what end, Private Burns, precisely?'

'Disrupting the enemy, er, infa-struncture, sir. It's better than nothing, ain't it?'

As it was his idea, Burns was awarded the honour, balancing precariously on Theo's shoulders, of reaching up and cutting the telephone wire. Whereupon the twelve picked up their kit and trudged back to the beach.

'I wonder how the others got on,' Theo puffed as they manhandled their drum down the cliff path.

'Expect we'll find out soon enough.'

CHAPTER 11

A few days later, the 130 men of 3 Commando who had
been on the ill-fated mission – grandly codenamed Operation
Ambassador – were ordered to assemble in a hangar for a
debriefing. Their commanding officer, Colonel Durnford-Slater,
would not be present, they were told; nor, Theo noted, was
Lieutenant Copeland or any other junior officer. Instead their
much-feared senior NCO, Sergeant Major Bolton, would be
addressing them. As they waited, nervously checking the shine
of their boots and straightening their tunics, anxious murmurs
circled the hangar like prayer.

'What's this about, do you think, Percy?' Theo whispered.

'*Burnsy*, for Christ's sake!'

'Sorry. What do you think it's about?'

'No idea. But I doubt it's for giving out medals.'

He was right.

'SHUT UP!' A glowering Bolton appeared, pacing back and
forth before the gathered ranks. 'Right, you feckless tossers!
I'm not going to stand here and tell you what a load of bollocks
last week's cock-up was, because you already know that, don't
you?'

'Yes, Sergeant Major!'

'A cock-up and a disgrace. What was it?'

'Cock-up and disgrace, Sergeant Major!'

Bolton then spent ten minutes angrily recounting the catalogue of disasters that was Operation Ambassador. Apparently, while Theo's B Force was busy roaming the wrong island, A Force landed on the right island, but couldn't find the airfield while C Force failed to find any island at all, spending hours steaming round in circles with a faulty compass.

'And that all adds up to one pathetic cock-up, don't it?'

'Yes, Sarnt Major!'

'That's right.' Bolton's voice lowered to a snarl. 'But what you don't know is, cock-ups have ramifications, and the ramifications of this cock-up is the Prime Minister himself is royally brassed off. So much so that 3 Commando is to be disbanded.'

Shocked murmurs circled the hangar.

'Dis-bloody-banded!' Bolton glared. 'And that's a fucking disaster by any standards, ain't it?'

'Yes, Sarnt Major!'

The result of this disaster, it emerged, was that the men of 3 Commando were to be redeployed. Some would suffer the humiliation of being RTU'd – returned to their old units as unfit for special duties. Others, meanwhile, would be sent to similarly less demanding postings. Only a fortunate few were to be saved, transferring to 2 Commando: 'In the forlorn bloody hope they can beat some sense into you!'

'. . . So in a moment Corporal Hatch and Corporal Stoddart will come down the line, and you will learn which is your fate. Is that all clearly understood?'

'Yes, Sarnt Major!'

Theo and Burnsy waited, watching anxiously as the corporals moved slowly through the ranks, clipboards in hand.

'Please don't let me be RTU,' Burnsy whispered, 'I hate the bloody infantry.'

'I can't be returned to my unit,' Theo mused, 'I don't have one.'

Eventually their turn came. 'Right, Burns, Trickey, apparently you both showed some pluck and initiative, so congratulations, you're both still in.'

'Really, Corp?'

'Yes really. So splash or crash, which is it?'

The two exchanged glances. 'What's that, Corporal?'

'Are you deaf? I said splash or crash! Do you want special ops messing about in boats? Or special ops messing about in aeroplanes? And get a bloody move on!'

'What d'you think, Burnsy?'

'Christ knows, but I'm buggered if I'm doing any more swimming, I damn near froze my bollocks off last week.'

'I've never been in an aeroplane. Um, shall we have a go at that?'

'Might as well. So that's two for crashing please, Corporal.'

The date was 20 July 1940.

Three days later, Theo, Burnsy and a coachload of former 3 Commandos arrived at a base somewhere in the countryside south of Manchester. 'Ringway Airport', the sign said as they pulled through gates on to a windswept airfield surrounded by hangars and huts on one side, and passenger buildings on the other. As they disembarked and formed up into lines, PE instructors in white vests stood by to greet them, at their head a major of the Royal Engineers.

'Welcome to Central Landing School,' he said. 'My name is John Rock, these gents are your instructors, and our job is twofold. First, to get you fitter than you've been in your lives, and second, teach you how to jump out of aeroplanes. Any questions?'

'What did he say?' Burnsy murmured.

'Not sure,' Theo replied.

'Good,' Rock concluded, 'off you go then, grub's in an hour, we start tomorrow.'

It was the first they'd heard of their destiny as parachutists. There were sixty in their intake. Apart from the commandos who knew each other slightly, all were strangers, but soon learned from the plethora of insignia and accents that they represented units from every corner of the kingdom: Welsh Fusiliers, Irish Guards, Scottish Rifles, lancers, hussars and grenadiers, infantry, cavalry and artillery; there was even one from the veterinary corps ('They said something about dogs'). Aged eighteen to thirty, from humble privates to a captain of the Coldstreams, they could not have been more disparate, yet, apart from pluck and enthusiasm, they had two vital bonds in common. All were volunteers, and all felt driven to achieve something different and exciting for the war effort. And the extra two shillings a day it paid.

Their training was strict, physically demanding, and necessarily experimental, for Central Landing School was only a few weeks old, and the business of training paratroops still in its infancy. There was no manual, no template, no equipment – and no precedent, so Major Rock and his instructors were obliged to improvise as they went, copy what they could from the German model, and develop techniques by trial and error. 'I've neither information nor instructions!' Rock wrote plaintively to his superior. Nor were his efforts universally applauded, as many in the military thought the entire enterprise a waste of time. Official letters came deliberately misaddressed to the 'Central Laundry Service' or 'Central Sunday School', new volunteers were inexplicably slow in arriving from their units, and vitally needed equipment went astray or failed to turn up at all. Billeted at a civilian airfield so as not to interfere with 'proper' military work, and grudgingly loaned six dilapidated aeroplanes and a selection of spare parachutes, Rock and his men did what they could to devise a workable programme. Early training methods included throwing recruits from the back of a moving lorry, dropping them by wire from a fifty-foot tower and, least popular of all, lying them on a stretcher suspended from the hangar ceiling and swinging them back and forth to test for airsickness. As for actual parachuting, the antiquated Whitley bombers supplied had no door suitable to jump from, so other methods of 'egress' had to be contrived. The first idea involved removing the gun turret from the bomber's tail and building a little platform out in the open there, complete with windscreen and handrail. On receiving the command 'Prepare to jump!' the trainee crawled to the end of the aircraft on elbows and knees and squeezed out on to the platform, carefully raising himself to a standing position and holding on for dear life. Facing forward at 140 mph and viciously buffeted by the slipstream, at the command 'Jump!' he pulled the ripcord to release his parachute and in a flash was jerked from the platform and whirled violently away. Called the 'pulling off' method, it was unsatisfactory in many respects, not least the violence of the 'pull' which rendered many men senseless and resulted in wildly oscillating and even damaged parachutes. Also having to open their own parachutes wasn't ideal, so work went on designing a 'static line' system whereby a tether attached to the aircraft pulled open the parachute for them as they jumped. Another drawback of the pull-off method was the slowness of the procedure. With some minutes elapsing between the dispatch of one man and the next, jumpers could end up landing many miles apart, which was useless in a combat scenario, especially at night. Further efforts were made to speed things up, but after little improvement, and two fatalities, the method was abandoned for something less complicated...

... although still hazardous, as Theo and his intake were to discover – but not until they'd completed ground training. That first morning they were roused rudely from sleep before dawn, turfed out on to the moonlit grass in full kit and ordered to run round the airfield, some three miles in circumference. Upon arriving back sweating and gasping, they were ordered round it again, only the other way. After breakfast of porridge, bread and jam they then cleaned and tidied their huts before reporting to stores where they were issued with exotic new boots with crêpe soles and laces at the sides, and an old-fashioned leather flying helmet with extra padding in the top. Then they were divided into groups to begin training as parachutists.

Theo's group was led outside to an apparatus called the Trojan Horse. This heavy wooden construction consisted of a platform supported by four legs fitted with wheels. The platform, which was ten feet off the ground, had a circular hole around which four men could sit, legs dangling, while the others took turns pushing the 'horse' over the ground. At the given order, the pushers accelerated the horse to a running pace whereupon the instructor shouted 'Number one go! Number two go!' and so on until all four jumpers had 'dispatched' through the hole to impact with the concrete ten feet below. This training, they were told, was about learning to land without injury, which involved bending the knees and rolling on to your back, and also jumping closely one after another without getting in each other's way. Due to difficulties pushing the horse and confusion over the jumping order, Theo's first attempt resulted in all four jumpers crashing painfully to the ground in a confused heap. Repeats followed until, bruised and dazed, they slowly got the hang of it, whereupon they were sent running round the perimeter again.

After lunch they were introduced to the parachute harness, a heavy webbing affair that passed over the shoulders, round the chest and waist, and up between the legs, to a central release point on the midriff. It was from this harness that the jumper hung from his parachute, therefore donning it correctly – and learning how to release it – was of paramount importance. Loose straps resulted in agonizing 'bites' when the parachute opened, particularly in the groin area, while fumbling the release mechanism after landing meant being dragged painfully over the ground. Both these scenarios were simulated, the first by having the trainee leap from a platform with his harness too loose, the second by taking him outside and pulling him face down across the concrete while he tried to release it.

In the evening the trainees changed into PE kit for an hour's 'physical jerks', and a run round the perimeter again for good measure, before collapsing on to their cots, battered and exhausted. A further two days of this 'synthetic' training followed, including classroom lectures on wind, drift and descent control, plus a closely attended demonstration of how a parachute was folded and packed. Then on the third morning they made their first jump.

Before it came a change of clothing, variants of which were constantly in development. After their early-morning run, wash and breakfast, they reported to stores where they regretfully handed in their crêpe-soled boots (too expensive) and less regretfully their leather flying helmets (of no practical use) to be issued instead with their old boots, and enormous doughnut-shaped headgear featuring a rubber ring held by a chin strap. Following this novelty came a curious new garment resembling oversize overalls with the legs cut off. This 'smock', they were told, was to be worn over their battledress, but under their parachute harness, the idea being that in a real scenario, a paratrooper would carry his weapons, supplies, rations, ammunition and other paraphernalia in his battledress pockets and webbing in the usual way, then don the smock over it before strapping on his parachute, so nothing caught up when he jumped. Copied from the German version or *Knochensack* – 'bone sack' – the sartorial effect was comical; the men immediately dubbed it 'maternity wear', but its practicality was quickly proven.

Duly attired in new smock and helmet Theo and Burnsy helped each other into their harnesses, this time with parachutes attached, and clumped outside into the sunshine with the others. Two barrage balloons waited, attached to winches mounted on the back of lorries and swaying gently in the breeze. Beneath each balloon was a metal cage with a hole in the floor.

'This is it, I'd say, Burnsy.'

'About bloody time.'

The lorries moved off, their balloons following behind like lumbering elephants, until they reached the middle of the airfield.

'Right!' The instructor rubbed his hands. 'Who's first for the long drop?'

It was quite bad, Theo decided afterwards, but could have been worse. The most unsettling part was not the coming down but the going up. They were dispatched in pairs, and when their turn came he and Burnsy clambered awkwardly into the cage, where an instructor bade them sit on either side of the hole while the balloon ascended. This took some time and all the while it swayed and jerked and strained on its wire like a bull on a tether. Disconcerting sounds emanated too, sighing and flapping and creaking, while the cage itself tilted and wobbled alarmingly. The net result was nausea and vertigo, made worse by the view, which was either straight up at the trembling skin of the balloon, matted and patched like a worn bicycle tyre, or straight down at a receding circle of grass dotted with upturned white faces, or straight across to Burnsy whose sickly grin offered neither humour nor encouragement. Undecided which was worst, Theo closed his eyes. Eventually the winch jolted to a stop and it was time to jump.

'Sit on the edge, legs together, arms at your sides, just as you practised.' The instructor clipped Theo's parachute line to the cage and checked it with a tug. 'Keep your chin up and listen for instructions from below. A good push off now, and GO!'

A shove from behind and he was plummeting, the breath sucked from his lungs. Rushing wind, then a crackling noise, a sharp jerk and suddenly he was floating. The transition was instant, the silence startling, the sensation magical, and relief surged over him like a wave. A whoop from above as Burnsy's parachute opened, a few more seconds of blissful floating, then: 'Keep your fucking legs together, Trickey!' from below. He looked down. The ground was already rushing up and he was drifting sideways; he tucked his elbows, bent his knees – a bone-jarring crash and he was down, tucking and rolling as best he could.

'Bloody shambles!' the instructor pronounced. 'Get it right next time or else.' But he knew he'd done well enough, and later that day he made a second jump which earned him the rare plaudit: 'Better.'

After three balloon exits the trainees moved on to aeroplanes. First, however, four of their intake were removed, two for refusing to jump from the balloon, and two for deciding to 'un-volunteer' for special ops. Nothing was said: they packed and left, and the training went on. The aeroplane jumps took place over a large country estate nearby called Tatton Park. Groups of ten jumpers called 'sticks' embarked the Whitleys at Ringway, flew to Tatton Park, jumped, and then marched the six miles back to base carrying their parachutes with them. The 'pulling off' jumping method had by now been replaced by the 'dropping through a hole' method, as per the balloon, the hole being where the Whitley's lower gun turret used to be. This was a vastly improved arrangement, for as well as being safer, it meant jumpers could exit in reasonably quick succession, as would be required on a mission. But it had one serious drawback, which became known as the 'Whitley kiss'. The hole in the floor was not so much a hole as a tube, three foot long and narrower at the bottom. In order to exit satisfactorily, therefore, it was essential the trainee adopt the 'thin as a pencil' pose and push himself off very precisely. Not enough push and his parachute caught on the lip, pitching him forward. Too much push and he hit the opposite side as he fell. Both resulted in painful injuries to head and face: bloody noses, split lips and broken teeth. 'Oh, hello,' the instructors would quip as another stunned victim gathered himself from the ground, 'kissed the Whitley again, I see.'

Days turned to weeks and bad weather delayed their final jumps; they were reduced to classroom lectures and endless PE. That and worried queuing for the telephone as German bombers struck London and elsewhere. Then at last the day dawned for their final qualifying jump, which was to be performed as an 'operational' demonstration before a specially invited audience of military chiefs, War Office officials and possibly even the Prime Minister himself. For the performance, four Whitleys were to take off from Ringway, each carrying a stick of ten men, fly in formation to Tatton Park, then drop them in a simulated attack on a building in the grounds. Theo and Burnsy's stick were to fly in the leading Whitley. In addition to battledress, smock and harness, each man wore a chest pouch containing smoke bombs and a whistle to add authenticity to the attack, and upon landing they were to make for a weapons cache where they would further arm themselves with rifles and bayonets.

The weather was clear, the autumn breeze slight, and the first three Whitleys took off as scheduled, climbing steadily into the sunshine over Ringway. There was then a delay with the fourth bomber due to technical problems, but since VIPs were waiting it was decided to press on with three, with the fourth following when possible. As they neared the target Theo's stick took up position, two men sitting on either side of the exit hole, the rest bunched closely behind. Minutes of tense waiting followed; then with a shout the instructor dropped his arm and out they went. The descent went well; Theo landed heavily but rolled quickly on to his knees, releasing his harness without difficulty. Hearing whistles around him, he dropped a smoke bomb and set off towards the arms cache, dimly aware of a crowd of onlookers to one side. Overhead came the drone of the fourth bomber with the final stick of men. He reached the cache, where he found Burnsy and the others busy collecting rifles.

'Bloody terrific, eh, Trick?' Burnsy grinned.

Then came a shout and everyone looked up. Hands pointed, necks craned, the VIPs turned to see. A figure, one of the men in the last stick, was tumbling rapidly earthwards, arms and legs flailing, his unopened parachute streaming behind him.

Everyone froze, the demonstration forgotten, watching in mesmerized silence as the figure dropped, struggling all the way, until it hit the ground with a sickening thump.

They finished the demonstration, or an abbreviated version. Afterwards, while the dead man was discreetly removed, they were lined up on the grass for the VIPs to inspect. The Prime Minister was not among them. Few made comments as they passed; their mood seemed distracted.

'Gliders, Geoffrey, is the way to go,' Theo heard one man say to his colleague. 'Why risk throwing them out of aeroplanes when you can pack a dozen in a glider, in full kit, and land them safely bang on the target?'

'You could be right.'

It was a 'Roman candle', their instructors told them later, a rare malfunction of the parachute whereby it deployed, but didn't open, just streamed behind like a horse's tail. Nothing to be done, they said, a chance in a million. It was a poignant climax to their training. The victim was a Yorkshireman called Gelling and well liked; now his locker was cleared and his bunk empty, as though he never existed.

A period of limbo followed. They formally passed out from Central Landing School, which was suddenly renamed Central Landing Establishment amid rumours it was to include 'other' forms of airborne training. They were also informed they were no longer attached to 2 Commando, but something called 11 Special Air Service Battalion which no one had heard of. In compensation they were officially designated paratroopers and awarded newly designed insignia featuring a winged parachute, which they sewed proudly on to the shoulders of their uniforms. Another intake arrived, so they moved out to barracks in nearby Knutsford to continue their PE regime and weapons training, and go on exercises which often involved forced marches of thirty miles or more. At the same time, with invasion fears looming, the Blitz in full swing and rumours of war in Africa, many began fretting about deployment, especially when they saw former colleagues going to fight. Bored with polishing boots and endless training, and fearful of missing out, some began requesting to return to their old units. Stagnation set in, and with it the suspicion that having created an elite corps, the powers-that-be didn't know what to do with it. To emphasize the point, and in time-honoured military tradition, they were sent home on leave.

Theo returned to Kingston where Eleni greeted him with customary fervour and horror stories about the bombings: 'My lovely haberdashing shop on Station Road gone, Teo, poum!' As for Carla, he learned better news: that her political status had been downgraded from 'A' to 'B', which meant she wouldn't be deported to Canada, but interned somewhere in Britain. Theo wondered privately whether International Research Bureau might be connected with this; Eleni said she didn't know the reason but warned him Carla was suffering low spirits and poor health. 'She jus' want go home South Tyrol, my dear.'

Next morning he took the bus to Kempton, riding up top to gaze out at rain-filled craters and smouldering rubble where once houses had stood, and noting how oblivious Londoners seemed as they hurried about their business.

The Kempton camp had grown since his last visit, and in the dank autumn drizzle looked and smelled crowded, depressing and unsanitary. Nor was it housing only Italians, he learned, but foreign dissidents and agitators of many persuasions and nationalities, including many outright criminals. Life for the inmates, already oppressive and unhealthy, was clearly also unsafe. Carla's appearance shocked him too: thin and wan as she entered the room, she burst into fits of tearful coughing when she saw him.

'What is it, Mama? Do you need the doctor?'

'It's nothing,' she gasped, 'just the *infezione*. Everyone has it.'

Nor was she cheered by her improved status. 'Canada, Scotland, what's the difference, Theodor, I'm still *undesirable*, no?'

He asked about the Blitz. She said they heard the sirens and bombs sometimes and trooped down to shelters beneath the grandstand. Then he asked about Josef and Eleanora, at which she shook her head and sighed. Since declaring war the Italian authorities were more tyrannical, more paranoid, more cruel to their own people than ever, she said, and she feared her father might never be released. As for Eleanora: 'Pah, let her go to Rodolfo in Rome, if she wants. I begged her to come here to England' – she gestured around – 'but for what point?'

Back in Kingston he telephoned Captain Grant at Baker Street, was told he was unavailable, so left a message. Then with nothing to do and no one to see, he lay on his bed and stared at the ceiling. Street noises drifted through the window; from farther off came the hooting of river traffic. He felt lonely and adrift, like a stick in a stream. Home was an empty boarding house in a country he didn't belong to, his family was scattered and broken, he had no friends outside the army, no trade but soldiering – which he felt inadequate at. He was a misfit, and a fraud. He rose and went to the washbasin, staring at the pale-eyed stranger in the mirror. '*Impostore*,' he sneered, and then ran the taps and began to wash.

'Theodorable!' Susanna Price opened her front door. 'You're alive! And just look at you, all posh and handsome in your uniform.'

'Hello, Susanna, you look well too.' She'd blossomed in the year since last he'd seen her. No more the gawky Juliet to his schoolboy Mercutio, she'd filled out, was taller and more assured, like a proper young woman. 'I wondered if you'd like to walk out?'

'I'm not supposed, on account of the Blitz.'

'We needn't go far.'

'I'll ask my dad.'

They stepped on to the blacked-out streets.

'Where shall we go?' she asked.

'I don't mind. Somewhere quiet.'

'Saucy!'

'Not like that. I just meant, you know, get away from things a bit.'

They set off down Wood Street; she slipped her arm through his.

'Things?'

He sighed. 'War, fighting, the army, living with men all the time. It gets a bit much sometimes, that's all. That and, you know, family difficulties.'

'I heard about your mum. Doesn't seem right.'

'No.'

They walked to the river at Turk's Pier and found a bench, staring out at the oily water and watching the barges pass. Away to the east searchlights swept the sky like silver wands.

'Are you, um, still walking out with Albert Fitch?'

'Don't be daft.' She nudged him. 'Albert's working in his dad's greengrocer's. He's going with that Stella Watt from Woolworth's.'

'Oh.'

'What about you? A girl in every town, you infantry types, isn't that right?'

'Not really, there's never any time. Anyway I'm not in the infantry now.'

'You left the East Surreys?'

'After I got back from France.'

'What was it like? France, I mean. I heard about Dunkirk and that.'

His mind went back. Caen, Blangy, St Valery, Veules, tanks and Gammon bombs, diving Stukas, fighting retreats, a man exploding in a red mist, another gripping his hand from a pushcart. Had any of it really happened? 'I never made it to Dunkirk. We – our unit, that is – we got cut off. It was quite bad, a lot of killing and, um, chaos. I didn't do very well.'

She leaned on his shoulder. 'You got home safe. That's all that matters.'

'No it isn't. But thanks anyway.'

'It does to me. Poor Kenny's mum is beside herself.'

'Still no news?'

251

'Nothing. More than six months. What happened, d'you think?'

Outside Major Wilson's tent was the last time he'd seen Kenny Rollings. The day he was chosen as a runner, because he could ride a bicycle and Kenny couldn't.

Why did you tell him I'm an officer?

Cos we'll get better jobs, you idiot! Kenny had said.

'There was this little village, near a river. We got separated. There was a lot of confusion, and fighting and retreating. Hundreds were captured, thousands, over the next week or two. There's a good chance he'll turn up.'

'Perhaps you could visit his mum. It might cheer her up.'

'I will.'

Back at the boarding house there was a message from Grant: 'Tomorrow 2.00 p.m.' He arrived early, was shown up to the fourth floor, and then had to wait an hour in a side room. International Research Bureau seemed much busier than before, although by now he guessed the name signified little of its purpose. Footsteps hurried up and down the corridor, telephones rang, doors squeaked open and banged shut again, voices spoke in urgent murmurs. Eventually Grant appeared, followed by two men, one a lieutenant of the Royal Signals, and the other a tall man with black hair and Mediterranean complexion, wearing a suit. Theo sensed immediately he was Italian.

Grant, as before, was chain-smoking and looked dishevelled and harried. 'Ah, Theo, there you are. Sorry, all sixes and sevens as usual. How was the training?'

'Oh, um, it was fine, thank you, sir. I passed, that is.'

'Yes I know.' Grant flicked through a file. 'Near the top of your intake too. Good show. So now, Theo, this is Lieutenant Tony Deane-Drummond, who is halfway through his jump course, and this gentleman is, er, Signor Rossi. Gentlemen, meet Officer Cadet Theodor Trickey.'

'Oh, um, only Acting – that is I never finished—'

'I wouldn't worry about that.' Grant checked his file. 'Soon sorted, so I believe.'

'Hello!' Deane-Drummond pumped his hand. 'Done with your jump course, you lucky beggar. I'm sick to death of running round that damned perimeter, and as for those wretched balloons. . .'

'Ah, yes, sir, much easier jumping from the aeroplane, although—'

'Watch out for the Whitley kiss – yes, I've been warned!'

Rossi stepped forward, scrutinizing Theo through narrowed eyes as they shook hands. '*Ciao, soldato,*' he said pointedly in a cultured Roman accent, 'Hello, *Private,*' and before Theo could draw breath he launched into a rapid Italian interrogation: birth, family, friends, education, vacations, contacts, politics, plus quick-fire questions on Italy's history, geography and culture. Theo responded as best he could, but had trouble keeping up and was thrown by the man's hostile demeanour. Suddenly, after five minutes Rossi stopped and turned to Grant.

'He's a northerner, so speaks like a mountain goat. Neither can I vouch for his integrity. But there's no foreign accent; he'll pass as a native.'

'I am a native,' Theo said, still in Italian.

'No, you're a Tyrolean separatist peasant who ran away.'

'*Scusi?*'

'Thank you, chaps,' Grant interrupted cheerily. 'And thank *you*, Mr Rossi, you've been a great help. Mrs Simpson will see you downstairs. Meanwhile I think we three will adjourn for a chat.'

Head reeling, Theo followed Grant along the corridor to his office, which was as he remembered, only even more cluttered. Throwing piles of papers to the floor Grant cleared chairs for Theo and Deane-Drummond, and lit up a cigarette.

'Well, that all seemed to go pretty well, don't you think, Theo?'

'Who was that man?'

'A business acquaintance. No one you need concern yourself with.'

'Um, I'm not sure, sir, he seemed. . .'

'Business-like. Yes, I know. Now, tell me, Theo, how are you feeling? Fit, ready and raring to go?'

'Go? Well, yes, of course, only I came about my mother—'

'No, you didn't actually, but we'll come to that. We'll also come to your mother too, no doubt, but in the meantime, how would you feel about a trip to Italy?'

'I. . . What?'

'Tony here has a proposition for you.'

'He does?'

'Yes. Only it's absolutely top secret. So whether you accept it or not, you can never breathe a word to a soul. Is that clearly understood?'

It was a special mission, the first ever for the fledgling parachute corps. It was called Operation Colossus, and was to take place in Italy. Over the next half-hour, Deane-Drummond, who was the mission's intelligence officer, outlined its purpose. A single troop of forty men, hand-picked from 2 Commando, or 11 Special Air Service Battalion as it was presently known, and led by a Major Pritchard, was to parachute into the Apennine Mountains, and blow up the main aqueduct supplying water to the southern province of Apulia, which included the strategically important cities of Brindisi and Taranto. Having blown the aqueduct, they were then to escape west across country to an isolated spot on the coast near Salerno, there to be picked up by the Royal Navy. Theo, as the only Italian speaker through parachute training thus far, would be going as interpreter.

'Only should the need arise,' Deane-Drummond added. 'Contact with the Italians, military or civilian, will be avoided at all costs, but you never know.'

'I see.' Theo nodded, trying not to appear shocked. 'When, did you say?'

'The next couple of months, January or February probably. There'll be a working-up period first, in Scotland, to acclimatize everyone to the conditions, mountain training and so forth.'

'So you're planning to cross the Apennines. On foot. In midwinter.'

'That's right. It's sixty or seventy miles, we estimate. We're allowing four days.'

'Should be right up your street, eh, Theo?' Grant quipped. 'You being a northern mountain goat and all that.'

'Yes, but—'

'You'll have to drop out of sight, the whole team. Until the operation's over. No going home, no telephone calls and so on. Assuming you're willing, that is?'

Theo looked up.

Grant was behind his desk, not smiling, but watching him closely. Smoke curled from an inch of ash hanging from his cigarette. 'Are you?'

'Sir. Operation Ambassador. . .'

'Was a total foul-up, we know. But not your fault. It was rushed, it was badly planned, it should never have gone ahead. Frankly it's a miracle you all got back in one piece, so we should count ourselves lucky. This one won't be like that. It's been meticulously planned, and you'll be thoroughly trained and properly equipped. This one's going to work.'

Silence fell. Deane-Drummond nodded encouragingly. Grant sat back.

'So?'

'Yes.' Theo straightened. 'Yes, I'll do it, but I want my mother released.'

'I understand that.'

'You know she's no threat to this country.'

'I believe that to be true. However, the internment of nationals from belligerent countries has nothing to do with the work of this bureau.'

'Then—'

'Nevertheless, you have my assurance that we will continue to do everything in our influence to advance her case. As has already been demonstrated.'

*

Eleni waited, her basket on her knee, staring round at the featureless room with its mildewed walls and grime-stained window. It was damp and cold. Her breath misted the air; her hat and coat remained on. Outside, snow dusted the grandstand roof, the compound was churned brown with mud, and thin smoke rose from a dozen hut chimneys. Finally Carla arrived.

'You didn't visit,' she said, her voice a croak.

'I been busy.'

'Of course.'

'I bring you things. For the Christmas.'

'That's very kind.'

'Not much. Biscuits, a packet of marge, tin a oranges.'

'Thank you.'

Eleni rose. 'Now I mus' go.'

'So soon?'

'Yes, very busy. You hear from Teo?'

'He came. He said he was going away, on training, several weeks. Eleni, please—'

'I mus' go.'

'I don't know what to say.'

'Say nothing. Your country attack my country. Nothing more to say.'

'I'm so sorry. But you must know I detest this invasion, I detest the Italian government, I detest Mussolini, attacking Greece is barbaric—' She broke off, convulsed with coughing. 'Sorry, I—'

Eleni waited, arms folded. Slowly the spasm subsided. 'You cough no better?'

'It's the damp. It's nothing. Eleni, please—'
'Syrup a ginger. I bring next time.'
With that she picked up her basket and left.

CHAPTER 12

Erwin Rommel, by coincidence, would fly into Italy on exactly the same night as the men tasked with blowing up the aqueduct.

Following his triumphant charge across France in the summer, he and 7th Panzer Division were repositioned to the Loire region, stood down and ordered to rest. This was much needed, for despite its successes both Ghost Division and leader were in a depleted condition. Not since breaking out from the Ardennes had Rommel slept a full night, eaten a leisurely meal or taken any time off. He was everywhere at once, always moving, never stopping, endlessly rushing back through the columns, cajoling, encouraging, berating, exhorting, then hurrying forward once more to the 'tip of the spear', there to lead the charge. His voice became a hoarse croak, he lost weight, injured his back and, despite his infectious confidence, he suffered anxieties which caused stomach pains, nausea and vomiting. 'I am somewhat done in, Lu dearest,' he wrote home, 'and I long to rest in your arms.' But rest had to wait, because barely was the 7th settled when secret orders began arriving from High Command to prepare for Unternehmen Seelöwe – Operation Sealion – and the invasion of Britain. A project Rommel passionately believed in, Sealion called for a combined air and sea assault across the English Channel, a feat not even Germany had attempted before. If successful, the conquest of the west would be complete, and the war in Europe over. If it failed, the Allies might yet regroup and prevail. The key, Rommel knew, was to strike quickly, before England could recover from the chaos of Dunkirk. Delay, even by a few weeks, might cost Germany dearly. Gradually Sealion's details arrived and he gathered his officers together to study them. Ghost Division, they learned, would spearhead the invasion, embarking on barges in Le Havre by night, and crossing for a dawn landing at Rye on the Sussex coast. Simultaneous landings would take place along a hundred-mile front between Ramsgate and Lyme Regis. Having secured the Rye bridgehead, the 7th was then to move inland to a town called Tunbridge Wells where they were to pause and regroup. But Tunbridge Wells, Rommel soon noted, seemed of little strategic interest. 'Yet only thirty miles from London,' he pointed out to his men, already mentally modifying his orders. 'Keep moving, strike fast, we could be first at the capital!'

Before any of it could happen, the Luftwaffe, which had performed so admirably over France, had to knock out the RAF and secure the skies over the Channel. Only then could the barges be safely launched. Days went by, weeks, 7th Panzer returned to full strength, July turned to August, the weather remained fair, the sea conditions favourable, but still no orders came to advance. Rumours spread that the Luftwaffe was losing in the air, invasion dates came and went, embarkation postponed to 30 August, then 9 September, then the following week of the 15th. And then the unthinkable happened, and without warning on 17 September Rommel received coded orders that Sealion was postponed indefinitely, and the 7th was to return to Germany.

By November he was home in Neustadt. He spent the winter there with his family, walking with Lucie, hiking and skiing with Manfred, building up his strength, restlessly following the news reports and awaiting new orders. Rumours were strong of a fresh spring offensive, not westwards on Britain, but eastwards into Russia, a prospect that both thrilled and awed him. What an epic undertaking: surely the 7th would be in the vanguard? Finally in February the summons came and he journeyed to Berlin for an interview with Field Marshal von Brauchitsch, commander-in-chief of the whole army. But it wasn't Russia he was destined for, he soon learned, or even Britain. 'Mussolini wants to invade North Africa,' von Brauchitsch explained, 'but is sure to make a hash of it. So the Führer commands you to fly to Italy and make arrangements for Germany to "assist" our illustrious ally in this venture. Having secured our involvement, you will then prepare to lead it.'

In the end, thirty-five men were selected from 11 Special Air Service Battalion to carry out the aqueduct mission. Dubbed 'X Troop' and led by former Welsh Fusilier and heavyweight boxer Major Trevor 'Tag' Pritchard, they consisted of five officers and thirty men variously trained in explosives and demolition, mountaineering, navigation, signals, and included two Italian speakers: Theo Trickey and a former Italian waiter called Fortunato Picchi. After a month's winter training in the Scottish Highlands the team returned to Ringway for night-jump practice, advanced weapons training and simulated attacks on a mock-up of the aqueduct. Secrecy was paramount: the men were kept segregated; no one was allowed to leave the site or use the telephone. By early February 1941 training was complete and X Troop moved to Mildenhall in Suffolk to await transportation to Malta.

Also in Suffolk, unknown to Theo, was a twenty-eight-year-old captain of the Cameronians, with whom his destiny would become entwined. His name was John Frost. Kicking his heels supervising beach defences along the Suffolk coast, Frost returned to his billet one night that February to find a War Office circular requesting volunteers for the Special Air Services. Bored with beach defences and with little idea what special services might entail, he filled in the form and sent it off.

Before boarding their flight to Malta, the men of X Troop were assembled in a hangar at Mildenhall for a send-off by a VIP. Impatient to get going, they felt they could do without it. Theo stood in line with the others, vaguely recalling the last time he'd paraded for a talking-to. More than six months ago, the fiasco that was Operation Ambassador had been an ill-conceived mission of unclear purpose with inadequate training and poor equipment. Not this time. This time the mission was clear and they were ready. Fit, focused, primed and raring to go, like racehorses at the starting gate. Properly equipped racehorses too. He tugged at the collar of his battledress, freshly pressed from the 'cleaners'. Their clothes had all been removed two days ago, then returned loaded with special additions: a leather-lined pocket for carrying grenades, another for a commando knife, a hacksaw blade sewn into the collar, 50,000 lire in the waistband, silk maps in the lining of the sleeves, a tiny compass hidden in a button. Cold-weather clothing had been issued, plus new rubber-soled boots, and special high-energy food of the sort polar explorers ate. Then there was the weaponry. Quite apart from high explosives for blowing the aqueduct, they were armed to the teeth with Bren guns, Thompson sub-machine guns, automatic pistols, extra ammunition, hand grenades and the commando knife called a Fairbairn-Sykes. They'd practised night jumping, night navigation and night warfare; they knew the layout and terrain by heart; they'd rehearsed assaulting and blowing the aqueduct so many times they could do it in their sleep. All they needed now, without further delay, was to get on with it.

The send-off was not as expected. The VIP turned out to be Admiral Sir Roger Keyes, a naval officer of pensionable age who was also Chief of Combined Operations and a keen supporter of the new paratroop corps. No one in X Troop had seen him before. Tall, gaunt, nearly seventy, he wore a concerned expression as he passed slowly down the line, pausing, unusually, to speak at length with every man.

Except one. 'Hello,' he said to Theo, 'and you are?'

'Trickey, sir, um, one of the interpreters.'

Keyes flinched slightly. 'Oh yes, Trickey. That's right. Well, the best of luck, old chap,' he said, moving swiftly on. And having met everyone individually, Keyes then made a long and unsettling speech about courage and sacrifice, during which he was seen to brush something from his eye, before concluding: 'I simply could not let you go without saying a proper goodbye.' At which he pulled himself to attention and saluted *them*. Clearly distraught, he then turned to go, but not before he was heard to mutter: 'A pity. A damned pity.'

The flight to Malta was long but largely uneventful. John Rock, the boss of Ringway school and now a colonel, flew with them for encouragement and support. Eight Whitleys had been allocated, four to fly the mission, two to make diversionary raids, plus two spares. All made it to Malta safely, but arriving overhead Valetta they had to wait while damage to the runway from the island's nightly air raids was repaired. Eventually they landed and were whisked away to a disused barracks for safekeeping. That night their leader Tag Pritchard called them together for a final briefing. As well as discussions about loading the Whitleys, sharing out of equipment, jumping order and myriad other last-minute details, they finally learned the plan for their escape from Italy.

'After the job's done we divide into teams,' Pritchard explained. 'We've a lot of rough terrain to cover and small groups will fare better than large. We travel by night and lie up by day. Not getting spotted is crucial, as is speed: we've sixty miles to cover in a straight line, probably double that allowing for the terrain. It'll be a tough slog, but we must do it in four nights, because on the fourth night the Royal Navy submarine HMS *Triumph*, currently berthed here in Valetta, will be waiting to pick us up.'

Amazed murmurs and low whistles were exchanged.

'Yes, I know, they're laying on the red carpet, so let's not keep them waiting. After we're picked up *Triumph* drops us back here, we relax on the beach and wait for a lift home. Any questions?'

'What's the procedure for the sub rendezvous, boss?'

'*Triumph* will surface after dark, then flash a V-for-victory on the hour every hour until dawn. As soon as we respond they'll send dinghies to pick us up.'

'What if we do get spotted en route?'

'Capture is not advisable. We fight our way out.'

'So, when do we go?'

Pritchard grinned. 'Moon's full, weather's clear. How about tomorrow?'

The final day was spent checking and rechecking equipment, then loading it into the Whitleys. The explosives and heavy weapons were packed into large canvas canisters suspended within the Whitleys' bomb bays. The rest was distributed among the men. Their mood as they worked was cheerful and optimistic, with much accompanying banter.

'Pay you a fiver if you carry the Bren, Fletch.'

'Money up front?'

'When we get back.'

'Not bloody likely!'

Theo busied himself packing. In addition to his regular duties and interpreting, he was also first-aider for his stick and carried the maps for the trek across the mountains. Along with food, clothing, weapons and ammunition, finding space for everything in his rucksack was a challenge. Halfway through repacking for the fourth time, he was summoned to a side office, where he found Deane-Drummond in discussion with a civilian introduced as 'Smith'.

'Mr Smith is a local representative of International Research Bureau, Theo. You know, Grant's lot from Baker Street. He's come to give you your orders.'

'Orders?'

'Listen carefully to what he says. I'll leave you in peace.'

Deane-Drummond left, and Smith produced an envelope which he told Theo to open and read. It didn't take long.

'It just says after the mission I'm to follow verbal instructions issued by you.'

'Correct.'

'What instructions?'

'Sit down.'

'No, thank you. What instructions?'

'Have you heard of an Italian anti-government activist called Gino Lucetti?'

'I. . . Who?'

'He led various protests and uprisings against Mussolini in the twenties and thirties, including an assassination attempt.' Smith waited. 'Ring any bells?'

'Something. . . In the newspapers, um, when I was at school. Isn't he in prison?'

'Yes. And that's the point.'

'What is?'

'He's been moved. He was at Santo Stefano, now he's at the Regina Coeli prison, in Rome.'

'I don't understand. . .'

'Just along the corridor from your grandfather.'

'What!'

'Just listen.' Smith produced another envelope, larger,

bulging with letters and documents, and money – Italian lire, Swiss francs and several British gold sovereigns stitched into a belt-like pouch. The documents, he explained, were identity cards, travel passes, letters of introduction: everything Theo would need to travel to Rome, spend time there and then leave again. The gold was to demonstrate 'sincerity'.

'Lucetti has supporters, a small but determined group calling themselves Partito d'Azione, Action Party, whose sole aim is to depose Mussolini and overthrow Italian Fascism. We need to make contact with them, so we can provide assistance. Do you understand?'

'No.' He could barely believe his ears. 'No, I don't. What is this, and what has it to do with my grandfather?'

'The only way to Action Party is through Lucetti. Once in Rome, you will visit your grandfather in prison, twice. On the first visit you will explain the situation and hand him these letters to give to Lucetti. They prove you are genuine. On the second visit your grandfather will pass you instructions from Lucetti on how to contact his followers in Action Party.'

'Yes, but—'

'You meet them, explain we want to help, give them the gold, obtain names and addresses, contact information and so on, then you leave.'

'Leave.'

'Yes, leave. You are an Italian medical student returning to your home in the north after visiting relatives in Rome. Once back in South Tyrol you cross into Switzerland, where you report to the British Embassy. It's all very straightforward.'

'Straightforward? But it's, it's not. . . I can't, I'm a paratrooper, on a special operation. We're a team, we've trained
for months, I can't just walk off—'

'We know about the operation, and this won't interfere in
any way. You fulfil the mission, you escape with the others,
then at an appropriate moment you slip away. Pritchard is fully
briefed; so is Deane-Drummond.'

'Appropriate moment.' Theo shook his head in bewilderment.
'And when's that?'

'That's for you to decide. When your services are no longer
needed, I'd say. When it's all over.'

'When the submarine picks them up, you mean.'

Smith glanced away. 'I wouldn't leave it that long.'

They took off at dusk. The flight time was only three hours, but
air raids were now a nightly event at Valetta airport, and they
couldn't risk getting caught on the ground. So the four Whitleys
headed out to sea, circled slowly up to ten thousand feet and
then set a circuitous course to bring them over the target at the
appointed time of 9.30 p.m. Two more Whitleys laden with
bombs headed for the nearby city of Foggia, where they were to
make a diversionary raid. The night was clear and cloudless with
a full moon and bright stars. Aboard the shuddering bombers
it was thunderously noisy and bitterly cold; the men huddled
down on the bare metal with cushions and blankets and tried
to doze. Soon they were over Sicily, then Italy itself, following
the west coast northwards, with the snow-capped peaks of the
Apennines glistening in the moonlight to their right. Then at

Agropoli they turned inland for the run in to the target. Aboard Theo's Whitley, Deane-Drummond was in charge, keeping in touch with the pilots by intercom. On this their first mission, the Paras were to use a new system of lights to control their exit: a red one would come on five minutes before the jump; a green one was the signal to go. It sounded simple: they hoped it worked.

'Fifteen minutes – hatch open!' Deane-Drummond wriggled down to the hatch, which was covered by a hinged lid. Withdrawing the bolts, the cover came off and a blast of icy wind tore through the Whitley. Shuffling forward, the men peered down through the hole and there, less than a thousand feet below, were the towering peaks and plummeting ravines of the mountains. It was a forbidding sight in the harsh moonlight: the terrain looked menacingly steep and thick with snow, sheer cliffs, craggy gorges and cascading white waterfalls; lower down was darkly forested with sinewy dark lines indicating tracks, and here and there the occasional glimmer of light from a lone farmhouse.

Fifteen minutes came and went, twenty; the Whitley seemed to be circling, as though searching for landmarks. No red light came on. Deane-Drummond called into his intercom and tapped his headphones, his face perplexed. Then a figure appeared, crawling up from the tail: the Whitley's rear gunner, waving urgently.

'Intercom's bust! You go in one minute!'

Frantic preparation ensued, the men quickly tightening harnesses and helmets, hooking their static lines on and taking up their jump positions either side of the hole, the first pair with legs dangling ready. Still no red light glowed, but suddenly the green light came on. 'Go!' Deane-Drummond shouted and away they went. Theo jumped third, jerking to attention as he dropped, making a clean exit down the tube into the freezing hurricane. Then followed the mad tumble, the tug on his shoulders, the world jolting upright and the familiar blessed floating, silent save for the rumble of receding engines. Swinging gently, he checked his parachute, raised his hands to the risers and tugged to turn into wind. He saw a line of white parachutes from his stick and coloured ones for the equipment, noting the drop pattern looked neat and tight. Below him the ground was approaching, the terrain thrown into harsh relief by the light. Somewhere a dog started barking. He glimpsed the lights of a farmhouse, saw a patch of cultivated soil and heaved left towards it. Just before impact he pulled down hard on the risers; he hit, tucked and rolled, rose swiftly to his feet, smacking the harness release with his fist while the canopy folded itself neatly on to the ground beside him. He'd made the perfect landing. And not two hundred yards away, hard and angular against the moonlit sky as it spanned a deep ravine, was their target, the Tragino Aqueduct.

No time was wasted on congratulations. Deane-Drummond gathered the stick together and they began searching for their stores. A few minutes later jumpers from two more bombers came tramping through the undergrowth, a breathless Tag Pritchard among them. Of the fourth Whitley's stick there was no sign.

'Right, Picchi, Trickey, those farmhouses, you know what to do,' Pritchard ordered. 'Meanwhile 3 Section set up a defensive position here while the rest of you get cracking rounding up the stores.'

Two farmhouses had been spotted lower down the hillside. A mission imperative was that no locals were allowed to leave the scene, in case they tried to pass word of the attack or telephone the authorities. All had to be rounded up and held secure until the job was done. Theo and Picchi descended a winding path, crossed a bridge over a stream and split up to investigate. Theo reached the first building, an ancient and dilapidated stone farmhouse. As he neared, the dog he'd heard earlier started barking again. '*Apri la porta!*' he demanded, banging on the door. Scuffling came from within, but the door stayed shut. He knocked again, adding 'Don't be afraid' in Italian for good measure. More scuffling, then the sound of a bolt sliding. The door opened a crack and an ancient face appeared.

'*Mi scusi, signore,*' Theo began, 'I am sorry to disturb you. However, I must ask you and everyone here to accompany me.'

The old man gazed at the alien apparition before him. 'You came from the sky?'

Within ten minutes he and Picchi had gathered them all together: two families, men and women from youths to ancients, and several children who ran around clapping and squealing with excitement. One man wore a battered uniform and cap. 'I am the stationmaster and very important,' he kept saying.

'Then do as we ask, and all will be well,' Theo replied.

Reaching the bridge they found the main party busy unpacking the stores.

'Will you shut those bloody brats up!' Pritchard barked. 'They'll be heard all over the valley. And tell those men they

271

can help carry the stores up to the aqueduct. It's a steep climb and time's pressing.' Pritchard knelt by the equipment. 'And where the hell's Captain Daly got to?'

'Hasn't been seen, sir, none of 'em have from stick four.'

'Well, we need him, he's got most of the detonators.'

Amid some grumbling from the Italians, especially the stationmaster, the crates of explosives were manhandled up a steep path to the aqueduct, and stacked against a concrete supporting pier. Despite the noise of tramping boots, barking dogs and excitable children, no one appeared in the valley, nor did their activity seem to attract attention. Halfway through proceedings, Deane-Drummond approached Theo, who was standing guard over the civilians, and trying to keep the children quiet with chocolate.

'Take a look at Boulter, would you, Trickey? I fear he's injured.'

Corporal Harry Boulter was in Theo's stick. He'd complained of a bad landing, and had been hobbling around, but was now sitting by the path grimacing with pain.

'Hello, Harry. How's the foot?'

Boulter rubbed his ankle. 'For Christ's sake, don't tell Tag, but I think it's broken.'

'Maybe we can bandage it. Shall we take a look?'

Together they unlaced Boulter's boot and began to ease it off, but at the first pull he yelped with pain. 'Christ, Trick, stop!'

In the end they cut the boot off with commando knives to reveal a darkly swollen foot at an odd angle. Moving it even slightly caused Boulter excruciating pain.

'It's broke, ain't it, Trick?' he gasped.

'We'll bind it up tight, fix you up with a stick. You'll get out with the rest of us.'

'No, I'm done for. You know the rules.'

Theo bandaged the foot, gave Boulter painkillers and was about to go in search of wood to cut a crutch when Pritchard called X Troop together. Suddenly everyone, even the Italian children, fell into an expectant hush.

'Daly's stick didn't make it. Let's just hope they came down safe somewhere and are already heading for the rendezvous. But as a result we don't have enough explosives to blow both ends of the aqueduct, nor the right detonators. So we've piled all the boxes around one pier and we'll blow the lot using a slow fuse and blasting cap. It's not ideal – let's just hope it works. Everyone now get back to those rocks for cover while I go forward and light the fuse.'

Theo translated for the Italians, who gathered the children and scurried for cover, X Troop following; meanwhile, Pritchard went forward up the hill, lit the fuse and then hurriedly returned. Nothing happened. The fuse was set for two minutes, but long after this the valley remained still and silent. Another minute passed, then everyone watched anxiously as Pritchard rose and crept slowly forward. His hesitancy saved him, for suddenly the valley was lit by an enormous flash which held him in frozen silhouette before the shock wave knocked him down. A second later a thunderous explosion shook the ground and a volcano-like eruption blasted high into the sky above the aqueduct. On and on it went, echoing round the valley like thunder; moments later debris began raining down – earth, stones, concrete, rubble – pelting them like hail. Slowly the fragments stopped falling and the sound of thunder faded to silence around the valley. A cloud of acrid dust and smoke then rolled down the hill, enveloping them like fog. The dog resumed its barking; someone began praying in Italian; choking and cursing was heard through the smoke. Then a new sound.

'Listen!' Pritchard climbed unsteadily to his feet. 'Listen to that, boys!'

The roar of water. Torrents of it, cascading to the ground like a waterfall over a cliff. They'd done it. Just six months after the first volunteers arrived at Ringway, the parachute corps had pulled off its first mission. Colossus had succeeded; the Tragino Aqueduct was blown.

Now all they had to do was get home. The time was 1.00 a.m.

Swiftly they made their preparations. With just five hours of darkness remaining, covering ground was crucial. While the others packed up, Theo and Picchi escorted the Italians back to their houses.

'Armed guards are being posted outside,' they warned them, as pre-arranged. 'You will remain inside with doors locked and windows shuttered. Anyone attempting to leave will be shot on sight. The guards will inform you when it is safe to come out.'

'Not sure mine believed me,' Picchi said as they trotted back. 'Yours?'

'Who knows.'

At the bridge the heavy Bren and Thompson guns were being dismantled and discarded, leaving each man with personal weapons only: knife, pistol and grenades. These plus spare ammunition, five days' food and water and a thirty-pound backpack would go with them to the coast. Nothing else. With Daly's team still missing, the remainder divided into three groups, each led by an officer. Theo was attached to Deane-Drummond's, as was Tag Pritchard, who joined them at the last minute. As the time for departure neared, he called Theo aside.

'Listen, Trickey,' he murmured, shrugging on his backpack, 'I've spoken to Boulter. He'll never make it. We're leaving him here.'

'Sir, if we make a crutch, we could take turns helping him, and I don't mind carrying his—'

'Not a chance. He knows the drill and so do you. Non-walking wounded stay behind. We're leaving him food and water, cigarettes and that, but can you make sure he's as comfortable as possible, you know, bandages, painkillers and so on?'

Boulter was propped against a tree. 'Hello ,Trick, you all set, lad?'

'I suppose so. Doesn't seem right leaving you, Harry.'

'Nonsense. We knew the rules when we signed up. Anyway, it saves me slogging over these bloody mountains.'

'Have you got everything you need?'

'I'll say!' Boulter forced a grin, his face white and waxy in the moonlight. 'I've enough fags and chocs to last a month!'

'Here's some things from first aid. Benzedrine if you need it, and these are morphine tablets, for if the pain gets bad. Don't take too many.'

'I won't.'

A shout from Pritchard: 'X Troop, stand to!'

'Trick.' Boulter grabbed his arm. 'Listen, lad, a quick favour. Two as it happens.'

'Anything.'

'There in the bushes, the boys dumped one of the Thompsons. Fetch it over here, would you? Bring the ammo bag an' all.'

'But you've got your pistol, surely?'

'Bloody pea-shooter wouldn't stop a fly. Get me the Tommy, there's a good lad.'

Theo retrieved the machine gun. 'You're not planning anything rash, are you?'

'Not a chance. Here.' Boulter produced a crumpled paper. 'I jotted this down. It's for the missus. See she gets it when you get back, will you?'

'*You're* going to get back, Harry.'

'We'll see. They don't take kindly to saboteurs around here, as we all know. See she gets it, Trick, promise?'

'As soon as I get home.'

'Good. And make bloody sure you *get* home.'

They shook hands. Theo stuffed the note in his pocket and hurried back to his group, already making its way up a steep path away from the site. Pritchard's plan was to ascend the mountain behind the ruined aqueduct, then follow the contour lines west, up and over the Apennines, before descending to the plateau beyond and thence to the rendezvous, where the

River Sele met the sea. The other two parties were to head there by different routes.

Difficulties hit them from the start. The path upwards soon petered out, so they were left clambering over boulders, or scrabbling hand over hand through undergrowth, the ground soft and cloying beneath them. Soon they reached the snowline and the climb became yet more treacherous, with icy rocks for hand-holds and hidden cracks and depressions waiting to catch the unwary. Soaked and frozen, men repeatedly missed their footing, stumbled and slid downhill, only to pick themselves up, battered and dazed, to begin the weary slog upwards again. After two hours Pritchard called a halt and everyone flopped gasping on to the snow. Fatigue dragged at them; without rest since the previous dawn, and following the exertions of the night, they were in dire need of sleep. But sleeping on snowy mountains was ill advised, and in any case time couldn't be spared, so after a few minutes Pritchard roused them and the march resumed. Having traversed the peak, they came next to a series of deep ravines which required them to slither down treacherous rock faces, desperately clutching at roots and boulders and praying they didn't plunge over a cliff. At the bottom of each ravine, fast-running streams and riverbanks knee-deep in sucking mud had to be negotiated, before they began the back-breaking ascent up the other side. They crested ridge after ridge, yet the line of distant hills they were aiming for never seemed nearer. Finally the starlit sky began to pale and, cresting the summit of the latest ravine, Pritchard called a halt, choosing an overhung ledge with a view below as their hideout for the day. Exposed and uncomfortable, the men nevertheless slumped to the ground and fell instantly asleep.

'Got a position, Trickey?' Pritchard asked as they pored over the map.

'Here, sir, by my estimate, a little above Calitri.'

'But that's no distance! And we must have gone fifteen miles.'

'Yes, sir, but only five or six as the crow flies.'

And as dawn broke, the town of Calitri became visible in the valley far below. As did the lie of the land. Villages and farms dotted the lowlands. Any remotely flat piece of ground had been cultivated, and soon they saw labourers heading to the fields through their binoculars. They could only hope none ventured to higher slopes. Behind them rose the mountain above the aqueduct, still disconcertingly near. By now they knew it would be swarming with Italian military searching for them. Sure enough during the afternoon a spotter plane appeared, combing the hills and valleys, stopping, circling, moving on as it searched. The men froze, face down among the boulders, hoping the dull green of their clothes camouflaged them. The plane strayed near, buzzed above for a few minutes, and then departed. Whether it saw them or not, no one could tell. By dusk all was quiet. They boiled water for tea and the Arctic pemmican ration which brewed into a glutinous fatty porridge the men pronounced inedible. The two officers forced it down as an example; Theo too ate it, having eaten similarly in the mountains with his great-grandfather, but most rejected it and fed only on chocolate. At sunset Pritchard and Deane-Drummond ascended the ridge, returning later with the unwelcome news that the team's next obstacle was a three-hundred-foot cliff.

'We did well last night,' Pritchard told them gravely, 'but not well enough. If we're to make the rendezvous we must cover more ground, and that means upping the pace and fewer rest stops. Nor can we wait for stragglers. You all know the drill: fall behind and you're on your own – and we don't want that. So check your packs again for unnecessary weight, chuck out all but the essentials and let's get going.'

Rucksacks were grudgingly unlaced and soon small piles of discarded clothing and personal effects were appearing on the ground. Theo watched, idly marvelling at the trappings some men chose to carry on their backs: books, shoes, a grooming set, a box of dominoes, a mouth organ; one man even had a framed photograph of his fiancée with him. His own pack was sparingly packed, as always, but as he watched his mind strayed to the package Smith had given him, including its weighty gold coins. But he could barely contemplate its existence, yet alone think of opening it.

The cliff nearly finished them before they started. Approaching in gathering darkness, it revealed itself as almost vertical. A goat track helped them up the first part; from then on it was slippery boulders, deep mud and loose shale occasionally studded with treacherous rocks that skittered away into the darkness when you stood on them. Using cut branches, hunting knives, bayonets or bare hands, they dug into the mire and clawed their way blindly upwards, gasping with effort and clinging to the slope in trepidation. More than once a warning shout from above was followed by the rumble and clatter of a landslip, and then sheets of icy mud and shale would slide down and around them like lava. Finally they hauled themselves over a crest to the summit and collapsed to the ground. Pritchard, near exhaustion himself, allowed them fifteen minutes to recover.

From then on the going was still tough, but marginally less so, and better progress was made. Obstacles still had to be circumvented, ridges traversed, hills climbed, ravines plumbed, and running water became a frequent feature of the journey, with one deep torrent sweeping two men off their feet and thirty yards downstream before they managed to struggle clear. But by 2.00 a.m. an estimated eight miles had been covered, with the hope of another five before daybreak.

Then they came upon a road. They spotted it far below, little more than a well-worn cart-track, winding in a generally westerly direction, like them. At first Pritchard would brook no discussion regarding its use, but did agree they could follow it from above. After struggling another mile, however, and with no sign of person or vehicle, he conceded that doubling their groundspeed outweighed the risk of discovery.

'Form up into ranks,' he said as they descended cautiously towards it. 'If anyone comes, start marching in time. Trickey, you shout orders, and tell anyone who asks that we're an Austrian unit on night exercise.'

It worked. The feel of firm ground beneath their blistered feet brought immeasurable relief, and with energy and enthusiasm renewed they immediately made better progress. Four miles went swiftly by; no vehicles passed, no humans were seen, but then they rounded a bend to find themselves amid a cluster of houses. A few lights showed in windows; the usual chorus of dogs started barking.

'Keep going!' Pritchard hissed. 'Now, Trickey!'

'*Sinistra destra, sinistra destra*, keep in time, you useless rabble!'

Curtains twitched, a light came on, the dogs barked, but they marched through the village and on without challenge.

As dawn neared, the search began for the next day's hideout, which meant ascending to high ground once more. They continued another mile but nothing suitable appeared; then with time running low the shadow of a hill loomed to their left, and they hastily departed the road and started to climb. They struggled up through the usual thick mud, and by the time they neared the top dawn was close. But the hill was devoid of trees, and they could see no useful clefts in the rock or large boulders to use as cover, while the summit itself was shrouded in cloud. 'Up there,' Pritchard ordered. 'Maybe there's some cover, and at least the cloud will hide us.'

The mist was damp and cold. They stumbled up into it and searched, but found nothing but a few straggly juniper bushes. With no other option, and fatigued beyond caring, they crawled into them, ate some chocolate and fell into exhausted slumber. Theo waited, munching dried pemmican until all were snoring. Then, retrieving his flashlight, he dug into his rucksack for the package from Smith.

It had been haunting him all night. He'd tried to ignore it, tried to banish it from consciousness, but it kept coming back, like a recurring bad dream. *At an appropriate moment you slip away,* Smith had said. But when? *That's for you to decide.*

His name was Andreas Ladurner, he read, which was a shock, but then also logical thinking by someone, he recognized, being the name he was born with and registered under in Bolzano. His place and date of birth were the same too, in fact very little was doctored or made up, not his height, hair or eye colour, not even the photograph which was from Kingston Grammar School, of him smiling vaguely in jacket and tie. In fact it wasn't a false identity, he realized, it was simply his 'other' identity, the one belonging to his other Italian self. Which made perfect sense, he had to concede. He was a legally registered citizen going about his lawful business and, if checked, this would be borne out by official records.

At least, it would be for as long as his other 'other' identity, the half-English one which had fled Italy to fight for the British, remained undiscovered.

He dreamed he was in his bedroom above the print shop in Bolzano. It was morning and the town's women were at market, gossiping animatedly as they shopped. They seemed far away, their voices tinkling like music, but getting nearer; then he knew he wasn't dreaming and straightened stiffly up, groggy with sleep, to find himself staring into the eyes of an elderly peasant leaning on a crook twenty yards away. The mist had gone and bright early-morning sunlight warmed the hillside; he and his compatriots lay in plain view.

'Um, Major Pritchard.' From down the hill rose the murmur of approaching women and the excited laughter of children. 'Major, I think you'd better wake up.'

Ten minutes later Pritchard's party was standing amid an animated crowd of women and children, all noisily inspecting the '*Angeli inglesi*' like sightseers on a village outing. They weren't hostile, they were curious, and amused; there was much pointing and passing of comment.

'What do we do now, boss?' one of Pritchard's men asked.

'Nothing reckless. We don't want civilians getting hurt.'

'I vote we fire a round over their heads and make a dash for it.'

'Dash where? We're surrounded.'

'Good point.'

'What are they saying, Trickey?'

'Um, they know who we are, I'm afraid, sir. English angels from the sky, they're calling us, the ones who blew up their aqueduct.'

'God, you mean they've been tracking us all along?'

'It rather looks like it.'

Another party was labouring up the hill, a more official one, possibly a mayor, accompanied by a civilian clerk and two elderly policemen in plumed helmets hefting ancient muskets.

'Now what? Home Guard?'

'Sir, if we don't make a break for it now. . .'

'Hold your ground, Corporal!'

The mayoral party arrived, red-faced and puffing, and elbowed its way to the front of the throng, which by now numbered a hundred or more. Having mopped his brow, the clerk, who was wearing a tightly buttoned suit with bow tie, produced notes and began to read a lengthy pronouncement. Theo listened, noting as he did so that men with shotguns and hunting rifles had appeared at intervals along the ridge of the hill above.

'Um, he says, in effect, that his excellency District Under-Secretary Caballo, here, is formally and, er, respectfully, arresting us for the wilful destruction of Italian government property, namely the water-conveying structure at Tragino, and that we are to lay down all weapons and submit—'

'Submit, my arse. I'm getting the fuck out—'

'How, Corporal?' Pritchard snapped. 'By shooting women and children? And have you see those lads up there? They've been trailing us the whole time, and those are telescopic sights on their rifles. How far do you think you'd get?'

'But, sir. . .'

'I'm sorry, everyone. It's over.'

They were disarmed, searched, escorted down the hill and marched into the nearby village of Teora, where they were met by a far less friendly crowd who jeered and spat as they passed. And waiting at the police station was another unpleasant surprise: two lorries were parked outside, one containing armed *carabinieri* military police, the other containing one of the other X Troop parties from the aqueduct. Led by Captain Lea, they too looked filthy and exhausted; some also showed cuts and bruises on faces and arms. Among them was a worried-looking Fortunato Picchi, nursing a bloody nose.

'A civilian was killed by one of our boys, Theo,' he murmured. 'It became ugly.'

Worse was to come. As they waited, the crowd began to shout angrily, chanting '*Viva Il Duce!* Death to the terrorists!' and surging menacingly forward until the *carabinieri* had to form a defensive ring round their captives. Meanwhile Deane-Drummond sidled up to Theo.

'Didn't expect you to still be here.'

'No, sir. Thought I should stay as far as the rendezvous.'

'Bad idea, by the looks of it.'

Then a car screeched to a halt and four men disembarked wearing the black shirts, jodhpurs and boots of the feared Fascist government militia. With them was the stationmaster from the farm by the aqueduct, the one who had protested his importance and complained about carrying the stores. Followed by the Blackshirts he set about searching among the prisoners.

'Him! And him!' He pointed to Picchi and Theo. 'Those are the Italian traitors!'

They were separated, handcuffed and bundled at gunpoint into the back of the car, which sped off, pulling up ten minutes later outside a municipal courtroom in a town Theo guessed was Caposele. Here they were again roughly searched, before being thrown into a dungeon-like cell in the basement. The cell was cold and bare, with concrete platforms for beds, a stinking hole in the ground for a toilet and a barred window looking out on a courtyard. They were given neither food nor water; no one came; they heard no sound of other prisoners. Minutes passed, then hours, and as they did so Picchi became more agitated and anxious.

'They're going to do for me, Theo.'

'No, Fortunato, don't say that. We just stick to the story, and we'll be back with the others before we know it.'

'It's all right for you, you look English and speak perfect English, and have British antecedents. But I don't, I'm Italian by birth, my parents are Italian, I look Italian, I even speak English with an Italian accent. It doesn't matter that I took British citizenship, they'll see it as treachery and they'll do for me.'

The afternoon wore slowly on. As the barred shadow of the window crept across the floor, Picchi took to sitting in a corner, hugging himself. Then suddenly the door crashed open and two guards hauled him out. Thirty minutes later he was returned and thrown to the floor, his face bloody, his chest heaving for breath.

'Fortunato!' Theo knelt at his side. 'My God, what happened?'

'They don't believe me!'

'What do you mean? Here, try sitting up, let me help you.'

'They don't believe I'm British. I told you. They say I am to be shot as a spy!'

Ten minutes later it was Theo's turn. The bolt banged and the two guards grabbed him, dragging him by the neck along a corridor to an office-like room with table and chair. In the chair sat one of the Blackshirts from the car. Theo stood, his hands cuffed before him, the guards waiting behind.

'Who are you?' the Blackshirt asked in Italian. 'And what are you doing here engaged in treacherous acts of terrorism?'

Theo said nothing. A moment later an explosion of pain knocked him to one knee as a fist hit him in the back.

'Answer!'

'Trickey,' he gasped in English. '71076 Private Theodor Trickey. That is all I'm required to say.'

Another punch followed by a vicious kick to the legs brought him to the ground. A storm of kicks and blows from the two guards followed, on his back, his ribs, his legs, too fast to follow, too brutal to assimilate. He curled into a foetal position and tried to protect his head with his arms. The assault went on, from feet and fists, and then suddenly he was dragged upright once more.

The Blackshirt lit a cigarette. 'You speak Italian like a native. It was heard by the guards, observed by the locals, witnessed by the stationmaster, so let us not pretend. Otherwise everything will go very badly for you, very quickly.'

'All right,' Theo panted, 'all right, I speak Italian. My grandparents were Italian, on my mother's side. But my father is English and I have British citizenship.'

The Blackshirt nodded, blowing smoke. 'This is your story. Rather like your friend's. I say it is all lies, and that you are both terrorist traitors and spies.'

'What?' Theo hesitated, head still dazed from the beating. 'But. . .'

'As traitors and spies you are liable to the ultimate punishment. I have two choices. I can throw you to the crowd who will lynch you, disembowel you, stuff your genitals in your mouths and hang you naked from lamp-posts until you are dead. Then they will drag your bodies through the streets and leave them for the dogs. . .'

'No, I—'

'Or I can execute you by firing squad. One at dusk, one at dawn, then hang your bodies in the square as a warning to others.'

'This is a mistake—'

'Take him away!'

After a further cursory beating in the corridor, he was returned to the cell and flung to the floor. He lay there, head ringing, mouth bloody, his body hot with pain, listening to the pounding of his heart, his own hoarse breaths and the receding footsteps of the guards. After a while he opened his eyes and forced himself to a sitting position. Picchi was in his corner, body hunched and rocking, muttering to himself.

'Fortunato?' Theo coughed, 'Fortunato, we must try and get out of here.'

'It's impossible. They know, they know!'

'No, they're guessing, but we must find a way to get out.'

'It's impossible.'

A pitcher of water and two stale crusts had been left in his absence. He crawled to the jug and drank greedily. Then he rose painfully to his feet and began searching the cell. He found nothing but cigarette ends and a piece of wire. Then he began examining the window. It was small, perhaps two feet square, and set high, well above eye level. It had no glass, but two vertical bars of wrought iron cemented into the sill.

'We have our blades.' Theo plucked at the stitching around his collar. 'The hacksaw blades, Fortunato. Come on, we'll take turns.'

'But they'll hear. Anyway I can't reach, I'm too short.'

'Then stand on my back.'

They tried. By stretching on tiptoe Theo could just reach the bars with one hand and saw the blade back and forth with the other. But it was exhausting work and he was soon numb with exertion and gasping for breath. He then had to crouch on all fours while Picchi stood on his back and stretched up to saw.

Repeatedly they had to stop, sometimes for minutes on end, when they heard footsteps in the courtyard or voices in the corridor. And all the while the sun's shadow crept across the floor. After a while, Picchi gave up and returned to sitting in his corner. Drenched in sweat, Theo too slumped to the floor for a breather. Evening had come, the building fallen quiet. He tried the piece of wire on his handcuffs but it bent and broke. The cuffs were old, however, and improperly fastened, and by twisting his hands he felt he might just get them off, albeit while losing some flesh. Spitting on his wrist he began working at it.

Then the door crashed open.

'You!' The guards pointed. 'Out!'

'No!'

They dragged Picchi up and out into the corridor and a moment later the door slammed and all Theo could hear were his friend's anguished cries as they hauled him away. Silence fell for some minutes, then he heard commotion in the courtyard: marching feet, shouted orders, a lengthy announcement. Jumping to the bars, he hauled himself to eye level in time to see the firing squad take aim, hear the shout *'Sparate!'* and watch the explosion of a dozen rifles.

He sawed. Blind to the pain, he wrenched the handcuffs from his wrists, retrieved both blades, reached up to the window and sawed, long into the night, long after his throat was burning up from thirst, the sweat was pouring down his neck, and his fingers were in shreds and slippery with blood. The bar was thick, but the iron poor and the blades keen. As one grew too hot to hold he swapped it for the other; as his right arm tired from hanging he turned his back to the wall and hung from his left. Some time around midnight he was still feebly sawing when he heard a sudden 'clink' and looked up to see the bar was severed. Still hanging from the other he then set about levering the broken one aside to create a gap. Finally it was done and, pausing only to check all was quiet outside, he jumped up one final time and wriggled out into the night.

It took him another hour to work his way back, cross-country, to the hill by the village. Moving swiftly but stealthily, keeping to high ground and pausing at the slightest noise, he reached it undetected, soon locating the juniper bush where they'd hidden. His pack was where he'd buried it. He retrieved it, drank water and ate pemmican, heaved the pack on to his shoulders and set off once more. The weather was overcast, with a cold wind blowing scud over the mountaintops. He had his flashlight, maps, food and water. And twenty-four hours to the rendezvous. By dawn he'd covered ten miles and reached the spa town of Contersi Termi where the fast-flowing headwaters of the River Sele rose. On the outskirts he stole men's working clothes from a line and fruit from an orchard. Avoiding the town he descended to the riverbank and began searching among the overhanging trees and mud banks until he found what he wanted, which was a *canoa di pesca*, a canoe-like fishing skiff beached among the reeds. Throwing his pack inside, he picked up the paddle and pushed off into the current.

It took all day. At first the going was wild and headlong with torrents of fast-flowing melt-water crashing in fearsome white rapids over the rocks and boulders. The *canoa* pitched and tipped alarmingly, repeatedly shipping water until he had to land and empty it. Gradually, guiding it with the paddle as he had learned in childhood, he descended the rapids to wider sections of quieter water. By late afternoon he was in the lower reaches, passing towns like Persano and Torrette, the river widening, turning brackish and slow, and he had to paddle harder. Finally at Ponte Barizzo he reached the lowland plain leading to the sea and with darkness falling he beached the skiff and set off on foot. The ground was open farmland, flat and exposed and criss-crossed with dykes and irrigation ditches. He kept to the riverbank which, though winding, was more wooded. Another five miles and he could smell the sea, and slowed his pace, probing cautiously forward, pausing to listen, advancing again. Then his boots trod into sand, he heard the crashing of surf and glimpsed the flashing of a light. He knelt, watching the light, but it was no submarine, it was a navigation mark, showing the point where the Sele joined the sea. He'd arrived. He sank to the dunes, taking cover beside a jumble of rocks, and fumbled for his flashlight.

He stayed until dawn. No one came. No third aqueduct party, nobody from Daly's missing team. And no submarine. Every hour on the hour he pointed his flashlight out to sea and signalled three dots and a dash, morse code for 'V'. No answering signal ever came. In a pouch in his pocket were his written notes of the aqueduct operation, the retreat and capture of the two escaping groups, details of the two missing ones, his arrest by Blackshirts, and the murder of Fortunato Picchi. He also had Harry Boulter's letter to his wife. Had the submarine come he would have handed them all to its captain. And stayed on board for the return to Valetta? Or taken the dinghy ashore again for the mission to Rome? He didn't know which, for it was a question he didn't dare ask himself. Now there was no option, so no need to ask it. Burying his report and army pack in the sand, he slipped Smith's packet into the pocket of his stolen clothes and crept away into the trees.

CHAPTER 13

Following my day-release with Inge Brandt in Bergen I return to Stalag XIB that evening together with the much-needed medical supplies. Driving in through those gates is a depressing moment, not just because XIB is such an appalling dump, but also because today is the first day I've spent away from everyone since leaving England, and it has made an indelible impression: the open air, the leafy town, the spotless hospital, Inge's quiet intensity, the drive in her car, the dreadful shock of the camp in the forest. Our strangers' embrace. I feel a strong urge to reflect upon it all in private, write it down even, but there's no privacy to be found in a POW camp, and I've nothing to write with, so I'm soon plodding into the overcrowded lazaret with its stink of pus, sewage and malodorous menfolk. I'm greeted warmly however, or at least the stores are, by our new CO, Major Philip 'Pip' Smith. During the day, following Colonel Alford's departure, Smith, being next in seniority, has assumed command of the medical team, and has clearly been busy organizing things. A quiet man, modest but determined, he's even visited Möglich, which is courageous of him, and after another 'supper' of boiled cabbage and potatoes he calls us together for an update.

'Möglich couldn't have been nicer,' he begins, 'so I don't trust him an inch. Bill Alford's threats must have got through, because he's promised to look at the stores and supplies situation, find some extra blankets, heating coal and so on.'

'What about the food? This slop is beyond a joke.'

'Yes, he says he'll look into that too, although don't expect miracles. In fact don't expect anything – he's a slippery bastard and no question. All we can do is cope as best we can and keep nagging him. Hopefully matters will improve in the next week or two. Meanwhile, at least we've got the supplies Garland brought back from Bergen.'

Murmurs of approval, then: 'So how was it, Dan?'

I'm taken aback rather, and oddly reticent. But I give them the basics.

'Bergen's pretty small, but the hospital's good, well staffed and equipped, and I'm sure our wounded will be looked after properly. The clinical director is trying to arrange further supplies for us too. She'll contact Möglich when she has news.'

'She?'

'Yes. Name of Brandt. Pretty helpful. Her husband was the major in charge of the Apeldoorn train.'

'Did you get out and about?'

'I. . . Not really. Didn't see much military activity either. The hospital staff were civil; the locals seemed, well, normal. That's about it.'

'Much bomb damage?'

'Not that I saw. As I say, a small town so probably of little strategic value.'

Not what they want to hear. What I'd seen in fact was ordinary people going about their lives with little sign of the suffering, submission and surrender we've been expecting and hoping for since crossing into Germany. Which is disheartening. Yes, common sense tells us the war is nearing its end, and yes, we're confident of victory, but here in the rural heartlands, there isn't much sign of it.

Pip Smith reads our thoughts. 'We're going to have to face it. We're stuck here for the winter at least.'

A dismal prospect, and over the next couple of weeks a dismal pattern evolves. Roused rudely at dawn by shouts of '*Heraus!*' and '*Aufstehen!*' we seven medical officers descend from our bunks after a freezing night on the unyielding slats and make our bleary way to the washroom, there to queue for the one toilet, and then the one basin, where we scrape painfully at our chins with blunt razors before returning for a 'breakfast' of coffee made from acorns and bread made from potato starch. Thus nourished, twelve hours of unremitting labour follows, attending to the three hundred wounded men in our care. The work is relentless and exhausting. We get half an hour for a cabbage-soup lunch, and by six or so in the evening, after more soup, possibly laced with shreds of rancid horsemeat, we're finished for the day, literally and figuratively. Some desultory chat, a half-hearted game of chess, a smoke of precious tobacco, then the doors and window shutters slam, the lights go out and it's back to the bunks for another freezing night on the slats.

It's an abject existence made worse by the overcrowding (we doctors are six to a room, the men up to twenty), the onset of winter, and most of all by the condition of the patients, which in many cases seems to be getting worse not better. By now their treatment is about after-care, or should be, as the business of managing their injuries – debriding dead tissue, setting bones, stitching up wounds – has long been completed. So the focus is on recuperation, that is keeping their wounds clean, draining pus, changing dressings, and building up their strength and resistance to infection. The problem is that their diet is so poor, the overcrowding so acute and the sanitary arrangements so awful that many are going backwards with their convalescence, with wounds becoming reinfected, fevers breaking out, healthy tissue turning necrotic and so on. To add to their woes a gastro-enteritis bug strikes, bringing extra suffering to many, including some doctors and orderlies. With little at our disposal to fight it with, all we can do is mop the vomit and look on helplessly. One victim particularly hard hit is Jack Bowyer, whom I visit most evenings.

'Hello, Sergeant, how are you tonight?'

'Bloody awful, Doc, since you ask.'

'Managed to scrounge you a couple of M&B.' I hold out sulfonamide tablets.

He lifts his head. 'Where the hell did you get those?'

'The French. Two packs of cigarettes.'

'Bastard Frogs.' He flops back. 'You should save 'em for the lads.'

'Doctors and orderlies take priority: you know that. We need you fit again.'

'Bollocks to priority. Anyway I'd only puke them up.'

'As you wish.' I check him over, starting with his pulse.

Looking weak and pale, his cheeks hollow, his eyes sunken and darkly ringed, he's a shadow of the man I dropped into Arnhem with. Wasting, like all the others, to a husk before our eyes. Anger. I'm starting to feel these days, for the first time, real anger at the Germans for perpetuating this misery. It's a novelty, I find. Helps focus the mind.

'You're going to get through this, Jack.'

He leans over to retch. 'Not sure I can be buggered.'

A few days later comes a development. Two. Firstly, another shipment of medical supplies from Inge Brandt; a sizeable load too, it arrives by truck, the French looking on with envy as we unload it. There's also a note, for me.

Dear Doctor Garland,

I hope you find these of value. I regret it is the last we can send. A directive has been issued: all spare medical supplies must be diverted to the Front; infractions will be punished severely. As a result, we will run short ourselves (although I will keep some for the women we visited).

Your wounded men continue to make progress. Two will be returned to you in the next few days; however, Private Trickey remains unconscious, stable but critical. I would like to retain him a while longer. Good luck on your journey. Remember our discussion.

Sincerely,

Inge Brandt

What journey? I wonder. Then I remember our conversation about trains, and realize she's being metaphorical. Or not. For as I'm helping unload the stores into our makeshift dispensary, I receive a sharp prod in the back from a rifle.

I turn in annoyance. 'What!'

'*Zum Kommandanten!*' the offending guard demands.

Irritation, fatigue, hunger, the incessant shouting, the unnecessary prodding: suddenly I've had enough. 'Go away, I'm busy.'

His eyes widen. '*Zum Büro des Kommandanten! Beeile dich!*'

Evidently Möglich wants me, and right now. But welling up inside, for the first time I can recall, certainly the first time since dropping into Holland, is a sudden and overwhelming urge to stand up to my enemy. Actually fight him, which since I'm an unarmed medic carrying cardboard boxes and he's a trained killer hefting a rifle, may be admirable, but rather foolish.

'I said, I am *busy*, you irritating lout!'

Instantly there's a metallic click as he chambers a round, and I'm staring down the barrel of his gun, which is levelled at my nose. Everyone stops, silence descends, a stand-off follows. Obviously rifle beats cardboard box, so my one-man rebellion is crushed before it begins, yet anger and obstinacy are overriding common sense and I stand there glaring at the man, waiting, daring him even to pull the trigger. Seconds tick as my resolve wavers, and then Pip Smith comes to the rescue.

'It's all right, Dan, we can manage the rest. You'd better pop over and see what the silly bugger wants.'

I follow the guard across the compound, buttoning my uniform and pondering what just took place. Uncharacteristic rashness, I conclude. Soon we reach the admin block and wait to be admitted, and I'm wondering what Möglich does want, and whether the guard will report my insurrection, and find I don't care much, although I do secretly hope he's sending me to Inge Brandt's again.

No chance. I'm frog-marched in: '*Links rechts, links rechts, halt!*' Beret off, stamp to attention, chin up and salute.

Möglich barely looks up. 'Stalag 357,' he says, waving a note. '*Morgen.*'

Returning from his office I bump into Padre Pettifer.

'Hello, old chap, why the long face?'

'I'm being transferred. To another camp.'

'Which one?'

'Stalag 357.'

'Ha!' He beams. 'Then fortune has favoured you, dear boy. By all accounts it's a holiday camp compared with this place.'

Pip Smith greets the news less cheerfully. 'For God's sake, I'm already short-handed! Now he's taking another bloody doctor. I'm sorry, Dan, I'll have to lodge an official complaint and try and stop this.' Off he stumps, only to return twenty minutes later saying the order apparently came from a 'higher authority' and there's nothing anyone can do to change it, not even Möglich.

I keep quiet and wonder which higher authority it could be, and then spend the rest of the day as the least popular man in camp. It's odd, but there's a definite change in attitude once the news circulates: suddenly I'm *persona non grata*, shunned by my peers as if I've betrayed them. Nothing is overtly said or done, but the resentment is palpable: You're getting out, we're not, and that's the nub of it. Nor can I pretend 'I'd much rather stay here with you chaps' or 'Maybe this new camp's no better' because everyone knows neither is true. Even the patients give me short shrift.

'You could refuse,' Jack Bowyer says when I visit him. 'You should, in my view.'

'How?'

'I don't know. Go on hunger strike or something.'

'I thought I already was.'

This raises a wry smile, which is a good sign as far as his recovery goes.

'I wish you were coming with me.'

'Now you're talking. Fetch my boots will you, Doc?'

We chuckle at the notion. 'Seriously though, it's the end for me, isn't it? As far as the Paras go.'

'Probably be some Paras at this new camp.'

'Not from Arnhem. Not from 1st Airborne. None who've been through what we have. Together.'

Next morning I'm roused even earlier than usual and spend twenty minutes washing and packing and clumping about in the dark trying not to disturb everyone. Irritated grunts and groans follow my progress, until eventually I'm ready, my worldly goods packed in my haversack, my beret on my head, my heart oddly heavy.

'Cheerio, old chap,' Pip Smith murmurs unexpectedly from his bunk. 'Good luck.'

Suddenly I'm saluting him in the darkness. 'And good luck to you, sir.'

'We'll need it. *Waho Mohammed.*'

'*Waho Mohammed.*'

My escort for the journey is a jug-eared youth of about seventeen. He signs me out at the gate and we set off on foot towards the gathering dawn. The weather is cold and clear; the tree-lined road silent save for the crunch of our boots. My guard speaks no English, and offers no comment or conversation, but after a while we find ourselves falling into step and are soon marching along at a good clip. The exercise and fresh morning air energize me, and as Stalag XIB slips steadily behind I find my spirits rising, as though a weight has been lifted. Pretty soon I'm whistling 'Colonel Bogey', which to my amusement my escort joins with, clearly unaware of the 'libretto'. After an hour we arrive in Fallingbostel, and continue through the town to the station, which I last saw from the Apeldoorn train. He buys tickets at the office; then, checking the station clock, he gestures that we have thirty minutes to wait.

'*Frühstück?*' I try some newly acquired German. 'Breakfast?'

'*Ja ja, Frühstück,*' and to my surprise he leads me to the station cafeteria where upon production of a chit we're served with rather better ersatz coffee and bread than at camp. The girl behind the counter even produces a pot of jam, passing it over with a shy smile. Outside the concourse is growing busy with morning commuters, mainly women, although also some men in uniform. Army, I note, with only a smattering of Luftwaffe and Kriegsmarine. Some glance my way but most do not, which is odd, for a British Tommy having coffee with a German officer at St Pancras would certainly raise eyebrows. Perhaps after five years they don't care any more. Or they've learned to look the other way, as Inge Brandt implied. For safety.

Sure enough, a little later, just as we're preparing to leave, the cafeteria doors swing open and two men in civilian suits and overcoats enter. Nothing about their dress or demeanour betrays their purpose or occupation – they could be bank managers or civil servants or even doctors for all I know – but an immediate frisson of tension passes through the room like a chill, and my young escort practically jumps from his skin. Especially when he sees them heading for us.

'*Papiere*,' barks one, snapping his fingers, and the youth nervously produces a bundle. Meanwhile the second man orders coffee from the terrified waitress by simply lifting his chin. I now sense exactly what these two are about and deliberately turn my back. A full five minutes then elapses, the cafeteria almost silent, while they drink coffee and pore over our papers. Meanwhile my escort is growing increasingly anxious.

'*Unser zug. . .*' he pleads. Our train.

'*Warten Sie!*'

We wait as ordered until, apparently satisfied that all is in order, the documents are at last returned to him. Then the first man turns to me, scrutinizing my beret and wings with undisguised contempt.

'Terrorist,' he says in English.

'Doctor,' I reply. 'And you?'

'*Heil Hitler.*' He flings out a Nazi salute, and the pair walk out.

A collective exhalation circles the cafeteria. Then conversation resumes as if nothing happened.

'Gestapo?' I say to my guard.

He mops his brow. 'Gestapo.'

CHAPTER 14

With the winter sun rising over the coastal plain to his right, Theo set out along the shoreline, speed-marching three miles north to the seaside village of Caselle. Time was now of the essence, time and distance, for his prison escape was more than twenty-four hours old, and though his pursuers couldn't know his exact location or intentions, X Troop had been caught making for the coast, so they'd assume the same and search accordingly. In his favour, they were chasing a desperate British Tommy, not a scruffy Italian labourer, so he entered Caselle unnoticed, mingling with workers waiting for a bus to the city. Squeezing aboard, nobody paid him heed and he was soon jolting north towards the factories and mills of Salerno sixteen miles up the coast. There he headed for the station, stopping at shops en route to buy clothes suitable for a medical student, including sports jacket, shirts, tie, cap and toiletries, and a small suitcase to carry them in. Finally buying new shoes, he buried his old clothes and army boots in rough ground behind the stadium, and under his new guise of Andreas Ladurner continued to the station, where he bought a ticket for Rome. With the cash Smith had given him plus the fifty thousand lire from his battledress lining, he was more than adequately financed, so as he waited he bought a shave and haircut, and breakfasted on coffee and *biscotti* at the station buffet. There, surrounded by the alien yet familiar chatter of Italian accents, and watchful for cruising *carabinieri*, he picked up a newspaper, scouring its pages for mention of the aqueduct raid. He found none, but to his shock did see photos of Erwin Rommel, in Rome apparently meeting military chiefs. By late morning he was aboard his train, rocking gently north out of Salerno, skirting the cone of Vesuvius and sprawling suburbs of Naples, and heading into the softer hills and plains of Lazio. The view was restful, the carriage quiet, the motion soporific, but he was too keyed up to relax, and passed the hours scrutinizing his fellow passengers and staring at his own hunted reflection in the window. At Cassini he was jolted from his reverie when the train suddenly stopped and armed *carabinieri* boarded, passing through the carriages checking everyone's papers. He waited, heart pounding, trying to appear calm and praying the check was routine; when his turn came the policeman flicked through his papers, holding up his *carta d'identità* and glancing between his face and his Kingston school photo before handing it back without comment. Twenty minutes later the train was on its way again, arriving at Rome's Termini Station early in the evening. He found a *pensione* nearby, checked in under the Ladurner name, clumped wearily up to his room and collapsed on the bed.

When he woke later, darkness had fallen and his room was shrouded in shadows. He blinked blearily at the ceiling, trying to marshal his thoughts. The flight from Malta, blowing the aqueduct, crossing the mountains, capture, interrogation,

Picchi's execution, escape, fleeing to the sea and the final fruitless wait for rescue. All in just four days: could it be possible? And now this. An insane mission to contact revolutionaries – and the chance to see his grandparents again – all just a few miles from where he now lay. With the sheet round his shoulders, he padded barefoot to the window and threw open the shutters. Raucous noise and cold night air greeted him, while below the city spread out like a twinkling blanket. Theoretically blacked out against air raids, lights still showed everywhere, the whole city refusing to be subdued, heaving and buzzing with irrepressible life. Car horns blared, horses clopped, street-sellers shouted, cooking and wood-smoke smells rose, mingling with the musical murmur of Romans on the streets. This was not his home, this Italy of the metropolitan south, and never had been, but as he watched and listened he sensed something elemental stirring within him, calling to him like siren song. Unable to resist, he donned his new clothes, descended the stairs and stepped into the night.

The next day he paid his first visit to the infamous Regina Coeli prison, located across the muddy waters of the Tiber beside the Mazzini Bridge. Unfamiliar with the old city's bewildering layout, finding his way took longer than anticipated and he arrived later than Smith's suggested time of noon. Then he expended precious minutes pacing the street outside, eyeing the prison's daunting façade and knowing his fate, indeed probably his life, hung on two slender threads: the papers in his pocket and the strength of his nerve.

'Who the fuck are you?' demanded the guard at the gatehouse.

'My name is Ladurner. I, um, I have travelled from South Tyrol to visit an inmate here, my grandfather, Josef Ladurner.'

'Then you've wasted your time, mountain boy. Visiting's over, and anyway all visits are by strict pre-arrangement only.'

'I understand this but have travelled a long way. The trains, you know.'

'Tell me about it.'

'And I do have the necessary permits. See here.'

Heated negotiation followed, plus a long and detailed scrutiny of his papers, which included permissions from the Ministries of Justice and Interior, and a letter of reference from a Fascist Party functionary, all forged, Theo presumed, like his identity card, by Smith and his team. Evidently, however, they passed muster and after a body search for contraband he was admitted through a series of heavy steel doors and corridors to a bare room furnished with metal tables and chairs. Then Josef appeared.

'Grandfather.'

'By all the heavens, Andreas, is it really you?'

'Yes, Grandfather, it is me.'

He was older, slighter, greyer and more stooped of posture, but the gleam in his eye was still piercing, his smile broad and his hair stiff and straight like a brush. 'My God, Andreas, look at you! I was told you might visit one day but, I mean, all the way from Bolzano, I never thought. . .'

They drew up chairs. In doing so Josef caught Theo's eye and nodded at the ceiling, indicating their conversation was monitored. And throughout it he switched constantly between Italian, German and Ladin languages and never once mentioned England, nor referred to Theo as anything but Andreas.

'How are your medical studies, my boy?'

'They are progressing, Grandfather. More importantly, how are you?'

He looked well, Theo had to concede, despite his incarceration, now entering its fifth year. Older, perhaps slower, and with, he noticed, a slight tremor to his right hand, but as Josef spoke of life as a political prisoner, a mischievous glint soon entered his eye, and he became earnest and animated.

'This place is stuffed full of great brains!' he murmured in Ladin. 'Academics and intellectuals, political thinkers, theologians and writers: it is a repository of wisdom and conscience. Oh, the discussions we have! And the arguments, of course, everyone has their own opinions!' He lowered his voice further. 'There is dissent too, and much mistrust, even among our own, but collectively we are a great thorn in Il Duce's side – you know, one he will not silence and cannot ignore.'

'Yes, Grandfather, but I trust you are being prudent?'

'Pah!' Josef's voice fell to a whisper. 'His time is limited. He knows it and so do we. Then we shall see!' He glanced at the ceiling again. 'You have something for me, I believe. . .'

'What? Oh, um, yes.' He fumbled at his pockets.

'Not now! When we leave, embrace me.'

'Right. Sorry.'

'And now...' He sat back. 'Andreas, dear boy, tell me what you can of your family, back in our beloved South Tyrol. Your mother, for instance, how is the dear lady?'

Interned like you, Grandfather, he wanted to say, imprisoned because of her birthright. But he thought better of it. 'She has been through a difficult period recently.'

'So I understand from your Uncle Rodolfo, whom you must also visit. . .'

'Yes I will—'

'. . . with great caution.'

'Ah, right, well—'

'. . . and also your grandmother whose condition worries me.'

'I will be sure to see her. In the meantime I am hopeful that Mother's situation will, um, improve soon.'

'I too. Let us thank heaven for that. Please pass her my very best wishes when next you see her. In Bolzano.'

They spoke further in generalities, of news from home, the continuing struggle for South Tyrolean autonomy, the progress of the war and Italy's expansionist aims, daily life in the prison, the food and exercise arrangements, then a guard entered and the visit drew to a close. They rose from the table, hugged briefly, Theo passed the crucial letter for Gino Lucetti, and the task was completed.

As he was led from the room Josef turned and spoke once more.

'One piece of rather sad news, Andreas.'

'Oh, yes?'

'Your teacher, at school back in Bolzano, what was the name?'

'Do you mean Herr Adler?'

'No, the other teacher. At the *other* school.'

'You mean Miss Angeletti. Nikola Angeletti at the, um, catacomb school.'

'That's her. Got arrested and thrown in jail. Up in Trento, when I was there. She died of maltreatment and starvation. Murdered by the oppressor. So young, so courageous, simply for teaching and trying to do right for her pupils. Come and see me again soon, won't you?'

His great-uncle Rodolfo lived in a tall house in the exclusive Rione XVI quarter, to the south of Villa Borghese. Upon ringing the bell he was admitted by a maid who showed no surprise at his arrival, but led him to an airy fourth-floor bedroom with ornate ceilings and an iron balcony overlooking the Borghese gardens. Signor Zambon was at the Ministry, she explained, his wife and daughter were out shopping, but he was to make himself at home. He dozed for an hour, to be awakened by the creak of footsteps in the corridor outside. These moved back and forth for a while; then his door squeaked open and an old woman appeared.

'Who are you?' she asked.

'Grandmother?'

'Who are you?'

'Grandmother Ellie, it is me Andreas – um, Theodor.'

'You must go!' she replied fearfully. 'You must go, there is danger and betrayal!'

'Where, Grandmother?'

'Everywhere!' Her once lustrous hair was wispy and white, her face pinched, and her eyes hunted anxiously about the room. She showed no sign of recognizing him.

'Grandmother?'

'Go! Before they come!'

Eleanora's mind was going, Rodolfo explained later over dinner. It was the strain of years of conflict in Bolzano, he said, which was Josef's fault, and Carla's. Eleanora had repeatedly begged them to moderate their fanaticism, but they never did, and it had destroyed her nerves.

'What about doctors?'

'Doctors have tried. They do nothing but issue pills which do no good. We take care of her as best we can, but often she doesn't recognize us. She refuses medication and wanders the streets, sometimes all night. If matters continue she will end up at the sanatorium.'

They were sitting in an elegant dining room drinking wine from crystal glasses and eating off flatware from Puglia. Rodolfo looked the same, perhaps more corpulent, but still urbane and stylish with expensive suits and smoothed-back hair. His wife Francesca too was the same as in Theo's memory: coiffed, haughty, suspicious. Only his cousin Renata was transformed, from the gap-toothed tomboy of their youth to a dark and Rubenesque beauty. Although Rodolfo had hinted as such in his letter to Kingston, actually seeing her was a revelation, and he had trouble not staring. The atmosphere at table was of polite curiosity and caution. Francesca spoke little and appeared hostile; Rodolfo was expansive and voluble as always, talking at length of Italy's reascent to global masterpower, while Renata nodded agreement and winked mischievously at Theo. Nobody mentioned aqueducts, his service with the British army, or indeed why he was in Italy at all. After dinner

Rodolfo suggested Renata take him into the old quarter to see the sights. 'But keep away from trouble spots,' he instructed, 'don't talk to undesirables and be home before midnight.'

He lent Theo a serge overcoat; Renata donned sable, took his arm and led him south along wide boulevards lined with municipal buildings sporting neo-classical arches and colonnades. 'Government quarter,' she said, quickening their pace, 'boring as hell. That's Treasury, there's Agriculture, Defence, over there's Justice. Come on, I want to show you something in Trevi.' Hurrying past the Piazza dell'Esedra with its famous Naiads fountain, they were soon entering narrower cobbled streets crowded with tightly packed, stucco-walled houses whose terracotta roofs were criss-crossed with wires and washing lines. Overhead women gossiped, babies cried, couples argued, somebody played a clarinet; at street level old men sat watching the crowds as they wandered the countless bars, *osterie* and restaurants.

'In here!' Renata pulled him down steps to a tavern thick with cigarette smoke and the noise of raucous singing. Elbowing her way through the crowd she dragged Theo up to a tiny stage where three musicians were tuning a violin to a trumpet and accordion. They wore leather breeches with white shirts and scarlet waistcoats and felt hats with goat brushes on the side. Soon they stepped forward and began to play.

'This isn't. . .'

Renata grinned. 'Just listen, Theo!'

It was like being transported to his childhood, to his grandfather's knee in the room above the print shop, listening to folk music on the gramophone while Josef thumped time with his boot: the real Tyrolean music of the mountains, rhythmic, melodic, alive with wit and energy. The tune sounded familiar and he began to clap in time; soon the whole bar was singing and stamping along.

'Thought you'd enjoy a taste of home!' she shouted above the din.

'It's amazing, Renata, thank you, it takes me right back!'

'Remember the ice-cream parlour, and Papa's sports car?'

'How could I not? I was in love with your curls!'

Later they walked slowly home, her arm through his, her head on his shoulder.

'What are you doing here, Theo?' she asked eventually.

'Has your father said anything?'

'Nothing. Only that you are passing through and won't be staying.'

'That is true.'

'Why, where are you going? To England again?'

'My mother needs me.'

'What do you do there?'

'It's complicated. Probably best if we don't go into it.'

'Are you spying on us? For the British?'

'Renata, that's absurd!'

'It's all right, I wouldn't tell. Although Mother thinks you are.'

They had returned to the area near the government quarter. Rounding a corner they arrived at a piazza with stone steps leading to an imposing square-fronted building. A line of black limousines waited below, while on the steps barriers had been erected with policemen to hold back a small crowd of onlookers.

'What is this place?'

'It's the opera. Must be some big-wig concert going on. Come on, let's see.'

As they watched from the barrier, the main doors opened and guests began to emerge, the women in evening gowns and furs, the men in dinner suits or uniforms. After an initial exodus, a second more important cluster appeared, about a dozen men in Italian army uniform, a few senior Blackshirts, several expensively gowned women, and in their midst a solitary figure in field grey, his boots highly shined, his cap and gloves in his hand, the unmistakable glint of the Iron Cross at his throat.

'Good God.'

'Look, it's General Rommel!' Renata clapped excitedly. Others in the crowd were joining the applause, cheering and calling his name; a photographer stepped forward, flashbulbs popping. Rommel appeared surprised at the fuss, but then offered a modest wave before descending the steps with the others. As he passed Renata, still clapping with excitement, he inclined his head politely. Then he saw Theo. And stopped.

His eyes narrowed. 'It is you,' he said in German, 'isn't it?'

'Yes, sir, I'm afraid so.'

Rommel began buttoning his gloves, then glanced back at the opera house. '*Amleto*, by Faccio, based on Shakespeare's *Hamlet*. Good story, rather indifferent music, I found. Do you know it? The play, that is.'

'Um, well, no, sir, not really.'

Rommel nodded. 'I shall have to start calling you Horatio.'

With that he continued down the steps to his limousine.

313

Late that night, footfalls sounded outside Theo's room again. There was a squeak as the door opened, but it was not his grandmother this time. He heard the sigh of falling clothes, felt the bed sheets lifting, then Renata's body was pressing against him, her breath hot on his neck. 'Just hold me, Theo,' she whispered. 'Hold me like a husband would.'

The next morning he awoke late with his head throbbing and the house empty. 'The family is out for the day,' the maid informed him brusquely. 'Furthermore, Signor Zambon instructs that you stay here no longer, but at a *pensione*, and he has left money accordingly.' No other explanation was offered, nor did she know when the family might return. 'Your presence displeases the Signora,' was all she said when pressed. Unsure if this was to do with Renata, or his clandestine dealings in Rome, but suspecting the latter, he breakfasted alone, packed his suitcase and departed.

He passed the day aimlessly touring Rome, its *piazze* and *viali*, its statues and fountains, its famous buildings and historic monuments. Unlike London, he noted, Rome was entirely untouched by the ravages of bombs, its residents and visitors appeared blithe and unconcerned, and, apart from uniforms and the occasional strident billboard, it was hard to believe Italy was at war at all. After viewing the Coliseum, the Pantheon and the Circus Maximus chariot stadium, he paused to rest in a bookstore where he researched *Hamlet*, learning that Horatio was the Prince's rather shadowy follower, who didn't really have a history, didn't fit into the narrative, but kept cropping up at key moments. Hamlet himself, he read, flicking to the end, died by poison at the hands of those he once considered allies, while his enemies marched on his homeland.

The hours passed slowly and uneasily, not helped by heavy rain and the nagging headache, both of which intensified in the afternoon, forcing him back to his *pensione*. This suited him, for, apart from feeling cold and ill, he had begun to imagine he was being followed, although with all the crowds it was hard to be sure. Stretching out wearily on the bed, he fretted over the next day's plan, which seemed to grow more impossible with each rehearsal. Return to Regina Coeli prison in the morning; bluff his way past the guards again; have a second meeting with his grandfather to receive instructions from Lucetti, and speak about Eleanora's health and Carla's imprisonment; magically engineer a rendezvous with Lucetti's Action Party cohorts; convince them of his legitimacy, exchange contact information and give assurances of support from the British government; finally make the soonest possible departure to the north, cross the border into Switzerland and report to the British Embassy for transportation home. Round and round his head the details swirled, while his teeth chattered, his body ached and the sheet grew damp with sweat. He dozed feverishly while outside rain lashed at the window and darkness fell. He heard the rumble of thunder and saw himself lying in a rain-filled ditch, in a black wood with artillery shells exploding all round. A figure rose beside him. 'Don't shoot till you smell their breath,' it said, then vanished in a crimson mist. Later he imagined rough hands hauling him away: his head was smothered, he couldn't breathe and his arms were pinned painfully behind him. Then he was dragged blindly downstairs and out into rain-washed streets for a jolting ride on the floor of a car, terrified by giddiness and suffocation. Then nothing but a long fall into the beckoning black.

Time passed, intervals of lucidity came and went like images at a magic lantern show. Waking in terror to a blacked-out room. A midnight cycle ride through a rainy forest. Lying on a hard cot, his hands shackled to the frame. Columns of men stretching into the night like a giant insect. Swimming towards a ship that never came nearer. A figure slumping before a firing squad.

Then he awoke to find a woman kneeling beside his bed. A candle burned nearby; he thought she was praying, and therefore he must be dying, but then her clasped hands unfolded a cloth with which she dabbed his brow.

'He lives,' she muttered, seeing his eyes blink.

'Water,' he croaked feebly.

She tipped a cup to his lips and then departed. Later she returned with a bowl of soup, but his wrists were still manacled, so she fed him by spoon like a baby.

'Where am I?'

'Don't speak.'

'Bathroom, I need—'

'Later.'

She left again. The next time he woke, daylight showed through the curtained window. He was still fastened to the bed, and the urge to urinate was overwhelming, but the fever had broken and his head was clearer. After a while the woman returned bearing a basin and chamber pot. She unfastened one hand and then stood by the window while he used the pot before returning to bathe him with the basin and cloth. She didn't speak but her eyes were anxious as she changed him into clean shirt and underwear before departing once more, locking the door behind her. He dozed. From the sounds of livestock and birdsong beyond the window he guessed it was mid-morning, and he was in the countryside. Later, heavy feet arrived at the door, the lock turned and two men entered, one dark and swarthy, the other slighter with shaved head and spectacles. The larger one stood nervously by the door while the bespectacled one drew out a notebook and pen.

'Name?'

Theo's head spun. So much complication in such a simple question. And who were these men? Kidnappers? Terrorists? Undercover police?

'I. . . I'm not—'

'Tell me your name!'

'Andreas Teodoro Giuseppe Vittorio Ladurner-Trickey.'

The man jotted. 'This will require verification.'

'By who? Who are you?'

'I will ask the questions. Why were you in Rome?'

'To visit relatives.'

'Lies. You are a spy and infiltrator.'

'No.'

'Then answer.'

'I. . . No.' A spark of rebellion flickered inside him, the product of his commando training perhaps. Or the beating from the Blackshirts. 'Not until you tell me what's going on.'

317

'You were apprehended, you are in custody. Say who you are and what you were doing in Rome or you will be executed as a spy.'

'You know who I am, you have my belongings, and my papers; no doubt you have stolen the gold sovereigns too.'

'Everything is being checked. Who ordered you to Italy? Speak now.'

The second man was nodding encouragement, his face pleading. Theo rolled over, turning his back on them both. 'You have my name, you have my belongings; I have nothing further to say.'

'Very well.' He heard the fountain pen screwing shut. 'We believe you are a traitorous infiltrator sent to betray us. Your uncooperative attitude supports this. I will now leave with my report and your belongings and return in due course with our findings. If my suspicions are borne out, you will then be executed. In the meantime you will remain here under lock and key.'

He spent the rest of the day shackled to his bed. Mostly he dozed; once the woman visited, clucking anxiously as she fed him bread and cheese. In the evening the larger of the men returned, standing by the door fingering his cap. Eventually he spoke.

'Il Capitano thinks you're a spy.'

'He is mistaken.'

'I am inclined to agree. Unfortunately it is not my decision.'

'What isn't?'

'What they do with you. I am Cockerel by the way. Cockerel is my code name. My real name is Francesco. This is where I live.'

'I see.' Cockerel's dialect was of the rural interior. 'And where is this?'

'To the south of Rome.'

'Are you Action Party?'

'I'm not supposed to say.'

'Was that your wife earlier?'

'Yes. Her code name is Sparrow. It is cold up here. If I release you from the bed, you can come downstairs where it is warm and meet the others.'

'Others?'

'Yes. But you must promise not to escape and I must lock you up after.'

'I understand.'

Five minutes later he was sitting in a rustic farmhouse kitchen, eating soup, bread and wine brought by Sparrow, who fussed about him as though he were a sickly relative. Also watching closely were about a dozen men of varying ages and appearances ranging from eager youths to wrinkled pensioners. Three women, including Sparrow, were also present. Cockerel appeared to be their spokesman.

'We are one of three cells in the southern Rome department,' he explained. 'All are named after great Italian heroes. Ours is Cellini after the master sculptor and soldier Benvenuto Cellini. There are perhaps twenty cells in all of Italy. We communicate via courier, by hand, using codes and never letters or telephone, although we are hoping to receive radios. From our allies.'

Theo nodded. Still dizzy and weak, he sat wrapped in blankets by the stove, chewing slowly on a crust. 'So you are Partito d'Azione.'

'That is not how we began, but we come under their patronage.'

'What are your aims?'

'Aims?' Cockerel bristled with indignation. 'To overthrow Fascism of course, depose the dictator Mussolini and restore socialism to our nation, nothing less!'

'Do you have weapons?'

'Of course! Well, no, not many. Some hunting guns, a few old carbines. We're hoping for more, obviously, from you – that is, our allies. Explosives and so forth. Along with radios.'

'I have a Springfield rifle!' a youth said excitedly. 'From 1890. It's a beauty!'

'Eighteen ninety, well, that's, um, quite old. And what about organization – you know, like a command structure?'

A pause. 'A what?'

'Ah.'

'We're pissing in the wind.' An old man called Crow spat noisily on the floor. 'We're a disorganized, under-equipped rabble!'

'Now, Crow, that is untrue, I Capitani provide support and instruction—'

'Bah! They are interested only in arguing politics. We are pensioners, farmers, baker's boys: what do we know of organizing revolutions or, or *command structures*!'

Silence fell. Theo looked round the kitchen. Heads were shaking; people stared at their boots; the women exchanged glances. Then Cockerel shrugged.

'I suppose we could do with some help in that department.'

*

He stayed two weeks. Confined at first to his attic prison, after a few days he was allowed out on the promise he didn't escape, so wandered about the farm like a sickly octogenarian, a blanket about his shoulders, sniffing the spring air, sunning his face, watching the goats and chickens before returning to his fireside chair to read and make notes. A few days more and with his strength returning, he began taking closer interest in his surroundings and his hosts, Cockerel and his wife. They had two sons, he learned, both drafted into the army but not heard from in months, and they were tenant farmers in this village on Rome's southern outskirts.

'I must have better confirmation of your identity,' he told them one lunchtime. 'Code names are well and good but the special operations people in London need to know who they are dealing with.'

'You are with special operations in London?' Cockerel asked incredulously.

Theo considered. 'I suppose I am.'

'So what is *your* code name?'

'Mine? I don't have. . .' Disappointment clouded their eyes. '. . . um, well, it's Horatio. But don't tell anyone.'

Most evenings the Cellini cell gathered at the farmhouse, there to chat, drink wine, tell stories, play dominoes and crack jokes. More a social club than a revolutionary organization, Theo decided; he saw little evidence of plotting or planning, apart from frequent enthusiastic toasts to *libertà!* or *democrazia!* and slowly, almost without realizing it, he found himself adopting the role of military adviser.

'Do your meetings not have agendas?' he asked one evening as a sing-song was getting under way.

'What for?'

'For things like, um, you know, priorities.'

'Priorities?'

'What needs to be done, who's going to do it, when, and so on.'

'Everyone!' Crow called out. 'Everyone listen! Horatio thinks our meetings should have agendas. To decide on priorities. What say you?'

Murmurs of misgiving, then: 'Why?'

Suddenly all eyes were on him, like children in a classroom.

'Well, look. You want us, your allies that is, to send you materials, like radios, and weapons and so on.'

'Grenades!'

'Yes, grenades, and—'

'Uniforms!'

'Uniforms, indeed. But the thing is, for them to risk sending aeroplanes to drop these supplies, you must give them something in return. Like information.'

'What information?'

'Things like troop numbers, and movements. Around Rome for example: where the main garrisons are, how many troops live there, air defences, navy ships at the docks and so on. Things that will help *them* to help *you* overthrow the government. When the moment comes.'

Which would be a long time, he knew, for the simple truth was they weren't ready. Apart from absent commanders, code names and good intentions, they had nothing: no structure, no organization, no relevant skills or weapons, nothing. They were children playing a game.

'Tell us about London,' they asked one evening a week or so later. Fed a diet of Fascist propaganda and censorship, his stories of the world beyond Italy were their favourite, and they would listen in rapt fascination. And in growing numbers too, he noted, with new recruits appearing nightly to sign up. Word of the Cellinis, despite his repeated warnings about security, was clearly spreading.

'London?'

'Yes. Our newspapers say it is flattened to rubble, with the vanquished people begging Il Presidente Churchill to surrender. Is this true?'

He thought back to a bus ride through the capital, sitting up top passing the wrecked streets, smoking craters and smashed buildings. And the people, chains of volunteers passing buckets, digging through rubble for a photograph, ornament or child's toy. Suddenly he felt proud to be part of it. Not the death and desecration, but the unity, the sense of common purpose, the gritty black humour.

'No, the Londoners don't beg for surrender, that is not their way. The bombing is cruel and merciless and yes there is much devastation, but Britain is not beaten, far from it, her spirit is strong, and even as we speak she reaches out to attack the enemy.'

Nods of solidarity, then Crow caught his eye. 'So, were you involved with that aqueduct incident down in Campania?'

A breathless hush filled the room. Theo allowed himself a faint smile. 'I have no idea what you're talking about.'

A few mornings later he awoke to the sound of a motorcycle racing up the track. As usual he was locked in his bedroom, but crouching at the window he glimpsed one of Cellini's youths aboard the machine. A moment later feet were crashing up the stairs. 'Horatio! Il Capitano is coming!'

The meeting took place in the kitchen. Theo was escorted downstairs by Cockerel to stand before the same bespectacled man, who was dressed in jacket and cap and sitting at the table. Upon it was a sheaf of documents and Theo's suitcase.

'Why is the suspect not shackled?' the man demanded.

'He gave his word,' Cockerel replied. 'And keeps it.'

'We shall see.' He held a photograph up to Theo. 'Do you recognize this person?'

'No.'

'No?'

'I will not speak to you until I have an explanation.'

'I see.' The man removed his spectacles. 'Then I will give you one.'

His code name was Leon; he was regional secretary of Action Party's ruling council in Rome. The party was still in its infancy and gaining strength every day, but was threatened by dissenting interlopers, competing factions, the State, government spies, secret police, and the Germans, whom nobody trusted. It had therefore to exercise extreme caution in its dealings with outsiders.

'Our objective is to overthrow Mussolini and restore a socialist democracy. By force if necessary. So we have many dangerous enemies. Which brings me to you.' Leon pushed

Theo's suitcase across the table. 'As far as can be ascertained, your story appears genuine.'

'Thank you.'

'But we can't be certain and cannot risk betrayal. Therefore we require a demonstration. As proof of your integrity, and the British government's commitment.'

'A demonstration.'

'Yes. You are supposedly a trained combatant and saboteur. Demonstrate it, and we will supply the information you require to pass to London.'

It was a set-up, Theo sensed immediately. Action Party hadn't the skills or training to mount operations, so were using him for its own political ends. He glanced uneasily at the photograph on the table. Worse soon followed.

'You do recognize him.'

'Yes.'

'Of course.' Leon picked up the photograph. 'Senator Ettore Tolomei, better known as the Undertaker of South Tyrol, scourge of the separatist movement you profess allegiance to. Many innocents has he arrested, including your grandfather; many more he has simply caused to disappear. He advocates the ruthless suppression of any opposition to the Fascist regime. He is a murderer.'

'What has he to do with Action Party?'

'He is one of Mussolini's closest allies and henchmen, and therefore our sworn enemy and a legitimate target. He has a villa not far from here – he uses it when the Senate is sitting. You will go there next Tuesday night and assassinate him.'

CHAPTER 15

He had four days. Before Leon departed, and with his mind
reeling, Theo secured consent for the mission to take place
under his sole control. He would pick his men, he insisted, and
plan and carry out the operation. No one from Action Party
or any other group was to come near. Leon, face impassive
behind his spectacles, agreed, then handed over a package
wrapped in cloth.

'It is a Webley. Old, but in full working order. British too.'

'So I see.' Theo hefted the pistol. 'Is this all?'

'One man. One bullet. What more do you want?'

The next morning he took Cockerel aside. 'Francesco, I need
three good men, and as much weaponry as we can gather.'

'Do you not trust Leon?'

'Action Party has enemies, the Cellinis have enemies, I have
enemies, danger and betrayal lie everywhere and our security
is deplorable. We can trust no one.'

'Then trust me.' Francesco stiffened to attention. 'I will be
your *tenente*.'

'Thank you. You'll be second-in-command, covering our
withdrawal.'

'But can't I lead—'

'No, I need you in the rearguard. Now, two more: fit, fast runners and, um, dependable men. The youth with the Springfield perhaps?'

'Starling, yes, he's keen, and the baker's boy too, Armando, would be suitable.'

'Code name?'

'He hasn't got one yet.'

'Tell him he's Nightjar and they're both to meet us here tomorrow for training.'

'Will do, *capo*.'

'And tell them at all costs to say nothing to anyone. Now, weapons. I must see everything you have.'

By Monday he was as ready as could be. Transportation was by baker's van, supplemented by bicycle. His three-man team was eager and had rehearsed diligently, but the weapons cache was woeful, amounting to one Webley, one Springfield, a couple of shotguns, sundry knives, and three rotting hand grenades of First War vintage.

'More,' he'd pleaded, when he saw them, 'we need much more.'

'Are we expecting trouble?' Cockerel asked.

'We'd be fools not to.'

So Cockerel put out the word, and then he and Theo set to work with petrol cans and wine bottles preparing Molotov cocktails. They also made something Theo called a jam-tin grenade, which was gunpowder from shotgun cartridges packed into a jam-tin with a wick for a fuse. 'It's in the army field manual,' he assured Cockerel. As they were finishing, the old man called Crow appeared on the track leading a mule.

'Artillery.' He gestured proudly at the mule. 'For your mission.'

'How do you know about our mission?'

'Doesn't everybody? It's a cannon.'

Theo examined the device that was strapped to the mule's back. 'It's very small. Is it a toy?'

'A toy! This weapon saw service in the Ethiopian war. Battle of Adowa, 1896!'

'I'm sorry. Does it have, um, cannonballs?'

'Of course! I have six. You light the fuse, drop one in, then fire by pulling this string like a flintlock. Straight up it goes, then *poum* into the ground like a mortar!'

And a while later one of Cellini's women also appeared, limping up the muddy track towards them.

'Good day, Greenfinch,' Cockerel said, 'are you in pain?'

'No, just damned uncomfortable.' Glancing round, she fumbled beneath her skirts and produced a bundle. 'My Giorgio works at the quarry at Velletri. He borrows these sometimes.'

'I see.' Cockerel opened the bundle. 'He borrows sticks of dynamite?'

'For fishing. On the lake.'

That night Theo addressed the Cellinis for the last time. The kitchen was packed, which was worrying, yet since everyone knew all about the mission, pretending it was secret seemed pointless. 'Tomorrow I must leave,' he began. 'If all goes well I will be reporting your good work to my superiors in a few weeks. If not I will most likely be dead in a ditch, or taken into captivity. In that event you must disband immediately and make no contact with each other until safe to do so. Thank you for your faith and,um, solidarity, I wish you good health and victory: *la salute e la vittoria!*'

Much singing, carousing and back-slapping followed, together with frequent toasts and copious glasses of wine and grappa. Theo yearned for solitude and calm and a good night's rest, but the Cellinis' buoyant mood was infectious and soon he found himself thinking of X Troop, and Colossus, and sitting in the hut at Valetta the night before the mission, joshing and joking with Fortunato, Harry Boulter, Tag Pritchard and the others. As though keeping a tradition.

The old man Crow sidled up to him, his eyes rheumy with wine. 'Wish I was coming with you, my boy.'

'Next time perhaps.'

'Indeed.' Crow leaned closer. 'So how will you do it? Deal with Tolomei, that is.'

Theo drained his glass. 'In my own way.'

Nightjar drove the baker's van; it belonged to his grandfather so only he was permitted to drive it. It was very old with a canvas roof and wooden frame with spoked wheels, and it poured smoke and lurched alarmingly, but Nightjar, who was eighteen, wiry and strong, wrestled it along the darkened lanes with practised aplomb. Beside him sat Theo with the map and Cockerel who gave directions, while the fair-haired youth Starling rode in the back steadying the weapons and equipment. All were darkly clothed, their faces blackened with charcoal; they spoke little, the only sounds the asthmatic rattle of the engine, the squeaking of springs and the clink of petrol bombs in the back.

A village appeared in the headlights. 'Up here, then turn right.' Cockerel pointed. 'Go on a little further... now pull in and stop. There, look, that's the driveway to the villa.'

They waited and silence fell; a dog barked, lights burned at a few windows, but otherwise the village seemed deserted.

Theo raised field glasses. 'Trees lining the driveway – they may be a problem. Then it narrows at a bridge over a stream before continuing to the main house. The stables are to the right.'

'Any sign of guards?'

'I. . . It's too dark to tell.' A lorry lumbered by; he lowered the glasses until it passed. 'We're exposed here. Time to reposition.'

Ten minutes later they were unloading the equipment by the side of a forest track. Dense woodland surrounded them; a half-moon showed through thin overcast and leaves rustled in the breeze. Soon they were ready and after final murmured instructions and a clasp of hands, Theo led the two youths into the trees. Weapons slung, they set a fast pace; underfoot was dry and the snapping of foliage sounded like gunfire, but for the moment speed was more important than stealth. Heavily laden, slashing at brambles with their hunting knives, soon all were gasping for breath as Theo took them on a compass bearing through the forest. Then suddenly they broke into clear ground at the edge of an ornamental lake. On the other side of the lake rose the dark outline of outbuildings; beyond these stood the taller profile of the villa.

Theo sheathed his knife and drew out the Webley. 'You know what to do. Wait five minutes before moving up. If you encounter guards, or hear gunfire at the house, withdraw immediately to the rendezvous with Cockerel and go home without waiting.'

'But, Horatio—'

'Those are my orders. Listen for the signal. And for God's sake be careful with the combustibles.'

He crept forward, skirting the lake and then advancing on the main house using the outbuildings for cover. All seemed unnaturally quiet, with the villa's doors and shutters closed, no guards patrolling, no dogs barking. A single light burned in a downstairs window. He scampered across the courtyard; then, pressing his back to the wall, he crept around the back, testing shutters until he found one loose. Prising at the window with his knife, he levered it open and slipped inside.

Tolomei was in the adjacent room, a wood-panelled study, sitting behind a desk lit by a table-lamp. His face was in shadow, and he appeared much older than in the photograph, dressed in suit and tie, his beard trimmed, grey hair combed, shoes shined. He looked like an old man expecting visitors. Who had fallen asleep.

Theo was behind him in seconds. 'Wake up, *senatore*.'

Tolomei started. 'Who—'

'Don't cry out, I have a gun to your head.'

'Are you going to kill me?'

'I'm going to finish you.' He fumbled papers from his pocket, smoothing them on to the desk in front of Tolomei. 'Sign.'

'What are these?'

'Letters. Sign them all. Quickly. Here is the pen.'

Tolomei began signing. 'You were not meant to get into the house.'

'So I imagine.'

'The place is surrounded, you will never escape.'

'We shall see. Now stand.'

'Why?'

'You're coming.'

A flash lit the night sky beyond the shutters, followed by a distant thump.

'What was that?'

'Time to go. Quickly, through the window there.'

'But I'm seventy, for the love of God!'

'Climb out or I shoot you.'

'Help me. There – that stool.' Another flash, now the crackle of gunfire, then an explosion of yellow flame. 'Joseph and Mary, my garages!'

They clambered out, Theo dragging him round to the front of the house where outbuildings were already ablaze. Dark silhouettes, some of them bearing weapons, scurried about the courtyard in confusion.

'Call to them, call them off, or we torch the house too.'

Tolomei needed no urging. 'Save the garages!' He waved frantically. 'Save the limousines, the lake – hurry, get water!'

Theo left him and doubled back around the courtyard; then he sprinted for the trees on the driveway. Spotting Nightjar and Starling by bushes he ran to them.

'Good work with the outbuildings.'

'One of the grenades was a dud but a Molotov did the trick. Where's Tolomei?'

'Busy saving his cars. Anything from Cockerel?'

'Not yet, but there are men on the driveway. Near the bridge – look.'

Theo peered. Five or six figures, some clearly armed, were advancing slowly up the drive towards them.

'What do we do?'

'I, um. . .'

'Horatio, that's our escape route, what do we do?'

Scottish boys in a lane, Germans creeping towards them. *You're the fucking officer!*

A flash, then a spurting thump on to the driveway as Crow's cannon fired.

'Horatio!'

'We charge them! Throw dynamite and shoot as we go. Now! Come on!'

The three sprang from the bushes and sprinted for the bridge, the Springfield and Webley firing as one. Figures on the bridge stood up, hesitating, startled, while others knelt to shoot back. As he ran, Theo felt fire rising in his chest, then a wild animal howl escaped him, exultant, primal, like the war cry of Highlanders charging tanks. Beside him Nightjar and Starling took up the shout, the three of them running and howling like wolves. As a second shell from Crow's old cannon thumped in, Starling paused to throw dynamite; the stick landed short but exploded spectacularly. A few shots hummed back in their direction but their enemy was confused, faltering. 'Stop!' Theo ordered then. 'Kneel, aim, shoot!' A third cannonball crashed and dynamite lit the night. 'Now move! Left into the trees – go!' They rose and ran, leaping into the woods like deer. In seconds the trees swallowed them; behind came chaotic shooting and confused shouts, and the tinkle of bells as an *autopompa* arrived. Soon noise was receding until only the crash of their feet and breathless hoarse gasps filled their ears. They lost direction, corrected it, then glimpsed a flash from the cannon, and heard Cockerel's anxious shout: 'This way, boys! Hurry, they're coming.'

He was by the van, his blackened face streaked with smut from the cannon, which stood at his feet, angled skywards, two shells remaining. Half a mile back along the forest track, headlight beams scoured the trees.

'Shoot the cannon towards them, there, deeper into the woods.'

'Who are they?' Cockerel fumbled for a shell.

'The enemy.' *Carabinieri*, police, Blackshirts, Tolomei's thugs, Action Party and its foes, Rommel, Aunt Francesca, a loose-tongued Cellini: the list was endless. The cannon flashed, the shell soaring skywards to explode into trees near the headlights.

'Now go. Leave the grenades, the jam-tins and the rest of the Molotovs.'

'But, Horatio—'

'It's all right. It's as we expected. Take the van, continue along the track, lights off until you reach the Telo road. Then head home, long way round as planned.'

'What about you?'

'I'll hold them, cause a diversion, then leave.'

'Can I take my Springfield?' Starling's eyes were anxious.

'Yes, but leave me the rest. And the bicycle.'

He set the Molotovs in the woods beside the track, a jam-tin grenade next to each. After lighting the fuses he sprinted back to the cannon, which he pointed into the trees. As the first of the Molotovs blew, bathing the forest in yellow and gold, he fired the remaining shell, throwing the grenades at random and loosing off with the shotgun. The result was a haphazard pattern of shots and explosions in all directions. Then, flinging aside everything but his suitcase, he picked up the bicycle and pedalled into the night.

He rode the remaining hours of darkness without pause, staying off roads and riding only dirt lanes and tracks, in the open one minute and plunged into dark trees the next, head down, legs pumping, like a frightened young messenger in France so long ago. When dawn broke he took to the roads, continuing hard north all morning, nearly thirty miles to the town of Monterotondo, then on to Rieti where, nervously circling the station, he dumped the bicycle and caught a local train to Perugia, changed on to a second for Siena, and finally a third to Florence, where he arrived in the evening. That night he dared not use a *pensione*, so hovered near the station, passing the freezing hours of darkness with the other tramps on the steps of the basilica. A policeman moved them on brusquely at dawn but nobody asked for his papers. The next day, still using local trains, he avoided detection through Bologna and then Modena where he boarded one bound for Verona, just a stone's throw from the southern frontier with

South Tyrol. With the architecture more Alpine, the landscape more rugged and snow-capped peaks gleaming to the north, salvation seemed tantalizingly close, but nearing Verona the carriage jolted, the brakes squealed, and the train lurched to a stop. Ten minutes passed, twenty, and nothing happened; soon passengers were becoming impatient.

'What the hell's going on?' one asked, leaning out of the window.

'Gang of *carabinieri* up front, looks like they're boarding.'

Theo collected his bag and moved swiftly rearwards. The guard was on the track watching proceedings. Theo quietly opened the door, jumped out and ran. A shout pursued him, but he kept his head down and sprinted, reaching the cover of woodland where he followed the railway line round a bend, crossed over and struck out westward. He walked for an hour, sticking to lanes and paths, then hitched a lift from a farmer on a tractor.

'Where are you heading, young man?' he asked.

'Lake Garda,' Theo replied.

'Twenty miles.' The farmer pointed. 'There is a bus, you know.'

Spectacularly beautiful, mountain-fringed and more than thirty miles long, Lake Garda stretches from Verona northwards deep into South Tyrol, its northern shore just forty miles from Bolzano. Theo had visited as a child with Carla, played on its beaches and ridden its passenger ferry. The bus dropped him at the dock where he caught a late-afternoon sailing and three hours later stepped ashore at Riva, where he made for the station. By midnight he was home.

Exiting the station, for a moment he stood shivering in the icy air, savouring the familiar townscape with its tall spires, cobbled streets and overhanging roofs. Snow crunched underfoot; a wintry moon bathed the town in silver. It had been four years since last he was there, and it felt barely a week. Yet Bolzano was now firmly under Italian control and as he walked towards the old centre he noticed Tolomei's handiwork everywhere. Shops all seemed to have Italian proprietors now; street names too were in Italian, while posters and advertising hoardings promoted Italian goods and services. The *tricolore* flag hung from municipal buildings instead of the crimson eagle of Südtirol. And rounding one corner, he found himself face-to-face with a huge billboard of Mussolini, twenty feet tall, glowering down on him imperiously in the moonlight. *Viva Il Duce!* the caption read. *l'Italia ha finalmente il suo impero* – Italy finally has its empire. Italian policemen patrolled the streets too, he saw, and he gave them a wide berth. And as he neared Laubengasse, its once familiar sign now Italianized to Via Padiglione, caution slowed him further, until he was stealing from shadow to shadow like a burglar.

The print shop was gone. It had turned into a hardware store. At first he thought he was mistaken and doubled back to check his bearings. But it was no mistake: his childhood home was no more. He stared in confusion. A light came on upstairs suddenly as someone moved rooms. Not only had the shop gone, but people were living in the apartment. He crept closer. 'Di Paolo', the nameplate said.

He lingered in the street, shivering with indecision. The hour was late and the temperature plummeting; he had only his student clothes and nowhere to go. If he stayed outside he'd freeze. He needed shelter: a shed or outbuilding or something. Then he remembered Mitzi. Mitzi Janosi, the girl he'd held hands with at the chocolate parlour, the girl he'd sat next to at catacomb school, the girl he'd kissed at the cinema. Her family lived fifty yards away: he knew their house. They'd signed the Option Agreement and stayed on as Italians; Mitzi's father was vehemently pro-Italy. Could they be relied on? Were they even there?

The door was opened by a woman wearing curlers and dressing gown.

'Signora Janosi, I am sorry to disturb you so late.'

A hand went to her mouth. 'Good heavens, it's the Ladurner child!'

She brought him in, made him hot tea, sat him by the parlour fire and roused Mitzi, who rushed downstairs in her night clothes, face wide with disbelief.

'My God, Teo, it is really you!'

They embraced tightly, clinging together like lost relatives. Theo found himself welling up with emotion. A month on the run, living on his nerves, danger at every turn, his childhood home gone and his family scattered. 'Thank God you're here, Mitzi.'

Her mother prepared food while Mitzi gave him the facts. The print shop had been taken over by an Italian family, she said, in accordance with policy. In refusing to sign the Option Agreement, Josef had forfeited his right to the property, so Italian settlers had been awarded tenancy. Di Paolo they were called, a nice enough couple from Milan, who kept themselves to themselves.

'They moved in after your grandmother left.'

'Where are all our possessions?'

'I believe she put them in the basement.'

'I must get to them.'

'You can't, Teo, they'd report you.'

'They are informers?'

'They are scared, like everyone. You know the Blackshirts came looking for you?'

'When?'

'Two days ago. They kicked on the Di Paolos' door and asked all kinds of questions. But once they saw they knew nothing, they left them alone. But they told them to report anything suspicious immediately.'

Theo nodded. 'Where is your father, Mitzi?'

'Genoa. He's deputy manager at the port. He comes home once a month. Don't worry, you're safe staying with Mother and me.'

'I couldn't ask that. Anyway, I must leave.'

'And go where?'

'It's best I don't say. But I have one important favour to ask.'

The following afternoon he watched from a doorway as Mitzi rang the Di Paolos' doorbell. Twenty minutes later she reappeared, laden down with climbing equipment, mountain-eering clothes, rucksack and skis. Back at the house she watched as he checked it over.

'Is it all here?'

'Yes, everything, thank you.' He glanced up. 'What did you tell them?'

'That my cousin lent you his climbing gear years ago, but now wants it back.'

'Did they believe you?'

'I'm not sure. They seem very fearful.'

The Blackshirts came early, pounding on the Janosis' door and then ransacking the house from top to bottom. But they found no trace, for by then Theo was long gone. Rising before dawn, he'd dressed for the mountains, in extra shirts and sweaters, thick socks and boots, backpack, skis, binoculars, gloves, maps. Then his notes and papers for Grant, and a package of food from Mitzi. 'I know you won't tell me,' she'd said, pushing chocolate in his pocket, 'so I won't ask.'

'Thank you.'

'But when you get there, please write and tell me you're safe.'

'I will. In the meantime can you post these?'

'Of course. What are they?'

'Letters. Important letters.'

Then they kissed and he slipped out into the darkness.

He caught the bus north to Merano. Waiting at the terminus for a second bus he picked up a discarded newspaper: *Senator Retires* ran a headline: . . . *following an unconnected incident at his Rome home, Senator Ettore Tolomei has announced his retirement from politics. 'I have striven my best to serve my leader and our peoples, but it is time for younger blood to take up the challenge. . .'*

By mid-morning he was aboard a smaller bus, winding its way westward along the valley of the River Etsch. Swelled with icy melt-water, the river rushed by just yards from his window, while the bus toiled steadily upward. The view beyond was harsh and forbidding, the valley walls rising steeply towards craggy, ice-covered peaks thousands of feet high, their summits lost in scudding cloud. Soon all vestige of green was gone, leaving only the snow-covered valley and ice-white mountains all round. The bus laboured on, rounded a series of bends, then a village hove into view half a mile ahead.

'What's that?' Theo asked the driver.

'Sluderno. Last checkpoint before the border.'

'Let me off here please.'

The bus driver eyed him. 'You speak like a *Südtiroler*.'

'I am. Born in Bolzano.'

'Sign the Option Agreement?'

He knew. A lone youth, dressed for the mountains, on the bus for Switzerland: he could only be a fugitive.

'No, sir, I'm a separatist.'

'Good.' The driver nodded. 'Me too. Take that track there to the right: it leads up the side of Urtirolaspitz. Be careful of that mountain, she's ten thousand feet and a bitch this time of year. And stay out of sight: border police watch it with binoculars. The summit marks the frontier. Once over, descend westwards by ski until you hit the road at Fuldera.'

'That's it?'

'That's it.'

'How far?'

'Eight or nine miles.' He grinned. 'But I'd say you've come a lot farther.'

'Thank you. I have.'

They shook hands. Theo descended from the bus and began the long climb out of Italy.

CHAPTER 16

As Padre Pettifer predicts, Stalag 357 is indeed a holiday camp compared with the nightmare of XIB. Only twenty miles or so down the railway from Fallingbostel, the layout is similar – the usual collection of huts around a compound, plus an admin block for the Germans – but thereafter all comparisons cease. For a start I'm greeted at the medical officers' hut by an orderly who insists on carrying my rucksack along to my 'bedroom', which although tiny is mine alone, featuring a real bed with sheets, pillow, blankets and bedside cupboard. After that I'm shown to a pleasant-looking 'lounge' with tables strewn with newspapers and magazines, a well-stocked bookcase, gramophone player, heating stove and a few scruffy but comfortable armchairs.

'Good heavens,' I exclaim. 'So, er, where is everybody?'

'Out and about, sir. They'll be back later. Meantime Major McKenzie suggests you relax for the afternoon.'

'Relax.'

'Yes, sir. Help yourself to Bovril and biscuits. Supper's at six in the dining room.'

Somewhat bemused and with little else to do, I duly select a magazine or two and settle down, Bovril in hand, to relax in an armchair. In no time I'm fast asleep. That evening over a veritable feast of Spam fritters, vegetable soup, bread, butter and Ovaltine, I meet my fellow medical officers, who are three captains like myself, an Australian dentist, and another padre. Also our senior MO, Major John McKenzie, who is a Scot. All have been prisoners for some years, McKenzie since the fall of France.

'Dunkirk?' I enquire over the soup.

'No, Normandy, during the 51st retreat.'

'51st?'

'51st Highland Division. Got cut off and surrendered. Thousands taken prisoner.'

'I never heard of that.'

'It was hushed up. Dunkirk was the big story.'

His tone discourages further comment, and around the table the others too seem reticent about discussing their capture and captivity, perhaps because they've heard it so many times. They are, however, curious about my story.

'You dropped by parachute?' The dentist looks shocked. 'A medical officer? It's a wonder you survived!'

'Well, I did have some training. . .'

'Arnhem, you say,' another asks. 'How far's that from Germany?'

'Only a dozen miles or so from the border, as the crow flies.'

'So the Allies could be here any time?'

'Well, I wouldn't say that exactly. The operation, at the end of the day, must be counted a failure. 30 Corps never made it, we didn't secure the Rhine bridgehead, we took terrible casualties, and the rest had to fall back. . .'

'Sounds like another cock-up,' McKenzie mutters.

'Yes, well, much was learned and we're optimistic about an early spring offensive.'

Wry laughter. 'Haven't we heard *that* before!'

Sarcasm too. And when I talk about Stalag XIB they're openly scornful.

'Six officers to a room? Preposterous. And no Red Cross parcels, you say?'

'That's right. No heating fuel either, pitiful medical supplies, sanitation's awful, and as for the food. . .'

'You should have complained!' McKenzie's fist hits the table. 'Immediately and in the strongest possible terms.'

'We did complain, sir, and still are complaining, I assure you. But the situation's complicated. We paratroops are regarded with some hostility by the Germans, and also we're the new boys in camp, which is largely run by the French, who've cornered the market in resources, so to speak.'

'Ah.'

And in that 'ah' lies the rub. For here in 357 the British hold sway, and they've had nearly four years to fine-tune it to perfection. Which accounts for the clubby if somewhat claustrophobic atmosphere. Red Cross parcels arrive like clockwork (hence Bovril, Ovaltine, Spam and myriad other luxuries including magazines and gramophone records), the commandant apparently is elderly, docile and wants no trouble, the guards too are mostly peaceable, with many 'tamed' using bribes of Red Cross chocolate and cigarettes. Once tamed they have no choice but to accede to further demands – or get posted to the Russian Front for corruption, so extra luxuries like writing materials, a tailoring and laundry service, the odd bottle of schnapps and even little outings are laid on. Life therefore for these long-term inmates, if tedious, is relatively untroubled, especially for us medics who as non-combatants are regarded benignly. Furthermore, after the weary grind of XIB, the workload is absurdly easy, as I find out following an excellent night's rest in my bedroom. Woken by the orderly bearing tea, I have a wash and shave in warm water, then a hearty breakfast of coffee and porridge sweetened with Red Cross jam, and I'm ready for the fray.

'Stalag 357 is not a hospital camp but a regular POW camp,' McKenzie explains, showing me round the medical hut. 'Five hundred or so prisoners; we have a sick bay with twenty beds, but if anyone gets seriously ill they're transferred to hospital. That just leaves routine medical matters for us to handle. We hold a daily sick parade here each morning after roll call; generally we're all finished by lunchtime. Any questions?'

One or two, but I decide to save them. 'No, sir. Thank you.'

'Good. Any problems come and find me, or ask one of the others.'

With that he leaves me in a well-equipped treatment room where I pass the morning curetting warts, lancing boils and mopping out running ears. The most serious case I see is of advanced *tinea pedis* (athlete's foot), which the bearer tells me he's had since the siege of Tobruk. I deal with that using a paste made from bicarbonate of soda, he hobbles out and I await my next case. The knock comes, the door opens, and the first thing I see is the Parachute Regiment insignia on his right shoulder.

'*Waho Mohammed*,' I say, scarcely believing my eyes.

A young man enters. 'Oh, hello, sir. *Waho Mohammed*. Er, where's Dr Rawlings?'

'He's been posted elsewhere, so I believe. I'm his replacement, my name's Garland. And you are?'

Jenkins, he's a private, he's twenty-two and tells me he's from Wolverhampton. He's slight of build for a Para, and rather pale and tense-looking. Once we have introduced ourselves, I wait for him to explain what's wrong. But he doesn't, he just sits there and talks, and some sixth sense tells me I should let him.

'11th Battalion you say, sir? Can't say I've heard of it. When was it formed?'

'Only last year, I think. Yes, March or April of forty-three. I joined it a few months ago. What about you, Jenkins?'

'Oh, I'm a Royal Engineer, sir.'

'Really? Which unit?'

'25 BD Company. Then I got to try for the RE's Parachute Squadron in forty-two. Did my jump training at Ringway, passed OK and got posted to Africa.'

'BD?'

'Bomb disposal.'

'Ah, yes, of course.'

'Anyway I joined 1st Parachute Brigade in Africa just in time for the invasion of Sicily. Right caper that was.'

'Is that where you were captured?' Jenkins has a slight tick in his cheek, I note, and he licks his lips frequently. Also, curiously, a small teddy bear pokes out from the top pocket of his battledress. He makes no mention of it, so neither do I. Proceed with caution, I tell myself.

'That's right. There was this mission, to capture a bridge – Primosole it was called, somewhere on Sicily, box-girder construction over a little river. We were supposed to take and hold it for Monty's lot to come charging through. But it was a cock-up from the start. A night drop: everyone got scattered so only a couple of companies made it to the bridge, then had a devil of a job taking it. Terrible casualties, I must say. . .' He breaks off to study the floor.

'Bridges do seem to present unique problems to paratroops.'

'It kept changing hands, you know. We'd have it, then they'd take it back and so on. Pretty soon there's bodies everywhere. Mates and that, dead and injured. Anyway, turns out Jerry's rigged the whole thing with explosives. . .'

'Which is where you came in.'

'Yes.' He turns his face to the window. 'Me and my section.' I wait. A minute passes, but that's all he has to say.

'How are you sleeping these days, Jenkins?'

'I never sleep.'

'Did Dr Rawlings ever discuss barbiturates?'

'What's the point? I'd only dream.'

'How can I help?'

'You can't.' He looks at me, his cheek twitching. 'Nobody can.'

A week later, 357's medical contingent, to my astonishment, goes into town for a drink. 'Out and about,' as the orderly put it on my first day, apparently really does mean 'out'. I'm sitting in the lounge smoking a pipe (a new affectation) and reading the *British Medical Journal* when the dentist hurries in wearing greatcoat and cap. 'Come on, Garland, everyone's waiting!'

Ten minutes later we're out of the gate and strolling down the road as though it's the most normal thing in the world.

'What's going on?' I whisper to the padre.

'Parole,' he murmurs.

Parole, it turns out, refers to a little-known clause of the Geneva Convention, with origins dating from Roman times. Storming across Europe, the Romans acquired more POWs than they knew what to do with, but they certainly weren't going to bother housing and feeding them all, so on their sworn promise never to bear arms again, the prisoners were free to fend for themselves. Many simply went home. In the present context parole means extra freedoms and privileges, such as tools to build a camp theatre, provided they aren't used for escaping, or art materials for painting lessons, on condition documents aren't forged with them. Or even a walk in the woods, as long as we don't wander off. Logical but mad, it's all based upon our solemn 'parole' as officers and gentlemen to play by the rules.

There's more, unbelievably. Another clause says that 'Officers on a Journey' are legally entitled to refreshments. This is why I was given sandwiches for my outing to Bergen, and breakfast at Fallingbostel Station. But in the case of 357's medical officers, it means beer-at-a-pub-while-out-for-a-stroll. Mad, as I say, but who am I to argue with the law? So, accompanied by a guard hefting sackfuls of our laundry, we walk a mile or so down a cobbled lane into a pleasant village, where he leads us straight into a cosy *Herberge*. Seating ourselves at a scrubbed oak table surrounded by genial old men who express no surprise at our arrival, a clandestine exchange of goods takes place at the bar which results in foaming mugs of *dunkel* beer arriving before us, served with a cheery wink by a suitably ample waitress.

'*Prost!*' everyone toasts, including the old men. I take a sip, taste something delicious and stout-like, and know I'm hallucinating.

'It's all perfectly above board,' McKenzie explains, seeing my expression. 'The landlord's sister does our laundry, the guard pays in cigarettes and cocoa powder, keeps a small percentage as commission and everyone's happy.'

Except that it's Red Cross cigarettes and cocoa powder we're trading in, I reflect, which doesn't feel right, especially when Pip Smith and the others need them so badly just a few miles away at XIB. Nor, call me old-fashioned, does it feel right fraternizing so chummily with the enemy, even if they're only old men and barmaids. And as I'm sitting there among British officers who see nothing wrong in this, I realize they've been captive so long they've stopped thinking like soldiers, and settled into institutionalized apathy like animals in a zoo. And soon a second mug of beer arrives and goes straight to my head, which is growing increasingly confused and uneasy, and before I know it I'm heading for trouble.

'Sir, could I ask you something?'

'By all means.'

'It's about one of the patients. A boy called Jenkins.'

'I've seen him. Explosives chap. Talks a lot.'

'Yes, that's him. The thing is I fear he's having some sort of breakdown.'

'Really? Based on what?'

'Well, a gut feeling.'

'Gut feelings aren't very professional, Garland.'

'No, sir. But I sense he needs specialist care. Or even a medical repatriation.'

'What!' His eyebrows shoot up. 'You want me to request a medical repatriation? Based on a gut feeling? That'd upset the apple cart all right!'

But this apple cart needs upsetting. And I'm about to kick it over.

'Yes, sir. There's another thing. A question.'

'Go on.'

'Why did you request me here?'

'I didn't. Rawlings got transferred, I merely told the commandant I needed a replacement. A few days later you showed up.'

'Yes, but why me? When they're so desperately short-handed at XIB?'

'I have no idea. Evidently you have friends in high places.'

I consider this, think of Theo, and Inge Brandt, sup more beer, then plough on. 'But you didn't. Don't, I mean. Need a replacement, that is.'

'What do you mean?'

'We're overstaffed. More doctors than required for the patient workload, that is. You don't need me.'

His eyes narrow. 'What exactly are you getting at?'

'I'd like your permission to escape.'

351

His mouth opens, then closes, and before I know it he's dragging me outside.

'Listen to me, Garland. There is absolutely no question of it. Nor are you ever to mention that word again, do you understand?'

'But why?'

'Because we have given our parole! And the instant anyone breaks it, all this' – he gestures angrily around – 'disappears in a flash. No more perks, no more schnapps or fresh bread, no more favours from the commandant or smuggled treats from the guards, and certainly no trips to the village for a beer.'

'With respect, sir, are we not forgetting our obligation as British officers?'

'Our obligation is to the patients!'

That old chestnut, and I'm ready for it. 'But I don't have any patients. None that can't be handled by someone else.' And this is my point. The point that's been befuddling my brain since I arrived at Stalag 357. That from the minute I departed the wreckage of the Schoonoord Hotel aboard a lorry of wounded men, I have been able to say, hand on heart, that they needed me, and continued to need me, from Oosterbeek to Apeldoorn, then from Apeldoorn and the hospital train to Fallingbostel, and finally to the nightmare of Stalag XIB. Now they don't need me. Nobody does, not even Theo, comfortably tucked up in his hospital bed in Bergen. I am surplus to requirements, and as such fully entitled – some might say duty-bound – to make a break for freedom.

'Listen, Garland, old chap' – McKenzie tries cajolery – 'I admire your spirit, really I do. What they say about you Red

Devil parachute bods is clearly true, gung-ho fearless action types and all that. But now is not the time for gung-ho, now is the time for cool heads and patience. This war will be over soon: everyone knows it, even Jerry. So bide your time, keep your head down and your mind on the job, and we'll all be home before we know it. Can you do that?'

I try. For a few days anyway, keeping my head down and my mind on the job, as he urges. But soon know it's hopeless. Paras don't think like that, even useless neophyte ones like me. It's to do with the training, and the mind-set, the *esprit de corps* and the reputation. Earning a red beret takes guts and determination, and when you finally put it on you sign up to something for ever. 'Old Paras never die,' the saying goes, 'they go to hell and regroup.' *Waho Mohammed.*

I make my preparations. They're not complicated – no tunnels, wire-cutters or elaborate disguises are required. Once a week we walk down to the village for a beer; I'll simply slip away while we're there. End of plan. Thereafter things become hazier, but according to my silk escape map (which I still have, along with miniature compass) we're barely fifty miles from the North Sea port of Hamburg. By lying low during the day and travelling cross-country by night I should easily make it in three nights, the aim then being to stow away aboard a cargo ship bound for Sweden.

The longer the delay the greater the risk, so I give myself a week to prepare. As the days pass the tension rises, and a heady mix of exhilaration and terror grips me. At night I lie awake trying to cover the eventualities, which seem to multiply: food, shelter, a torch, avoiding detection, the freezing weather at night – and also recalling everything that's happened since I arrived in Holland, and the people like Sykes, Warrack, Redman and others who have escaped, and poor Cliff Poutney lying dead by the tracks. During the day I maintain my normal routine and duties, feign nonchalance and hope to God nobody catches on, although in my heightened state of paranoia I'm convinced McKenzie and the others sense what's afoot.

There's only one person I feel it necessary to confide in.

'How are you feeling today, Jenkins?'

'All right, thanks, Doc. OK if I come in?'

'Of course. I could do with the company.'

He pops in most days, ten minutes, an hour, to sit and talk, pace the floor in agitation, or just stare into space, teddy bear in pocket. I encourage these visits, chat if he wants, keep quiet otherwise, but make no demands, ask no probing questions, and certainly don't suggest he 'confront issues'. He's severely traumatized, I have no doubt of that, mentally exhausted too and a nervous wreck. My role, if I have one, is simply to be there. For as long as he needs. Which is why he must agree to me leaving.

'Really?' he says, when I explain, then goes silent, nodding and fidgeting and licking his lips. The teddy comes out; he fingers it, cheek twitching. I scarcely dare breathe.

Then he looks up. 'I'd rather you didn't.'

And that's that. My only patient wants me to stay, so the escape is cancelled. Part of me, if I'm completely honest, is greatly relieved.

'Well, of course, Jenkins, if that's—'

'But you absolutely should.'

'What?'

'I'd rather you didn't, but you absolutely should. I'd go too, but don't have the nerve. Anyway I'd only foul things up.'

'Are you sure?'

'Totally, no question, we're Paras, aren't we? Anyway, must dash!' And he hurries for the door. But then he stops, and turns, face twitching. 'Are you going like that?' He nods at my battledress.

'Well, yes, it's all I've got, apart from my jumping smock.'

'You'll stand out like a dog's balls.'

Thursday comes, Friday, and then the big day finally dawns, clear and cold. By now I've assembled a few supplies. Three days' rations including dried fruit and chocolate, a water canteen, flashlight, schnapps for emergencies, tobacco for my pipe and a blanket which I'll conceal beneath my smock for the walk into town. I take better care than usual washing and shaving, polish my boots and clean up my gaiters, dust down my beret. I stand before the mirror and straighten my tie. I came into this war wearing this uniform, I tell myself, so I'm bloody well walking out in it too. Then a knock comes, and my eyes widen with alarm in the mirror. 'What is it?'

It's Jenkins, bearing a bundle. 'Got you these.'

'Hello, Private. Good heavens. . .'

He opens the bundle; it's an overcoat, hat and scarf.

'My God, but where—'

'Don't ask.' His head's twitching and the clothes tremble in his arms, but there's a lopsided grin on his face. 'The greatcoat's modified French army, so with the hat and scarf you'll look like a civvy, as long as no one looks at your feet.'

I slip the coat on. It's blue, and a little tight but wonderfully warm. 'Well, goodness, Jenkins, this is marvellous.'

'Stop you freezing to death at night.'

'Yes it will. How can I ever thank you?'

'By getting home.'

'Yes, well, I'll do my best.'

'I mean it.' He produces an envelope. 'Give this to my mum. Please. And explain – things. You know. . .'

'All right.' I pocket the letter. 'But you're going to get home too, Jenkins.'

'We'll see.'

'You must. We're going to get you fixed up.'

He's nodding, but doesn't meet my eye.

'Stay as positive as you can, like we talked about, and just take each day as it comes, yes?'

'I'll try.'

'Good man.'

We shake hands, take our leave, and I can only hope for the best. I then pass the morning attending to the Saturday sick parade, which, although routine, at least keeps my mind occupied with its bellyaches, sore throats and haemorrhoids. As the hours pass I sense a change coming over me, a sort of quiet resignation, and talking to the patients I begin thinking of home and parents and friends, and I find myself talking to the patients more, asking them about their homes and families, and asking whether they've written to them recently, because they're sure to appreciate it.

At noon I finish, tidy up and head off for the medics' hut for lunch. Halfway there I'm unsurprised to see Major McKenzie coming my way.

'Nice overcoat,' he says, falling into step. 'Do you have a moment?'

'Of course.' He knows, I immediately guess, yet I detect no hostility. Nor do I feel any. We stop, and talk, rationally and without rancour.

'How was sick parade?'

'No problems.'

'Good. Listen, I've just come from the commandant's office.' He unfolds a note. 'Bergen Hospital. The clinical director there, a Dr Brandt. You know her?'

'Yes, I do.'

'She's been arrested.'

'What for?'

'Commandant didn't say, nor I suspect does he know. The notification came from the medical services directorate.'

'Inge. Christ. Does it mention her husband?'

'No. But it seems someone's watching out for you. Apparently you have a patient at Bergen Hospital, a Private Trickey?'

'Yes.'

'He's been transferred out.'

'Transferred where?'

'His previous POW camp. Stalag XIB.'

'But he's critically ill! And that place. . . It's a disgrace – it has nothing. He'll die.'

'Sorry, Garland, I'm just passing the message.' He waits, tapping the note on his palm. 'So, what do you want to do?'

'I. . . I beg your pardon?'

He smiles. 'I know what you've got planned. And how you plan to do it. That's your business – you know my views, but I'll not interfere. Or I can get you transferred back to Stalag XIB. To be with your patient. It's entirely up to you.'

I gaze round the muddy compound, at the dreary wooden huts, the guards in their towers and the barbed-wire fences. Overhead thickening November clouds have ushered away the morning's clear blue. Seagulls pick over the camp rubbish dump; one of them cries, mournfully, like a summons to the sea. I draw my new overcoat tighter, and feel something in one pocket. I reach in and touch a teddy bear.

'So what do you want to do, Daniel?'

CHAPTER 17

Erwin Rommel left Italy for Africa shortly after X Troop blew up the Tragino Aqueduct. Busy with his new mission, Operation Colossus was of no interest to him, although he did hear of it and expressed surprise at how easily the British seized the target: 'No armed guard?' he queried of his Italian host. The reply was a shrug.

A sign of things to come, for as von Brauchitsch had intimated, Mussolini was indeed making a hash of things in Africa. With grand visions of expanding the new Roman Empire across the entire continent, he deployed huge armies there, including fourteen divisions into Libya. Their job was to kick the British out of neighbouring Egypt, and so seize control of its key ports and vital Suez Canal. 'Once this is achieved,' Mussolini told his generals, 'all of Africa will soon follow.' But his Egyptian campaign was a disaster. Despite overwhelming numbers, Italy's forces were ill equipped, poorly led and unwieldy. Setting off eastwards from the Libyan port of Tobruk, they advanced to the Egyptian border, crossed sixty miles into it, halted and dug in. So the British attacked and drove them out again. Worse was to follow. With a force barely a fifth their size, the Tommies then set off in pursuit, driving the

Italians back along the coast into Libya, taking Tobruk, Derna and Benghazi on the way, until finally halting at El Agheila, where the entire Italian 10th Army surrendered. Rommel read the reports in disbelief. The figures were staggering, with ten Italian divisions lost and over 130,000 prisoners captured, together with hundreds of tanks and artillery pieces. British losses by comparison were fractional. Worst of all, they were now poised to advance on Tripoli itself, and thus take control of the entire southern Mediterranean. It was this catastrophe, first and foremost, that Rommel was ordered to stop.

But it was a delicate business, for Italian national pride was at stake. Vain and arrogant as ever, Mussolini initially refused all offers of German help, until Hitler made him see sense. Even then strict conditions were attached. The campaign must continue under Italian auspices; all German forces were to be under Italian control; and the German commander, whoever he was, must take orders from an Italian general, whom he would defer to at all times. Hitler assured Il Duce the matter would be sensitively handled. He knew what Mussolini wanted was a tactful underling who would keep a low profile and do as ordered. What he got, however, was a voracious predator with no time for niceties. The Desert Fox had arrived in Africa.

Right from the start Rommel took the initiative. Studying the situation before even setting foot there, he saw the British were strung out for hundreds of miles right across Egypt and Libya, and immediately recognized vulnerability. Telephoning the Luftwaffe he requested they bomb the British supply line at Benghazi.

'We can't do that!' came the reply. 'The Italians haven't authorized it.'

Rommel telephoned his Italian superior, General Gariboldi. 'Under no circumstances!' Gariboldi scolded. 'Italians own property in Benghazi, they don't want it bombed!'

Rommel telephoned Berlin, and the following night the bombings began. Next he flew to Tripoli to plan his offensive. The British front line was 250 miles east, so that's where he wanted his forces. Again Gariboldi baulked; he wanted no advance at all, but a tight defensive ring round Tripoli itself. Rommel telephoned Berlin again. 'Do what you have to,' came the reply. He sent his forces forward; they were still dangerously small, just two Italian divisions and one German one: 'Not my beloved 7th Panzer,' he wrote to his wife, 'their destiny now lies in Russia. But these are eager boys, Lu, I will forge them into an Afrika Korps to be proud of.' The attacks started, catching out the British, who fell back a full 200 miles to Mersa el Brega, then another 150 miles to Benghazi, then still further, Rommel in hot pursuit, following the same tactics he'd learned in the First War in Italy, and perfected in the charge across France: drive hard, move fast, don't stop, lead from the front. Gariboldi was aghast, Hitler thrilled, German High Command anxious. Within two months Rommel had pushed the British back to within a hundred miles of the Egyptian border. 'Next objective Suez!' he wrote to Lucie. Just one obstacle remained before this. And even he knew it would not be an easy one. Its name was Tobruk.

*

John Frost sat in his office at Hardwick Hall totting up numbers. His foot rested on an upturned waste-basket, a walking stick leaned against the wall, an opened bottle of aspirin stood on his desk. Three days earlier he'd finally reported to Ringway to do his jump training. He'd been putting it off: the battalion needs me here, he kept telling himself, the paperwork's not finished, I can't spare the time, not until the recruitment process is complete. Then suddenly it was complete, virtually three full companies signed up, plus an HQ company in support. 2nd Battalion was done, he realized, up to full strength. Then checking the list he saw that every man on it had completed the parachute course except one, and if that one didn't do it soon, they'd deploy without him, which was ironic since he'd recruited them in the first place. So he'd gone to Ringway, spent two days in the hangar looking at blackboards and jumping from tables and rickety scaffolding and a wired contraption called the windmill. On the third day he'd donned his parachute for real and climbed into that infernal balloon, and hung on for grim death while the beastly thing jerked and swayed upwards like a kite on a string. Then he'd jumped out and it had scared him half to death, but the canopy snapped open, the descent was smooth and his landing was textbook: neat, tidy and barely a bruise. The instructor grinned. 'One more like that, sir, and you're done with balloons!' So he'd gone straight up again, laughing and cocky and leaping through the hole like a professional. But he started swinging in the descent this time, and landed hard, cracking his head and tearing a ligament in his foot. Now the medics said no jumping for a fortnight at least, so while everyone else was off on leave, celebrating, socializing and sewing parachute wings on their uniforms, he was stuck in the office shuffling papers and hobbling around on a stick.

Everything had happened so very fast. Within a couple of weeks of filling in the form for special air operations, he'd been summoned to London for a series of interviews, which resulted in his appointment as adjutant to the 2nd Battalion of the 1st Parachute Brigade. This sounded impressive, except that neither existed. 'It's a big push by Churchill,' his new boss, Brigadier 'Windy' Gale explained. 'He wants a division-sized force, along the German model, and he wants it now. General Browning will lead the division; we'll be its first parachute brigade.'

Three battalions were needed to form the new brigade. Gale already had one: the 11 Special Air Service, formerly 2 Commando, which he renamed 1st Battalion. Frost's job, he soon learned, was to form 2nd Battalion: that is find, interview and sign up five hundred men, from scratch. Another captain, Stephen Terrell, was to form 3rd Battalion, also from scratch. Time, Gale told them, was of the essence. Barracks had been allocated near Chesterfield in Derbyshire, and a massive recruitment drive was under way, with enrolment officers visiting every army unit in the realm to drum up volunteers.

Frost and Terrell moved into the new barracks and waited for them to arrive. Soon a trickle appeared, wandering up from Chesterfield Station each day like pilgrims to Mecca. But almost immediately the two adjutants noticed a problem, in that many recruits were completely unsuitable. Slackers, miscreants, troublemakers and outright criminals: an age-old military tradition was being played out, they realized, with commanders seizing the opportunity to get rid of their worst troops instead of sending their best. Gale soon put a stop to the practice, but much time was lost. Slowly the situation improved, but then Frost noticed Terrell was getting better recruits than he. Hurrying down the road in puzzlement he found a corporal hiding in the bushes, with orders to send everyone to Terrell first, before sending the rejects on to Frost. Not to be outdone, Frost duly posted his own tout further down the road, Terrell followed suit, and soon both were virtually camping at the station.

Common sense prevailed and gradually the numbers crept up. Once a man was accepted he was issued with a coloured lanyard to denote his battalion, and after introductory training at Hardwick Hall he was packed off to Ringway to learn how to be a parachutist. At one point Frost noticed an abundance of Scotsmen applying from various Highland regiments, and, being a Cameronian himself, decided to form one of 2nd Battalion's three companies as entirely Scottish. Cheekily pencilling his own name as possible company commander, the legendary C Company, 2nd Battalion was born. Unknown to him, in less than six months he would be leading it on one of the most daring raids of the war.

He sat back, examining his lists and absently rubbing his ankle. A knock came and a young man appeared, a private, unkempt, wearing rumpled battledress, shabby boots, and with his hair too long.

'Selection's over,' Frost said irritably, 'you might as well go back to the station.'

The youth didn't move, merely stood there holding his cap and looking vaguely around. He had parachute wings sewn on his shoulder, Frost then noticed, the old version too, as issued to the very first Ringway graduates. Yet he looked young, with a continental complexion as if tanned from a good holiday, clear blue eyes, and fair hair with full lips and an unperturbed expression. Which all looked familiar.

'Wait a minute!' He delved into a drawer. 'Yes, look!' He pulled out a sheet. 'You're him! You're Trickey, Theodor Victor Trickey.'

'Yes, sir.'

'From 2 Commando – I mean, 11 Special Air. . . Christ, you're from X Troop!'

'Yes, sir.'

'Well, for heaven's sake.' Frost struggled to his feet. 'Let me shake your hand!'

Minutes later the two were seated across from one another, Frost listening intently as the youth recounted his story. He did so dispassionately and concisely, Frost noted, in a clear if accented voice, and without emotion or embellishment, as though filing a report.

'And that's all, sir,' he said at the end.

'Nobody else got away.'

'I don't believe so, although Captain Daly's party never—'

'No, I'm telling *you*, Private. Nobody else got away. We heard via the Italian Red Cross. Daly's team got picked up, Harry Boulter too, after mounting a grand defence of his position, so everyone in X Troop is in captivity. Except the other interpreter, poor what-was-his-name. . .'

'Picchi, sir. Fortunato Picchi.'

'Picchi, yes. Bad business, that.'

'Sir. May I ask... how, um, do you know these things? And also, why am I here?'

Frost smiled. 'We know about them because X Troop are our people now. Even if they're in captivity. And you're here, I presume, because your, ah, special ops officer in London sent you here. After he debriefed you. Correct?'

'Yes, sir, that's true, but why?'

Frost spread his hands. 'Because this is your home.'

'Home?'

'Yes. You see, your old unit, 2 Commando, which then became 11 Special Air Service, is now part of 1st Parachute Brigade, which is based here. You're on our payroll!' He waved a sheet. 'In fact we've been expecting you since we heard from special ops that you'd made it back to England.'

Trickey looked uncomfortable. 'I um, I had to visit my mother, sir – that is, my parents. Sorry, it's complicated, it took longer than—'

'Good God, don't worry about that! You've earned weeks of leave.'

'Thank you, sir.'

'No, thank *you*, Trickey.' Frost studied the sheet. 'Your mother's situation is, er, improved, I gather.'

'Yes, sir. Well, she's been released from the internment camp.'

'Excellent.' Frost tossed the sheet aside. 'So all we have to do is decide what to do with you.'

'Sir?'

'Well, strictly speaking you're in 1st Battalion, because that's where the rest of your old unit ended up. How do you feel about that?'

'All right, sir, I suppose. Only might it not be, um, a bit odd, being the only one there from X Troop?'

'My thinking precisely. So tell me, have you ever worked with Scotsmen?'

'Yes I have. With the 51st Highland Division in France last year.'

'What d'you make of them?'

'I like them, sir. Wonderful soldiers, very brave. And, unusually, humorous.'

'Indeed. So the thing is, I'm just putting the finishing touches to 2nd Battalion's roll. And C Company is all Scots, and could definitely use a young officer with your skills and experience on the staff.'

'I, um, I never actually finished OCTU.'

'We can look into that.' He opened his drawer, withdrew three items and placed them carefully on his desk. 'See these?'

'Sir?'

'This' – he gestured grandly at the first item – 'is the new shoulder patch for all British airborne forces. It depicts the mythical hero Bellerophon astride Pegasus the winged horse. Rather beautiful, don't you think? Next, we have this beret, also for the airborne forces. General Browning's wife chose the colour; she's the novelist Daphne du Maurier, you know, and apparently very fond of maroon. Fetching, no? Finally this' – he picked up a slender lanyard – 'this denotes our battalion, 2nd

Battalion, which I would be delighted if you'd consider joining.'

Trickey fingered the lanyard. 'Why yellow?'

'Stands out better! Everyone will know who we are, even the enemy!'

'I see. Good idea.'

'Precisely. Care to join us?'

Trickey smiled. 'I'd be honoured.'

'Then it's all settled. Welcome to the Parachute Regiment.'

Keep reading for a preview of

FREEFALL

BOOK II

in the

AIRBORNE TRILOGY

CHAPTER 1

At six pm Lieutenant Charteris appeared round the door of the hut.

'It's on boys,' he said breathlessly, 'get your stuff together.'

Heads shook knowingly, wry smiles were exchanged. 'Aye aye sir,' someone sighed, 'soon as I finish my newspaper.'

'Yes and I've darned my socks.'

'I mean it!' Charteris protested, 'it's really happening. Tonight!'

'That's what they said last night.'

'And the night before, and the one before that.'

'Yes but this time it's true. Listen!' He opened the door wider, beyond it the moonlit field lay motionless.

'Listen to what? I cannae hear a thing!'

Charteris grinned. 'Precisely!'

'So . . .'

'The wind,' Theo sat forward. 'It's gone.'

'So it has.'

'Christ boys it's on!'

Fifteen minutes later the one hundred and twenty Scotsmen of C Company, the 2nd Parachute Battalion, were crammed aboard army buses, singing lustily as they lurched along narrow

1

Wiltshire roads to the aerodrome at Thruxton. There they disembarked to find twelve black-painted Whitley bombers dispersed around the perimeter being prepared for flight. Fuel bowsers hurried to and fro, engineers kicked tyres and screwed down cowlings, flight crews checked maps, radios, signal flares and code books, while gunners loaded and tested their weapons. Meanwhile beneath each bomber, ground crews carefully manhandled equipment canisters into the Whitleys' bomb bays, and attached their parachute lines ready for release over the target.

A wan-looking airman in RAF greatcoat was watching proceedings to one side.

Theo rubbed his hands against the cold. 'All right, Charlie?' he asked him, although it came out as *a-reet*.

'Yes thanks. Looks like we're really going, doesn't it?'

'It does rather.'

'Can't quite believe it. All that running around on cliffs and messing about in boats, I think I persuaded myself it wasn't actually, you know, real.'

'I know what you mean.'

'Now I'm scared stiff I'll mess everything up. For everyone.'

'You won't, you'll be fine.' Theo regarded the airman. Inserted late into the team as a 'technical expert', Charlie Cox was the typical boffin, intense, nervy, bespectacled, and slight – childlike in size compared to the huge Scotsmen noisily disembarking the buses around them. Theo had been told to stay close to Cox. A few minutes later he finally learned why.

'Well good evening everyone!' Major Frost, standing on a chair, grinned broadly at his men, ranged in an attentive semi-

2

circle before him. They were assembled in one of Thruxton's cavernous hangars, no-one outside C Company had been allowed in, and Company Sergeant-Major Strachan had locked the door shut behind them. Up to that moment, only Frost and his officers knew details of the assignment they were tasked with, now it was time to tell the men who would carry it out.

'Thank you for your patience this week, I know how difficult it has been, especially having trained so hard.' Frost checked his watch, 'But in two hours from now we will be embarked upon a mission of great importance. Its codename is Operation Biting, and its aim is to seize a radar facility belonging to the enemy. This facility sits on a cliff on the coast of Normandy, our job is to secure it and the area around it, so that our RAF radio technician, Sergeant Cox here, can dismantle it and bring key components back home for analysis.' A hundred pairs of eyes turned on Cox who forced a wan grin. 'Now, we need not trouble ourselves with the technicalities, our role is to deal with the enemy, but let me assure you that success will save thousands of Allied lives. Also may I remind you, this is the first operation ever assigned to our battalion, and therefore a great honour and responsibility.'

Theo glanced at the men around him, listening to their leader in rapt silence. Almost all were Scotsmen, many still wearing their Highland insignia, in defiance of regulation. Bobble hats, Glengarry caps, Tam o'Shanters, some displaying the coloured 'hackles' of their regiment; he saw Black Watch, Seaforths, Camerons, Argylls, Gordons, and was reminded of an insane attack against tanks in France, four boys charging down a lane to their deaths, and an entire division desperately fighting for its life. At home in Scotland these men would squabble like feral cats, but in battle he'd seen them die gladly for one another. It's what made them so special.

'We go in by RAF and we come out by Royal Navy.' Frost was saying, 'We operate in four groups, exactly as trained, and deploy according to known enemy disposition.' He stepped off the chair to pull a sheet from a blackboard, revealing a chalk-drawn map. 'This is our target, the radar unit, close to the cliff edge here. It's manned by Luftwaffe technicians who may be armed. Lieutenant Vernon's team, which includes Sergeant Cox and our German speaker Trickey, will take it. Oh, and there's a three-hundred foot drop over the edge so watch your step! A quarter mile north is the radar-receiving building and guard house, which is where the main enemy concentration is expected, so Lieutenant Timothy and his group will deploy there to stop anyone approaching. Leading south from the radar unit is our exit route, which is a steep footpath down to the beach area. Intelligence suggests this is guarded by a second enemy detachment located in this blockhouse down on the shore, with more enemy garrisoned in the village of Bruneval just inland from the blockhouse. So Captain Ross and Lieutenant Charteris will bring their teams there and secure the beach for the Navy landing craft to pick us up. Meanwhile my team will oversee operations, help with the radar unit and mop up as required. The DZ is a quarter mile inland from the radar station, here behind these trees, after the drop we all assemble there, then take up our positions as stealthily as possible. The signal to commence attack will be four blasts on my whistle. We must be off the beach by 0300 hours latest. Our drop time is midnight, so we emplane at 2100.'

Frost concluded with a goodwill message from their divisional commander, General Browning, then everyone was told to disperse to their groups for more detailed instructions. Theo waited with Cox until they were summoned forward.

'All set Sergeant?' Frost asked Cox.

'Yes, sir, I . . . I think so.'

'Trolley ready, tool kit packed?'

'Yes, sir. Checked everything myself.'

'Good man.' Frost glanced at Cox's uniform, a lone patch of blue amid a sea of khaki. 'I'm sorry we couldn't fix you up as a temporary Para, Cox. I tried, you know, but it's RAF regulations apparently.'

'It's all right sir, I don't mind.'

Frost dismissed him then turned to Theo.

'Will he be all right, Trickey, he looks like a rabbit caught in headlights.'

'It's just nerves sir, I think he'll be fine.'

'He'd better. Everything depends on him.'

'It's the jump. That and the responsibility. He'll be better once he lands and starts work.'

'Let's hope so. Now listen. Stick to him like glue. Your interpreting services will be needed at the radar unit, sorting out the Jerry technicians and so on, ideally we'd like to nab a couple if possible. But I can't emphasise enough the importance of speed, for we must get off that cliff before they call up reinforcements. Boffin types like Cox get bogged down at the slightest thing, so just make sure he gets the guts out of the blasted apparatus quickly, then get it and him down to the beach, you got that?'

'Yes, sir.'

'Good.' Frost paused and passed a hand over his face. His eyes were bloodshot, his face fatigued, he looked weary and old beyond his twenty-nine years. Five consecutive days and nights this ordeal had been going on. And many weeks of training before that. To cap it all the final dress rehearsal, which had involved scrambling over a Dorset cliff in pitch darkness to be picked up by Navy landing craft, had been absolute chaos, with men getting lost in the dark, several falling and injuring themselves, and the Navy landing at the wrong beach. Now this. Five times the mission had been set then cancelled, five days of careful preparation and nail-biting anticipation, only to receive the 'cancelled-due-weather' phonecall at the last moment. Then today he'd been told the window had finally closed, that the February tides were now wrong and the moon too weak to mount the operation. After all the effort it was heartbreaking, and yet secretly a relief, and he'd begun preparing to stand everyone down, even allowing himself the notion of a weekend's quiet leave to recover. Then suddenly a higher authority intervened, possibly Churchill himself, the telephone rang and he was told one final go might be attempted, *if* the weather cleared. All afternoon he waited, and slowly, impossibly, the winter clouds parted, the mist melted and the wind dropped to a zephyr. 'Fancy a crack at it Johnny?' General Browning quipped over the phone at tea-time. 'Good luck, and make sure you're home for breakfast!'

'The RAF uniform, Theo,' Frost said, 'I wanted Cox added

6

as an extra, you know with false name and Para uniform and everything. In case it all went wrong and we got captured. At least he'd have a chance if he looked like one of us.'

'Yes sir.'

'But the point is, if it does all go wrong, the War Office is adamant.'

'About what sir?'

'He has too much technical knowledge. About our radar, our countermeasures, our research and development.'

'Sir?'

'So he can't be taken alive, Theo. Under any circumstances. Do you understand?'

***

FREEFALL

will be published in 2018
To keep in touch, sign up for our newsletter at
www.headofzeus.com